The Choice Is Theirs

Big Track Bascomb—a bull-like sheriff who has to choose between the votes of the people who give him power and the respect of the son he loves

Loretta Sykes—a proud black girl who must submit to the brutal debauchery of her body if she wants to stay alive

Breck Stancill—an unyielding aristocrat who is torn between the tradition of the past and a love that violates all taboos

Charles Peck—a militant who has to choose between the directives of his northern supporters, and his own intimate knowledge of the South

And over every choice, the grim shadow of

THE KLANSMAN

William Bradford Huie's raw and searing novel of the new South

Paramount Pictures presents ·
A William Alexander—Bill Shiffrin Production of
A Terence Young Film ·

THE KLANSMAN

Starring

Richard Burton

Lee Marvin

Co-starring

Cameron Mitchell
Lola Falana
David Huddleston
Linda Evans
Luciana Paluzzi
David Ladd

With

O. J. Simpson as Garth

Produced by William Alexander
Directed by Terence Young
Screenplay by Millard Kaufman,
Samuel Fuller
Based on the novel "The Klansman" by
William Bradford Huie

Technicolor ®

William Bradford Huie

THE KLANSMAN

A DELL BOOK

Published by
DELL PUBLISHING CO., INC.
1 Dag Hammarskjold Plaza
New York, New York 10017

BIG TRACK

SOMETIMES Big Track Bascomb felt good. He felt like he was bettering himself, getting somewhere and having something. Other times he felt scared. He just didn't know and wasn't sure. Only three people knew he ever felt scared: his wife Maybelle, his son Allen, and Breck Stancill. Nobody else would believe that Big Track could feel scared. He looked too strong.

At 8:30 P.M. on Sunday, April 11, 1965, Big Track felt good. He liked the car in which he was riding. It was a special-built, air-conditioned Buick Wildcat four-door sedan, saddle brown with tan leather upholstery. On the side of each front door was a foot-high gold star and the lettering:

SHERIFF
ATOKA COUNTY
ALABAMA

Built into the car was a "police pack" which ratioed its gears to where it could hit eighty from a standing start in nine seconds and hit one-twenty in four more seconds. On top was a 640-candlepower streamlined red light which could burn steadily or flash continuously, and on the left side was an 850-candlepower streamlined white spotlight. Under the hood was a siren which, once turned on, screamed hysterically until turned off. Inside the car was firepower: a derringer concealed in Big Track's pocket; an Army .45 automatic on the front seat; a shotgun in a rack above the windshield; a carbine under the front seat; and, in the trunk, a submachine gun, a tear-gas gun, grenades, nightsticks, a blackjack, and extra handcuffs and leg irons.

Whenever the car stood at its Reserved parking place on the courthouse square in Ellenton, folks examined it and exclaimed

over it like tourists aboard the battleship *Alabama* in Mobile
Bay:

"I feel sorry for any pore s'nuvabitch that gets chased by Big
Track in this booger."

"Big Track takes off like a astronaut at Cape Kennedy."

"With this spotlight Big Track can read your tag number at
midnight from a mile away."

"Other night I was home, in my own bed, tending to my
woman, when I heard this si*reen* open up. It sounded 'way off,
clean across the Big Hollow. But it scared me so I couldn't
finish my home work."

"When Big Track takes off in this thing he thinks he's back
in Korea in a tank piling up dead gooks all around him."

"If Old Long Ears [President Johnson] really wants to kill
them gooks in Vietnam, he ought to send Big Track and this
Wildcat."

Big Track Bascomb possessed horsepower, candlepower, firepower and sirenpower. Moreover he looked like power. Thirty-
six years old, he weighed 245 and stood six-four in his bare,
size-fourteen feet which had given him his name. His mother
named him Buford, but kids named him Big Track, so now the
Buford was forgotten and even on ballots it was Big Track Bascomb with no quotation marks.

Some folks in Ellenton said he looked like Marshal Dillon
on *Gunsmoke.* They said that when Big Track, khaki-clad, in
his calf-length boots, walked around the courthouse square, or
across to Cora's Café, or to Flack's Barbershop, or to the jail,
speaking and waving to everybody, joshing, inquiring about
crops and miseries, they said it was just like Marshal Dillon
in Dodge, visiting the Longbranch, or Delmonico's, and jawing
with Chester or Festus, Doc or Mis' Kitty.

But there were differences between Big Track and Marshal
Dillon. The marshal wears the high-crowned ten-gallon Western
hat. Big Track wore the Southern cattleman's hat, which is also
turned up on both sides but which has a low crown. Since Big
Track was meatier than Marshal Dillon, in thighs, chest, fore-
arms and jaws, the low-crowned hat made him appear stocky,
like Pope John wearing his borsellino in the Vatican rose garden.
Big Track's thick sandy hair was close-cropped, and his skin
was a shade redder than most men's. He usually looked serious
but he could smile. He could whoop and holler when the Ellenton High School Blue Devils made a touchdown; he could
holler louder, even throw his hat in the air, if his son made the

touchdown. In his fantasies he pictured himself as General Patton, or as a fullback for the Baltimore Colts, his favorite TV team. And, unique among all the marshals, sheriffs and troopers, real or TV, Big Track, when he walked, carried in his gun belt not a revolver but the old Army Colt .45 automatic with which he could behead a lizard at forty feet.

General Patton, too, favored the old automatic.

Another difference between Big Track and Marshal Dillon was money. The marshal is paid thirty dollars a month. Big Track was paid fees, like a doctor or lawyer. He owned his own cars, including the Buick Wildcat; he hired and paid his own deputy, his own clerk and his own jailer; and he operated the county's jail at his personal profit or loss. His income was neither guaranteed nor limited. By law he was "High Sheriff of Atoka County, Alabama, the highest official of the county." His sworn duty was "to make each citizen of this county secure in his person and possessions." His income "in the American way" depended on his "diligence, vigilance and devotion to duty."

"And don't ever forget the biggest difference between me and Marshal Dillon," Big Track often said. "He don't have to get re-elected. I do."

A second reason why Big Track felt good was that his son, Allen, was with him. Allen was seventeen, lithe, six feet tall, 180 pounds, the high-school touchdown-maker. Inevitably he was called Little Track. With his close-cropped sandy hair, he looked like Big Track. But he had some of his mother in him, so he was finer-textured and not so big-footed. He moved faster. He was driving and Big Track sat beside him, relaxed, chewing his cigar, enjoying watching the boy enjoy pushing the Wildcat at a steady eighty along the white concrete strip through the pine forest.

"I'm glad we come on this trip together, Al," Big Track said. "We've had a good time. I could'a sent Butt Cut after this punk. But I wanted you and me to have a trip together."

"Sure, Dad," Allen said. "We've had a good time. Best time we've had since we went to the Orange Bowl and saw Alabama and Texas."

The punk was in the back seat. He was a male Caucasian, nineteen, who had murdered an old man during a filling-station holdup at a rural crossroads in Atoka County. He had been arrested in Mobile, 277 miles south of Ellenton, and held for Sheriff Bascomb. Big Track had considered sending his only deputy, Elmer "Butt Cut" Cates, then had decided to go himself.

The punk was secure because the Wildcat had been built to transport offenders as well as overtake them. Shatterproof glass, re-enforced with steel mesh, divided the car at the back of the front seat. The back doors could be locked and unlocked only from the outside. The shatterproof windows could be rolled down only with a key. In addition the punk was in handcuffs, with the cuffs chained to a steel bar in the middle of the back seat. The punk could not overhear normal conversation in the front seat.

Big Track switched on the overhead light in the back seat and glanced at the punk. Then, satisfied, he switched off the light.

"This punk thinks I hate him," he said. "He'd like to cut my throat with a dull knife. But I don't hate a punk; I just don't know what else to do with him but cage him. Before a wild kid turns into a punk, when he's stealing hubcaps, or tires, or even a car, or even when he sets the schoolhouse afire, I keep trying to help him. Just as soon as I pick him up, before I book him, I call his daddy or mama, or the welfare people, and I try to talk to him. I try to get him in the Army: God knows the Army helped me. But once a wild kid turns into a punk, once he makes his mind up not to try to better hisself, once he gets the snakes in his guts and the scorpions in his head, once he uses that knife or gun, what can anybody do but cage him? Or burn him, like they'll do this one? Hell, this one shot that old man just to see him fall. He already had the old man's money, the old man was just standing there helpless with his hands up, and this punk shot him just to see him fall."

The Army did indeed help Big Track. Generations of Bascombs in Atoka County had never had anything or got anywhere. They were not White Trash: the half-assed, thieving, trifling Trash who won't work. The Bascombs would work and they wouldn't steal, but they never got anywhere. Not one Bascomb had ever finished high school, or owned the ground under his feet, or had a bank account, or been allowed to buy anything on credit that couldn't be repossessed. They all lived in shacks in the woods or on the edge of Ellenton, and each shack had a secondhand washing machine on its front porch and looked as though its TV aerial might tip it over in a high wind. The Bascombs all worked in the woods, around the peckerwood sawmills, logging, offbearing, setting blocks, or wheelbarrowing sawdust; and they all prayed, sang and shouted at country Baptist churches, and hoped they'd find Glory in Beulahland.

Born in 1929, the year the Depression started and the saw-mills stopped, Big Track had been hungry when he was three, four and five years old. That he lived to be six and older was due to welfare vegetables, Franklin Roosevelt and the Federal minimum-wage law. By 1945 Big Track was the educated Bascomb: he reached the ninth grade before he dropped out to work in the woods and at filling stations and at trying to learn to fix cars. In 1947 he was trapped by his manhood. Under big moons, in warm summertime, lying on pine needles with Maybelle Abernathy, he couldn't control himself; and when she budded he had no healthy choice but to become an eighteen-year-old married man. (The Abernathys lived in the woods, too; and they shot as straight, and as readily, as the Bascombs.)

In the Wildcat Big Track swallowed hard and shook his head. I don't know how me and Maybelle stayed alive, he thought. We couldn't't'a made it without Breck Stancill. He let us move into a shack on his land, and he talked young Doc Parker into letting Maybelle have the baby in that new hospital he'd set up in a empty store building. A lot o' credit's got to go to Maybelle. That little skinny yellow-headed country gal has always had grit in her craw. She ain't never been scared in her life. She's always told me that we was gonna better ourselves and get somewhere and have something, and that our kids was gonna be somebody.

Big Track often shook his head and marveled at the way things turn out. That growth in Maybelle which had scared him and forced him to see the preacher, that growth had become the son who could score the touchdowns, and push the Wildcat at a steady eighty, and make his father throw his hat in the air. Not many sons ever make their fathers throw their hats in the air. Even more marvelous: Allen Bascomb was now in the eleventh grade, and he was an A student. Not only did he know about forward passes, he also knew about sines and cosines, and he could listen to Huntley and Brinkley, even to Eric Sevareid, and understand every word they said.

Big Track didn't know what a gene is, but he knew something of the wonder of genes: how from a woodcutter and a char-woman can come a Caruso, from a tailor and a washerwoman can come a Steinmetz, and from a Bascomb and an Abernathy can come an Allen Bascomb. And he knew what many of the immigrant families reaching America knew: that for Bascombs and Abernathys to get somewhere and have something, un-lettered parents must strive and save and sacrifice, and appreciative children must strive, aspire, study, accomplish and acquire. Big Track thought this two-generation effort was "the American way." Maybelle had told him it was.

As for the Army: skilled Americans go to the Army reluctantly and at financial loss. In 1950, when he was twenty-one, Big Track, who was unskilled, went to the Army proudly and at financial gain. He bettered himself when he became an Army private: he wore warmer clothes, and he put more bread in his son's mouth and more cash in Maybelle's thrifty hand. The Army bettered itself by employing Big Track because soldiering was an employment at which he could quickly become skillful. He took to weapons. There was war in Korea; it was not a popular war; so the Army badly needed gook-killers, and Big Track became expert at gook-killing. Young second-lieutenant platoon leaders, just out of West Point, wanted Corporal Bascomb, later Sergeant Bascomb, with them on night patrols. One night a "human sea" of screaming gooks, bugles blowing, attacked the patrol; and when relief arrived the only man alive and standing fast was Sergeant Bascomb, surrounded by thirty-nine dead and dying gooks.

The free world was grateful. By battlefield promotion Sergeant Bascomb became Lieutenant Bascomb; and in the White House rose garden, with Maybelle and a four-year-old boy looking on, President Truman saluted Big Track and placed around his neck the Congressional Medal of Honor. That night Maybelle and Big Track and their son slept in the Mayflower Hotel as guests of the grateful people of the United States of America.

The people of Alabama and Atoka County were grateful. Big Track and Maybelle returned to a new $12,000 gift home, with all-electric appliances, in Ellenton, and to membership in the First Baptist Church. Big Track became a deputy sheriff until 1958, when he was elected sheriff. He became post commander of the Buford Bascomb Post, American Legion; vice president of the Lions Club; and commander of the Ellenton Gun Club. In 1962, the year George Wallace was elected governor of Alabama, Big Track was re-elected sheriff.

"Son," Big Track said, "there's just one thing me and you and your mama want now. We all know what it is, and we're all aiming at it. You're gonna go to West Point. The congressman has promised to appoint you. So next year I'm gonna get re-elected, and I'm gonna get that congressman re-elected if I have to hold a gun on every voter in the district. You're gonna go to West Point. Being the son of a Medal of Honor winner helps your chances, and being a all-state halfback damn sure ain't never hurt the chances of any boy tryin' to get in West Point. So you're gonna go. When a man comes out of West Point he can give orders from the start. Flunkeys carry his gear and make up his bunk. Nobody never looks down on him. He travels in a reserved seat, and goes right on up the ladder. I know because I seen it. That's what you're gonna have, Al."

Big Track and Allen had left Ellenton early Saturday morning. They drove south, through Tuscaloosa, then southeast to Montgomery, and stopped at the State Capitol. The Selma-to-Montgomery March by hundreds of supporters of the Negro Movement had ended two weeks earlier. Big Track and Allen, and everybody else in Atoka County, had followed it on Huntley-Brinkley and *CBS Reports*.

"Now we'll hear the other side," Big Track said. "We'll hear it from the governor and the troopers and Jim Clark."

The governor first had himself photographed standing between Big Track and Allen, welcoming them to the Cradle of the Confederacy. They dwarfed him, but he liked it because he boasted of being a "fighting *little* judge."

"We'll give this picture to *Life* magazine," he said. "Let 'em show the world how the fighting Governor of Alabama is supported by a great halfback and a great soldier."

The governor led them to a window and pointed to where the marchers, "males and females together, white and black," engaged in a "mass urination," right there in the streets, "just opening up and letting fly by the numbers," so that urine "flowed down the gutters like spring rain."

"That's the sort of troublemakers that Johnson and Bobby Kennedy and Katzenbach and Earl Warren sent into this great state," the governor said. "Punks, whores, scum, degenerates, kooks, atheists and perverts, all controlled by Communists. Everything you heard on television is lies told by liars who hate me and you and Alabama. Just let the troopers show you the true pictures and affidavits. They'll turn your stomach."

Big Track and Allen were shown enlarged photographs of some of the beatniks in the Selma March: the arms of white females around the necks of Negro males; the hands of Negro males on the rumps and breasts of white females; a Negro male and a white female kissing and "sucking each other's tongues"; a Negro male and a white male kissing; and a Negro male and a white male lying under a tree each with a hand in the other's crotch.

"Old Long Ears calls that the Great Society," a state trooper explained. "Looks real great, don't it?"

"Yeah, that's Bobby Kennedy's Freedom Now," another trooper added. "That's Sweet-Jesus Freedom after We Shall Overcome."

A third trooper asked: "Why didn't Huntley and Brinkley show them pictures? Then people could'a knowed what the march was all about."

A Montgomery policewoman's affidavit read: "There were white and Negro people all over the Ripley Street side of St. Margaret's Hospital. Many of them were kissing and hugging. One couple on St. Margaret's lawn were engaged in sexual intercourse: a skinny, blond white woman and a Negro man. After they were through she wiggled out from under him and over to another Negro man lying near them and he mounted her."

A second affidavit read: "One organization in the march had its headquarters in a building with a large room up front which was used for an office. Off this room, in back, was a smaller room in which were about twelve to fifteen canvas cots. Men and women used this room for sex freely and openly and without interference. I saw a priest take off his front-assed collar and his pants and have intercourse with a Negro girl. On another occasion I saw a Negro man, one of the leaders of the march, and a red-haired white girl on one of the cots together. They engaged in normal sexual intercourse as well as an abnormal sex act which consisted of the two manipulating the other's private parts with their mouths simultaneously. They made no effort to hide their actions, and several persons saw them, including at least one white man wearing a front-assed collar. Everybody seemed to think nothing of it."

A third affidavit: "In the Jackson Street Baptist Church I saw numerous instances of boys and girls of both races hugging, kissing and fondling one another openly in the church. On one occasion I saw a Negro boy and a white girl engaged in sexual intercourse on the floor of the church. At that time the church was packed and the couple did nothing to hide their actions. While they were in the actual act of intercourse, other boys and girls stood around and watched, laughing and joking."

When Big Track and Allen were leaving the Capitol, the governor came out of his office and spoke to them again. "We're gonna win this war, Big Track. We've lost a few battles but we're winning the war. All we got to do is fight, fight, fight! Stand Up For Alabama! The real Americans are already behind us, and the rest of the decent Americans are gonna get sick of this Nigger Business the minute it touches them. We're fighting a war and we're gonna win."

"Well, Governor," said Big Track, "we been mighty lucky up in my county. The outsiders ain't tried to bother our niggers yet, and I'm hoping they won't try."

"They'll try. But you can handle them. I'm counting on you. Just remember they are punks and perverts, particularly the ones claiming to be priests or preachers. If you need any help the troopers will give it to you."

The trooper who was the governor's bodyguard grinned. 'I can't see Big Track needin' much help. A man who can kill thirty-nine gooks in one shooting match ain't likely to need much help handling a few punk agitators."

Driving toward Selma, along the route of the march, Big Track was told over the Wildcat's two-way radio that a trooper would meet him at the spot where Mrs. Viola Liuzzo was slain by Ku Klux Klansmen for having participated in the march. The trooper was waiting, and he showed Big Track and Allen where the Detroit woman's Oldsmobile stopped off the road after she was shot.

"We want you to get the truth of this, Big Track," the trooper said. "You heard Old Long Ears go on the television and get all hot in the collar about Ku Klux killing this pore innocent woman. But he didn't tell it all. He just told what suited him to tell. When we stripped this woman we took off a dress and a slip, and she was wearing some kinda little old girdle up here around her hips. But her crotch was bare's a possum's ass. She wasn't covered up between her legs like a decent white woman's supposed to be. She was bare-legged, bare-assed and bare-cunted, and she was in that car at night with a stiff-peckered, Freedom Now, black buck setting right close up next to her."

Big Track asked: "Did the doc find any . . . any sign that she'd been popped that night?"

The trooper shrugged. "Course not. Them niggers used rubbers on her. We found rubbers scattered the whole fifty-one miles from Selma to Montgomery."

After Big Track and Allen resumed their journey, driving on toward Selma, Big Track said: "Al, you're a little young for me to be lettin' you listen to all this friggin' talk."

"I'm seventeen, Dad. And big for my age."

"I know how old you are. But I aimed for you to spend most of this trip studyin' your history and geography lessons. Not listenin' to talk like that."

"We've talked pretty straight for a couple of years now. I'm not a child. I'm getting ready to go to West Point."

"Yeah, I know. Maybe it's all right. But your mama sure wouldn't like me lettin' you listen to talk like that."

A few miles farther Allen asked: "Dad, did that woman from Detroit deserve to be killed?"

Big Track chewed his cigar and didn't want to answer. "It's hard to say. I won't say she deserved to be killed. I don't know enough about what all she'd been doing. Or what kinda fool notion she had to bring her 'way off down here. She might or might not been lettin' niggers pop her. But one thing's sure. She had four young kids of her own up in Detroit. She oughta been home keeping her kids from being scared and helpin' them to better theirselves."

After more reflection Big Track added: "There's something wrong with a thirty-nine-year-old woman who runs off with a gang like that and leaves her own kids wonderin' why she's gone and when she's coming back. There's something she ain't findin' at home that she wants mighty bad."

At Selma they lunched at Holiday Inn, attracting attention with their obvious well-being: their identical dress, their height, their calf-length boots, their ruddy health, their physical power, their father-and-son camaraderie. Big Track wore no gun or badge: only the khaki pants stuffed into the boots, the khaki shirt and a neat khaki tie. Since Big Track was barely nineteen years older than his son, some observers guessed they were brothers.

When Winston Churchill, during the Second World War, first saw General Claire Chennault standing at the edge of a crowd, he asked who the man was with the awesome appearance. When told, Churchill shuddered and said: "Thank God he's on our side." The West Point careerists in Korea thanked God that Big Track was on their side. George Wallace took comfort in the assumption that Big Track and Allen were on his side. Many Americans, perhaps most Americans, watching Big Track and Allen at lunch, would have felt friendly toward them: "Glad they are on our side."

Allen wanted to see places in Selma he had seen on television: the Brown Chapel African Methodist Episcopal

Church, headquarters of the marchers and demonstrators; the new stone-and-glass courthouse before which the demonstrators stood, night and day, for a week; the restaurant in which troopers slew Jimmie Lee Jackson; the tree under which Rev. James Reeb was bludgeoned to death; and the Edmund Pettus Bridge at which, before TV cameras, troopers tear-gassed marchers, and beat them to the ground where they were run over by horsemen of Sheriff Clark's posse.

After visiting these places, guided by another trooper, Big Track and Allen met Sheriff Clark at his office.

"I tell you, Big Track," the sheriff said, "you had to see it to believe it. I never thought I'd live to see a fine old cultured American city like Selma ravaged by a filthy mob. Perverts! Whores! Liars! Thieves! Scum of the earth! To think that such scum could have the protection of the courts and the President of the United States! Whatever it costs us we've got to stop it. This is a war we got to win. Just look at our pictures and affidavits. They'll boil your blood."

Big Track and Allen looked at more pictures like those they had seen in Montgomery. In addition there were pictures of beer cans, whiskey bottles and contraceptives scattered on the Brown Chapel churchyard. All the affidavits were sworn to by Selma police officers:

". . . There were many colored girls and white boys laying in the same sleeping bags. Several of these white boys told me they come here to join in the march because they was guaranteed $15 a day and all the pussy they could get. I also seen a white girl about 17 years old and four colored boys get into the back of a truck and close the doors. They were in the truck about 45 minutes, and when they opened the door to get out the girl was dressing."

". . . I saw white females building up their sexual desires with Negro males. After a few minutes of rubbing and kissing, a Negro male would lead a white female off into the Negro housing project. I watched this procedure many, many times."

". . . I saw two young white men dressed as priests and four young Negro girls, all holding hands and hugging. One tall priest was observed for several days around Sylvan Street, always in the company of the same Negro girl. Always they were holding hands and rubbing up against each other. I saw a white man and a Negro female laying together under a blanket in the middle of the street just before daylight. There was much movement by both parties beneath the blanket. The white man, the day before was wearing a priest's collar. Next day he was wearing a sweat shirt and dungaree pants."

". . . One night about 200 demonstrators were singing in the street and I observed a limp-wristed white male standing in the front row with a blanket over his shoulder and a black male's shoulder. This white man had his arm around the Negro and at one time he kissed the Negro in the mouth with a long, lingering kiss."

". . . I stopped a 1957 Ford driven by a Negro man. There was another Negro man in the front seat and a Negro man and a white girl about 24 years old in the back seat. The girl tried to conceal her race by pulling her coat over her head. She was also scrambling around trying to get her dungaree pants on. When I got these people out of the car the white girl's dungaree pants were unzipped down the side, and the Negro man's pants were unzipped who had been in the back seat with her. The girl said she was from California."

About 4 P.M. Big Track and Allen left Selma and drove the 160 miles south to Mobile. En route they didn't talk much. They were uncommonly quiet. A tied-up baseball game, in extra innings, was on the radio. Allen turned it on for a few minutes, then turned it off. He said: "Dad, we both watched a lot of the Selma march news on TV. Not all those people looked like kooks. Was . . . frigging . . . was that *all* that march was about?"

"Well," answered Big Track, "I guess there was a few good people in the march. Just mixed up and thought they might be doin' some good. But in a white man's mind all that this agitation comes down to is frigging."

"Why? Can't a Negro vote without frigging a white girl?"

"I don't know. Maybe. Maybe a few good, sound niggers can. But maybe friggin' goes with votin'. Most white men in Alabama figure that once we let the bars down, once niggers mix in white schools and churches and courthouses, once the nigger feels like he can lay his hand anywhere a white man can, then you're just bound to get more and more frigging."

"Is that why all those pictures and documents we looked at, why they were all about sex and nothing else?"

"It just comes down to that, Al. It's what it all comes down to. A white man just naturally hates to think about a black hand on a white girl. The very thought of it makes him sick.

And if he sees in his mind a nigger actually climbing a white woman and doin' her like a bull does a heifer, a red-blooded white man goes crazy as a bat. It's just more'n he can bear. He wants to kill somebody, and he damn sure will kill somebody if he ain't kept from it."

During another long silence Big Track again felt himself becoming uneasy. I'm afraid Al's taking all this a little too much to heart, he thought. Him and me ought to be laughing, feeling good, going into Mobile for a Saturday night. Fancy dinner at Constantine's. Plenty of soup and oysters and strawberry tarts. After dinner the wrestling matches. Unless he's dyin' o' cancer any man'll laugh and yell at a wrestling match. Then sleeping at a fancy motel. Al'll like that. But I made a mistake lettin' him look at all that friggin' evidence. He's not as tough inside as a lot o' boys. And then, by god, I made a *second* mistake.

To get his son's mind off all that frigging, Big Track decided to explain to him the second mistake his dad had made.

"One thing I'd just as soon'd not happened," he began.

"What's that?"

"I'd just as soon we'd not been in that picture with Wallace."

"I thought you liked Wallace."

"Well, it ain't easy to explain. Let me start this way. You see, in all my goin' around, to sheriffs' conventions and Legion conventions and to the Army, I met one real American who stands head and shoulders taller'n the rest. He's Harry Truman. He's a great man, Al, great like in your history books, and when he talks I listen. He's been for helpin' the nigger in some ways. But he thinks all these troublemakers coming down here from the North ought to stay at home. Whatever Truman says, that's what I try to do. At least I think about it a lot."

"And Truman doesn't like Wallace."

"He sure as hell don't. I kinda like Wallace. He don't know it, and nobody else knows it but your mama and now you, but I didn't vote for him in '62. But he's a fighter. The trouble is, in politics you got to look after Number One. I can help Wallace get re-elected but he can't help me get re-elected. Lots o' voters in Atoka County like him. Some of 'em think he's Jesus. But there's a good many that don't like him. I got to get votes from all kinds. I'm making money as sheriff, a whole lot more'n I could ever make doing anything else. I got to have that money, for you, for your two sisters to go to the university, and for all the other things we want that we ain't got yet. So it was all right for us to see the governor and shake his hand, but I didn't figure on no picture. It could hurt us."

"Maybe the picture won't be published anywhere."

"Like hell it won't. Wallace'll see to that. It'll be in the Birmingham *News,* and the Legion *News,* and the Lions Club *News,* and it damn sure will be looking at us next week on the front page of *The Northwest Alabamian* in Ellenton."

"Well, don't worry about it, Dad," Allen said. "It can't hurt much."

"Maybe not," said Big Track. "But I ain't got to the worst part. When it comes to helping you get in West Point, what good can Wallace do? The Medal of Honor was give to me by President Truman and the United States of America. It's the United States of America that's got to pay your way to West Point. Wallace is fighting a war with the United States. He's got about as much influence with the United States as he's got with the N-double A-C-P. If you and me are Wallaceites, somebody may be standing in the door up at West Point tryin' to keep you out."

After the wrestling matches Big Track and Allen walked around in Mobile for a few minutes, stretching their legs, then went to the motel, turned on the TV and got ready for bed. Both of them felt lonely. Big Track remembered nights when he walked streets in San Francisco and Tokyo looking for excitement. He didn't look for excitement in cities any more, not even during Legion conventions. A public servant can get in trouble at night in a city, trouble that can cost him an election and embarass his family. When Big Track wanted excitement the place for him to look for it was in the woods in Atoka County where he could control the situation.

Allen began feeling lonely when he unpacked their hand bag. On one bed he laid his father's pajamas, on the other bed his own. He could feel his mother's hands on the cloth. She had made both pairs, washed them, ironed them, packed them neatly in the bag. Along with the two toothbrushes, one razor, one tube of toothpaste and one can of shaving cream. Maybelle Abernathy Bascomb was a backwoods girl with an eighth-grade education who had got knocked up and had to get married at seventeen. But with her family she had lived by one rule: she was always *there.* Except for the eight days and nights when she was in the hospital, bearing her two daughters, no child of hers had ever waked up or come home from school and not found her *there*. Allen had heard her say: "A mother's put in this world to keep her children and her husband from being scared. Every day she's got to say to her family: 'Hold your head up. Work hard. Be honest. Get your lessons. Say your prayers. Your mother or your wife loves you and thinks you're the most important living human. You're gonna be somebody and have something.' "

Allen Bascomb, for all his size and seventeen years and football skill and good grades, was virginal and a baptized Baptist who believed in Heaven. He had never doubted that his mother and father loved him and that he loved them. In all his life he had spent only fifteen nights away from his mother: those eight nights when she was in the hospital and seven nights when he was away with his father.

After Allen was in bed and the TV turned off, Big Track sat on the side of the other bed and said: "Son, there's one more thing I want to talk about on this trip. Set up so I can see your face."

Allen propped up on his pillows and said: "What's that, Dad?"

"Well, we mentioned it a little before. But we can't talk about it easy in Ellenton. It's something you and me need to talk about, man to man."

Allen smiled. "I know what you mean, Dad. Okay, let's talk about it."

Big Track shifted his weight and cleared his throat. "It's tough for me to talk about because of the spot it puts me in. It looks like I'm saying that what I done was a mistake, and that you're the mistake. And that ain't true. It's just that times change, and you can't afford to do what I done."

"You mean," said Allen, "that I can't afford to risk knocking up a girl and having to get married like you did?"

"That's it."

"It worked out all right for you and Mama, didn't it?"

"Well, *now* it appears it did. I got your mama, and no man ever got a finer wife. We got you, and no couple ever got a finer son. But it sure didn't look like it then. We mighty near starved to death! And things was different. I wasn't goin' nowhere. 'Cept to the Army. If you do what I done you'll never get to West Point."

"You don't need to worry. So far I haven't taken any risk."

Big Track got up and drank a glass of water. When he sat back down he said: "It's that 'so far' that's worryin' me. I been rememberin' how I was when I was your age. Hell, I was running around in the woods learnin' about girls. Most of what I learned I learned from your mama. But I wasn't thinking about much else but learning. And now . . . well, a sheriff is sort'a in the sex business. He knows a awful lot about what's goin' on. He has to. And I been thinking that, by god, with all that's going on, it ain't very likely that you're gonna go on, for the next year or so, while you're waitin' to finish high school and get to West Point, without tryin' to learn a lot about girls. You're a big, fine-looking boy, smart as a whip, a football hero, and now it's spring and the sap's rising. Hell, you're just naturally gonna put more pressure on, and there's girls around, even nice girls, who might give in to you. Ain't that right?"

"Well, Dad, I'm human," said Allen. "Sure I'm human. You know I've got a girl. Billie Jean. She'll be seventeen next month. She's my girl. You like her: she's pretty and smart and she's a cheerleader. Sure we've been doing a little exploring."

Big Track nodded knowingly. "That's how the trouble always starts. You start exploring. Then one night you explore too far and bingo! you want to do it ever' night and she's got you. Even if you're lucky and don't knock her up, she puts the pressure on you to get married. And married men don't go to West Point. They wind up privates scrubbing latrines."

"You want me to be a priest?"

"Hell, no, I don't want you to be a damn priest. I want you to be a man and a general in the United States Army. That's why I been thinking. You see, all the trouble, all this teen-age knocking up and gettin' married and more trouble, it comes from boys and girls gettin' out in the dark together and exploring when neither one of 'em knows a damn thing about what they're doing. I hear experts talking about it on TV. I ain't no TV expert: I'm just a red-necked country sheriff dealin' with it ever' damn day. But here's the way I see it. It's natural for a seventeen, eighteen-year-old boy to explore. He's got to prove to hisself that he can do what a man's supposed to be able to do. That's natural. Maybe it's right. At least nobody can stop it. So the thing to do is to find the way to keep out o' trouble. And I know the way. The only way is for a boy to do his exploring with a woman who knows what the hell she's doing, and who won't let herself get knocked up, and who don't expect to get married."

"You mean a whore!"

"Hell, no, not a whore! Hell, in Atoka County we got women who know what they're doing, and who can let a boy prove he's a man, and still they're not whores!"

"You know these women?"

"Sure I do. I'm the sheriff."

"And you want to arrange such a woman for me? And you want me to leave Billie Jean alone?"

"Naw, son, I ain't sayin' you ought to leave Billie Jean *alone*. Let her be your girl. Go places with her. Dance with her at the Legion Hall. Hug her a little. Kiss her a little. That's natural. If you love her, tell her you love her. But tell her if she wants to marry you she'll have to wait five or six years and get herself a college education. A girl can wait. A boy . . . well, he ain't likely to."

When Allen said nothing, Big Track cleared his throat and went on: "I don't know any better way to do it, Al. I thought about it a lot. Your mama's losing sleep over it. I know it sounds funny . . . a daddy telling his boy he'll get him a woman. But me being the sheriff, and knowin' so much about everybody, it makes it different. Maybe most daddies can't do this for their boys, but I'm in the position to do it for you. A daddy who wants his boy to go to West Point and not think about gettin' married till he's twenty-three, twenty-four years old . . . hell, a daddy like that, he's a helluva sorry daddy if he don't try to find some way to keep his boy out o' trouble."

Except about football it was the longest conversation they had ever had together. Big Track wondered if he was being too hard on the boy. Allen felt disturbed: the whole day had disturbed him. He wished he was at home, in his own bed, with his mother sewing in the next room. Or parked in the woods with Billie Jean's saucy head on his shoulder. But he wanted to help his father—his big-hearted, big-tracked father —who sat there in his pajamas and big bare feet almost pleading with him.

"I don't know, Dad," he said. "I don't know whether I'd want to do any exploring with a woman you got for me. It sounds a little like sending a young bull over to a cow, instead of turning the young bull in with a heifer. When I'm with Billie Jean I feel like I know more'n she does. So I feel good when we're exploring together. And what about this? Suppose a man really loves a girl, and he just wants to learn about girls with her, and he doesn't ever in his life want to get that close to another woman? What about that?"

Big Track shook his head. "I don't know how to answer that, son. All I know is that if you do all your exploring for the next year with Billie Jean, or some girl like her, then you may not ever go nowhere or have nothing."

They sat looking at one another. Allen could think of nothing more to say. Big Track said: "If a man's got no education, if he ain't going nowhere, hell, he can learn about girls with girls. If he gets married at eighteen or nineteen, maybe it's to the good. But if a boy's smart, and going somewhere and have something, hell, he's just got to stay out of the woods with girls until he's through West Point."

Now Allen knew he had to say something. "I see what you mean, Dad. I'll think about it."

"You think about it, son. And promise me this. Promise me you won't go no further with Billie Jean, or any other girl, till you talk to me about it first. Will you promise me?"

Allen nodded. "I promise."

Big Track got into bed and turned off the light. He felt relieved. For six months he had been trying to get around to talking with Allen. Now he had got around to it. He believed he had done some good. At least he hoped so.

On Sunday morning Allen and Big Track drove south, along Mobile Bay. They crossed the new bridge to Dauphin Island, and walked along the beach picking up shells. After lunch they returned to the Mobile docks and visited the battleship *Alabama*. In 1964 the United States gave the ship to Alabama, and school children paid to have it towed from Seattle, through the Panama Canal, and installed in Mobile Bay as a tourist attraction and as "a shrine, a perpetual memorial to the valor of American arms in two Pacific wars."

It was a bright, warm April Sunday afternoon. Hundreds of tourists were aboard the ship or along the dock. Martial music paraded from many loudspeakers: "Dixie," "Anchors Aweigh," and "God Bless America." Flags waved. Spirits were lifted by the tonic of spring sunshine and pride of race and country.

"This old ship helped us kill a lot o' gooks," Big Track told Allen.

When Big Track signed the visitors' book he was recognized by employes of the Tourists Bureau, so a photographer was summoned to pose the great Medal of Honor winner visiting the *Alabama*. Big Track was photographed in color, standing on the dock gazing with pride at the fighting ship, and standing on the main deck pointing out to his son the pictorial record of enemy planes shot down by the ship's guns. The crowd learned the big man's identity, so he was recruited by fathers and mothers to pose with their seven-year-old sons, sitting on guns, leaning on guns and looking at guns.

Big Track grinned and said: "I feel like I'm running for governor."

Around 3:30 P.M. Big Track and Allen went to the Mobile County jail and picked up the punk. Then they headed due north, on U.S. 43, which crosses western Alabama, south to north, from Mobile, through Demopolis, Tuscaloosa and Ellenton, to Muscle Shoals and the Tennessee line. During the five-hour trip to Ellenton they stopped twice. The first stop was at a filling station and rest room. To take the punk to the rest room Big Track opened one of the car's back doors, and using a second set of handcuffs, cuffed his own right wrist to the punk's left wrist. He then unlocked the cuffs which the punk had been wearing, let him step out of the car and walk to the rest room, where Big Track stood by him while he urinated. Big Track then returned him to the car and cuffed him into the original position.

The second stop was at a drive-in sandwich stand. Big Track ordered cheeseburgers, coffee and lemon meringue pie for himself and Allen, to be eaten in the car. He ordered a hamburger and coffee for the punk. While the sandwiches were being made, Big Track put the punk in leg irons and uncuffed his hands so he could eat. When Big Track was back in the front seat, out of the punk's hearing, Allen said: "Dad, don't you think we ought to order pie for him, too? He can see us eating, and I hate for us to eat pie and not give him any."

Big Track laughed. "Okay, son." He called the car-hop and told her to make it three pieces of pie. "On your say-so, Al, we'll give the punk pie and lose money on him today. We get paid my food and lodging and ten cents a mile for comin' and gettin' him. We'll have to feed him for three or four months till they get through tryin' him and givin' him the chair. We get sixty cents a day for feedin' him, and we got to make a living out o' that. So the punk won't get much more pie on this earth. He'll get plenty o' them turnips and lima beans and fatback that Hattie knows how to cook and make go a long way."

When the trays arrived Big Track removed the knife, fork and spoon from the punk's tray, opened the back door and handed it to him. "I don't want him rammin' a fork in my belly when I get back there to cuff him again after he finishes his eatin'."

By 8:30 P.M. they had passed through Tuscaloosa and were nearing the Atoka County line. The curves became sharper and more frequent, the hills higher, with more bluffs and boulders visible in the lights. Big Track and Allen knew that the great dark stretches were gorges and vistas of loblolly pine. The infrequent lights were in big chicken houses.

"Yeah, we've had a good trip," observed Big Track, yawning. "But home'll look good to us. Seems like we been gone a week."

Allen was glad to see the city limits sign and turn down the familiar street, past the high school, to the courthouse square. The clock in the courthouse tower was striking nine when the Wildcat stopped at the little new pink-bricked, two-story jail.

Big Track didn't know it, but inside his jail trouble was waiting for him.

BUTT CUT

AT 11:30 A.M. on Sunday, while Big Track and Allen Bascomb were picking up seashells on Dauphin Island, Sheriff's Deputy Butt Cut Cates sat in the jail in Ellenton reading:

A gale of chivalrous passion and high action, contagious and intoxicating, swept the white race. The moral, mental and physical earthquake which followed the first assault on one of their daughters revealed the unity of the racial life of the people. The Ku Klux Klan was the resistless movement of a race, not of any man or leader of men. The secret weapon with which they struck was the most terrible and efficient in human history. These pale hosts of white-and-scarlet horsemen struck where the power of resistance was weakest and the blow least expected. Discovery or retaliation was impossible. Not a single disguise was ever penetrated. All was planned and ordered as by destiny. The accused was tried by secret tribunal, sentenced without a hearing, executed in the dead of night without warning, mercy or appeal. The movements of the Klan were like clockwork, without a word, save the whistle of the Night Hawk, the crack of his revolver, and the hoofbeat of swift horses moving like figures in a dream, and vanishing in mists and shadows.

It was a passage from *The Clansman*, a novel published in 1905, from which a film was made. When released the film, too, was titled *The Clansman*, but this was changed to *Birth of a Nation*. In 1960-65 *Birth of a Nation* was the "theme film" of the Ku Klux Klan. It was used to recruit new members and reassure old ones. It was frequently shown in small town drive-in theaters, after which Klan recruiters said prayers, set fire to a cross, and led the singing of "Onward Christian Soldiers" and "The Old Rugged Cross."

Because *Birth of a Nation* was endorsed by Woodrow Wilson, and because *The Clansman* contains quotations from Abraham Lincoln which can comfort Klansmen, all Ku Klux Klansmen are taught to regard Presidents Lincoln and Wilson as their benefactors. Many Klansmen learn and recite passages from *The Clansman* as though they were Bible verses.

Butt Cut was not reading the novel, *The Clansman;* he didn't read books. He was reading "Passages from *The Clansman*," featured in a mimeographed URGENT Four-Bell Ku Klux Klan *Bulletin.* He read further:

> Lincoln said: "The American is a citizen king or nothing. I can conceive of no greater calamity than the assimilation of the negro into our social and political life as our equal. A mulatto citizenship would be too dear a price to pay even for emancipation."

> The physical touch of a negro is pollution.

> This Republic is great, not by reason of the amount of dirt we possess, the size of our census roll, or our voting register. We are great because of the genius of pioneer white freemen who settled this continent, dared the might of kings, and made a wilderness the home of Freedom. Our future depends on the purity of this racial stock. The grant of the ballot to negroes is a crime against human progress.

Butt Cut's nickname was common in a county where the principal occupation was the growing and processing of pine trees, either for lumber or pulpwood. "Butt cut" means massive might close to the ground. The first log cut from the base of a felled tree—the butt cut—is the more massive, more noted for circumference than length. Twenty-nine years old, Butt Cut Cates was five-feet-six and weighed one-ninety. He was a human bulldozer. From the day he dropped out of the seventh grade until he was twenty-five he drove a pulpwood truck and learned "every pig trail in Atoka County." This knowledge of terrain was one of the reasons why Big Track, in 1962, made him his only deputy.

With a gangling, fast-breeding, redheaded wife and four stumpy sons, Butt Cut's ambitions were both financial and po-

litical. He wanted to see himself sheriff "before too long." He
wanted to see Earl Warren impeached—whoever he was. And
he wanted to see George Wallace inaugurated President of the
United States.

Butt Cut was not the jailer. That position was filled by Big
Track's formidable old-maid sister, Hattie Bascomb. She lived
in the jail, cooked for the prisoners, cleaned up, handled visitors, and thoroughly "ran things," spelled only at times by Big
Track or Butt Cut. With Big Track out of town, Butt Cut was
spelling Hattie while she attended the Baptist Church half a
block from the jail. As he read, Butt Cut felt sure he identified
Hattie's contralto in "Dwelling in Beulahland."

Butt Cut shook his head. He thought: We damn sure got
one thing in Atoka County that nobody else's got. We got the
onliest full-time, thirty-two-year-old, virgin jaileress who
wears a mustache and sings bass in the Baptist choir!

He read more of "Passages from *The Clansman*":

Can the negro be educated? History has the answer.
Since the dawn of history the negro has owned the conti-
nent of Africa—rich beyond the dream of poet's fancy,
crunching acres of diamonds beneath his bare, black, flat
feet. Yet he never picked one up from the dust until a
white man showed to him its glittering light. His land
swarmed with powerful and docile animals, yet he never
dreamed a harness, cart or sled. A hunter by necessity,
he never made an axe, spear or arrowhead. He lived as
an ox, content to graze for an hour. In a land of stone
and timber he never sawed a foot of lumber, carved a
block, or built a house save of broken sticks and mud.
With league on league of ocean strand and miles of in-
land seas, for four thousand years he watched their sur-
face ripple under the wind, heard the thunder of the surf
on his beach, the howl of the storm over his head, yet he
never dreamed a sail. He lived as his fathers lived—stole
his food, worked his wife, sold his children, ate his
brother, content to drink, sing, dance and sport as the
ape.

And this creature, half-child, half-animal, the sport of
impulse, whim and conceit, pleased with a rattle, tickled
with a straw, a being who, left to his will, roams at night
and sleeps in the day, whose speech knows no word of

love, whose passions, once aroused, are as the fury of the tiger, they want to set this thing to rule over the Southern people!

The mimeographed bulletin from which Butt Cut was reading was one he had just brought from the post office. Either as a sheriff, or as a past post commander of the American Legion, or as a Medal of Honor winner, or as commander of the Ellenton Gun Club, Big Track was on the free mailing list of twenty-four organizations dedicated to the proposition that America is being destroyed from within. He received not only the regular bulletins but also all the special Condition-Red Alerts and Now-Hear-This Alarums.

Every day Butt Cut brought from the post office an armload of revelations and exhortations. "Americans beware! Now is the time for every real, red-blooded, God-fearing, Bible-reading citizen to stand up, fight, suspect his neighbor, man the ramparts, sharpen his aim, keep his powder dry, and otherwise bestir himself to save Freedom from the Red socializers and mongrelizers!"

Butt Cut read nothing else but this "post-office literature" because he knew from the governor that the TV and the daily newspapers belong to the socializers and mongrelizers. At Flack's Barbershop or at Cora's Café he often explained: "The onliest way for a real American to git the truth is to git it from a organization that has its own experts keepin' tabs on the Reds. Like the Klan and the State Sovereignty Commission, and the State Committee for the Preservation of the Peace, and the State Troopers. Even after the experts git the truth, the onliest way they can git it to us is to bring it, man to man, or mail it to us in a plain *in*velop."

Every day Butt Cut skimmed through his post-office literature and scissored out what struck him as the direst warnings and the shockingest exposures. Once each week he took his accumulated clippings to Hardy Riddle, superintendent of the Atoka Lumber Company, and Hardy's secretary made two hundred Xerox copies of each clipping. Then Butt Cut taped the copies to bulletin boards at the courthouse, the city hall, the post office, the Legion hall, the Masonic Temple, Cora's Café, Flack's Barbershop, the high schools, and the larger churches of the county. He also kept a stack of clippings atop the flush tank of every public WHITES ONLY toilet in Ellenton.

"It's the patriotic duty of the sheriff's office," Butt Cut said, "to try to git the truth to as many real red-blooded Americans as has eyes to see."

For immediate copying and distributing to his bulletin boards and toilets, he now scissored out the final "Passages from *The Clansman*":

> You must sink to the negro's level if you walk as his equal in physical contact with him.

> If you dare put a negro on this jury, or open your mouth as to what occurred in this room, I'll kill you.

> Men of the South, the time for words has passed. The hour for action has struck. We will execute tonight!

> You call us midnight assassins? It is the question of who should possess the power of life or death, the men who love a community or those who would degrade it. For less than Southern white men have suffered from those who would degrade them, kings have lost their heads and empires perished before the wrath of freedom.

Butt Cut frowned as he thought of the gut-grinding conflict which had grown out of his bulletin-board activities. One citizen of Atoka County—only one—had ever publicly displayed any objection to the efforts of "the sheriff's office to git the truth to real, red-blooded Americans." That *one* was Breck Stancill.

Every other citizen, preachers and teachers included, either appreciated or tolerated Butt Cut's efforts. But not Breck Stancill. Breck lived on Stancill's Mountain, five miles from Ellenton, and whenever he came to town and happened to notice one or more of Butt Cut's clippings on a bulletin board—no matter how many eyes were watching—he performed an unchanging ritual. He walked to the board, hung his aluminum walking stick in the crook of his arm, took out his pocket knife, and loud enough for every watcher to hear, he spoke one word: "Trash!" He then cut the Scotch tape, jerked off the clippings, crumpled them and tossed them into the nearest trash basket. He walked away without speaking another word.

Even if Butt Cut was watching, or Big Track, or Hardy

Riddle, Breck never changed the routine. On one heart-stop-
ping occasion, which everybody heard about, Breck was in the
barber chair and Ed Flack was cutting his hair. Hardy Riddle
was in the next chair. Five or six good men were sitting
around, jawing, waiting their turns. Big Track and Butt Cut
came in.

Breck spoke to them, passed the time of day, as friendly as
anybody. But when Ed Flack finished the haircut and gave
Breck the final dusting and handed him his walking stick, and
Breck got out of the chair, everybody quit talking and tensed
up.

Breck paid Ed Flack, put on his hat and started out. Then
he noticed the bulletin board. When he began his routine, all
the bystanders got ready to duck or run, figuring that Butt
Cut couldn't take it before Hardy Riddle and Big Track and
the whole damn county!

Then Breck said "Trash!" A little louder than usual. Everybody heard it. Hardy Riddle's jaw hardened. Big Track
looked at the floor. Butt Cut's face lost color. But nothing
happened. Breck crumpled up the clippings, and went over
and threw them in the can where Ed Flack threw the dirty
towels. Then Breck walked out.

When Breck was gone, nobody in the barbershop said a
word, not until Ed Flack cleared his throat and started talking
about the Alabama-Tennessee football game.

An hour later Butt Cut went back to the barbershop and
put up more clippings. And in the sheriff's office, with the
door closed, he tried to have a showdown with Big Track
about it.

"How long we gonna let that one-legged bastard keep treat-
in' us like yellow dogs?" he asked Big Track.

"I don't know," said Big Track. "I don't know if he's treat-
in' me like a yellow dog or just you like a yellow dog. When
he says 'trash' I don't know if he's calling me trash, or you
trash, or Hardy Riddle trash, or if he's just calling what you
put up there trash."

"He's spittin' in my face," said Butt Cut. "He's spittin' in
yo' face. He's spittin' in the face o' law and order and the
Constitution. He's got no right to tear down what I put up.
And he's causin' younguns to start doin' it. He's gittin' to be a
sort'a hero in the high schools. Two or three football players
are startin' to tear down what I put up. I ain't got their names
yit, but I'll git 'em. We got to stop it, Track! How we gonna

enforce the law if everybody gits to thinkin' that me and you's afraid to tangle with Breck Stancill? I tell'ya right now I ain't gonna let that s'nuvabitch spit in my face again!"

Big Track exhaled a cloud of cigar smoke. "Yeah, y'are," he said. "At least for a while yet. When Breck spits in'ya face just use'ya handkerchief or'ya sleeve, and go paste'ya bulletins back up, like Hardy Riddle tells'ya to. There's lots'a reasons why you ain't gonna tangle with Breck Stancill. First off, he's one-legged. That right leg was blowed off six inches above his knee at Iwo Jima. He was a Marine lieutenant, a platoon leader, and a goddam good'un. He got the Silver Star and the Purple Heart. He's the only man in this county who's killed as many gooks as me. Him and me stood side by side when the Army and the Legion buried Alvin York up in Tennessee. The night Sergeant York lay a corpse, the Legion held a meetin' in a motel up there in the Tennessee mountains and Breck did some o' the speaking. Breck writes letters to Harry Truman, and the President writes back to him."

"Then why ain't he a red-blooded American? Did he get his balls blowed off same as his leg? What's he doin' bein' a lousy nigger-lover and spittin' in my face for doin' my patriotic duty?"

Big Track answered: "Ain't nothing wrong with the color o' Breck's blood. Ain't nothing wrong with his balls, from what I hear. And he ain't a nigger-lover, even if he has got that bunch'a old nigger relief-hounds livin' out there on the mountain with him. He's just a one-legged man who don't like Ku Klux. He thinks George Wallace is a piss-ant, and he ain't afraid to say so. That's the only difference between him and you."

Butt Cut was puzzled. "What the hell, Big Track!" he said. "You takin' up for that s'nuvabitch? After what he just done to both of us? After what he's *been* doin' to us for a year or more?"

"Naw," said Big Track. "I ain't taking his side. I ain't saying I like what he's doin' to you—and maybe to me. I ain't saying I wasn't itchin' to call his hand over there in the barbershop. I'm just tellin' you the way it is. If I ever tangled with Breck I'd have my own wife to fight. Maybe my own boy. It goes back to '47 when I wasn't nobody around here but a pore, scared kid with a knocked-up wife and my own daddy in bed with his back broke. We was hungry and didn't have no place to sleep. The man who give us a shack to live in and something to eat and went to bat for us was Breck Stancill. And, hell, he was just four, five years older'n me, and just back from the war and the hospitals, still falling around and cussing, tryin' to learn to walk with that tin leg and ride his horse in the woods. He's been my friend. He got mad at me last year when Willie Washington was lynched—he blames me for it—and he blames me and you for what's happening to that white woman—Nancy Poteet—that Willie raped. But if I was hungry today I could still set down at Breck's table and eat."

Butt Cut pulled his cattleman's hat down tight. He said: "The s'nuvabitch may be yo' friend. But he ain't mine. And he's gonna get knocked flat on his one-legged ass!"

"Well," said Big Track, "whoever does the knockin' better knock fast. Because Breck can take his right hand and break a man's neck with it. He learned karate in the Marines. He's been leanin' on that right arm and right hand for twenty years. He rams his right fist in a barrel o' rice clean up to his elbow just to keep in practice. And he can shoot a lot straighter'n you can."

"He don't scare me," sneered Butt Cut. "I got friends. They know ways."

"They sure do," said Big Track. "They can shoot Breck's dog. They can shoot his horse. He loves his dog and horse. They can fire his woods. He loves them pine trees he grows: he sets 'em out just as careful. They can hide in the bushes and shoot him in the back. They can overtake his pickup and shotgun him in the head while he's driving. Maybe that's what'll happen. But, by god, I ain't gonna do it. And as long as you work for me, you ain't gonna do it."

A few minutes before noon a Chevrolet pickup pulled into the jail's parking lot, and two men got out and rushed up to the jail's outside door. Butt Cut let them in. They were Sy Shaneyfelt and Tag Taggart, and they were Night Hawks, or armed lookouts, for the Ku Klux Klan. Sy, thirty-two, worked in a filling station; and Tag, twenty-eight, "fixed cars" at his shack on the edge of Ellenton.

"Where's Big Track?" Sy asked.

"Out'a town," said Butt Cut.

"When'll he be back?"

"Not'll tonight. Maybe nine, ten o'clock."

"Then you got to git movin'. Fast. One'a the sonsabitches got in here last night. The main one we been lookin' out fer."

"Not Josh?"

"Yeah. Josh."

Butt Cut reached into a desk drawer and pulled out several posters, like those of "Wanted Men" the Western sheriff always has on television. These posters had been circulated by the Klan, and the poster on Josh offered two photographs and this information:

REV. DAVID JOSHUA "JOSH" FRANKLIN, Male Caucasian, 24, 5' 11", 170 pounds. Crew-cut brown hair. Hazel eyes. No beard. Goes bareheaded, even in the rain. Wears a white "priest" collar, a black, short-sleeved "priest" shirt, blue dungarees, and rough, heavy, high-topped, tan GI shoes. Born: Ames, Iowa, March 2, 1941. Northern Presbyterian. Long police record in Birmingham and Selma. Known Communist. Agitator, Socializer. Mongrelizer. Holds prayer meetings with niggers, praying for the Lord to lead niggers to the ballot box. Lives with niggers, eats with niggers, kisses nigger girls in public and holds hands with them. Can *always* be found in a nigger girl's bed on Saturday nights. Other nights maybe, but he *always* gets "chocolate milk" on Saturday night.

"That's him," said Tag. "I hate to think of it, but that Red s'nuvabitch was right here in Atoka County last night, right here amongst us, gittin' his Saturday night chocolate milk and singing 'We Shall Overcome.' "

"Where's the s'nuvabitch now?" asked Butt Cut.

"Well, that's just it," said Sy. "We don't know 'zactly where he is right now. But here's what we do know. He come in here last night in a green Chevy sedan with a Birmingham plate. He had a bearded nigger with him. They went to Stancill's Mountain and hid the car behind a nigger shack. You 'member a nigger gal named Loretta Sykes?"

"Yeah," said Butt Cut. "She lit a shuck fer Chicago coupl'a years ago."

"That's her. Well, last week she came back. We figger she joined the Apes-and-Alligators [NAACP] up North, and they sent her back in here to sort'a 'prepare the way' and 'spy out the land' and fix a nest fer Josh and his agitators on Stancill's Mountain."

Tag said: "She's stayin' in a shack on the mountain. It's

one o' them three shacks you see on the right hand side when
you come up on the first hump o' the mountain. Josh and the
bearded nigger stayed there maybe three hours last night.
Maybe one of 'em's still hiding in there."

"Did you see Josh? Or the car?"

"Naw, we didn't see nothing," said Sy. "We was tied up fer
a while last night down at Awful Annie's. You seen us there.
We're telling you what we just got on to. Josh got in and maybe
got out without us seeing him. We didn't get on to it till about
a hour ago."

"Is Loretta out there on the mountain now?"

"We seen her there not more'n twenty minutes ago. That's
what we come runnin' in here for. You got to git out there
and grab her."

"This is D-Day, Butt Cut," Tag said. "This is what we been
expectin'. They're startin' in on Atoka County right now. We
got to move fast and nip it in the bud."

Butt Cut hesitated. "I got to wait a few minutes till Hattie
gits back from church," he said. Then he asked: "Is Breck
Stancill out there on the mountain? Did'ya see him anywhere?"

"Naw," said Tag. "He ain't out there today. His pickup's
settin' right up here at the bus station. He took the eight-ten
bus this morning fer Birmingham—to spend Sunday with that
woman o' his'n. He ain't likely to be back till the ten-twenty
bus tonight."

Butt Cut felt excited as he got in his white Ford sedan and
pulled out of the parking lot. His car didn't cause talk like Big
Track's Wildcat, but it was adequate. It had the gold stars, the
red light, the siren, and it was armed just as heavily.

As he left the parking lot Butt Cut had to move slowly because the Baptists were still pouring from their church, in
their Easter outfits, clogging the sidewalk and the street, shaking hands, laughing, patting each other on the back, praising
the sermon, complimenting the ladies' hats, and admiring the
dogwoods and the azaleas. Two blocks farther Butt Cut was
caught in a similar jam at the Methodist Church, and even
when he reached the countryside he had to drive carefully because the country people were leaving their churches, crowd-
ing the road, hurrying home to their Sunday dinners.

Perhaps it was the sight of all these good, happy, Christian
people; perhaps it was the weight of command, with Big
Track 277 miles away; but for some reason Butt Cut felt a

heavier burden of responsibility than he had ever felt before. These good and happy people were looking to him to protect their way of life. They were in their Sunday clothes, some of them carrying Bibles, hurrying to good dinners, while he was in uniform, carrying guns, hurrying to confront an agitator in a "stinking nigger shack." The good people didn't want to wear uniforms or carry guns or confront agitators in "stinking nigger shacks." They wanted Big Track and Butt Cut to "handle it."

Except on TV Butt Cut had never seen an agitator. He knew how to handle murderers, thieves and moonshiners. But did he know how to handle an agitator? He felt almost as if he were standing before all the white people of Atoka County —all 11,642 of them—and all of them were looking straight at him, and pointing their fingers at him, saying:

"Butt Cut, we done seen what'all's happened in Birmingham and St. Augustine and Mississippi and Selma and Montgomery. We done seen it all on TV. We done seen them dogs, and tear gas, and water hoses, and cattle prods, and picketing, and singing, and demonstrating, and limp niggers sprawling and being carried off to jail. We don't want none o' that in Atoka County. Not a *damn* bit of it! This is a happy, peaceful, quiet little rural county where you can walk down a street or road at midnight and not be afraid of nothing. This county ain't a jungle like New York or Chicago. We want our good niggers —all 4,877 of them—to be protected. We expect you to protect them. We don't want no agitators coming in here bothering our niggers. That's what we got you and Big Track for. If you want to keep your job, you keep the agitators out. If anything even looks like it might be starting to develop, you nip it in the bud."

Butt Cut remembered statements made to him by Big Track.

"Hell," said Big Track, "being sheriff o' this county before '62 was easy. I cooperated with the four city cops here in Ellenton, looked after the city and county prisoners, and collected my turnkey fees. Out in the county I cooperated with the state troopers on the highways. I cooperated with the FBI on interstate car theft. I chased a few bootleggers and 'shiners, and handled a little shootin' and cuttin' on Saturday night. I rounded up kids stealin' hubcaps and bicycles. But in '62 Wallace was promisin' he'd stand in ever' schoolhouse door and keep niggers out. To get re-elected I had to promise I'd stand on the county line and keep agitators out. So now bein' sheriff is a military problem. I got to protect the county from invasion. It's like settin' up a perimeter defense against gooks in Korea or Vietnam. I'm defending a hundred-mile perimeter against sneakin' mongrelizers. I got to have lookouts like the Klan Night Hawks, and I got to have Reserves like the members of the Ellenton Gun Club."

As he hurried toward Stancill's Mountain, Butt Cut felt as if he were activating Big Track's military defense plan. In his mind he could see the map of the county as a defense problem:

A rectangle, 20 miles by 30 miles; a perimeter of 100 miles; an area of 600 square miles; 384,000 acres. With the courthouse in the center of the county. With a fourth of the county's 16,519 people living within the city limits of Ellenton. With another fourth living within three miles of Ellenton, around the two big lumber mills, the heading mill [wooden kegs] and the yards for collecting pulpwood. With the other 8,000-odd people scattered through the county in the pine forests, at crossroads settlements, and on forty-acre farms with chicken houses, three-to-ten-acre cotton allotments, and pastures with small herds of cattle.

In his mind Butt Cut could also see the county's three Negro settlements which would be the targets of the invaders: two "niggertowns" near the mills, and the forty Negro shacks strung along the gravel road on Stancill's Mountain. And because the county's scattered rural population had declined by four thousand Negroes and two thousand whites in twenty years, across the countryside Butt Cut could see empty and rotting shacks, some of them with GONE TO CHICAGO scrawled over a flapping or fallen front door.

Butt Cut decided that this was no ordinary day in his life. He was on no ordinary mission. His excitement increased as he neared the foot of Stancill's Mountain. He felt that what he was about to do could affect what he wanted. It might decide when he was to become sheriff. It might even help decide great issues, like when Earl Warren was to be impeached or George Wallace elected President.

While hoping the sheriff's car would not come, Loretta Sykes had been expecting it. She watched Butt Cut get out of the white Ford, and she waited for his call from the yard:

"Hello! Anybody home?" Then she opened the door and faced him.

"You looking for someone, Sheriff?"

"Yeah," said Butt Cut. "You Loretta Sykes?"

"Yes, sir."

"Anybody else in the house?"

"Only my mother. She's ill and in bed."

"You sure nobody else's in there?"

"Yes, sir, I'm sure. Would you like to step in?"

Butt Cut eyed her closely. "Naw," he said, "we'll just stand out here and talk. Come on out."

"May I get my sweater?"

"Okay. But don't keep me waitin'."

Loretta stepped inside and put on a blue sweater over her short-sleeved gray dress. She was twenty-two and about the size of Leslie Uggams. She was darker than Miss Uggams, but not as dark as Sammy Davis, Jr. (Alabama Negroes describe their color in relation to TV personalities.) Most persons would have called her "nice-looking" but not a beauty or a high-yellow sex trap. She appeared neat, intelligent and capable; and in Chicago she earned $105 a week as a secretary for Montgomery Ward. Her hands were her best feature: long, graceful, efficient.

When she and Butt Cut stood together in the yard, they both knew that eyes in two other shacks were watching them.

"How long you been up in Chicago?" he asked.

"Three years," she said. "Well, *almost* three years. I left in May, the day after I finished high school in Ellenton. You know how we 'go Greyhound' when we get that high school diploma, Sheriff."

"Yeah. Out'a Slavery and Up to the Promised Land. When'd'ya git back?"

"A week ago yesterday."

"What'd'ya come back fer?"

"My mother has cancer. She's a terminal case. Dr. Parker says she has two or three months to live. There was no one else to nurse her, and she wants to die and be buried here on Stancill's Mountain. So I had to take a leave of absence from my job and come back."

Butt Cut's jaw hardened. "Don't lie to me, nigger! That ain't the reason you come back!"

Loretta flinched. She had told herself that things *must* have changed a *little* in Atoka County between 1962 and 1965.

Now she knew better. She knew that Butt Cut would subject her to the old Ordeal by Humiliation. He had begun by calling her a nigger. Next he would spit the obscenities at her. She began to wonder if she shouldn't have listened to her neighbors at sunrise that morning and either "grabbed that Greyhound bus" or "gone and told Mistah Breck before he got away."

She said: "Dr. Parker will tell you that I'm telling the truth. So will Mr. Stancill."

"Well, that ain't the onliest reason you come back," said Butt Cut. "It ain't even the main reason."

"I don't know what you mean."

Before those words were out of her mouth Loretta knew they were a mistake. She remembered that nothing infuriates a Butt Cut like a "Chicago nigger playin' dumb" with him. He snapped: "Like hell you don't! You know goddam well what I mean. Now don't fuck with me, nigger! You ain't in Chicago now. You know goddam well what I'm doin' here. Yo' ass is in a sling and'ya know it. Who was here with'ya last night?"

Loretta hesitated. All morning she had considered what she should say, even how she should dress. She had thought of using the old defense: lying, playing the sloven who "don't know nuthin', Mistah Sheriff: I wasn't even home last night." Then she had decided to make a normal appearance, to tell the truth and take her chances. This was 1965—time to quit lying and running, even in Atoka County.

"Two men were here last night," she said.

"One of'm was Josh?"

"You mean Reverend Franklin? Yes, he was one of them."

"Who was the bearded nigger with him?"

"Charles Peck."

"The Big Pecker, huh?"

"He didn't tell me he was called that."

"But he showed'ya why, didn't he?"

When Loretta made no reply, Butt Cut went on: "You let them two Communist agitators come in'ya house and spend the night with'ya?"

"They came to my door," Loretta said slowly. "I didn't know they were coming. I would have preferred that they not come. I'm here to help a good woman get in her grave with some dignity. So I'm hardly in a position to become involved in the Movement here. I had never met either of them. Reverend Franklin says he is a Presbyterian and a Democrat. Mr.

Peck is with Dr. Martin Luther King. Once they were at my door I couldn't refuse to let them enter. They stayed about an hour and left. I don't know where they are now."

Butt Cut rocked on his heels and stuck his right thumb in his gun belt. "Well, that's a bunch'a lies and you know it. But at least you confess that this house was used fer conspirin' last night."

"No, sir, I don't think I'm 'confessing' to any misbehavior," said Loretta. "Two men came here. They aren't criminals, are they? You don't have a warrant for their arrest, do you? They came here. We talked. That's all we did."

"What'd'ya talk about?"

"The Movement."

"We Shall Overcome?"

"If that's what you call it."

"Freedom Now?"

"Yes, sir. They talked about a new voting-rights bill they expect Congress to pass this summer. They talked about trying to get a thousand Negroes registered to vote in Atoka County by the end of 1965."

Two figures flashed through Butt Cut's mind: 1166 to 793. That was the vote in the sheriff's race in 1962. With not one Negro voting, Big Track had beaten a white opponent by less than four hundred votes. What would a thousand Negro votes mean?

Butt Cut asked: "Last night or this morning, why didn't you report this conspiracy to the sheriff's office?"

"I didn't know it was a conspiracy. Besides there is no telephone out here."

"Well, you're guilty of conspiracy against the peace and dignity of Atoka County."

Loretta lowered her head and tried to think of something to say or do. She considered saying: "Sheriff, look at this pitiful, weather-beaten, unpainted, rotting, two-room shack in which I was born. It has no plumbing, not even a kitchen sink. We used to use tar paper to try to keep the wind and the rain from coming through the walls, the roof and the floor. Now we use a clear plastic that Mr. Stancill gives us. When I was fourteen Mr. Stancill gave me a rebuilt old typewriter and told me it could spell FREEDOM for me if I could become the best typist in America. Can you imagine, Sheriff, how many hours I beat on that old typewriter in that shack? How hard I studied my shorthand and typing in high school in

Ellenton? How hard my mother worked to keep me fed and clean? How in Chicago, I worked during the day and went to business school at night? And after all this effort, Sheriff, to escape from Atoka County, to escape from dirt, dung, decay and degradation, can you imagine that I would ever come back here *one day* except to repay part of my debt to a dying mother? As much as I admire the Movement, can you imagine that, even to help the Movement, I would risk coming back here even for one hour!" Loretta only *considered* saying that. But she didn't say it. She knew it would further "contrary the Court."

"Now here's another crime you're guilty of," Butt Cut continued. "You know it's against the law fer a nigger gal to . . . to shack up with a white man. They got a fancy word fer it, but it means shacking up."

"You mean cohabitation?"

"I mean fucking," said Butt Cut, again using obscenity to try to degrade. "We know damn well that Josh gits his chocolate milk on Saturday night. Big Pecker gits it ever' night. He gits vanilla when he can, but he'll take chocolate milk if he can't do no better."

Loretta shook her head. "Nothing like that went on here last night."

Butt Cut snickered. "I bet it didn't! I just bet it didn't! I can just see you now, standin' up before a jury, swearin' that you and Josh and Big Pecker spent Saturday night in a shack in the woods together, and all'ya done was say'ya prayers and count nigger votes and sing 'We Shall Overcome'! Can't'cha just see a jury in Ellenton believin' that shit!"

After a pause Butt Cut added: "I'm takin'ya to jail. Fer further investigation."

"Won't you let me make bond? So that I can stay here with my mother?"

"How could you make bond?"

"Mr. Stancill will make it for me."

"He ain't here."

"He'll be back this evening. I believe Dr. Parker would sign my bond."

"It ain't time to talk about bond yit," said Butt Cut. "I ain't finished investigatin'. Let's go."

For the first time Loretta felt afraid. Despite the warnings of her mother and her neighbors, she had refused to believe that she had endangered herself seriously by allowing Josh

Franklin and Charles Peck to enter the house. She asked:
"Will you let me go inside and tell my mother and get a few
things?"

"Fer just a minute," he said. "But I'll go with you. I don't
want to spend a Sunday afternoon chasin' yo' black ass
through the woods."

Inside the shack not one word passed between Butt Cut and
the dying woman who lay in the old iron bed. She looked at
Butt Cut, who didn't take his hat off, and she knew that words
wouldn't help.

Butt Cut looked around. He noticed the pictures of Franklin and Eleanor Roosevelt. Those pictures had replaced Lincoln's in 1934 when James Farley distributed millions of
Roosevelt pictures as part of his successful campaign to take
the Negroes away from the Republicans. Butt Cut noticed
the old typewriter which had spelled FREEDOM for Loretta,
and the TV set which was newer and larger than his own. The
Federal Government had not brought plumbing to such
shacks, but through the Tennessee Valley Authority and the
Rural Electrification Authority it had brought electricity.

The only words spoken were by Loretta. When she had put
a few things in a handbag she went to the bed, knelt by her
mother, kissed her, and held her hand. "Don't worry, Mother," she said. "I'll be back before dark. The neighbors will
look after you while I'm gone. No harm is coming to me. You
get your rest, and look at TV, and I'll be back in time to
watch Ed Sullivan with you."

Her mother clung to her daughter's hand, choked on fear,
and prayed to God while tears wet her leathered cheeks. What
else can you do when you're old and worn out, and you've got
a cancer in your liver, and you're only hoping to see another
spring and hear a few more birds sing and watch a few more
flowers bloom?

Her mother knew that only God and Breck Stancill could
help Loretta now. And Breck wouldn't be back for nine
hours.

LORETTA

THE NEWEST and most marvelously automated building in Atoka County was the jail. This seemed strange because so few
citizens ever saw inside it, either as prisoners or visitors.
Moreover, in total assessed property value, Atoka was the
poorest of Alabama's sixty-seven counties. Why had the poorest county built what, in relation to its size, was the most expensive jail in the state?

Willie Washington was part of the answer. In 1964, after
he raped Nancy Poteet, Willie was taken from the old jail by
Ku Klux Klansmen and lynched. Television cameramen then
entered the old jail and exposed its squalor. This so embarrassed the people that they pressed their board of revenue to
build a new jail "second to none."

Big Track was part of the answer. In their embarrassment
some of the people said: "It ain't fair to Big Track. He's our
only citizen with a national reputation. He's a Medal of Hon-
or winner and a great sheriff. It ain't patriotic for us to let him
be looked down on on TV because he's running a filthy, stinking old jail. We got to build Big Track the shiningest, sweet-
smellingest jail in the whole country."

Then, too, the Negro Movement may have helped build the
new jail. By 1964 the people could see that in order to protect
their way of life they might have to jail many outsiders and
local troublemakers. This would bring more TV cameramen,
so the county would need a TV-worthy jail.

After deciding to build the new jail, members of the board
of revenue became prospects for the jail salesmen. It isn't
widely known, but in the United States there are companies
which compete with each other in designing, selling and
building new-model jails just as Ford, Chevrolet, GE, West-
inghouse and RCA compete with new-model cars, refrigera-
tors and TV sets. Every year these companies produce jails

which are safer, more convenient and easier to keep clean, vermin-free and odor-free.

The result was the new Atoka County jail, a two-storied marvel of safety, convenience and cleanliness, to serve both the county and the city of Ellenton. It looked more like a bank than a jail. It was low and sturdy, like a pink granite tombstone. From the outside no bars were visible, for there were no windows except in Hattie Bascomb's snug apartment. It was air conditioned; ultra-violet light substituted for sunlight. It was designed to keep thirty suspected offenders safe, clean, and segregated four ways: Caucasian males and Negro males on the ground floor, and Caucasian females and Negro females on the second floor.

Strictly speaking, the jail was not a prison, and its inmates usually were not prisoners. A prison is for convicts, persons who have been tried and convicted of offense. A jail may temporarily house convicts, but primarily a jail houses persons who are only accused or suspected of offense and are therefore, under the law, presumed to be innocent. If you are a citizen of the United States, only a judge or a jury can imprison you. But any sheriff's deputy can jail you. So you should be more concerned about the "safety" of jails than of prisons.

If you were accused of offense and brought to the Atoka County jail, you entered the front door which during weekdays was not locked. You stood before the jailer's desk and emptied your pockets. Then you were led through the first barred door and into the Delousing Room. There you stripped, and every article of your clothing was taken to be fumigated, cleaned and perhaps pressed. Jets of hot, soapy water attacked every square inch of your body. Then came the sprays—the bug killers and more potent cleansers. You didn't dry with a towel; no towels were used in the jail; you stood in a hot blast of air until you were antiseptically dry.

If you had an observable infection, you remained in the Delousing Room until a doctor or nurse examined and treated you, perhaps removed you to the hospital. When pronounced clean and jailworthy, you slipped on paper shoes and a blue, pajama-like, terry cloth garment, fresh and sweet-smelling from the jail laundry.

Big Track, Butt Cut or Hattie then led you to a solid steel door which was the entrance to a "block" of four cells and a Day Room. You passed through this door alone, and it was locked behind you. Then the jailer, standing safely outside the steel door and speaking through a baffle, directed you to walk straight ahead, past the Day Room, perhaps past other cells either empty or occupied, to your assigned cell. When you reached this cell door, the jailer, by electrical impulse, caused the door to slide open. You entered, and the door closed and deadlocked behind you. (Deadlocked means unshakeable, utterly immovable, even to .001 of an inch, except by electrical impulse from a cabinet outside the cell block.) Then, "safe" as a baby who has just been born and scrubbed, you sat on your bunk and contemplated the modern jail.

The cell was a steel and concrete box: five feet wide, nine feet deep, seven feet high. All sides were solid except the one which included the door. That entire wall was a steel grating. The vertical bars were four inches apart, the horizontal bars twelve inches. The bars were high-carbon, homogenous, tool-resisting chrome steel. By wearing out five thousand hacksaw blades you could cut through one bar. In the grating was a "pass through" large enough for a food tray. Four feet beyond the grating was another solid wall.

The bunk was a steel shelf, two feet three inches by six feet three inches, and only twelve inches from the floor so that you couldn't hurt yourself seriously by falling off. The mattress was foam rubber encased in washable plastic which admitted no bugs and instantly betrayed any effort to hide a razor blade in it. The thin pillow was of the same materials. The blanket was spun glass, permeated with bug repellent. Hercules couldn't tear it.

Music and radio news flowed from invisible speakers ten hours a day. Roy Acuff and "The Great Speckled Bird" and "The Wabash Cannonball." Elvis Presley and "Hound Dog." A full program of religious and country music by the Grand Old Opry.

At the back of the cell, in less than fifteen square feet, was a toilet-basin-and-shower marvel to match anything in any sleeping car. In no way could you damage it. In no way could you turn water on or off. The toilet was indestructible cast aluminum. There was no seat except the bowl. You couldn't flush it; it flushed automatically sixteen times a day at ten minutes after the hour. At no time did you possess more than four squares of toilet tissue: it came to you at 8 A.M. and 4 P.M. on the food trays. If, in protest, you wanted to clog the toilet, you had to use your garment or blanket. Automation defeated you. The toilet shut itself off, and a red light flashed in the jailer's office.

The shower was equally independent. Morning and evening the Voice announced that the shower would operate in five minutes. You slipped off your garment and assumed your shower position. The hot soapy water poured for one minute. Then came the rinse water for one minute, first warm, then turning cooler. When the water shut off you learned not to reach for a towel; you stood fast and received the drying blast of hot air.

Drinking water? Every hour on the hour it bubbled for a minute through a "bubbler" at the indestructible aluminum basin. If you were male, daily shaving was required. On your morning food tray was a locked safety razor and plastic cups of shaving cream and toothpaste. Suitable water in the basin reached you; the Voice told you when it was coming. You returned the razor and cups to the tray. You kept only a comb and toothbrush, both always visible. Over the basin was a "mirror" made of polished indestructible steel.

The two meals a day were cheap, clean and filling. If you pleased the jailer, your cell door would slide open, and the Voice would direct you and other inmates of your cell block to the Day Room. The door of the Day Room would deadlock, and you and your fellows could smoke, play cards and read paperback murder mysteries and westerns. While your cell was empty the jailer would inspect every square inch of it. Later the Day Room door would open, and the Voice would direct you back to your cell. Whenever there was movement between cells and Day Room, the jailer stood outside the block and watched through bulletproof glass. The steel door to the block was never opened until every prisoner inside the block was behind the deadlocked door of either the Day Room or his own cell.

Neither escape nor revolt nor the harming of a jailer was possible unless a jailer became careless. You couldn't communicate with any other prisoner except those in your cell block. You could protest by "noise or nuisance"—by screaming or by spitting, vomiting, urinating or defecating on the floor. If you resorted to "noise or nuisance," a jailer and two strong trusties would lodge you in the Deranged Room. It was soundproof and nuisanceproof. It was six feet wide, eight feet deep, seven feet high. It was lined—floor, ceiling and walls, including the door—with four-inch-thick foam rubber. The rubber floor was shaped and slanted like a shower bath with a drain in the center. The drain was an "Oriental toilet." A recessed light in the ceiling was always on, and its intensity, from dim to bright, was regulated by a rheostat outside the room.

You were placed in the Deranged Room naked so that you couldn't foul clothing or use it to strangle yourself. You were observed at intervals through a round, shockproof glass, eight inches in diameter, recessed in the rubber. You could throw yourself against the walls or floor, beating your fists, heels or head against soft rubber. You could sit on the floor, under the light, and scream and/or slobber, vomit, urinate or defecate. You could continue this until you were exhausted, or until a doctor arrived with an injection of thorazine to tranquilize you. Every hour the room would flush itself, like a toilet, with hot, detergent-laden water, cleansing both itself and you. The inescapable hot, drying, antiseptic air followed.

Not one in ten of the people of Atoka County had ever seen inside the jail. But everybody had heard about it, and everybody was proud of it. TV cameramen were welcomed, even invited. Everybody believed the jail to be the safest, cleanest, most humane jail in Alabama, probably in the whole country, perhaps in the whole free world.

Loretta Sykes was trying to restore her appearance after being washed and deloused on entering the jail. In her blue terry-cloth jail pajamas and paper shoes she stood in her cell before the steel mirror combing and setting her hair. Since she was the only Negro female in the jail, she was alone in the block reserved for Negro females. She placed her left hand against her bosom and felt how fast her heart was beating. She was terrified, but she was educated enough not to panic but to reflect on what had happened, what mistakes she may have made, and how she might help herself.

When she was fourteen her mother told her: "Lord, child, you got to learn to look after yo'self! When a colored girl gits out'a her mammy's sight, she ain't got *nobody* to take her part. A white girl's got a daddy 'n' de High Sheriff 'n' mos' ever'body to take up fo' her. But a colored girl? Even iffen she's got a daddy, iffen he raised a fingah he gits his haid blowed off. And yo' ain't got no daddy. I can't rightly say who yo' daddy wuz. Three o' fo' men wuz a-tendin' to me purty reg'lar 'fore you come, and hit don't matter much which'un

planted de seed whut sprouted. A colored girl lak you, whut's
smart 'n' purty, yo' got to be lak a vixen. Yo' got to look 'way
off 'n' smell them dawgs a-comin' so's yo' can run 'n' hide 'n'
make sho' *no-body* evah gits yo' in a tight place."

Loretta sighed. This time she had not been as smart as a
vixen. So she was in a tight place. As helpless as a snared
rabbit.

Her encounter with Hattie Bascomb had been degrading,
and also frightening because it was hopeless. Butt Cut had
brought her into the jail office and fingerprinted her. Then
Hattie handled the delousing and the lodgment. Hattie was a
rangy, big-boned, broad-shouldered, narrow-hipped woman in
tan slacks and matching shirt, who walked like a man and
wore her brown hair cut almost like a man's. Even when she
was in a pink dress and veiled hat, singing in the Baptist
choir, she looked like a dedicated policewoman or Army
nurse. She led Loretta into the Delousing Room and said:
"Strip!"

"You mean everything?" Loretta asked.

"Every stitch. And put 'em in this basket."

While Loretta undressed, Hattie sat in a corner of the room
where she could control the sprays from behind protective
glass.

"Now git in that first stall," Hattie ordered. "When I turn
on the sprays, run'ya fingers up through'ya hair. Lift'ya hair
and turn'ya neck to the sprays so ever' inch'll git sprayed."

Loretta objected: "Do I look like I have nits?"

"We don't take chances," Hattie said. "You're in my house
now. So do as I tell'ya."

When that spraying was finished, Hattie said: "Move into
the next stall and spraddle yo'self over that spray. Spread'ya
legs and straddle it, just like you was mountin' a mule. Then
take yo'hands and spread yo' butt." In that position Hattie
sprayed the pubic hair and perineum for crab lice.

"Now move out and stand there while the poisons finish
their killin'. I'll be back in a few minutes."

Loretta stood and remembered with shame how, when she
was a child, her mother picked nits from her head and crab
lice from her crotch. Now she resented the spraying more because she knew that once it would have been good for her, and
that it was still good for many Negroes and some whites who
entered the jail. She hated Hattie for spraying her because she
knew Hattie knew she didn't need spraying; she knew why

Hattie sprayed her; and she knew Hattie knew how she would feel and why.

When Hattie returned she ordered Loretta into the shower stall. The hot, soapy water cascaded onto her head and beat against her body. Then Hattie pointed a battery of four miniature fire hoses at her.

"Stand against the wall," Hattie said, "or it'll knock'ya down. Face the wall first, and when I tell'ya to turn around cup'ya hands over'ya teats so the water won't bruise'ya."

While the jets slammed against her body, fore and aft, Loretta gritted her teeth, held her breath, and through her tightly closed eyes saw those Negro youths sprawling under the Birmingham fire hoses.

"Now stand there before the body dryer till it turns off," Hattie said. "Then sit under this hair dryer. I'll be back to git'cha."

Hattie Bascomb hated Loretta Sykes because Hattie knew what Loretta knew about her. Loretta knew that Hattie hated her for this knowledge.

In 1948, when Hattie was fifteen, a tree fell on her father. It broke his lower back, crushed part of his pelvis. But it didn't kill him. It partially paralyzed him. He lived for seven years, in a shack in the woods, in bed; and since his wife was dead and his other children were gone, his youngest daughter, Hattie, was trapped. She had to live with him, and nurse him, until 1955 when his death freed her at twenty-two.

Thad Bascomb was forty-five when the tree hit him. The trouble was, the tree didn't cripple him sexually. It stimulated him. He couldn't read; he was illiterate. He didn't have a TV set; that was before everybody got TV. So he had nothing to do but lie there, indulge in sexual fantasy, admire his phallus which seemed to stand at perpetual attention, and shout for his daughter to "go git me a woman to come 'n' tend to this!"

Hattie Bascomb may have been the only white girl in Alabama to have to hurry through the woods, to Negro shacks, to bargain with Negro girls to come and tend to her father's erect phallus. And while the tending-to was going on, Hattie stood in the yard, or in the barn if it was raining, and listened to her father command, entreat, encourage, shout and groan in ecstasy.

Like a wife trying to persuade her husband to quit drinking, Hattie tried to persuade her father to practice continence, first for reasons of decency, then for reasons of economy.

"Pa," she argued, "we just ain't got the money. These nigger gals won't tend t'ya fer nothin'. I got to pay 'em. And the Workmen's Compensation just gives us sixty dollars a month. How we gonna eat? How'm I gonna cover my own nakedness with a dress fer Christmas?"

Sometimes Thad would quiet down for a few days. But the rule was that Hattie had to go naked and eat fatback so that she could hand the money to Negro girls who could do for a white-man-with-his-back-broke what his daughter couldn't do.

The effects of those seven years on Hattie were predictable. She hated every male on earth. She hated every Negro female. After Big Track's heroism made the Bascombs prominent, and Hattie became the jailer, she knew that every Negro female in Atoka County knew her story; and she hated this knowledge. This left only one sort of human creature which Hattie didn't hate: a white female. So white females in the jail knew how to get plenty to eat, drink and smoke. Some of them let Hattie tend to them.

Hattie lived on her hates and on her two blessed assurances. Her Blessed Lord, whom she served with song. And the Blessed Assurance that once she had a desirable white female in her possession she could tend to her more satisfactorily than any male could.

Hattie also knew something about Loretta. Everybody knew it. Loretta knew they knew it.

What Hattie and everybody knew about Loretta was that from the time she was fifteen until she was nineteen and went off to Chicago she avoided Negro males. She was, they said, "a Stancill nigger, smart and clean, with her teats a-growin' so fast they wuz a-bustin' out'a her blouse." On many afternoons, after she got back to Stancill's Mountain on the school bus, she hung around Breck Stancill's house. She helped clean up for him. Breck gave her a rebuilt typewriter and she learned to type his letters. Since Breck lived alone out there in the woods without a wife, everybody, white and Negro, could see plain as day that he was lifting Loretta's skirt. Nobody doubted it. Nobody ever disputed it. Jesus Christ Himself could never make anybody believe anything else.

But it wasn't true. The truth was that Breck Stancill gave Loretta about the same advice that Big Track later gave Allen Bascomb.

Breck had come in from the woods and was grooming his

horse, a palomino named Dan. It was a hot afternoon, so Loretta took him a pitcher of iced tea. It was her sixteenth birthday, and she had on a new red dress and had her hair fixed different. She wanted him to notice her and he did. Then he said: "Loretta, go in the house and look on my desk and bring me that letter from Montgomery Ward." When she brought the letter he said: "Sit down over there on that bench and read it to me."

Breck went right on working, not using his aluminum walking stick but steadying himself against the horse as he worked. Loretta read:

DEAR MR. STANCILL:
In reply to your letter let me emphasize that we are indeed hiring capable and personable Negro girls from Alabama with high school educations.

We regard such a girl as the best buy for Montgomery Ward on the Chicago labor market. The reasons, I'm sure, are readily apparent to you.

The ambitious Negro girl from Alabama wants to move rapidly from serfdom to the middle class. So she is the most acquisitive member of our society today. She will save on food to buy a refrigerator. So she becomes a good customer for Montgomery Ward as well as a dependable employee. We have found that Negro buying power is ACTIVE buying power.

The white girl we hire may quit when she gets married, or when her first child comes. The Negro girl from Alabama is much less likely to quit. She wants that little FHA home too much, with all that can go in it. She demands much more of her husband than Negro women once could demand. She wants her children to go to college. So she continues to work, often throughout her employable life. This doubly benefits Montgomery Ward: the longer she works the more she buys.

Please convey our best wishes to Miss Loretta Sykes. Urge her, by all means, to study hard, to become an expert typist, to learn all she can about the operation of business machines. Then, when she has her diploma, assure her that Montgomery Ward will be waiting to welcome her, to help her, and for her to help us, build the Better Life for All Americans.

Sincerely. . . .

When she finished reading neither Loretta nor Breck said anything for a while. Loretta was thinking and rereading. Then Breck said: "You understand what all that means?"

"Yes, sir. I think so. It means I got to work."

"Sure does," said Breck. "You're a smart girl. Nice-looking. A valuable human being. You want to go somewhere and have something. You don't want to live like your mother lives. You want your child to know who his daddy is. You want the daddy to marry you, and cherish you, and help you acquire a home, a Chevrolet, and an all-electric kitchen. You want your kids to go to college. That's good. I admire you for it."

Breck lifted Dan's left fore hoof and examined a loose shoe. Then he continued: "But if you want to join the middle class you must value what they value. To belong to the regulars you must be regular. So besides working here's something else you must do. Keep your skirt down and your legs crossed. Sex without prospect of marriage is for the irregulars. It isn't for strivers. When you finish high school and get up to Chicago working for Montgomery Ward, don't drop your guard. Don't let any selfish, reckless, irresponsible bastard, black, white or blue, get you in a tight place. Find you a man who wants exactly what you want. Then marry him and hitch him to the plow. Make him bring home the pay check, and be a daddy to his kids, and stay home on Saturday and mow the lawn."

Loretta, on her sixteenth birthday, had been solemn and a little scared when she said: "I know what you mean, Mistah Stancill. I'm gonna do *exactly* what you say."

Now, sitting on the bunk in the jail cell, scared half to death, she almost smiled as she remembered. She had, in fact, done exactly what Breck Stancill told her to do. Except that she hadn't yet found "Mr. Right," so now she was an aging, twenty-two-year-old virgin. She remembered the question she had then asked Breck: "Mistah Stancill, why haven't you done what you're telling me to do? Why haven't you gone off somewhere and done something big? Why don't you have a wife, and children in high school, and a new house, and a big Cadillac? All you got is a Chevy pickup, and this little old log house, and Christopher [an Irish setter] and Dan [the palomino]. You don't even have a TV!"

Breck chuckled. "I'm not a shining example, am I?" he said. "Somewhere I guess I lost my desire to acquire. Maybe it's because I was born with three thousand acres of land that won't grow much but rocks and pine trees. Ever since I got back from the war all I've wanted is just to live and help live, in the woods where it's quiet. These old people I inherited, like your mother, I want them to have their shacks, welfare commodities, relief money, TV, and Hope of Heaven. Since they all want it, I want them to be buried here on the mountain, where there won't ever be any progress so it'll always be quiet, and where they can all be together on that Great Gittin'-Up Mawning. But you young ones, I want you to continue the exodus. Hurry it up. The boys who go to the Army, I don't want them to come back. There is nothing to come back to. The rest of you, get your high school diplomas, grab that Greyhound for Chicago or wherever the jobs are, and get you a hundred-foot lot and an FHA house in the New Order. Serfdom in Alabama has had its day, and I want to see it die decently."

Because, by April, 1965, Loretta already had gained a foothold in the Chicago middle class, and because her mother wanted only to die peacefully as a serf on Stancill's Mountain, Loretta had not welcomed Charles Peck and Rev. Josh Franklin when they came to her door and identified themselves on Saturday evening. She had been almost hostile.

"Why have you stopped *here?*" she demanded. She had motioned them off the porch and joined them in the yard so her mother couldn't hear. "My mother is dying! I've come back only to nurse her. Don't you know you'll attract lightning to this house?"

"Relax, baby," said Charles Peck. "Lightning's everywhere now. Everybody's got to risk lightning."

"We don't want to bring harm to you," Josh said. "But since we know you are an NAACP member in Chicago we thought you might be willing to help us here on Stancill's Mountain."

"Here!" said Loretta. "There's nobody here anymore. Less than thirty shacks are occupied. There are no families: just the ones who are left. Maybe a dozen young people, waiting to go to the Army or somewhere else. Maybe forty old people waiting to die."

"They all count, baby," said Peck. "They all got to learn where the ballot box is. Else how we gonna keep the Big

Tracks from being sheriff and the Wallaces from being governor?"

Loretta relented enough to agree to talk a few minutes. While Peck was hiding the car among some trees, Josh said: "Since your mother is dying and I'm a preacher, perhaps you'd like me to go inside with her while you talk with Charles?"

In the moonlight Loretta looked at his blue dungarees and rough, high-topped shoes, at his bare head, crew-cut hair and youthful, tanned white face, and she smiled.

He said: "I guess she wouldn't take me for a preacher, would she?"

"She might make allowances. She likes for preachers to come to see her. Except she has never met a white preacher. That may be a problem for her. Have you got a Bible?"

"Oh, yes. In the car. I carry some of the tools of the trade. But perhaps your mother would like it if I used her Bible."

"Do you know how to talk and pray about Heaven?"

"You mean the old-time-religion Heaven?"

"I mean my mother's Heaven."

"I could try. Is that what you want me to talk about?"

"It's what I want you to talk to her about. Nothing but Heaven. Oh, grave, where is thy victory? Tell her about the white wings and the streets of gold and the sweet music, and the big fish frys and watermelon cuttin's, and especially about the Great Gittin'-Up Mawning. Don't tell her about us building a new Heaven on earth. Just tell her about the old Heaven beyond the sky."

"I'll do my best," said Josh, moving toward the house.

"Wait just a minute," Loretta said. "Wait about five minutes. She's watching Lawrence Welk now. It's one of her favorites. She particularly likes to hear Norma Zimmer sing 'In the Garden.' She looks forward to it all day every Saturday. It goes off at eight-thirty. Then we'll go in. I'll turn the TV off and tell her who you are, and tell her that you are one of the white preachers who now try to comfort Negroes. And you can talk and pray with her for twenty-nine minutes, until just before *Gunsmoke* comes on. She looks forward to it, too."

"You mean the Lord must wait on Lawrence Welk? And take His turn between Welk and *Gunsmoke?*"

"That's right," said Loretta. "I'm sure the sweet Lord my mother knows wouldn't want one of His dying chillun to miss a minute of those shows."

While Josh tried to comfort her mother, Loretta and Charles Peck sat in chairs on the porch. They talked about Atoka County, the Negro settlements, the Negro schools, and the Negro teachers whom Peck denounced as "collaborationists who already got their Chevrolets, their flush toilets in their FHA houses, and their M.A.'s from Columbia University at state expense, and who ain't takin' no chances on contrayin' The Man."

"Don't be too hard on the teachers," said Loretta. "I guess I think pretty much like they do. I pay my NAACP dues, so I support the Movement. But what I want most is to persuade the white people of Chicago, in the next year or so, to let me and my husband buy one little FHA house in one quiet suburb, so we can raise a family and work for Montgomery Ward and live happily ever after."

Peck nodded. "I know you, baby. I tabbed you on sight. You ain't no Han'kerchief Head. But up there on your coiffure is a little patch o' lace, not as big as a man's hand, but just about as big as what Jackie Kennedy puts on before she goes in to Confess. You're in the Movement up to yo' polished fingertips, but not up to yo' elbows. You're eatin' good, and you got your own private flush toilet up in Chicago, so you ain't too much troubled about yo' pore brothers and sisters who still got nits in their hair and grit in their ovah'halls."

Physically, Peck was a Negro Butt Cut Cates. Built like a fireplug. His face was broad and as dark as that of the late Nat King Cole. He wasn't a beatnik, but he wore the mustache and goatee of the Movement, and on his broad face they made him look like the portraits of Henry VIII would look had Henry been a Negro. With his khaki pants and red sports shirt he wore the calf-length boots that Big Track wore, so he was a fireplug with boots on. He was twenty-four and a graduate of Fisk University, Nashville, Tennessee. His speech often was that of a field hand with a degree in mathematics.

What further set Peck apart in the Movement was his boisterous humor. Dr. King had no fiercer disciple, but after a day of street demonstrations Peck liked to drink beer and amuse the faithful with imitations of Dr. King whom he called "De Lawd." Except for reversal of the ecclesiastical role, he was to Dr. King what Friar Tuck was to Robin Hood. He often explained that the Movement was not characterized by a celibate priesthood.

"We are an army of liberation," he preached. "And every

good soldier in every army of liberation remembers to liberate a generous woman to comfort him before the next battle." When reminded that the Ku Klux called him Big Pecker, his reply was: "Well now, brothers and sisters, let's be charitable with our Brothers of the Sheet. It ain't necessarily so that a Kluxer is wrong in ever' instance."

Peck asked Loretta who The Man was on Stancill's Mountain.

"His name is Breck Stancill," she said. "He's probably the only white man in the county you can talk to. He may not like you. He's about forty now, and I doubt that he likes many men your age who wear beards. But he'll sit on a stump and talk with you. And you don't have to be afraid of him."

"You don't think he's a Kluxer? At least in his heart?"

"Not in his heart or head or any part of him. The most famous crime in this county's history was committed right here close to where we're sitting. In 1861 Mister Breck's great-grandfather, Judge Landers Stancill, owned all this land and lived in Ellenton. He opposed Secession and wanted to end slavery. So Confederate military police and local hot-heads who later became Klansmen, they hanged Judge Stancill to a tree, right here on Stancill's Mountain, about a quarter of a mile up that road. Mister Breck passes the spot every day. You don't think he has forgotten, do you?"

Peck whistled. "We don't often run into that story. Up in Tennessee, yes, but not in Alabama. Sure, Alabama had men like Judge Stancill. Many of them. But in a hundred years of lying and Kluxing and Wallaceing, and slobberin' over films like *Gone with the Wind* and *Birth of a Nation*, the Stancills have been forgotten." After reflecting a minute Peck asked: "But if Breck Stancill's not a Kluxer, why does he let his tenants live in these old rundown shacks?"

"Oh, you know the answer to that," said Loretta. "My mother, these other people, they're not really Breck Stancill's tenants. Not any more. He owns the land, and they live here, but only one woman and maybe two men ever do any work for him. He just lets them live on here till they leave or die. After the Civil War and on down to back before I was born, the Stancills owned a lot more land. Cotton land down in the bottoms. The shacks were built up here to get away from the fever. Everybody thought folks were less likely to catch the fever in the summertime if they lived up here, and drank mountain spring water, and rode back and forth to the fields.

Then, like other folks, the Stancills kept leaving the county, and they sold off the cotton land, and cotton gave way to cattle and pine trees. Not many tenants were needed here any more. While Mister Breck was off fighting the war, his sisters both left, his father died in Germany, and his mother sold the house in Ellenton and went to Florida and married again. When Mister Breck came back, one-legged, all that was left was the mountain, and a lot of old shacks, and a log cottage up on top that his father had built for his other woman. That's the way it is now. Mister Breck lives in the cottage, and everybody just waits to leave or die."

"Baby"—Peck grinned—"the Chamber of Commerce of Atoka County ain't never gonna like you. And I still think Mistah Breck Stancill must be a lot better off than you make him out to be. He owns a whole mountain, doesn't he?"

"That doesn't mean much," said Loretta. "You must remember, first, that nothing is worth *much* in Atoka County. Not compared to cities or rich counties. I happen to know about Mister Breck's business because I used to type letters and records for him. He's got about three thousand acres. But land in pine trees is worth five dollars per acre per year. At the most. And you have to plant trees and fight fires and pay taxes. So Mister Breck is poor, not rich. If he didn't draw a little VA pension, for his leg, he wouldn't have as much cash money in a year as I have. The Negro relievers feel sorry for him because he doesn't even have a TV."

"I give up," said Peck. "He must be a kook of some sort."

"Maybe he is," said Loretta. "He just reads and writes letters and works in the woods. He does have a radio. But no telephone."

When Josh, Peck and Loretta were all standing in the yard again, and Josh and Peck were leaving, Peck put his arm around Loretta and said: "Thanks, baby. Thanks for all the information and Southern hospitality."

"You're welcome," she said. "Thank you, Reverend Franklin, for comforting my mother. She told me it was a blessing. You'll have a star in your crown."

"I was glad to try," said Josh. "I wonder if I sounded convincing, talking about Heaven? It was the first time I have ever tried."

"Nothing wrong in talking about Heaven, is there?" asked Loretta. "Even if it's true that 'evah'body talks about Hebben ain' goin' there'?"

"Well, next week, baby," said Peck, "there won't be no Hebben in Atoka County. Just Hell, like war is. We'll be calling the troops out'a school and demonstrating in Ellenton. Me and Josh'll be standing down there in the street at the courthouse eyeball-to-eyeball with old Big Track and old Butt Cut and all the other Kluxers."

Loretta shuddered. She had expected it; now she knew it. "I hope you don't get hurt," she said.

"We'll survive," said Josh. "It can't be any worse than Selma. Except we won't have as much publicity and support."

Again Peck squeezed Loretta. "I was thinking, baby," he said. "Maybe some night I might slip back up here, through the Confederate lines, up here where it's so peaceful and quiet, and you and me could sit under the trees and smell the magnolias, and like one of them Southern belles in *Gone with the Wind,* you could comfort me on the eve of Armageddon."

Loretta smiled but shook her head. "Don't come back," she said firmly. "You know my situation here. You know I can't do any more for you. As for the comfort, I'm strictly a square, remember? I don't comfort troops. You get your comfort from the camp followers. From the girls with the long stringy hair who wear the old tennis shoes."

"Okay, baby," Peck said. "But if you hear me runnin' through the woods some night, with them dawgs after me, don't harden yo' heart against me. Find me a cave to hide in."

Sitting on the bunk in her cell, Loretta wondered again why she hadn't ordered Josh and Peck to leave the minute they reached her house. Then she sighed, and guessed that their prompt departure would not have helped her. The report that they had *stopped* at her house probably would have brought the sheriff to investigate.

The door to the cell block opened and Hattie Bascomb set a food tray in the pass-through for Loretta. Hattie didn't speak but turned quickly to leave.

"Miss Bascomb!" Loretta called.

"What you want?" Hattie answered.

"Can you tell me anything about when I'm to be released? The loudspeaker says it's four o'clock, and I need to be back to my mother's house before dark."

"I don't know anything about your case," Hattie said. "My job is just to keep you clean and fed."

The steel door closed. Loretta picked at the Sunday dinner. Cornbread chicken dressing with pieces of baked chicken in it. Lima beans. Turnip greens. A piece of plain, homemade cake. Coffee.

Loretta sipped the coffee and listened to the music. Only sacred music was played in the jail on Sunday. The old song was "Walking My Lord Up Calvary's Hill."

LIGHTNING ROD

"OUR HEAVENLY FATHER, as we gather in Thy Holy Name on this Sabbath afternoon, we pray for knowledge and strength. Help us to know what we must do, and grant us the strength to do it. We stand alone, O Lord, besieged by Thy enemies, as Thy people have so often stood before. Step by step our once-Christian nation is being delivered to godless Communism. Thy altar has been banished from our schools. Those bearing the Mark of the Beast are being forced into the innocent company of our children, and the seed of the Beast is being planted in Christian wombs. Everywhere the God who directed the building of America is being proclaimed dead. His people are being driven before mobs in the street. In this desperate hour, O Lord, five of Thy servants are gathered here on our knees in secret. No man knows we are here: only Thou knowest. As devoted fathers and patriots, as red-blooded, Christian, Anglo-Saxon Americans, we want to stand up for Jesus and America. Guide us, O Lord, comfort us, protect us, assure us, strengthen us, to the end that Thy Blessed Rule on this earth may be secured and extended. We ask it all in Thy Name. Amen."

Having prayed that prayer, the Reverend Mark Alverson, pastor of the Pentecostal Baptist Church, Ellenton, Alabama, got up off his knees. So did his four companions: Vernon Hodo, Sy Shaneyfelt, Tag Taggart and Butt Cut Cates. These five were an Action Squad of the Ku Klux Klan. Vernon Hodo was the Exalted Cyclops, or commander, of the Atoka Klavern. Reverend Alverson was the Kludd, or chaplain. The others were Night Hawks, or lookouts and executioners. The meeting place was Vernon Hodo's office on the main lumberyard of the Atoka Lumber Company. Hodo was the company's "woods boss," and the yard and offices were deserted on Sunday except for a watchman who was also a Klan Night Hawk.

"It's four o'clock," said Hodo, looking at his watch. "The nigger girl's been in jail two hours. By now every nigger in the county knows we got her. Every nigger knows she was sent back in here to stir up trouble. Every nigger knows that the two Reds called Josh and Big Pecker spent last night with her on Stancill's Mountain. Every nigger knows that the Reds expect to lead demonstrations in Ellenton next week. Every nigger knows we know all they know. So every nigger expects us to *do something!* This leaves us no choice. We got to act! Now!"

Vernon Hodo spoke quietly. He was a quiet man: an artisan, expert in maintaining cutting edges on all the tools used to harvest trees. In his mid-forties, thickening around the middle, he was bald except for a grayish fringe. He wore the steel-rimmed spectacles which many such artisans wear; and he examined men with the same eye that he laid along the edge of every axe and power saw before he put a gang to work in the woods.

"You agree with me, Preacher?" Vernon Hodo asked.

Hodo and the preacher were dressed better than Shaneyfelt and Taggart. They were skilled and older; Shaneyfelt and Taggart were young, unskilled laborers. Hodo wore a blue-and-white-checked sport shirt, open at the neck. Only the preacher wore a suit and necktie. He was dressed as he had been for his morning sermon. Butt Cut wore his sheriff's uniform.

The preacher was a rangy, good-looking man, forty-five, with coal-black hair which he parted in the middle and combed back. He had been educated in a Baptist seminary. He believed in eternal damnation for unbelievers. He preached it. This had caused him to break with the regular Southern Baptists. They, too, believed in eternal damnation, but there was the matter of emphasis. Alverson preached "just too much hellfire and brimstone." So he built his own church. Many people thought he was a good man. He was no more vain, vulgar or venal than most men. He helped the poor. He visited the sick. For believers he preached a comforting funeral. His children made good grades in school. His wife, far from being dried-up and pickle-faced, was fat and jolly.

If the preacher was evil, it was because of belief. He believed that the Bible supports the belief that Negroes are more bestial than other men. He believed that the "Beast" visions of Daniel and John are warnings against Negroes. He didn't want to risk either his daughter or his son marrying a Negro.

So as a Klan chaplain Reverend Alverson thought he was like other chaplains. A chaplain may be any minister of God who encourages men who are fighting to defend or extend cherished beliefs. The Ku Klux Klan, to Mark Alverson, was the church militant.

"God has never wanted His people to be pacifists," said the preacher. "Whenever His people are threatened by the godless, God despises pacifism. Even the Savior was capable of anger and furious action. I think we must do whatever is necessary to give the enemy a sign that we shall not be moved. Violence, even wars, can be prevented by giving proper signs. Our nation could have prevented two world wars just by giving signs to the enemy that we would fight."

Every head nodded, and Butt Cut said: "And we got to do it fast. The Commies know we got the nigger gal. So by morning some Commie lawyer may present a writ. Or Breck Stancill could get back tonight and be knocking on the jailhouse door with a bond in his hand."

"How about a parade?" suggested Tag Taggart. "A motorcade. We call out the whole Klavern. Put on the sheets. Load up in fifteen, twenty cars and drive slow through every niggertown in the county."

"We could take the gal with us," said Sy Shaneyfelt. "Maybe show her off in a few places and let the niggers think we're gonna lynch her. We could use a little dynamite. Maybe burn down a nigger church."

"I'm opposed to burning churches," said the preacher. "Does more harm than good. People everywhere see the ashes on TV, and even people who aren't Communists contribute money to build them back. You can't destroy a church by burning it."

"We've paraded before," Butt Cut said. "Lots'a times. And burned crosses. And popped off dynamite. We got to do a lot more this time iffen it's to be a sign."

"Then why don't we just do it and get it over with," said Taggart. "Let's don't put it off no longer. Let's take the gal up to Stancill's Mountain, hang her right there where Judge Stancill was hung, shoot the living shit out of her—excuse the language, Preacher—and leave her right there for everybody to look at."

That suggestion quieted them for a moment. Each man reflected on it. Then Vernon Hodo cleared his throat, adjusted his spectacles, and said: "That won't do. Not now. Not in April, 1965. We're an Action Squad, all right, but the action's got to be smart now. A lot of burning, dynamitin' and killing's already been done. In Mississippi they took three out'a jail, shot 'em, buried 'em under a dam. In Georgia an Action Squad killed that nigger from Washington. Around Selma they killed one nigger, one white woman, and one white preacher. So let's think about this for a minute. What we need to do is something that won't *show*. Something that won't bring a crowd of reporters running in. Something that nobody can make a picture of. If we use fire or dynamite or a noose or guns, or even if we just beat the shit out'a the girl, we leave something that can be showed on TV. We need to do something that hurts niggers and nigger-lovers but can't be showed. Or even talked about on TV."

Butt Cut, Sy Shaneyfelt and Tag Taggart were perplexed. But the Reverend Alverson thought he saw what Vernon Hodo meant. "You mean some form of torture?" he asked.

"Yeah," said Hodo. "I mean using a nigger against a nigger. I learned that trick in the woods a long time ago. I've handled lots'a niggers, but I got my first time to ever hit one. I always had another nigger do it for me. Nothing hurts a nigger like having a smart white man just sit back and watch another nigger beating the living shit out'a him."

Butt Cut asked: "You mean you want this nigger gal beat up by a nigger?"

Like a comedian timing his punch line, Vernon Hodo delayed his answer. Then he said: "I mean Lightning Rod." He grinned as Butt Cut and Sy Shaneyfelt broke into grins. But now the preacher was perplexed, so Hodo explained to him.

"I guess you don't know Lightning Rod as well as the rest of us do, Preacher," began Hodo. "He's a big purple-black buck nigger, stout as a Jersey bull. He's crazy, or feeble-minded, or a moron, or something. He can't talk, just grunts at you. But he understands when you tell him to do something. They say that when he was a kid he was struck by lightning. And since lightning never strikes twice in the same place, the niggers say he's just as good as a lightning rod to have in the house when it's thunderin' and lightnin'. That's why they call him Lightning Rod. He lives with two old nigger women relief-hounds down on the edge of the lumberyard. Well, in the head Lightning Rod's not all there. But between his legs he's all there plus two or three extra inches. So he's hard on a woman. Especially if she tries to fight him off. He uses his fists, knees, teeth and elbows on her, and when he gets in there he *stays*. Maybe the lightning fixed him so he can stay longer'n other men."

Vernon Hodo lit a cigarette. Then he went on: "Well, Lightning Rod has made money all his life by white boys getting him out in the woods, or behind lumber piles, and paying him to show 'em his long blacksnake. They still do it. And on a Saturday afternoon, in the woods, when a white gang is paid off and the boys start to drink a little before they go home to their wives, or down to Awful Annie's, they been known to have a little fun with Lightning Rod. They catch a nigger gal somewhere, or they hire one for a lay without telling her what's gonna happen, then they form a circle in the woods, put the gal in the circle, and turn Lightning Rod in on her. I ain't never witnessed it, but the boys tell me it's a show better'n anything on TV."

"I seen it once," said Sy Shaneyfelt. "It's a good show, all right. Better'n coon-on-a-log, or dogs fightin' a bear, or a cock fight, or two lady rasslers in the mud, or a mean bull after a skittish heifer. I seen a young nigger gal fight Lightning Rod like a wildcat. He'd jump and grab at her, like a big black ape, but she'd dodge and jerk away, and he'd scramble after her, with his blacksnake sticking out there, looked like it was a foot long. While he was chasing her you could hear him grunt: 'Heh, heh, heh!' When the gal'd try to jump or break out of the ring, we'd knock her back, and she'd spit right at us, then spit at Lightning Rod. Finally, Lightning Rod knocked her down and jumped on her, and you never saw such a fight. Spittin', scratchin', bitin', kneein', elbowin', gougin'. But there was a hundred pounds difference in their weights. And when he started usin' them big knees on her, the gate just had to open, And, brother, he nailed her! When he hilted that blacksnake in her, her legs come up off the ground and she grunted just like a cow does when the bull drives it all the way to glory. That gal was one mess when old Lightning Rod got through with her."

The Reverend Alverson was shaken. "That's bestial," he said. "Vernon, you know I can't approve such an action." Then he sighed and remembered that he had come to the meeting prepared to approve murder. After a minute's reflec-

tion he became philosophical. "But I concede it's what the
Romans did to us Christians, and worse. Russians did it to
Germans in 1945. Such shows are common in the cesspools of
New Orleans. And no doubt there'll be several in niggertown
right here tonight. And niggers, as Sy says, can be likened to
the beasts of the field. The Bible likens them to beasts. So
what you propose, really, is that we do nothing but allow two
niggers the opportunity to prove again that niggers are bestial.
And every nigger in the county would learn that we have witnessed their bestiality. One way to keep an inferior race in its
place is to keep its members humiliated by what they know
about their own race."

Slowly but with conviction, Reverend Alverson nodded.
"Yes, reluctantly, and with some misgivings, I approve." (The
Kludd must approve planned acts of violence by the Ku Klux
Klan.)

But Tag Taggart objected. "It just don't seem like enough
to me," he said. "Hell, no nigger gal minds bein' raped much.
If that's all we gonna do, how's it gonna be a sign? If we gonna let this bitch off that light, how we gonna scare niggers so
they won't try to demonstrate, or try to register to vote, or try
to git in our schools? It looks to me like we gonna waste a
whole goddam Sunday doin' nothin' but helpin' Lightning
Rod git a piece'a ass!"

Vernon Hodo was a patient leader. So he handled Taggart
patiently. "You didn't listen close to the preacher, Tag. The
preacher told you how this action can do good. Butt Cut's
told me about this particular nigger gal. She's real uppity.
She's been in Chicago acting like she's white. She's got her
hair straightened and her fingernails painted. She'll think she's
too good for a pore dumb nigger like Lightning Rod. So she's
gonna be a mess when he gets through with her. A bigger
mess'n she'd be if Butt Cut worked her over with a rubber
hose. And remember this! She was sent back here to help lead
the Revolution. But tomorrow morning, or soon's she's able to
travel, she's gonna be on that Greyhound to Chicago. Every
nigger is gonna see her turn tail before the first battle starts.
How's that gonna make niggers feel? You think about it and
you'll see my proposition's smart. The gal gits mauled and
turned loose, and what can she do? Nothing. Lightning Rod
can't talk. She can't run to Huntley and Brinkley. All that
happened was that after she was turned out'a jail she laid for
some nigger. Is she gonna pose for TV pictures showing how

a nigger beat her up? Is she gonna claim that Ku Klux let a
pore nigger rape her? Wouldn't that be funny? How'd she
prove it? Who ever heard of a nigger raping another nigger?
It don't happen. So this is smart! No TV story or pictures.
Nothing for outsiders to latch on to. Just every nigger in this
county gittin' the message that the Klan is on the job, ready to
make it hard on any black s'nuvabitch that gits out'a line."

"I'm for it a hundred per cent," said Butt Cut. "I'm for it
for all them reasons plus another good reason. This gal in jail
is one'a Breck Stancill's niggers. He fucked her all during the
time she was in high school. He give her the money to go to
Chicago. It's gonna grind his guts when he learns that we let
Lightning Rod graze in one'a his pastures. And anything that
grinds Breck Stancill's guts just tickles me to death."

That erased Tag Taggart's objections. "I hadn't thought'a
that angle," he said. "That makes the proposition all right
with me. Because we all know that before this fight's finished
we gonna have to settle with Mister Breck."

"Well," said Vernon Hodo, "let's don't plan on crossing
that bridge unless we have to. Personally I got nothing against
Breck. I do business with him. He's the best tree farmer in Alabama. But he's got that one Stancill failing. In a showdown a
Stancill just naturally can't help but take the nigger's part
against the white man."

"I hope he don't push us too far," said the preacher. "He's
got a lot'a good about him. But a hundred years ago men of
God got on their knees and tried to pray and reason with his
granddaddy. But his granddaddy wouldn't reason. So he
stretched a rope. Maybe it's just a fact of life that every
hundred years God-fearing white Christians have to hang a
Stancill to keep things right in Atoka County."

The meeting adjourned after these further understandings:

Sy Shaneyfelt and Tag Taggart were to find Lightning Rod,
"keep him in tow," and ready him for his performance by giving him two or three jolts of corn whiskey. They were to
bring him to the jail at 7:30 P.M., by which time Hattie Bascomb would be lifting her voice in song in the choir of the
First Baptist Church.

Butt Cut would move Loretta Sykes to the jail's soundproof
Deranged Room. If Big Track returned during the action, it
was assumed he would cooperate.

Vernon Hodo would arrive at 7:35 to witness the action.
As for Reverend Alverson, he explained: "The timing poses a

difficulty for me. At seven-thirty I am supposed to be in my pulpit to bring the Sunday evening message. But I'll arrange for a substitute. As a chaplain in the United States Army in 1944 one of my duties was to be present at executions. A prison chaplain must be present whenever the State of Alabama employs the electric chair. So, as your chaplain, I must be with you tonight. I must stand with this Action Squad of the Ku Klux Klan to prove that your action is not a crime but is a deterrent to crime. The sole purpose of our action will be to help defend a Christian way of life."

The land which became Atoka County, Alabama, has never made any man rich: no Indian, no white settler, no Negro slave, serf or freeman. It is land on which some men have found freedom and status, but from which no man has accumulated wealth.

Lying between the Tennessee and Tombigbee rivers, this land was never claimed by any Indian tribe. No Indian village ever existed on it. No Indian ever cleared a foot of it, or planted a hill of corn on it. To the Indians it was hilly, rocky, less fertile than land in the Alabama Black Belt or the Mississippi Delta; so they used it only as a communal hunting ground, not worth claiming and fighting for. The Creeks, the Choctaws, the Chickasaws, they all hunted there freely, for bear, deer and wild turkey.

This land was "opened up" by General Andrew Jackson when he cleared a military road through it to support his campaigns against the Indians. One of Jackson's young lieutenants, from the Abbeville district of South Carolina, was named Fowler Stancill. After the Battle of New Orleans, in 1815, Fowler Stancill invested most of his mustering-out pay in a fourteen-year-old Negro boy, and the two walked from New Orleans to the area of Ellenton. At two dollars an acre, with four years in which to pay the two dollars, Fowler Stancill took up land and became the first settler in what was to become Atoka County. He was not the first *white* settler; he was the first settler of any color.

By 1820 every acre of Atoka County's 384,000 acres had been taken up by white men, many of them from South Carolina. They came in flatboats down the Tennessee River to Muscle Shoals, then walked or rode down the Old Hickory Trail. Fowler Stancill married another settler's daughter, and in 1817 the first child was born in the county. His name was

Landers Stancill, and in his forty-fourth year of life he was to
be hanged for opposing secession and advocating gradual abolition of slavery.

Some of these settlers couldn't bring or buy slaves. They remained yeomen: free but without status. Because they worked
"like a nigger" in the sun they were "rednecks." Other settlers
brought and bought slaves, for slave-owning meant status.
The "rich" planter sold raw cotton in an up-and-down foreign
market, and with his profits, if any, he bought more land and
slaves to grow more cotton to gain more status. But these
"rich" planters were always in debt; they were never "monied." This is why slavery failed long before it was abolished. It
couldn't create significant amounts of capital. It couldn't support industry. It couldn't diversify. Slavery could give status.
In rare cases, where the land remained fertile, slavery could
give wealth to a planter's family. But it couldn't create mass
buying power. For what did the "rich" planter buy for his
slaves? Coarse cotton cloth, cheap shoes, primitive plows and
hoes, mules, molasses, fat pork and corn meal. The rednecks
could buy for themselves little more, often less, than the planter bought for the slaves. So the South in general and Atoka
County in particular, because its land wore out quickly, had
too many producers and too few consumers. Atoka County's
postbellum planters were even less "monied." They were
"rich" only in worn-out land, serfs and status.

The houses in Atoka County told the money story. From
Fowler Stancill's arrival in 1815 to the end of the Second
World War, the most expensive house built in the county was
the $12,000 home built by Philip Stancill in Ellenton in 1890.
Philip was the son of Landers Stancill, the grandson of Fowler Stancill. Philip's grandson, Breckenridge Stancill, was born
in that $12,000 house in 1924.

In the Philip Stancill house, as in the few $10,000 houses
built in 1850, or 1890, or 1910, the carpentry was second-
rate, the stone work was third-rate, and the plumbing, if any,
was fourth-rate. For where were the artisans? From slavery
and serfdom came a few Negro artisans, but not many, because once a slave became skilled he was too valuable to be
worked even part-time as a field hand. He was "leased out" by
his owner. The artisan slave or serf became the freed slave or
serf; and like the white yeoman who became skilled, he often
went North or to Mobile or New Orleans.

Money began coming to Atoka County only after the New

Deal, with the TVA, the REA, the FHA and the minumum-
wage law; after the expansions, particularly in aluminum for
bombers, forced by the Second World War; after the growth
of the lumber and pulpwood industries; after the big cotton
farms became tree farms; and after the small farmers, all of
them white, began raising poultry and cattle along with ten-
acre allotments of cotton at a government-supported price.
Between 1945 and 1965 many FHA houses were built,
costing between $8,000 and $14,000. Building itself became
an industry which attracted and sustained artisans, all of them
white. And in Ellenton in 1965 there were two new homes,
each costing in the neighborhood of $100,000.

One of these "conspicuous consumption" homes belonged
to Dr. Ted Parker, for doctors, between 1945 and 1965, became the first truly "monied" men Atoka County had ever
seen. In almost every town of any size in Alabama the talk-
causing new home was a doctor's; and there was a saying that
"the only way a doctor can keep from getting rich now is for
the s'nuvabitch to get in jail for not paying enough income
tax."

The other expensive home in Ellenton belonged to Hardy
Riddle, superintendent of the Atoka Lumber Company and
the encourager of Butt Cut's bulletin board operations.

Just as being an Army hero had helped lift Big Track Bascomb from "nothing" to a $12,000 home and the position of
sheriff, so had being a football hero helped lift Hardy Riddle
from "a little something" to a $100,000 home and executive
position in the county's largest industry. Back in the thirties,
after starring for the Ellenton Blue Devils, Hardy went to the
University of Alabama on a football scholarship and played
in the Rose Bowl. He was an all-American center and line-
backer, expert at both advancing his teammates and stopping
his opponents. Displayed on his desk at the lumber company
was his motto: WINNING ISN'T EVERYTHING, BUT IT SURE
BEATS THE HELL OUT OF LOSING.

Nor was Hardy's influence confined to the lumber company. An "athlete's heart" had kept him out of the wars, so he
had stayed at home and used his popularity, his friendliness,
his good looks and his winning habit to get his finger in just
about every pie in the county. As a bank director he headed
the committee which approved every loan over $500. He was
part owner of the Atoka Inn, the new motel where the Rotary
and Lions clubs met. He was the silent partner in an insur-

ance agency which also "handled real estate." He was on the
Board of Stewards of the First Methodist Church. He was the
unofficial executive officer of the Atoka County Establishment:
the man to see if you wanted votes, money or "something
done."

In 1965 Hardy was fifty, still muscular, vigorous, with a
full head of graying hair. He was a big, shaggy man who wore
sport coats and sporty, narrow-brimmed hats, smoked pipes,
and had a face which might have been hewn from hickory.
He was relaxed, friendly, able, successful, confident, and he
would have been liked in almost any group except perhaps a
labor union and the NAACP. His blowzy wife, whom he
called Mama, was "in everything," and they had a yardful of
well-adjusted children and grandchildren. Hardy kept in shape
by playing handball in his basement with the young Methodist
Minister of Song.

Hardy Riddle's "connection" with Big Track Bascomb was
typical of the way he operated. In addition to Butt Cut and
Hattie, Big Track had a third employee, Trixie Cunningham,
who "ran things" at the sheriff's office in the courthouse. Trixie was an auburn-haired divorcee, about thirty-five, one of
those neat-looking, sharp, sensual women who know how to
meet the public as well as handle paperwork. Trixie was an
asset to Big Track, political and financial: she could call every
voter in the county by name. She was loyal to Big Track. But
she wasn't Big Track's "woman." She was Hardy Riddle's
"woman." She used what she had to make Hardy, not Big
Track, think he could conquer the world. Her working for Big
Track had been Hardy's idea. Hardy loaned Trixie to Big
Track, just like he loaned him money and votes, to help him
get ahead.

Whenever he bothered to think about it, Big Track knew he
wasn't happy with the "Trixie situation." He knew what folks
were saying:

"Hardy's got Trixie in there to tell him what's going on before she even tells Big Track. And she tells Hardy in bed."

"That Hardy don't miss a trick. He makes Big Track buy
his tail for him, and even watch out for him while he's gettin'
it."

"Trixie takes Big Track's money and does her tricks for
Hardy."

"Old Hardy never lets Big Track fergit that a all-American
outranks a Medal-of-Honor winner."

"Big Track, Butt Cut, Trixie and Hattie, they all dance when Hardy fiddles."

Big Track didn't like it. More than once he caught himself thinking about taking Trixie to the woods and teaching her that the man who feeds the cow has a right to drink at least a little of the milk. But Big Track needed Hardy and Trixie to get re-elected and to send his son to West Point. No matter how many votes Big Track delivered to the congressman, that congressman would never appoint to West Point a boy from Atoka County who wasn't recommended by Hardy Riddle.

After the meeting of the Klan Action Squad at the lumberyard, Exalted Cyclops Vernon Hodo drove to Hardy Riddle's home. He stopped his car in the driveway and rang the bell at the side door. One of the children let him in and led him to the basement where Hardy was in shorts and gym shoes practicing his handball. He pulled on a sweat shirt and sweat pants and sat down with Vernon. No drinks were ordered or brought because it was not a social visit or a meeting of equals. It was the boss of the Atoka Lumber Company being disturbed on a late Sunday afternoon by an employee with an urgent report too confidential to be telephoned.

"Skipper," said Vernon, "I guess you already know we're likely to have a little street demonstratin' next week?"

Hardy grunted. "We'll handle it just like we planned," he said. "I'm gonna talk with Big Track, tonight if he gets back in time. If not, first thing in the morning."

"Then I guess it won't surprise you," said Vernon, "to learn that the Klan has a little action laid on for tonight. I thought you'd want to know about it."

"Yeah, I want to know about it," Hardy said. "But I don't want to know what you're gonna do. I might have to put my hand on a Bible sometime. So it's not good sometimes for a man in my position to know too much. Just enough. What I want to know is what you're *not* gonna do. So I'll ask some careful questions and you give me careful answers. You're *not* gonna kill anybody?"

Vernon shook his head. "Absolutely not, Skipper."

"You're sure?"

"Absolutely. Not a chance."

"You're not gonna maim anybody? Like cutting his balls off, or cutting up his back so I got to look at pictures of 'Alabama racist atrocities' on Huntley and Brinkley? Or so my stockholders got to read in the *Wall Street Journal* about what 'barbarians' we are in Alabama?"

"No, sir, Skipper. We got more sense'n do that."

"You're not gonna burn a building down or use dynamite, so I got to look at some more'a that kind'a pictures?"

"Not a chance, Skipper. We learned better'n that."

Hardy thought a minute, to see if he had thought of all forms of atrocity which can be publicized. Then he said: "Okay. I guess it's all right. You know how I feel, Vernon. I told you four years ago when we were thinking about you organizing this Klan here. My only interest is the continued orderly development of Atoka County. We have fine, Christian people here, great opportunity, and we're moving for the first time in our history. A Klan, through periods of trouble, if it's run right, can be a useful adjunct to police power. So far, you've run it right, and you've seen my appreciation in your pay check. The way for a Klan to be useful is to just *be there!* The generals call it a 'deterrent force in being.' Just be there, but don't do much, except burn a few crosses and sing 'The Old Rugged Cross,' and if you have to take some agitator out and talk to him, maybe touch him up a little, make sure you leave him feeling just sort of chastised, so he can't run to the FBI about it. Make him feel that you're really his friends, just his good, Christian neighbors trying to keep him in line, so everybody can get along. A Klan should just *be there,* so everybody knows it's there, and knows what it can do if it has to. A Klan is not being run smart if it takes action that attracts outside attention."

"I know how you feel about that, Skipper," said Vernon. "You're one hundred per cent right. But you understand my problem. Some Klansman is always standing up in the meetin' sayin' 'Hell, if I'm gonna be a Ku Klux I want to Kluck!' That means he wants action. He don't want to keep coming out at night, missing good shows like Red Skelton and Andy Griffith, and not seeing no action! It's like trying to keep a good army without ever doing no fighting."

"Sure, I know, Vernon," said Hardy. "But you've proved you can handle that. You've done a great job. Whenever these Kluxers have got too big a hard on to go cutting or killing or burning, you've taken them down to Awful Annie's and let 'em do a little drinking and jigging at the expense of the Atoka Lumber Company. We've charged it off to Community Relations Expense. And the Willie Washington lynching helped you out a year or so ago. It gave the boys action without hurting as much. The TV reporters couldn't call it a 'civil rights atrocity.' Willie had it coming to him. He caught that poor young white mother stranded out there in the dark on the highway, so he threw a gun on her and made her take the blacksnake. Lynching Willie just saved the state the cost of electricity to operate the electric chair. But right now we don't want any sort of Klan publicity. Not just two weeks after three killings in Selma! So tonight you make damn sure that none of those Kluxers get trigger-happy, or dynamite-happy, or club-happy, or knife-happy right now when we got to handle these little demonstrations in Ellenton."

Vernon Hodo shifted his weight in the chair. "That brings me to a last question, Skipper," he said. "Then I got to run and let you get back to your handball. Everybody wants to know just how much we gonna give these niggers if they keep up demonstratin'."

"I don't want to talk much about that," Hardy said. "That's something that don't do to talk about. But I'll tell you we're gonna give a little bit. Not much, but enough to be smart. We've got fine colored people in this county, and we've always been good to them. You and I know that some of the best workers the lumber company's got are colored. Hell, it was them who turned Willie Washington over to Big Track! They were ashamed of him. So we're gonna let two or three Negro kids go to every white school. Hell, the roof don't fall just because a couple of scared black kids attend a white school! We're gonna let a few Negroes vote, and one or two sit on a jury now and then. We're reasonable! We're not gonna do any standing in the door or drawing any lines. That's George Wallace crap. It's good for George, but not for Ellenton. You just tell the Kluxers not to get their bowels in an uproar. Negroes will keep leaving Atoka County. That's inevitable. We got new machines coming in to cut labor costs in the woods and in the mills. The Negroes who stay here are gonna keep on being hewers of wood and drawers of water. We won't have any Negro girl secretaries, or Negro bank tellers, or Negroes counting money at the supermarkets. And, just like in Chicago, we won't have any Negro carpenters or plumbers or electricians or painters or bricklayers or garage mechanics. So the Kluxers have nothing to worry about. But don't tell them all this I'm telling you, Vernon. They'd talk it, and it might foul things up. Just feed it to 'em gradually. Let 'em horse around a little tonight, but not much. Tell 'em to keep their shirts on.".

A thought caused Hardy to grin, and he added: "I mean tell 'em to keep their sheets on."

As the Exalted Cyclops was leaving, and Hardy Riddle was pulling off his sweat pants, another thought came to Hardy. "And Vernon," he said, "I want to see Big Track tonight at nine-ten. No earlier, no later. Between eight and nine on Sunday I look at *Bonanza*. Just before ten I go to bed and look at the *CBS Sunday News*. When it's over I turn my light off. So tell Big Track to be here at nine-ten. Or, if you miss seeing him, leave word for him with Butt Cut or Hattie."

Lying on the bunk in her cell, listening to Ernie Ford sing "I Know My Savior Cares," Loretta Sykes was losing her fight to remain calm. Five hours alone in the cell block had frightened her more than the encounters with Butt Cut and Hattie. It had been five hours of waiting, listening and fearing, and the cumulative effect was now causing her lower lip to tremble unless she exerted conscious effort to control it. I must remain calm, she thought. I must not scream. I must keep my senses. As part of her effort, she tried to stand aside, outside herself, and compare in intensity the fear she felt now with fear she had felt at other times in her life.

One night when she was nine her mother barricaded herself in the pantry against a berserk Negro man with a butcher knife. Loretta ran nearly a mile to Breck Stancill's house. Breck was in his nightshirt, his leg off. With no time to strap it on, he hopped to his pickup and raced down the road, with Loretta at his side certain that they would find the pantry torn apart and her mother dead. At the shack Loretta watched Breck, hopping on his left foot, attack the man and take the knife away from him.

Then there was her first night away from Stancill's Mountain, on the bus to Chicago when she was eighteen. Alone, on a rear seat, she never closed her eyes. She prayed, watched the dark, flat fields of Indiana, and knew she was homeless, uprooted. Each time the bus stopped and the lights went on, she looked for a friendly face. But she saw only neutral or hostile faces entering the bus. The first morning at Montgomery Ward's her legs almost collapsed when she was told to walk into the office of the personnel manager. Twice in Chicago, returning to her sister's house from night school around

11 P.M., she was chased by gangs of youths intent on gang-raping her. But she dodged and ran and hid, like the vixen her mother raised her to be.

This time, she thought, I'm more afraid than I have ever been. There is more danger. They've caught me, so they feel compelled to do *something* to me! It's dark outside by now, and they can't just walk in here and hand me my clothes and tell me to go home and forget it. They are just like the boys who chased me in Chicago. Had those boys caught me, each boy would have felt compelled to prove himself on me. To avoid ridicule, even self-ridicule, he would have had no choice. The Kluxers are like that. They have been standing guard against outside agitators. Now they have caught one. So they have no choice. They, too, in some manner, must prove themselves on me. Will they kill me? Why not? They killed in Mississippi, they killed in Selma, they even killed girls in church in Birmingham. Why shouldn't they kill in Ellenton?

At 7:10 P.M. Butt Cut arrived at the jail so Hattie could go to church. She was ready, in her pink dress and white hat, with a white pocketbook in one hand and a hymnbook in the other.

"Before you go," said Butt Cut, "how about movin' the nigger gal fer me? Put her in the Nut Cage."

Butt Cut, without telling Vernon Hodo or anyone else, had decided to implicate Hattie. At least to some extent. He didn't want her telling Big Track that she had been told nothing. When she hesitated he said: "We got fourteen other prisoners in this jail. Eight male niggers, four male whites, and two female whites. If I have to teach the nigger gal a little lesson before I turn her loose, you don't want them others listenin', do'ya? Them cell blocks damn sho' ain't soundproof."

Hattie said: "Big Track ought'a be back in another hour'a so. Why don't you wait till he gits here? He ought'a decide things like that."

"He might git back too late. We got a tip that she might be sprung most any minute. You don't want her just walkin' out'a here, do'ya? Like she wasn't guilty? Without bein' taught nothin'? And showin' ever' nigger in the county that we can't lay a hand on filthy agitators?"

No, Hattie didn't want that. So she shook off her doubts and said: "Okay. But don't do nothin' you know Big Track wouldn't want'cha to do."

Hattie laid down the pocketbook and hymnbook, picked up the keys, and went to the cell-block door. "Okay, Loretta," she called through the baffle. "Bring your comb and tooth-brush and come heah."

As her cell door slid back and the cell block door swung open, Loretta obeyed. She felt relieved that whatever had to happen seemed about to happen. But she almost fainted when Hattie opened the door to the Deranged Room and motioned her in. Like peering into a cave, Loretta looked into the bare, dimly lighted room and gasped: "Is it . . . is it a gas chamber? Are you going to smother me?"

"Do what I tell ya," ordered Hattie. "Git in there."

Loretta put her hands to her face and began crying. "Please . . . Miss Bascomb . . . please help me. Don't shut me up in there and go off. Please help me."

"Git in there, nigger," Hattie repeated sharply. "Don't start cryin' on me. I don't owe'ya nothin' but a hard time."

Hattie grabbed the comb and toothbrush and shoved Loret-ta through the doorway. Loretta sank to her knees, crying. Hattie said: "Now give me that suit'cha got on. Strip it off. Quick."

Loretta raised her head, still pressing her hands to her cheeks. "You mean . . . stark naked? Please, Miss Bascomb!"

"You want me to call Butt Cut to come'n strip'ya?"

Slowly, Loretta managed to slip out of the prison suit. Hat-tie snatched it up. Loretta sat naked on the sponge-rubber floor, looking up at Hattie. Before Hattie closed the door, like pouring scalding water from a kettle down on a trapped rat, she poured hate down on Loretta.

"You should'a stayed up there in Chicago and not come back in heah makin' trouble. Now'ya can work at tryin'ta save yerself by usin' them three holes that ever' black bitch is so expert at usin' on a stiff white dick."

Again, alone, Loretta struggled to calm herself. She stood up and examined the cell. She found that the entire floor was spongy. So were the walls. By jumping she could touch the ceiling, and it, too, was spongy. She knew she was in a sound-proof cell because once she had seen a TV show about a girl dreaming she was in such a cell. The girl was screaming, but no one could hear her: no sound came from the soundtrack. The girl became even more hysterical on realizing that she couldn't hear herself: no matter how "loud" she screamed she couldn't hear a sound.

To learn if she could hear herself, Loretta spoke the words she always used to test a typewriter ribbon: "Every good boy does fine." She felt relieved to hear her own voice, though it sounded as if she were speaking through a handkerchief. She noticed the Oriental toilet in the center of the floor: an aluminized hole to squat over, like a child or an animal does in the woods. She noticed the yellow light in the center of the ceiling, directly above the toilet. It was burning at half-light. Loretta knew she couldn't regulate it. She couldn't choose darkness or light, dim or bright; those choices would be made outside. When she found the circular observation window she shrank from it, into a corner so that her nakedness couldn't be observed. Then she noticed a second window, in another wall and at a right angle to the first. This meant there was no corner in which she could not be observed.

Facing the door, and as far from it as she could get, Loretta sat down. From what Hattie had said the first attack on her would be sexual. Loretta knew about most forms of sexual attack. She was lacking in personal experience but not in knowledge. She had seen all the sights of a primitive, rural childhood, heard all the talk. In Chicago she had seen urban sights, heard urban talk. She had even read a modern marriage manual. So she was a knowledgeable, adult, tethered virgin awaiting attack.

How could she resist? She didn't know judo or karate. Her nails were not claws. They were typist's nails, too short to be a defensive weapon. Her teeth were clean and white, but they were not fangs. Her knees? Her elbows? Her quickness in dodging? Her ability to wriggle, like the greased pig clutched at by boys at a county fair? Could these help her in a six-by-eight-foot crib? What about submitting? Assisting in her own defilement? Doing like the jokes say? Contributing a wiggle to abbreviate the attack? Or, as Hattie suggested, what about using alleged African magic to tame the snake?

Had Loretta not been so afraid of losing her life, she might have worried about being impregnated or infected by her attackers. She might have wept at the prospect of losing her virginity to a man who hated her. She had wanted to lose it to a man who loved or, at least, liked her. But pregnancy, infection, defloration were minor worries now. Loretta wanted to live.

She noticed a white mask at one of the observation windows. She had to look twice before she could realize that it was real, that it was a Ku Klux Klan mask, and that a human face was behind it. The face was that of the priest, the medicine man, the Reverend Mark Alverson, come to bless the rite. The Exalted Cyclops had decreed that the victim was not to see a bare white face during the rite. This was according to Klan law, according to much ancient practice, and it was prudent. The masked face is the unidentified face.

Another mask appeared at the other window, after which masks seemed to be taking turns at both windows. Loretta became so absorbed watching this alternation of masks that for a moment she forgot to be afraid.

Then the door was jerked open. A naked and frightened man was pushing inside, and the door was closed. Lightning Rod stood looking around the cell and at Loretta.

Instantly Loretta understood. She recognized Lightning Rod. She had never known him, but he had been pointed out to her when she was in high school. She had heard descriptions of the rite sometimes celebrated in the woods on Saturday afternoon by white employees of the Atoka Lumber Company. She had once talked with a girl who had survived the rite. Every literate Negro in Atoka County knew that Lightning Rod was the poor white man's proof that all Negroes are bestial and simple-minded.

Now they have drafted him to tear me down, thought Loretta. They can't bear the idea of Negroes voting, being educated, and earning $105 a week as skilled workers. So they are going to watch Lightning Rod nail me with his horse cock and imagine they are watching the nailing of every Negro who strives and aspires and hopes. They'll rivet their eyes on the horse cock and say to themselves: "See there! That's what every red-blooded, God-fearing, Anglo-Saxon white man's got to fight to protect his womenfolks from."

For the first time since her arrest Loretta began to lose her fear. Defiance began to replace it. She thought of trying to communicate with Lightning Rod. Since the masked watchers probably couldn't hear words spoken inside the cell, why shouldn't she say to Lightning Rod: "Can't you see that we both are victims of men who despise us? So let's refuse to entertain them. Let's sit down together and compel them to kill us or leave us alone. Or, since your horse cock is your claim to attention and a source of income, if you feel you must put

it in me to preserve your reputation, then let me submit so
that, at least, we can deny our enemies the pleasure of watching me resist."

But communication was impossible. Just as a battered old
prize fighter assumes his fighting stance when he hears the
crowd, so Lightning Rod, on seeing the masked faces at the
windows, went into his crouch fully prepared to attack. Loretta decided then that she would never submit. To the limit of
her strength she had to resist, even if he knocked out her
teeth, gouged out her eyes, or choked her to death.

The watchers found the contest exciting. Perhaps it was
worthy of the coliseum. Bear-baiters would have liked it. Lovers of bull-fighting might have seen something beautiful in it.
It would have looked impressive on color TV. The entire in-
terior of the cell, the sponge rubber, was a luxurious green,
like Kentucky "blue" grass after April rain. Loretta's skin was
like melba toast, and Lightning Rod was as black as Sir Lau-
rence Olivier playing Othello for the screen. Quickly, they
both began to sweat, adding sheen, like a photographer adds
with glycerin. The light was golden, and as Butt Cut kept
playing with the rheostat, varying the intensity, the light
seemed at times to gild the struggling figures. It was shining
ebony on burnished bronze on velvety green, with splotches of
turkey red, like Loretta's lips, or Lightning Rod's tongue, or
blood, or the head of the horse cock.

In Saigon before all the wars, on the walls of opium dens
there were carved, gilded figures of human beings engaged in
phallus worship. Always the central figure was the man with a
phallus so large that he needed community assistance to help
him carry it. The scene in the Ellenton jail was something like
that.

The trouble was the contest was too brief. Had the arena
been as large as a boxing ring, Loretta might have dodged and
darted until Lightning Rod lost his breath. But the arena was
no larger than a cockpit. Or had Lightning Rod been a gentle-
man and refrained from hitting, gouging and choking, his success might have remained in doubt long after he knocked her
down and jumped on her. But Lightning Rod played by jungle
rules. He tolerated squirming only as long as it pleased him.
Then WHAM! the stunning backhand across the face. Once
Loretta was stunned her maidenhead caused a few beats of
delay. But it was no problem; the watchers didn't notice it.

Then Lightning Rod hilted his horse cock and enjoyed half an hour of varied and complete conquest.

During this half-hour, since Loretta seemed unlikely to scream, the Klansmen opened the cell door for more convenient observation. They stood around, lit cigarettes and smoked them through their masks, and made comments, like farmers whittling, jawing and chewing tobacco while a bull is servicing a heifer.

"That's something to see, ain't it," said Vernon Hodo. "I swear to God I never thought he could git all that thing in her."

"Nigger women are made for it," Reverend Alverson explained. "He'd tear something loose in a white woman. But nigger women are made for it. They breed easily and drop children like cows drop calves."

"It'd'a been a lot better if we'd took 'em out in the woods," said Sy Shaneyfelt. "We could'a give her more room to dodge in. She had a lot'a fight in her. Maybe more'n that gal I told you about. But in this cubbyhole she didn't have much chance. He was all over her like a blanket."

"We couldn't risk takin' 'em to the woods," said Vernon. "We might'a attracted attention."

When Lightning Rod had all he wanted, he sat slumped in a corner, like a tired old black lion sitting on his haunches near the ruins of a carcass. Loretta lay on her side, sobbing quietly, her eyes closed, as they had been through much of the performance.

"You boys better git the Champ out'a here," said Vernon to Sy Shaneyfelt and Tag Taggart. "Give him the rest'a that pint'a corn and this coupl'a bucks. He's a good boy. I'll let my wife see if I ain't got some old clothes to give him."

"I guess I'll be going too," said the preacher. "I don't seem to be needed here any more. I hope what we've done tonight serves the holy purpose we intended it to serve."

"It's bound to help," said Vernon. "Nobody who's here'll ever mention it. Or admit it ever happened. Except the gal. She'll tell a few niggers, then light a shuck back to Chicago. The niggers'll git the message. They'll know who's on the job and still lookin' down their throats."

In the jail corridor the Klansmen removed their masks and robes, Lightning Rod put on his clothes, and they all moved into the jail office. Hattie Bascomb came back from church, nodded to them, and went into her apartment to take off her

Sunday clothes. Sy Shaneyfelt and Tag Taggart, with Lightning Rod, went out the back door; the preacher went out the front door, leaving Butt Cut and Vernon Hodo.

"What'cha gonna do with the gal now?" asked Vernon.

"I guess I'll leave her there in the Nut Cage till Big Track gits here," said Butt Cut. "I'll tell him what we done. Then I'll do what he says. I guess he'll want me to take her back out there on the mountain and turn her black ass a'loose."

"Okay," said Vernon. "I guess I'll call it a day. I guess we've done all the damage we can do. If Big Track gits here in time, tell him the Skipper wants to see him at nine-ten. Not much later because the Skipper goes to bed in time for the ten o'clock news."

After Vernon went out the front door, for some reason Butt Cut walked back to the Deranged Room. The door was closed, so he looked in through a glass. Loretta was still lying there, on her side, her back to the door. For the first time Butt Cut noticed the amount of blood. Loretta was lying in blood, and across the back of her leg blood was running onto the floor.

At that moment Butt Cut heard voices in the jail office. Big Track and Allen, with their prisoner, were home from their trip to Mobile.

BRECK

"WHAT'S WRONG?" asked Big Track as he and Allen walked into the jail office with the prisoner. Butt Cut looked worried.

"I got to tell you some'pin," said Butt Cut. "In private."

"Okay," said Big Track. "Let's cell this punk in a Day Room till we find time to process him."

After celling the prisoner, Big Track, Butt Cut and Hattie stood in a corridor while Allen remained in the office. Hurriedly Butt Cut told of arresting Loretta and of what had happened in the Deranged Room. They all went and saw that Loretta was bleeding seriously.

"Must'a started her monthlies," said Butt Cut.

"Maybe," said Big Track. "But that's a lot'a blood. She's gonna be in bad shape if it don't slow down pretty quick. See what'cha can do, Hattie."

As Hattie entered the cell, Big Track and Butt Cut moved toward the office. "Hardy wants to see you," said Butt Cut. "Right now. At nine-ten. For sure he wants to see you before ten."

In the office Big Track told Allen to wait in the Wildcat for him. Hattie reported: "I ain't sure what's wrong with her. She says her monthlies ain't due for a week. We better do something. I give her some Kotex."

Big Track thought fast. Like he was back in Korea under night attack. Then he said: "It ain't safe fer us to claim that this nigger wasn't never in this jail. You jailed her in broad daylight so ain't no tellin' who might'a seen'ya. So both of'ya listen close. You jailed this nigger fer investigation at two P.M. Let the record show it plain. Both of'ya was here. At seven-fifteen tonight, about two hours ago, you released her. Let the record show it plain. Both of'ya was here. You released her just before Hattie went to church. That's how'ya remember so plain. The last thing either one of'ya saw of her she was walking out that door and down the street in perfect health."

"I got it," said Butt Cut. Hattie nodded.

"We all three got it," said Big Track. "That's the way it *was*. We ain't never gonna mix it up. Now here's what we do now. Butt Cut, you bring the Ford to the jail door. Then you take the Wildcat and drive Allen home. Tell Allen to tell Maybelle I'm tied up and may not git home 'fore midnight. Then you drive back here, listenin' out fer me on the radio. Hattie, you go git the nigger ready to move. Plug up that bleedin' somehow, put her clothes on, and make sure that nothin' o' hers is left in the jail. Lock her in the back seat o' the Ford without lettin' anybody see'ya. Then you come back in here, clean up the Nut Cage, fix the record just right, and you listen out fer me."

"Le'me take the nigger," urged Butt Cut. "I know how to do it."

"Just do what I tell'ya," snapped Big Track.

Big Track then telephoned Hardy Riddle. "Skipper," he said, "I just got back. Yeah, fine trip. I took my boy down to see the battleship *Alabama*. Yeah, we seen the governor and Jim Clark. The governor sent'cha his regards. Skipper, I just can't make it by'ya house any time soon. I got a coupl'a rows to hoe."

"Anything I ought to know about?" asked Hardy.

Big Track hesitated, then said: "I guess not. Just routine. And I got'ta git up early in the morning to tend'ta any demonstratin' that might come off."

Maybe it was because Big Track had hesitated. Or maybe it was because Hardy had felt uneasy ever since his talk with Vernon Hodo. Whatever it was, Hardy said: "I'm not much sleepy tonight, Track. I think I'll watch the late movie. So why don't you call me in an hour or two, after you get caught up."

"Okay, Skipper," said Big Track. "If you're sure I won't be waking you up."

Big Track went to a desk and, far back in a bottom drawer, he found a "zip gun" he once took from a Chicago Negro. It had been fashioned from a piece of half-inch pipe about five inches long. Its crude plunger could explode a .38 cartridge and propel a slug into a brain. Big Track slipped it into his pocket as he headed for the door.

With Loretta in the Ford with him, Big Track drove toward Stancill's Mountain. He didn't drive fast because he was thinking. As always he thought of protection: of protecting his family, his income, his good name as a Medal of Honor winner, his son's appointment to West Point. He wanted parents to keep wanting their children to pose with him for snapshots on the battleship *Alabama*. He wanted to keep hearing cheers when he was introduced at American Legion conventions. He wanted to keep feeling that he could still stand proudly before President Truman. He wanted to keep feeling that if he ever got hungry again he could sit down at Breck Stancill's table and eat.

If they just hadn't'a left this nigger bleeding so much! he thought. Then I could'a turned her loose and she couldn't'a caused trouble. She wouldn't'a had no evidence. It'd just'a been her word, and nobody believes a nigger woman ever gits raped. But if I turn her loose *now* what does she do? She's got to run to the Atoka Hospital. Dr. Parker sees the evidence, and she tells him Ku Klux did it to her in the jail! She tells Breck Stancill. Since she's tied in with outside agitators, she tells them and they tell the FBI. Maybe they tell Huntley and Brinkley. And all this telling comes right when we got demonstratin' and publicity to bother with. Sure, it's her word against Butt Cut's and Hattie's. But it causes me trouble. So I got no choice. To look after my interest I got to shoot her and leave her in a ditch. When I hear about it I investigate and find that agitators or some other niggers robbed her and shot her with a zip gun. That causes a little talk. Maybe it gits mentioned on TV. But that's the end of it.

Loretta, stunned, hurt, humiliated, horrified, was beginning to think again. She saw the big man with the big, round shoulders and the big hat in the front seat. She knew him. Every Negro did. Every Negro learned as a child to scurry before the approach of the High Sheriff's big, menacing car; to be afraid; and to watch pop-eyed from behind bushes as the car passed slowly and menacingly by. The High Sheriff was driving Loretta toward the woods, not the hospital. So she knew he was going to shoot her.

But Big Track questioned himself further. He didn't want to act hurriedly. A big man who's trying to better himself and his family can't afford a mistake. I wish I had time to talk it over with my wife, he thought. Maybelle's always knowed in a minute what's best for me and her and our kids. She always starts by asking this question: "Track, is it right? We can't go far wrong doing the right thing." That was Maybelle talking.

Big Track remembered himself talking: "Folks, my opponents in this sheriff's race keep saying that I'm a natural-born killer. That since I killed so many gooks in Korea I just naturally kill too quick as a sheriff. My opponents keep harpin' on the fact that I've killed two white men and one nigger since I been wearin' a badge in Atoka County. Well, here's my answer: I ain't never killed nobody on this earth who wasn't at that very minute tryin' his best to kill me. That's the kind'a man I am. As long as you keep electin' me sheriff, no man, white or black, needs to worry about me killin' him unless he's tryin'ta kill me or tryin'ta kill one'a you good folks whose lives and property I'm under oath to protect with my own life."

Was Loretta Sykes trying to kill him? Was she trying to kill anyone else? If he killed her, could he ever stand up and make that claim again? Or did her being tied in with agitators make her such a threat to property that he was sworn to kill her?

Again Big Track considered what might happen when Loretta was reported missing and her body found. Wouldn't Huntley and Brinkley call it a "civil rights atrocity"? Wouldn't FBI agents, as in Mississippi, come swarming in with a million Federal dollars to buy evidence from Ku Klux? He thought: What if I drove by Hardy Riddle's and asked him what to do with this nigger? Hardy don't want nothing happening that Huntley and Brinkley can call a "civil rights atrocity." Hardy is dead set against any killing, or maiming, or cutting, or burning, or dynamiting. But then Hardy ain't always looking out fer the best interest of me and my family. Hardy's just thinking about "the continued orderly development of Atoka County."

Big Track slowed down and turned into an abandoned side road which ran through trees to an abandoned, Gone-to-Chicago shack. He stopped the car, got out, and opened one of the back doors. But instead of reaching for Loretta he leaned down and spoke to her.

"You're a Stancill nigger, ain't'cha?"

"Yes, sir," she replied. "I was born on Mr. Stancill's place. My mother still lives in a shack on the mountain. That's where I was arrested."

"I've knowed Breck Stancill all my life," said Big Track. "He befriended me. I use'ta live in one'a his shacks on the mountain. I was livin' there when my boy was born. Maybe you remember us. So I was just thinkin'. You reckon me and you could make a deal?"

"A deal, Sheriff? What do I have that you could want?"

"Well," said Big Track, "I could do a lot fer you. And you could do a little some'pin fer me. You could help y'self and help me, too. But it'd mean you bein' honest with me. It'd mean you making me a promise and me trustin' you to keep it."

"Sheriff," said Loretta, "I'm going to bleed to death if I don't get to a hospital. You know that, but you're not moving toward a hospital. And you won't let me try to get there. So you brought me here to finish killing me, didn't you?"

"Well, that's just the question," said Big Track. "Ain't no law says I got'ta kill'ya. I ain't never killed nobody that wasn't tryin'ta kill me. I don't want'a kill'ya. Instead'a killin'ya, all of a sudden I can start playin' on yo' side. I can save'ya life. I can be the best friend'ya got. I can grab that radio and have Dr. Ted Parker meet me at the Atoka Hospital. The doc's been my friend for eighteen years. He brought my boy into this world. I can turn on that si*reen* and in ten minutes I can have you in the Emergency Room. Then, in a day or so, when you're in good shape, I can help'ya git back to Chicago. I can help'ya mother. I always try'ta help Breck Stancill's niggers."

"And what's the little something you want me to do for you, Sheriff?"

"Nothing much a'tall. Just be close-mouthed. Like ever' woman in yo' shape ought to be anyway. Just don't talk much. And what little you do talk, tell it right. Later tonight, or tomorrow, when the doc has'ya in good shape, I'll bring the tape recorder and you can tell it to me. Just like it happened. You was arrested by Deputy Sheriff Cates. He had a perfect, legal right to arrest'ya and hold'ya a reasonable time fer investigation. He treated'ya good. When he found nothing to hold'ya on, he turned you loose at seven-fifteen tonight. You was walking down the street toward the bus station to git a taxi to take you home when a car stopped by'ya. A young nigger man offered'ya a ride to Stancill's Mountain. He was short, stocky, black, about yo' age, and had a little beard. You thought'cha knew him so'ya got in with him. Then'ya saw'ya didn't know him. He drove'ya right here, right where we are now, and three more young niggers was waitin'. That gang'a niggers did t'ya what was done. They done it in the car right here close to this old shack. Then they threw'ya out and took

off, and I happened to find'ya, right now. You'd staggered out
in the road tryin'ta hail help. Like the Good Samaritan I
grabbed'ya up and rushed'ya to the hospital."

"But I won't be telling the truth, Sheriff," said Loretta.

"Maybe you won't," said Big Track. "But you'll be telling it
right. Everything that's right ain't always true. You know
that. You try tellin' it any different and folks'll say you
dreamed it up. You'll just be a lyin', agitatin' nigger sent back
in here from Chicago to try'ta shame the sov'ern state of
Alabama."

"I don't have any choice, do I?"

"Yeah, you got a choice," Big Track said. "Same choice I
got. Do right or suffer. When some'pin like this happens I
got'ta make it look like it happened like folks think it ought'a
happened. I got'ta do right or lose everything I got and want.
You and me's in this together. All you got'ta do is be close-
mouthed and play ball with me. And you got to be *goddam*
careful what you say'ta two men: Breck Stancill and Doc
Parker. I want them two men to think well'a me and my wife
and my boy."

"I understand, Sheriff," said Loretta. "I promise. Now
please hurry."

Hattie Bascomb reached for her pencil when she heard Big
Track on the radio: "Hattie, git on the phone and see if Doc
Parker's still at the hospital. If he ain't, find him and ask him
to meet me there. I'm bringin' in'a nigger female. Assault victim. Loretta Sykes. Same one'ya let out'a jail at seven-fifteen.
Put out a report to the state troopers. I'm lookin' fer four nigger males. Ages eighteen to twenty-two. Probably riding in a
'59 model white Ford two-door. All of 'em may have blood
on their pants. And Butt Cut, y'meet me at the hospital."

Hattie's report to the state troopers was broadcast at 9:47
P.M. Three minutes later a press association reporter in Bir-
mingham called the jail and asked for further information on
Loretta. As a public servant and friend of the Alabama press,
Hattie told him of Loretta's arrest and release: what the jail
record showed. About 10 P.M. Doctor Parker began examin-
ing and treating Loretta. At 10:05, outside the hospital, Big
Track and Butt Cut sat in the Wildcat in conference.

"You surprised the hell out'a me, Track," said Butt Cut.
"You sure you handlin' this thing right?"

"I got'ta figure all the angles," said Big Track, lighting a cigar. "I got'ta look after the sheriff's office. That means you and me. If I'd'a been here earlier today I might'a handled things different. But I wasn't here. I had to act on the situation I found at nine P.M. You learn that fightin' wars. Things are always happenin' that ain't according to plan. Men are always actin' in ways you don't expect. The commanding officer's got to make new decisions ever' time he gits a new situation report."

"You reckon that nigger gal's gonna play ball with'ya?"

"I can't tell. We'll stand by here till I git the doc's report. Then we'll see what the situation is."

At 10:10 Big Track went into the hospital's waiting room where several persons sat watching the *CBS Sunday Evening News*. At 10:13 the reporter, Harry Reasoner, was handed a typescript from which he read: "Finally, a winner of the Congressional Medal of Honor is in the news tonight. Former Sergeant Buford 'Big Track' Bascomb, who won the nation's highest award for valor in Korea, is now sheriff of Atoka County in rural northwest Alabama. Tonight Sheriff Bascomb is looking for four men he has charged with criminally assaulting an attractive young Negro woman from Chicago. The alleged victim, Miss Loretta Sykes, twenty-two, is said to have been slated to help lead civil rights demonstrations which are to begin in Atoka County tomorrow. The Justice Department says the FBI will help the Sheriff investigate what appears to be yet another civil rights atrocity."

Hardy Riddle jumped out of bed. "What the goddam hell!" he roared. "The stupid sonsabitches! Publicity is just what we didn't want! Now we get the goddam crowds and cameras! Big Track, like George Wallace and Jim Clark, becomes a TV star!" He grabbed his bedside telephone and began dialing the jail. Then he flung the phone back in its cradle. A phone can be dangerous as a rattlesnake, he thought. I better wait for them to come to see me. It's not good sometimes for a man in my position to know too much. I might have to put my hand on a Bible.

Maybelle and Allen Bascomb also heard the telecast. In her pajamas and robe, ready for bed, Maybelle had been sitting in her living room listening to her son tell of his trip to Mobile. After the telecast, Allen said: "Dad's on a spot. I better go and see if I can help him."

"Don't go, son," Maybelle said. "I'm sure your daddy wants you to stay here. Excitement may go on for several days. But you stay away from it. Let your daddy handle it. He's a good man. He knows what's right. You got to go to school in the morning. Just like nothing happened. Your schooling comes first in this family. That's the way your daddy wants it."

After hearing the telecast Big Track hurried back to the Wildcat and Butt Cut. "Goddam!" he said, "they already got it on TV. All bigger'n hell!"

"What'd they say?"

"Plenty. Me and the Medal of Honor and that goddam *civil rights atrocity* that Hardy Riddle wanted us to keep from havin'. Right this minute Hardy must be havin' a runnin' fit!"

"Oh, shit!" Butt Cut whistled and shook his head.

Hattie came on the radio: "Track, you better git on down heah! Everybody in the world is tryin'ta git'cha on the phone. I just got a call from across the water. From London, England!"

"Git Trixie on the phone," Big Track said to Hattie. "Tell her I said'ta git out'a bed and git down there and help'ya."

"What we gonna do, Track?" Butt Cut asked nervously.

"Keep'ya shirt on," said Big Track. "We been through this before. The night Willie Washington was lynched. With wars goin' on, and earthquakes and typhoons, everybody in the whole world all of a sudden gits interested in whether one Alabama nigger lost his balls before the Ku Klux shot him! There must'a been a thousand rapes in New York tonight, but everybody's dyin'ta hear about one little bit'a nigger screwin' in the backwoods'a Alabama!"

A nurse's aide came running out of the hospital and up to the Wildcat. "Sheriff," she said, "folks is tryin'ta git'cha on the hospital phones. Folks from 'way off some'ers."

"Tell 'em I'm busy, honey," said Big Track. "And don't run so fast."

"But they want'ta hold the lines open," she persisted. "Till they can talk to you or the doctor."

"Then tell 'em to hold on. We'll git to 'em after a while."

Hattie came back on the radio: "Track, you been on TV? I'm gittin' calls sayin' you're on TV."

"Yeah, I been on TV. I'll tell you about it when I git time."

"One thing bothers me," Big Track said to Butt Cut. "The TV says I'm looking fer four *men*. My report to the state troopers said I was looking fer four *niggers*. But the TV says I'm lookin' fer four just plain *men*."

"Then I better git on my horse," said Butt Cut. "I better go tell four *men* that the TV's wrong. That we're just looking fer four *niggers*."

"You can tend'ta that later. I got some'ers else fer'ya to go now. The TV says the Justice Department admires me so much that they're sending the FBI to help me catch them four men."

"Oh, shit!" said Butt Cut. "That means the sonsabitches will start arrivin' here in'a hour. At least ten pairs of 'em. Ever' pair in a new Hertz Chevy. Ever' damn one of 'em looking exactly alike in his necktie and hat and coat. Ever' damn one of 'em smiling and telling'ya how much he wants to help'ya and not believin' a fuckin' word you tell him."

"We'll handle the Bureau boys," said Big Track. "They ain't so bad. But listen to me close. I want'cha to go out to that spot where the nigger gal was jumped by the four niggers. I told'ya where that shack is. You can't miss it. When'ya git there, before'ya turn in on that old road, stop'n study them tire tracks. Ya'll see it's the Ford's tracks. That's where I pulled in. Drive the Ford on in, then back out and drive in a coupl'a times, so there'll be lots'a tracks."

"I get'cha."

"Well, git this, too," said Big Track. "Before'ya go out there go by the jail and look in the refrigerator. Must be seven, eight cans'a beer in there. Open'em, pour the beer out, and take the empty cans with'ya. Git two or three different brands'a cigarettes and smoke a dozen down to butts. Then when'ya git to where them niggers was waitin'ta rape this girl scatter the beer cans and the butts all around like niggers'll do. Git it? But make sure'ya wipe them empty cans. Don't leave'ya prints on 'em."

"I know jest how'ta do it," insisted Butt Cut.

"Okay. Keep'ya ear cocked'ta the radio. I'll be out there soon's I can. When the doc gits her fixed up I may need'ta talk some more'ta the victim. You guard the scene'a the crime. The Bureau boys'll be out there crawlin' on their hands and knees, sniffin' ever' blade'a grass."

The 10:20 bus from Birmingham was a few minutes late, so it was 10:27 when Breck Stancill stepped off the bus and walked toward his sky-blue Chevrolet pickup in the nearby

parking lot. He had "spent Sunday with a woman," so he was
dressed up. Instead of his usual faded khakis he was wearing
a gray tweed suit, a blue shirt and blue tie, and a narrow-
brimmed, dark blue hat. He carried a small blue airline bag
and a walking cane. In his slightly jerky gait he walked rapidly across the parking lot because he was tired and wanted to
get home. Cities and women tired him, which partially explained why he lived alone on a mountain, why he didn't own
a regular passenger car, and why he always rode the
Greyhound bus to Birmingham. He liked to read while he
rode.

A Negro boy, about thirteen, had been sitting in the bed of
the pickup. He jumped out as Breck approached.

"Caleb, what you doing here?" Breck asked.

"Trouble, Mistah Breck," said Caleb gravely. "Mama sent
me in heah to wait for you and tell you."

"What sort of trouble?"

"Loretta. The sheriff come and got her after church. He put
her in his car and drove off."

"Does anybody on the mountain know why?"

"Naw, suh," said Caleb. "Except'n two men come up on
the mountain last night. One of 'em was white, the other'n
colored. They talked to Loretta."

Breck unlocked the cab. "Well, get in here," he said, "and
we'll go see."

Breck Stancill was a responsible man. Forty-one years as a
Stancill, including three and a half years as a United States
Marine, had taught him not to shirk responsibility. So he
didn't often ask: Am I my brother's keeper? But once in a
while, when he felt tired and dispirited, he thought of all the
days and nights when some Negro had come running to hand
him trouble. Breck then smiled his wriest smile and thought: I
wish to hell my great-great-granddaddy, Fowler Stancill, mus-
tered out in New Orleans in 1815, hadn't bought a Negro boy
and brought him to Atoka County. And that sea captain in
1619, lying off Virginia with the first cargo of slaves, I wish
that s'nuvabitch had been fired on and denied permission to
land.

At the jail Breck stopped, got out, and tapped on the glass
of the front door. He could see Hattie Bascomb and Trixie
Cunningham inside. Trixie came and let him in. She knew
Breck well because after her divorce she had played every

card in her deck trying to become Breck's wife before she gave up and became Hardy Riddle's woman.

"Trixie, what about Loretta Sykes?" Breck asked.

"I just got here, Breck," said Trixie. "Hattie'll be off the phone in a minute. She better tell you."

Hattie gave the telephone to Trixie and came and stood with Breck. Hattie, of course, knew Breck, too, but not as well as Trixie knew him.

"A lot's happened, Mister Breck," said Hattie respectfully. "Butt Cut got word that Loretta might be tied in with some'a these agitators that're due in heah this week. He went up on the mountain and she told him two agitators had been'ta see her. So he brought her in for a while this afternoon while he investigated to see if that was all it was. He didn't find nothing else, so at seven-fifteen, just before I went to church, we turned her loose. She walked right out'a that door and down the street in perfect health. When Big Track got back from Mobile around nine, he made a little run out toward the mountain, just to see if any agitators was comin' in tonight, and Loretta must'a flagged him down out there. Big Track says she told him four niggers jumped her. We ain't had a report on her yet."

"Where's Big Track now?"

"At the hospital," said Hattie. "He's waitin'ta git Dr. Parker's report. The state troopers is helpin' look for the four niggers. The whole thing's done been on TV."

"Thanks, Hattie," said Breck. "If you can reach Big Track on your radio, tell him I'm on my way up there to see him."

When Breck was gone Hattie said to Big Track: "Track, Breck Stancill's just been in heah. I told him what's happened. He's on his way to see'ya."

"Is he hot in the collar?" asked Big Track.

"Didn't seem to be," said Hattie. "He thanked me for telling him. He's all dressed up. Must'a been some'ers."

"That's good," said Big Track.

Hattie turned to Trixie: "Where'ya reckon Breck's been?"

"He's been to see his Birmingham woman," said Trixie. "He's that kind'a man. He wants a woman he can visit at his pleasure. But he don't want to live with her. He's got to have his privacy."

"Maybe that's because he's got his niggers," said Hattie. "A white man who's got niggers ain't got much use for a white woman."

There she goes, thought Trixie. Trying to throw off on me. She used to have to hire nigger girls for her daddy, so she's got to think that every white man prefers a nigger girl. And because she knows I know what she does here in this jail with white girls, she's trying to belittle me by saying that Breck Stancill tried me out and turned me down because he found it better with a nigger than he did with me.

"I never believed that about Breck," said Trixie. "I don't believe he ever touched a nigger girl in his life."

Of course you don't, thought Hattie. How can any self-respecting, Anglo-Saxon white woman let herself believe that the man who's on her tonight was on a nigger girl last night? Everybody in Atoka County knows Breck Stancill got what he wanted from this nigger girl, Loretta, until he sent her off to Chicago. Then it was your turn, Trixie. You'd just got your divorce and your settlement from old Roy Cunningham. Everybody knows Breck Stancill sampled your tail every time he wanted it for six months. Then he decided it wasn't as good as what he'd been getting from a nigger.

Hattie said: "If, like you say, Breck never touched this nigger Loretta, then what's he doing down heah on Sunday night bother'n hisself about her? Do'ya happen to know any white woman he'd bother hisself this much about?"

The telephone interrupted Hattie's assault on Trixie, and while Hattie talked with a Memphis reporter Trixie fumed under her stylish, reddish-brown coiffure. Big Track knew better than to put these two cats in the same cage. Normally he kept the peace by keeping them a block apart. Trixie's cage was his courthouse office, Hattie's was the jail, and they spat at each other a few times each day over the radio or telephone. Only in emergencies did Big Track risk them in the same cage, and tonight they were in Hattie's cage.

Trixie Cunningham was still capable of loyalty to Breck Stancill. She not only *believed* that Breck had never touched a Negro girl, she *knew* it. She remembered Breck saying to her: "I guess I'm some sort of sexual queer, Trixie. The only women I can desire are those I don't feel too sorry for. And since I feel sorry for most everybody, I have a hard time finding women to try to get into bed with. I can chase only those who can afford to run. Thank God, you fill the bill. I love getting you in bed because you're so goddam fortunate and adequate. You're the country girl with looks who comes to town, goes to work for the middle-aged storekeeper, marries him, divorces him, and at thirty you are free, with a home, an Oldsmobile, and twenty thousand dollars in the bank. You could prosper anywhere. So my enjoyment of you can be unrestrained. It's a confrontation of adult and consenting equals. Or maybe I'm boasting. Maybe it's a well-fed tigress confronting a mutilated man."

Only a blind and perverted woman like Hattie, thought Trixie, could imagine that Breck Stancill could screw a nigger girl who was owing to him. If Breck ever screws a nigger female, she'll be a rich and powerful one. He'd be incapable with any female of any color he suspected he had the advantage of.

Trixie had also understood when Breck explained why he wouldn't consider marrying her. "You wouldn't like being married to me, Trixie," he said. "During that year I spent in hospitals, coming back to life, I didn't resign from the human race. But I did resign from the rat race. I had spent almost three years with a rifle platoon. From Tarawa to Iwo Jima. Three years learning to kill and survive. Then the world blew up in my face and I thought I was dead. In the months that followed I learned to mark the calendar. I learned that every day in a man's life has a number on it. So I swore I'd never waste one day that was left to me. Sometimes at night I'd see the faces of men I had killed. Most of them I suppose were young Japanese farmers with their gift for making plants grow. Somehow I got the idea that I owed it to them just to experience life every day I could. I felt that somehow they might see through my eyes when I planted a tree. Or watched two orioles build a nest. Or a doe teaching a fawn to walk. Or wild turkeys feeding at twilight. That's why I'm a tree farmer on Stancill's Mountain. That's why I ride my horse through the woods most every morning at sunrise with my dog running before me. I don't want any *thing* on earth. I don't want to compete or acquire, or menace any living thing's joy of being alive. Each night I try to feel that I've spent that day experiencing the wonder of life. That's the chief reason I can't marry. No woman like you could share such an existence in the 1960s. You want to strive and make progress and get ahead and acquire. So you need to share the life of a builder. You need to belong to an acquisitive man, not to me."

Trixie remembered the afternoon on Stancill's Mountain when she told Breck she had decided to take up with Hardy Riddle.

"I hate to think of losing you," Breck said. "Any man who loves feeling alive would hate to lose you, Trixie. You're a sensitive, sensual, luxurious woman with life in every muscle. But you have to leave me. I understand why. In a small community a woman like you can't be a single man's woman indefinitely. You'd be looked down on. There is no publicly acceptable excuse for a single man not marrying you. But you can be a successful married man's woman without being looked down on. He can't marry you because of his family. People accept that. They'll talk about you, but they'll envy, even admire you. So it's proper for you to belong to Hardy Riddle. He's the most acquisitive man in the county. On balance, he's not evil. The worst thing I know about him is that he secretly believes that a Ku Klux Klan, if run right, can be, in his words, 'a useful adjunct to police power.' But many otherwise good men believe that. Hardy's an authentic all-American. An alliance between you and him ought to be satisfying. It's certain to be profitable."

In any conflict among Breck Stancill, Big Track and Hardy Riddle, Trixie was capable of secretly helping Breck. But as she fumed under Hattie's assault, she wished Breck would go home and quit appearing to be concerned about the welfare of a Negro girl that nothing much had happened to. Breck's concern for Loretta didn't make him a nigger-lover. Not to Trixie. But it did to Hattie. So it made Trixie vulnerable to Hattie's assault. And Trixie Cunningham was not the sort of woman who could enjoy being vulnerable to a woman like Hattie Bascomb.

At the hospital parking lot Breck told the young Negro who was with him: "Caleb, you stay in the car. Curl up in the seat and go to sleep. I'll lock the doors so nobody can bother you. Don't open a door no matter who tells you to. As soon as I finish in here I'll take you home."

Breck happened to arrive at the hospital just as Big Track was leaving the Wildcat and its radio to go inside to Dr. Parker's office. They spoke and Big Track said: "The doc's just told me to come in. He's ready'ta gim'me his report."

"I'll go in with you if you don't mind," said Breck.

Big Track wasn't sure whether he minded or not. He felt uneasy as they walked together into the hospital and down the corridor.

When Big Track and Breck walked together, with their hats

off, the differences in them were startling. Big Track was seven inches taller and five years younger. Big Track weighed 245; Breck, 160. Breck's brown hair was thinning, and graying in the temples. Big Track's sandy crew-cut looked youthful. Breck's ruddy face was lean; the bone structure could be sensed if not seen; there was no fat on his jaws. Big Track's face was fatter. Breck's eyes were blue and wide open; Big Track's were hazel and half-closed. Breck, despite his slight limp, walked erect, narrow-hipped, square-shouldered. Big Track slouched: round-shouldered, heavy-hipped. Breck looked well-knit, well-bred; Big Track looked coarse, bred from scrub.

The man they were going to meet, Dr. Theodore Roosevelt Parker, was the least vulnerable man in Atoka County. He was much less vulnerable than Breck Stancill because his $100,000 home and his $400,000 hospital were both fireproof and insured. Breck's trees were neither. No one could seriously damage the doctor: not with boycott, slander, damage suits, punitive tax assessments, competition, fire or dynamite. He, or a member of his family, could be assaulted, but not with impunity. Born in Florence, Alabama, he was graduated in 1941 from the University of Tennessee Medical School in Memphis. After serving in the Army he set up in Ellenton in 1945 with nothing. In twenty years he built his own hospital, trained much of his nursing and technical staff, and now he had two younger doctors as associates. He was established and respected.

A dark, taciturn man who smoked a collection of pipes, Dr. Parker was the sort of doctor about whom his patients circulate stories. One of them was about when a delegation of Ku Klux Klansmen called on him. The five Klansmen, led by Vernon Hodo, complained that the hospital's chief X-ray technician was a local Negro girl who the doctor had "sent off" for training; that this was also true of the dietician; that several nurses and nurse's aides were Negroes; and that the waiting room was not segregated.

"Now, Doc," said Vernon, "you know how much we all think'a you. You're our doctor. You brought our kids into this world. But Alabama's got a great governor now who's tryin'ta keep things like they ought'a be. So we just want'a ask'ya to treat the white folks a little better in this fine hospital that we're all'sa proud of. God-fearing, Christian, Anglo-Saxon white folks deserve better'n to have'ta sit in a waitin' room with niggers when they're sick. We got good, Christian white girls who can learn about X-ray machines. And our great governor, who won't even serve likker in his mansion, he deserves everybody's help in tryin'ta keep things right in Alabama."

Dr. Parker raised his hand and said: "That's enough! You're wasting my time. This hospital treats human beings. It hires and trains human beings on the basis of skill and devotion. The day we start taking advice from Ku Klux Klansmen, or from peckerwood politicians who please Klansmen, we'll close the door. Now get out!"

Big Track thought of that story as he and Breck waited in the doctor's office. He thought of the first time he met the doctor: back in 1948, when the hospital was in an old store building, and when he was nineteen and scared and looking for a place for his pregnant wife to have their son. Breck was with him then, to pay the bills.

The doctor hurried in, spoke, and said: "Loretta's going to be all right." He lighted a pipe and continued: "Now first, about the legalities. Loretta Sykes is my patient. She is of age, conscious, competent, and no next of kin is present. She has rights, the first of which is the right of privacy. Without her written permission I could not describe her injuries to anyone, not even to the sheriff. But when I explained this to her she insisted on giving me such permission covering both of you."

Big Track shifted in his chair and crossed his legs. He hoped he was prepared for whatever came next. Dr. Parker began to speak as though he were testifying in a courtroom, because he was in fact delivering a formal report to the law. "When Loretta Sykes was delivered to this hospital she was frightened, upset, distraught, and bleeding from the vaginal area. I quickly determined that the bleeding was not menstrual. Chiefly, the bleeding was from the hymeneal ring which had been torn. Most women bleed very little when their so-called maidenhead is ruptured. But in a few cases there is unusual vascular concentration in this area and women bleed freely, even dangerously. A year or so ago I had a girl in here who bled a week. I thought I'd never be able to stop it. Additionally, Loretta Sykes had suffered torn tissue in the vagina. I used a local anesthetic and sutures to make repairs. I found numerous sperm cells. So I can report as medical fact that until this evening this girl was a virgin. She has been subjected to violent intercourse with very deep penile penetration. From what I know of her, and from what she told me, it is my opinion that she is the victim of a criminal act."

So many questions occurred to Big Track that he didn't know which to ask first. He chose: "What'd she tell'ya, Doc?"

"I haven't questioned her at length," said the doctor. "I've been too busy treating her. But she said the man who did it was a Negro."

"Just one nigger? Or two or three?"

"She didn't say that more than one penetrated her. Others may have assisted or been present."

Big Track had crossed the first hurdle. With more confidence he moved toward the second. "Now, Doc," he said, "about you saying that you think this nigger was a *virgin* . . . !"

"That isn't an opinion," said the doctor. "That's a medical fact which I have observed and reported to you. A ruptured hymen is an observable fact, like a broken leg."

"But, Doc, goddam!" said Big Track. "It may be a fact to you but it ain't gonna be to nobody else! Because nobody's gonna believe it. Everybody knows that ever' nigger girl gits popped by the time she's thirteen. You expect folks to believe that a nigger girl, raised out here on Stancill's Mountain, went to school right here in Ellenton, been up in them Chicago slums fer three years, you think anybody's gonna believe that she come back in here carryin' a cherry! I'm the sheriff! I'd have to look a long ways to find a good Christian white girl her age who's still got a cherry. I'll make a fool out'a myself if I tell the state troopers, and the FBI, and the TV that a twenty-two-year-old nigger virgin got raped in Atoka County, Alabama, tonight!"

"I see your problem," said the doctor. "But I don't know what else you can do except do right and tell the truth. You've done right so far. You found the girl, rushed her to me, reported the crime, and you're looking for the criminals, trying to bring them to justice. No one can criticize you to this point. Now I have treated the victim and reported the truth to you. Who can criticize you for repeating what I report to you?"

Big Track turned to Breck and asked: "Breck, you believe this girl was a virgin till tonight?"

"You want me to dispute the doctor?" asked Breck. "You want me to swear that she lost her cherry to me eight years ago?"

"That's what everybody thinks," said Big Track. "And a sheriff's got to worry about what everybody thinks. You and the doc don't have to worry. You ain't got'ta git re-elected. I'm the one who's got'ta handle this thing the way folks want it handled. I'm the one who's got'ta git on TV and stand up fer Alabama!"

"The best way to stand up for Alabama," said the doctor, "is to tell the truth. And since you must consider what folks think, maybe you could help yourself by explaining why Loretta was a virgin. Make your voters understand that Loretta is a striver. Breck encouraged her, so for years she has worked at bettering herself, getting somewhere and having something. Like many Negroes she already belongs to the middle class. And middle-class Negro girls must preserve their virginity more carefully than white girls. They must prove that all Negroes are not amoral. They want to be well thought of. They want good, God-fearing, Anglo-Saxon, middle-class white people to be willing to live in the same block with them."

"Now, Doc," said Big Track, "you know I can't say nothing that'd look like I was building up this nigger girl. The TV's done said she's a civil rights agitator expectin'ta lead demonstrations in Atoka County."

"You might try changing that, too," said the doctor. "It's a lie. Loretta's here to help her mother die of cancer of the liver. Her mother's my patient. Loretta's been calling me from Chicago for a month or so, getting reports on her mother. She's been paying the bills. One of her bosses, a white man at Montgomery Ward, called me to see if he could help. Loretta Sykes is thought well of. She is a decent, smart, hard-working, ambitious, Christian, American-Negro girl, down here for the sole purpose of helping her mother. That's the truth."

"The girl's the victim. not the criminal," said Breck.

Big Track got to his feet. He was scared and wanted to leave. But he needed the doctor and Breck. He wanted them to think well of him and his wife and his boy. He was dependent on the doctor. So he couldn't leave without coming to terms with them. "I need help," he said. "You're the two best friends I got. You helped my boy be born. You got education. I ain't. Hell, I ain't Jesus Christ! I'm just a country sheriff that's got'ta deal with demonstrations and TV and a civil rights atrocity. So tell me some'pin I can tell the state troopers. You should'a been with me yesterday and heard what they told me about Mrs. Lyeuseo. Tell me some'pin like that!"

"I understand what you need, Track," said Breck. "What you have been told here makes Loretta Sykes seem worthy of respect. She appears to be an innocent victim. But the people who keep you in office won't accept her as an innocent victim. They will destroy you if you present her as such. You need to do to Loretta what the Ku Klux and others are doing to Mrs. Liuzzo. The Detroit woman, they insist, was not the innocent victim of Ku Klux; she was the criminal because she neglected her children and went on crusades during which she allowed Negroes to screw her. You need to give Loretta the same treatment."

"That's it," said Big Track. "You hit the nail on the head. If this nigger girl was a virgin saint, then rapin' her was some'pin to do some'pin about. But if she ain't nothin' but a agitatin' nigger atheist who's been screwed by everybody since her tits started to grow, then who gives a damn! You're right, Breck. I need'ta tear her down. If I can't tear her down, I damn sure can't build her up. I got no choice. Hell, you should'a been with me yesterday. I was in the governor's office and in Selma. I could curl'ya hair by tellin'ya what the troopers know about all the fuckin' these agitators are doing. The governor hisself told me they're a bunch'a punks, whores, kooks, atheists and perverts, all controlled by Commies."

Dr. Parker got up. "I have nothing else to say," he said. "I'm a doctor. I'm supposed to be sane. I can't talk or tolerate doubletalk. You're the sheriff, Big Track. Do right, tell the truth, or hand in your badge."

No one spoke for several seconds. Big Track rubbed his jaw like he had been hit. Then he said: "I'm tryin', Doc. Just two more questions. Can I talk to Loretta now? I need'ta git some more descriptions."

"No," said the doctor. "She wants to talk to Breck a minute about somebody staying with her mother. She needs to rest. You come back in the morning."

"Then here's my last question," said Big Track. "I got'ta go out and start talking to troopers and FBI agents and reporters. I may have'ta talk a lot fer a week. Suppose I don't tell everything just like you told it to me? Nobody's likely to ask me if this girl was a virgin. That idea ain't gonna pop into nobody's mind. Suppose I leave out a few things and git mixed up on some others? What you gonna do, Doc?"

"That'll be up to Loretta," the doctor answered. "I have no right to discuss her case except at her direction. But tomorrow

she can talk with anybody she chooses. If she talks, then asks
me for confirmation, I'll tell the truth."

"You gonna talk, Breck?" asked Big Track.

"I'm a tree farmer," said Breck. "Not a talker. I think
you'll do what's right, Track. You're the best sheriff this county ever had."

MAYBELLE

THE ATOKA HOSPITAL was the most visited institution in Atoka County. This was because the people of the county were friendly. Each day the local radio station broadcast the names of patients admitted the previous day, so whenever a person remained in the hospital for several days he could count on being visited by most of his relatives, many of his friends, even a few of his casual acquaintances. But this visiting was not interracial. Whites visited whites; Negroes visited Negroes. In the first twenty years of the hospital's existence, from 1945 to 1965, no white man, unless he was a doctor or a policeman on duty, visited a Negro patient. A few white women visited their Negro cooks. But certainly no white man had ever visited a Negro girl. So when Breck Stancill, after hearing Dr. Parker's report, visited the private room occupied by Loretta Sykes at 11:20 P.M., he gained invidious distinction and caused ugly talk.

One nurse said to another: "Why would a white man like him be troubling hisself at this time'a night about a nigger girl who's tied in with agitators, who don't even work for him, and who says another nigger humped her?"

"Beats me," replied the other nurse. "Must be something there that won't stand the light'a day. It sure ain't natural for a white man to trouble hisself over a nigger."

Breck knew his visiting Loretta would cause such talk. He wished he knew how to avoid it. He didn't want distinction, invidious or otherwise. He wanted peace and the good will of everyone in the county. But he also knew that invidious distinction was part of his heritage. The Stancills had always been called "unnatural" in their dealings with Negroes.

They were called "unnatural" in 1840. In Alabama there was a state law against teaching Negroes to read. Fowler Stancill, then forty-seven, along with his son Landers, ignored the law. Not only did they teach their slaves to read, they also encouraged them to become artisans, Christians and freemen. So by 1840 the Stancills had set themselves against many of their fellow slaveholders and against every unskilled, barely literate redneck. The Stancills were on the collision course which would bring Landers Stancill to the end of a rope in 1861. When Breck Stancill, in 1957, encouraged Loretta Sykes to seek freedom by learning to type, he was only doing what Stancills had been doing for a century and a half. In 1964 when Breck began ripping Butt Cut's Ku Klux clippings from bulletin boards he was obeying the same "unnatural" impulse which caused Landers Stancill in 1857 to oppose secession and advocate gradual emancipation in speeches and letters to editors.

When Breck entered the room Loretta was crying and half asleep from sedation. The light was shaded and turned against a wall. "They tore me down, Mister Breck," she sobbed. "I'm like a vixen that's been caught and torn by the dogs. I won't ever be able to strive again."

"Sure you will," said Breck. "In a few days you'll be back in Chicago striving harder than ever. Think of the thousands of women in Europe who were raped during the war. Some of them by dozens of men. Most of those women came back to lead normal lives."

"They weren't Negroes, already weighed down with disadvantages. They weren't Alabama Negroes striving to make it in Chicago when the dogs caught them."

"Some of them had similar disadvantages," said Breck. "And they lacked your advantages. They didn't have a sheriff to rush them to a hospital. They didn't have a doctor to protect them against disease and pregnancy. In three days you'll be healthy as ever."

"What about Mama, Mister Breck?"

"Don't worry about her. Dora is with her. Dora sent Caleb to the bus station to wait and tell me about you being gone. Dora will stay with your mother."

"Then who'll cook for you?"

"Don't worry about me. I can cook for myself. In a pinch I can always break out a K-ration. What's important is that you sleep and forget."

Loretta thought Breck looked tired, standing there beside the bed, holding his hat, leaning on his cane. It seemed strange to see him dressed up. Only three or four times could she remember seeing him like that. Her mother had said: "Child, when a colored girl gits in a tight place she ain't got nobody to take her part." Loretta knew she was lucky to have a white man to take her part.

Standing again in a hospital room, looking down at Loretta, Breck remembered his own days and months in hospitals. Loretta's face, stunned, drained of hope, reminded him of other faces after other assaults. Just as he had searched men's faces, even his own face, he searched her face and was glad to see no cuts, bruises or abrasions which would leave permanent scars. He looked at her graceful, efficient hands, lying there on the cover sheet, and he felt thankful they had not been damaged. He remembered looking at his own hands and feeling thankful that the blast had spared them.

As he looked at Loretta, Breck remembered reading how, in one of the South Pacific cultures, when a man rescues a woman from drowning she acquires the legal right to expect him to help her for the rest of her life. Why not? Wasn't his motive selfish in that he preferred to rescue her rather than watch her die? Hasn't his action compelled her to continue carrying the burden of life? Why shouldn't he help her? It's the same when a man encourages a girl to strive, Breck thought. If by her striving she gets hurt, he should help her, shouldn't he? The most reckless act on earth is for one human being to encourage another. To encourage is to incur continuing obligation.

"Mister Breck," Loretta said, "before you go, would you give me a little advice?"

Breck wanted to say "No." To advise can be as reckless as to encourage. But with Loretta he was already obligated. "I'll try," he said. "For what my advice is worth, I'll try."

"The sheriff is coming here in the morning," said Loretta. "He's bringing his tape recorder. He wants to record my story of what happened."

Breck waited for her to continue. When she didn't continue he tried to guess why. Was she saying that she didn't want to tell the truth? Or that Big Track didn't want the truth? Breck said: "From what you are not saying I gather the truth won't do?"

"That's right," said Loretta. "The truth won't do."

"Does the sheriff know the truth?"

"Yes, sir. But if I told the truth he'd have to prove it was a lie. The truth just can't be. So I promised him a lie. He made a deal with me. He let me live and brought me to the hospital, and I promised not to tell you or the doctor about the deal. The sheriff doesn't want you to know. He wants you to think well of him and his wife and his boy."

Breck moved close to the bed and lowered his voice. Loretta was talking "killing talk," the sort of talk which results in killing. "Hush, Loretta!" he said sharply. "This is not the time or place for you and me to talk 'killing talk.' You're hurt and half asleep. Now listen carefully! Keep your promise to the sheriff. Be brief and don't accuse any identifiable person. But tell the sheriff what you promised to tell. Let him record it. Make him believe that you told me and the doctor only what you promised to tell us. Then refuse to discuss what happened with any other human being. Don't talk to any FBI agent or reporter or civil rights worker. Tell them to see the sheriff. Tell them you've told the sheriff all there is to tell. You understand?"

"Yes, sir. But will that be right?"

"Right can wait," said Breck. "You're already a casualty, so you deserve to be safe. Not even the Marines expect their wounded to expose themselves. You tell the sheriff whatever makes him feel safe. Then you'll be safe. If what's right and what's true are to be established here, let people who aren't yet casualties take the risks."

As Big Track drove away from the hospital in the Wildcat at 11:10 P.M., he spoke to Trixie and Hattie on the radio. "Any Bureau boys showed up yit?"

"Not yet," said Trixie.

"Le'me know the minute they do. I want'a come in there'ta meet 'em. I'm takin' a run out to the scene'a the crime. Is Butt Cut out there?"

"Yeah. He's in contact."

"I'm right with'ya, Track," put in Butt Cut.

"Trixie," said Big Track, "git on the phone and tell Hardy Riddle I can't git there for at least another hour. Ask him if he still wants me to come by."

Hattie said: "Track, what's the doctor's report? I got three reporters I promised'ta call and give it to."

"Well, here's the gist of it," said Big Track. "The doc says it's the brutalest rape he ever seen. Them niggers tore her up and left her bleedin' like a stuck pig. And she ain't no agitator; she's a damn good nigger. Them outside agitatin' niggers grabbed her right off the street, just after dark. They didn't give her no chance'ta run. They jumped out of their car, grabbed her, took her out and tore into her. She's in bad shape. She told the doctor how them niggers done her. She'd told the niggers flat out on Saturday night that she wouldn't help 'em in their agitatin'. So they grabbed her and tore her all to hell. The doc says she'd'a died if I hadn't'a found her when I did and then moved quick."

"What about white agitators?" asked Hattie. "Didn't the nigger girl see one white'un amongst them that was tearin' into her?"

"Can't say for sure about that till morning," said Big Track. "The victim's gone to sleep now. The doc give her a shot. I'll question her real close tomorrow when I got the tape recorder. We'll git the whole story then. Tell the reporters you'll have it for 'em 'long about noontime."

Trixie said: "Track, Hardy still wants you to come. No matter how late it gets. He said ring the bell at his basement door."

At the scene Butt Cut already had scattered the empty beer cans and the cigarette butts. He had set up a floodlight which, with his flashing red light, had attracted several carloads of white teenagers who had been parked in the woods and who wanted details of the rape. Butt Cut had allowed the teenagers to run their cars in and out of the side road, obscuring tire track evidence.

"Looks okay," said Big Track to Butt Cut. "Looks just like a bunch'a sorry niggers laid around here for a while, waitin' fer some'pin to hump. Now lets git some more points straight before the Bureau boys start askin' questions. You got a tip about Loretta Sykes bein' tied in with agitators. Who give'ya the tip?"

"Well, uh," began Butt Cut. He stopped, then blurted: "I disremember."

"That won't do," said Big Track. "Here's what happened. Pay attention. You was sittin' there in the jail readin' the Sunday paper. The phone rung. What sounded like a young nigger woman said: 'Mistah Sheriff, we-uns is a-callin''ta tell'ya that agitators was a-runnin' 'round in Atoka last night. They sho' was. They was up on Stancill's Mountain. Everybody give 'em a cold shoulder 'ceptin' that Loretta Sykes that's back in heah from Chicago. Seems mighty like she's tied in with 'em.' That's what this young nigger woman told you on the phone. Now repeat it back to me."

Butt Cut stumbled through a version of what his anonymous caller had told him.

"That'll do," said Big Track. "You work on it. Keep runnin' it through'ya head till'ya git it down pat so you can tell it to the Bureau boys. You tried hard'ta git the nigger's name who tipped'cha, but she rung off on'ya."

"I got it," insisted Butt Cut. "I can hear that nigger talkin' to me just as plain."

"Then get this," said Big Track. "You went out and found the girl. You was polite to her. She was polite to you. Then you didn't really arrest her, you just took her in protective custody while you cleared up her good name."

"That's what I did," said Butt Cut. "Them's the very words I told her. I just needed a little time to investigate."

"Sure," said Big Track. "You was trying to protect her and the county. You knowed she was a Stancill nigger so'ya couldn't believe she was tied in. So'ya pitched right in to investigating. First you looked through our jail records. Then'ya got Trixie on the phone and she come down to the courthouse and looked through our records in the sheriff's office, seeing if Washington had ever caught her with any Commies. Then'ya called the city. Who was on duty over there this afternoon?"

"Les Woodall. I run into him two or three times."

"Okay. You called the city police and asked Deputy Chief Les Woodall to check and see if they had anything on Loretta Sykes. He called you back and said she was clean as a whistle. Then you made one more call. To 'Fessor Elmore."

"What'd I call that nigger fer?"

"You called the principal of the Atoka County Training School and asked him if he remembered having any kind'a trouble with a girl named Loretta Sykes. The 'fessor told'ya that Loretta was smart and she didn't git knocked up while she was in school and he couldn't believe she'd ever let herself git tied in with agitators. Now'ya got all that?"

"Yeah I got it," said Butt Cut. "I called Trixie and Les and the nigger 'fessor. I got it."

Big Track and Butt Cut saw Breck Stancill's pickup stop on the side of the road. He got out and walked toward them. Lowering his voice, Big Track told Butt Cut: "Be nice and friendly with him now. He's on his way home from the hospital. He was with me and the doc, and he talked with the girl. Tell him that this afternoon, before you went to see the girl, you drove up to his house to tell him you needed'ta talk to one'a his niggers. But you couldn't find him. Tell him you're sorry about what happened."

"If you say so," said Butt Cut. "But the one-legged s'nuva-bitch won't believe me. He'll just nod his head and look at me like he thinks I'm trash."

"Just do what I tell'ya."

When Breck was within a few feet of them he stopped and asked: "Is this where it happened?"

"It's where the girl told me it was," said Big Track. "She flagged me down right out there in the road. I figure the nig-gers knowed she was in jail, and they was waitin'ta catch her when she was turned loose. They planned to catch her in town before she got on the bus. Just like they done. If they'd'a missed her in town, they'd'a followed the bus and caught her when she got off and started walking up the mountain to her shack."

Breck turned to Butt Cut and asked: "Who told you that she had been entertaining agitators?"

"Some nigger woman on the phone," Butt Cut answered. "She wouldn't give me her name. I was 't settin' there in the jail, readin' Little Orphan Annie, when the phone rung and this young nigger woman said agitators had been sneakin' around in the county last night and ever' nigger had give 'em the cold shoulder 'ceptin' this girl Loretta."

"She must'a made 'em mad last night," said Big Track. "She must'a told 'em she wouldn't help 'em. Maybe one of 'em got a hard on for her, so they grabbed her today and tore into her."

"Yeah, I guess that's how it was," said Breck. "She told me a few minutes ago it was Negroes. Just like she told you and the doc. So it must have been like that."

"Well, hell, you know how it is, Breck," said Big Track. "Ain't nothin' as hard on a nigger as other niggers. Ain't no white man ever treated a nigger half as bad as the nigger gits treated by other niggers. You know that."

"Yeah," said Breck, like he was tired of the subject. "Well, I got to get home. I got to be planting trees at sunup. Don't make any more out of this than you have to, Track."

"Hell, you know I won't, Breck," said Big Track. "You know me. It ain't my fault it got on TV. Somebody called the girl a civil rights worker, and you know what them three words does to Washington and TV. It drives 'em crazy."

"Yeah, I know," said Breck. "But the girl won't help Washington or TV. She won't say one word to anybody but you. So you turn the damper down and let her go on back to Chicago and forget it."

Big Track felt relieved. "Sure, Breck," he said. "You can count on me. You know that."

As Breck was about to walk away Butt Cut said: "Mister Breck, I want'cha to know that I didn't intend to talk'ta yer nigger without talkin'ta you first. Before I ever spoke to her I come up to yer house lookin' fer'ya. But you wasn't home. I'm sorry she got tore up."

"Thank you, Butt Cut," said Breck. "That was considerate of you."

Big Track and Butt Cut watched Breck get in his pickup and drive away. Butt Cut said: "I got'ta hand it to ya, Track. You sure handled this thing right."

"Maybe," said Big Track. "We'll see. Now I got to go and touch three more bases. You stay here about another hour, and if the Bureau boys don't show up, take down the light and go home. If I need'ya you'll hear me on the squawk box."

When he was again underway in the Wildcat, Big Track said on the radio: "Trixie, git on the phone and call Les Woodall at his house. Tell him I hate'ta git him up but I need'ta see him. Tell him to step out on his front porch and I'll be there in five minutes."

In his nightshirt and overcoat Les Woodall was waiting when Big Track arrived. Quickly, Big Track instructed him how, when he was asked, he was to confirm that Butt Cut had telephoned him for information on Loretta Sykes, and he, for the City of Ellenton, had pronounced her clean as a whistle. Then, back in the Wildcat, Big Track told Trixie to call "that nigger 'fessor Elmore" and have him waiting on his front porch.

Professor Leonidas Lincoln Elmore, forty-two, with a Master of Arts degree from Columbia University, was a good man, an efficient school principal, a devoted husband, and the proud father of two smart sons. But he had one failing. Eleven women teachers worked under his supervision. Teachers are the elite among Negro women in Alabama. Because they are so superior in wealth and education, they seldom have husbands, and the professor couldn't always resist the carnal temptation. So one night, under a harvest moon, when Sheriff Bascomb suddenly threw his flashlight into the back seat of a

Chevrolet parked in the woods, instead of flushing two teenagers, he caught the professor in the very act of tending to his
fourth-grade teacher.

Big Track was considerate. He retreated and waited for the
professor to "git hisself together" and come out and talk to
him. "I'm sorry, 'Fessor," said Big Track. "I didn't know it
was you. This land belongs to the Widow Blasingame. The
widow's sort'a soured on the vine, so she's posted her land and
asked me to see that it ain't used for the purpose you just
been usin' it fer."

"Well, Sheriff," the Professor stammered, "I . . . uh . . ."

"Fergit it, 'Fessor," said Big Track. "Plain or fancy friggin'
between grown folks of the same race ain't against the law as
long as I'm yo' sheriff. And we got plenty'a woods that ain't
posted. Just be careful not to throw out no cigarette and start
no fire. So you move on down a mile'a so and find you another place and start all over. I done fergot all about it."

The professor was so grateful that he now readily remembered that during Sunday afternoon he had received a telephone call from Deputy Sheriff Cates. He had informed the
deputy that Loretta Sykes was the valedictorian of the Class
of 1962, and, of all the graduates of Atoka County Training
School, she seemed the least likely ever to become tied in with
Communists.

"I appreciate'cha helpin' me, 'Fessor," said Big Track. "If
everybody, white and black, tried to help each other like you
and me, all this race trouble would be over in a minute. The
TV wouldn't have nothing to talk about but Vietnam."

En route from the professor's house to Hardy Riddle's
house, Big Track stopped at the jail and briefed Trixie Cunningham. He helped her remember how, at Butt Cut's telephoned request, she had spent much of Sunday afternoon in
the sheriff's office at the courthouse examining reports of the
House Un-American Activities Committee, the State Sovereignty Committee, and the State Committee for Peace and
Dignity. And in no report had she found any warning that the
United States or Alabama or Atoka County should beware of
Loretta Sykes.

At 12:20 A.M. Big Track rang the basement bell at Hardy
Riddle's $100,000 house. When Hardy opened the door Big
Track said: "Skipper, let's talk in my car here in your drive-
way. I got to be where I can hear my squawk box."

"Okay," said Hardy. "Just a minute." He stepped back in-

side and pulled on one of his old red University of Alabama
dressing robes, with a white "A" over his heart. Then they sat
in the Wildcat.

Hardy was worried. Since hearing the television report he
had been trying to put two and two together and figure what
had happened. "Track, did we have to get on TV?" he asked.
"Wasn't there some way you could have kept us off?"

"I didn't want to git us on TV," said Big Track. "But I
don't know what else I could'a done. I got back at nine
o'clock and found a mess on my doorstep. I had'ta git rid of
it. And I had'ta do it so it wouldn't hurt this county or this
state."

"Well, let's see if I understand it," said Hardy. "I don't
want to know too much. I just want to know enough so I can
talk intelligently to the powers-that-be in the back room of the
bank. Earlier today I got the impression that a little action
was to be taken tonight to sort of warn the Negroes not to listen to the agitators. I don't know what action was to be taken,
but I understood that nobody was to be hurt seriously enough
to attract outside attention. Now am I to understand that
there is a connection between that little action and this rape
you've put on TV?"

"There sure is a connection. That little action was in the
wrong place and on the wrong nigger. The wrong place was
my jail, and the wrong nigger was Loretta Sykes. She was the
wrong nigger because she's got two white men who'll stand up
for her. Doc Parker and Breck Stancill. Both'a them can tell
you and me both to go to hell. So they're dangerous men. You
got'ta be careful how'ya mess with men who can tell everybody to go to hell. When I got back I faced a situation where,
if the nigger was turned loose, she'd run straight to the hospital and tell Doc and Breck and the FBI and the agitators
where it was done and who done it."

"Why did you have to turn her loose? Why didn't you
patch her up, then take her out of the state?"

"In another hour Breck would'a come looking for her. If
I'd'a held her and tried'ta sneak her somewhere, I'd'a just
showed everybody that it happened in jail, so I'd'a made it ten
times worse."

"But there must have been *some* way you could have kept
it quiet and kept her from talking?"

"There sure wasn't," said Big Track. "I could'a kept her
from talking. I could'a killed her, or let her be killed. Then

we'd'a had the situation where a civil rights worker is arrested and then turns up missing and dead. That damn sure wouldn't'a kept it quiet. We'd'a never heard the end'a that."

"Even after you put her in the hospital, couldn't you have kept it off of TV?"

"No way that I know. Not without looking suspicious and making it worse. She was a rape victim. Rape is a capital crime in Alabama. A man's supposed to burn for it. I had to be looking fer rapists. When I'm looking fer rapists I got'ta tell the state troopers. I told 'em. Every big newspaper in the state's got men who listen to the troopers' radio. That's how the story got on TV. I couldn't help it."

"But good Lord, Track!" Hardy protested. "Isn't this Negro girl bound to talk? She's alive and on TV! She's bound to think she's been done wrong. The agitators know her, and they'll be after her. Isn't she bound to tell them what happened and where?"

"I figure she's bound *not* to tell," said Big Track. "She ain't no ordinary nigger. I talked to her. She's got education. She's what Doc calls a striver. She knows I did the best I could for her under the circumstances. She don't want trouble. She's already talked to Doc and Breck. She told 'em a nigger done it, and she didn't dispute where I said it happened. And she ain't gonna talk to nobody else but me and Breck."

"But what about Breck? Surely he's going to learn the truth?"

"If he does learn it," said Big Track, "I figure he'll see that nobody else learns it. I know Breck Stancill purty well. I know him better'n anybody else in this county knows him. Sure, he thinks George Wallace is a piss-ant. Sure, he hates Ku Klux. He's bound to: they hung his granddaddy. He spits in Butt Cut's eye, calls him trash, and jerks his clippings off'a billboards. But Breck knows how far'ta go. He knows what a killin' situation is. He recognizes killin' talk when he hears it. And he don't want'ta have'ta kill nobody, and he don't want nobody'ta have'ta kill him. He's laid by in the killin' business. So I figure when Breck eases up close'ta a killin' situation, he's bound to back off and live and let live."

"That's a dangerous way to live, isn't it?" asked Hardy. "You wondering what Breck knows and what he might do, and him wondering what you think he knows and what you think he might do?"

"Yeah, it's dangerous," said Big Track. "But I been through a war. So's Breck. In war you git used'ta living across the

road from a fellow who might kill'ya and who might not. It
ain't so dangerous if each fellow knows how the other fellow
thinks."

Suddenly Hardy Riddle noticed that the night air was chilly.
He had become uncomfortable. He thought he might be
catching cold. He wanted to go back inside his house and go
to sleep. He felt irritated with Big Track for keeping him up
past midnight, for subjecting him to the risk of a cold in the
night air, and for causing him worry. What Hardy did not feel
was guilt. Yet again he had become guilty of a capital crime.
He possessed criminal knowledge which he intended to help
suppress. His first crime had been the lynching of Willie
Washington. He had become a criminal then by having what
the law calls "prior knowledge" of a crime which he did not
disclose to the law. Having undisclosed criminal knowledge
makes any man just as guilty before the law as the rapist or
the murderer. But Hardy Riddle, despite his being a steward
of the Methodist Church, couldn't feel that he was twice a
criminal. What kept him from feeling it was his belief that a
Ku Klux Klan can be "a useful adjunct to police power." Belief can narcotize a man against guilt.

Big Track sensed Hardy's irritation. And this irritated Big
Track. Because Big Track felt that Hardy had subjected him
to needless risk. Why hadn't Hardy dictated that the "little action" be taken in some place other than the jail? And that it
not be taken against the "wrong nigger"? But Big Track
couldn't afford to irritate Hardy. If possible, before they parted, he had to mollify him. So he said: "Honest, Skipper, I
don't think there is much here for you to worry about. I don't
believe many folks'll want'ta talk about it. Because when'ya
git right down to it, nothing much happened. A nigger girl got
roughed up by a bunch'a niggers. That ain't much. Being on
TV makes it sound like more'n it is. And there ain't much
more gonna happen. Tomorrow, and for a few more days, a
dozen outside agitators, with a few nigger school kids, will be
standing around down there at the courthouse trying to feel
like Somebody. They'll sing 'We Shall Overcome' and 'I Shall
Not Be Moved,' and they'll listen to theirselves being called
dirty, black-assed, mother-fuckin' niggers. They'll see theirselves on Huntley and Brinkley fer a night'a two. Then the
girl who got roughed up will go back'ta Chicago, the outsiders
will go back where they come from, the school kids'll be back

in 'Fessor Elmore's school, and you can git back'ta developing Atoka County."

At 1:30 A.M. Maybelle Abernathy Bascomb was knitting. Her son and two daughters were in their rooms asleep; and Maybelle, wearing a neat pale blue gown and robe to match, sat working in her bedroom. She knew that when her husband came home, no matter what time it was, he'd expect to find her awake. He'd want her to greet him, to listen to him, to reassure him, to bathe his back, to bring him milk and pie, and to give him sexual comfort before they went to sleep. Tonight especially he'd want all her ministrations because he had been gone for two days and one night and he'd be tired, worried and afraid.

Maybelle was thirty-five, five feet two, and weighed 112 pounds. When she slipped off her highheels she could stand under Big Track's extended arm. The question about Maybelle was: how could a little woman who looked so soft work so hard? Determination didn't show in her face or manner, only in her record of performance. Her blond hair was still soft, fresh, alive. The skin on her cheeks, throat, neck and thighs was still moist, rose-tinted and downy. She was a proud, primitive, pretty, tireless female who came out of the woods scarcely able to read, but who knew how to hold a male and make him work, how to raise a healthy family, and how to get somewhere, have something, and become somebody.

That hers was a shotgun wedding never bothered her. She had done what a backwoods girl is supposed to do: use sex artfully to trap a desired mate. At fourteen her mother told her: "Girl, when'ya spot the man'ya want, don't court too slow. And when'ya court make sure'ya make him think from the start that he can do it better'n any man on earth. Just let him learn gradual that you can do it better'n any woman on earth." Maybelle continued to use sex artfully. She was first her husband's female, then his homemaker and mother of his children. In her six-room house her bedroom and bathroom were off-limits to her children. They belonged to her and her husband. They were a secret place of physical excitement, release, composure and whispered confidence. Maybelle never needed a Viennese psychiatrist to tell her that sexual surfeit is nature's tranquilizer and sleeping potion.

Maybelle, however, did need Dr. Parker to show her how

not to have children. After her son was born, the doctor fitted
her with a pessary which she was never too lazy to use properly. Her first daughter didn't arrive until her son was seven,
after Big Track won the Medal of Honor, after he was given
the home, and after he became a deputy sheriff with a chance
for promotion. Her second daughter arrived after Big Track
became sheriff. So Maybelle knew how to plan pregnancy.

Each year Big Track sent a Christmas card to every voter
in the county. The card was always a greeting from "the Bascomb Family to Your Family," and it featured a new color
photograph of the Bascombs. The voters liked to keep up with
the growth of Big Track's children and to argue over which
one favored Big Track and which one favored Maybelle. The
card for Christmas 1964 showed Maybelle standing proudly
in the center, flanked by Bettee, nine, and Joanie, six. The
three females looked fair, petite, blonde and curly. Behind
them, bronzed, crew-cut and sandy-haired, towered the two
males: Allen, sixteen, and Big Track.

The twelve-year-old Bascomb home, a tan frame bungalow
with a carport, was five blocks from the courthouse, in an
area of $10,000 GI and FHA homes. It was larger than the
other homes. It stood on a hundred-foot corner lot and had
two bathrooms. Overall it was 32 by 48 feet, so it contained
1,536 square feet, larger than most ex-soldiers could afford.
The organizations which presented it as a tax-free gift to Big
Track included the City of Ellenton, Atoka County, the civic
clubs, and the Atoka Lumber Company. In 1953 it would
have cost an ordinary purchaser $13,500. But the builder was
an American Legionnaire, so he donated his profit and sold it
to the organizations for an even $12,000.

The home belonged outright to Big Track and Maybelle,
but under the circumstances Maybelle encouraged people to
regard it as semipublic property. Along with the expensive
homes of Hardy Riddle and Dr. Parker, it was one of the
homes which people drove past on Sunday afternoons when
they were riding around comparing shrubbery and flowers.
Maybelle was known for her pink dogwood trees, her jonquils
and tulips, her azaleas, gladioli and hollyhocks.

In the living room of the Bascomb home was a shrine unlike anything in Alabama. It dominated the room and filled
the wall space at one end, like the crucifix in a cathedral. The
centerpiece of the shrine, on the pale-green wall over a wide,
bleached-maple bookcase, was the framed citation: the official

account of how Sergeant Bascomb slew all those gooks. To the right and left of the citation, and slightly lower, were framed, inscribed photographs of President Truman and General MacArthur. The Truman inscription: "I would rather have won the Medal of Honor, like Big Track Bascomb, than have been President of the United States." The MacArthur inscription: "I rise and proudly salute Sergeant Bascomb, a valorous American who fought unselfishly and well for a Great Cause." Below the citation was the framed, *Life* magazine photograph of the ceremony in the White House rose garden when President Truman presented the medal to Lieutenant Bascomb. Identifiable were Maybelle and her small son, the two United States senators from Alabama, and the congressman who promised to appoint Allen to the United States Military Academy.

The shrine was framed, right and left, by two flagstaffs, bearing the Stars-and-Stripes and the flag of the American Legion. The medal itself lay in a casket, under glass, atop the bookcase where it could be looked down on. Also atop the bookcase, in clear plastic sheaths, were *Life*'s photos of the three Bascombs touring Washington as guests of the President. Big Track, Maybelle and Allen at the Lincoln Memorial reading the Gettysburg Address; at Mount Vernon looking out over the Potomac; at the Tomb of the Unknown Soldier; on the steps of the Capitol with the two senators and the congressman; in the Library of Congress reading the Bill of Rights parchment; and relaxing in their suite at the Mayflower Hotel.

The top shelf of the bookcase was filled with scrapbooks and other plastic-protected photos. Big Track the private soldier. Big Track the national hero. Big Track at national Legion conventions, greeting Eisenhower, Stevenson, Kennedy, Nixon, Johnson, Goldwater. Big Track with John Wayne, Gary Cooper, Jack Benny, Jackie Gleason. Big Track remembering with a sick and aging Sergeant York. Big Track at the Statue of Liberty. Big Track with his arms full of bathing beauties at Miami Beach. Big Track caught between the fists of Jack Dempsey and Gene Tunney. On the lower shelves of the bookcase were the hero's weapons and battle gear. The M-1 rifle which he fired so accurately. The "grease gun" which spat streams of lead. Grenades (defused) like the ones he hurled against the human sea. The Colt automatic for gooks who got close. The bayonet, his last resort. His helmet and canteen.

Each year Maybelle allowed the first-grade teachers at every white school in the county to bring their children to the house in school buses. She arranged a date for each teacher. She watched anxiously while the children punished her rugs and fingered the precious photos. She tried to help the teachers maintain order. Women's clubs, church groups and Boy Scouts visited the house. Occasionally a car from some far-off state would stop, and strangers would ask to see the medal and the citation.

Except for these periods when it served its public function, the living room was the television room. Allen and Big Track, often with guests, looked at sports, the astronauts, and news reports. The girls saw their programs in the late afternoon, then Allen and sometimes Big Track and the girls watched *Rawhide, Wagon Train, Gunsmoke, The Virginian, Bonanza,* Andy Griffith, Red Skelton and Jackie Gleason. Maybelle watched *Ben Casey* and *Doctor Kildare.* Other than school books and comic books, in all the house there were only two books: The Holy Bible and *The Life of Jesse James.* Neither Big Track nor Maybelle had ever read a book. They subscribed to no newspaper or magazine, and the only publications which reached the house were those which came automatically, like the Ford and Chevrolet magazines, the *American Legion Magazine, The Alabama Baptist,* and various tracts like those of the John Birch Society, the Minute Men, and the Ku Klux Klan.

Maybelle had neither time nor inclination to read. She worked. In the kitchen, in the laundry, in the yard, at sewing, at cleaning, at marketing, at fixing her hair or that of her daughters. What she knew of the world she knew from her family, from television, or from her preacher. She knew that two wars were on: one between the Army and the gooks in Vietnam, the other between the police and the rebellious Negroes in the United States. Because her husband was both an Army man and a policeman, and her son would be an Army man, Maybelle felt involved in both wars. She didn't want the wars to hurt her family's effort to better itself.

She feared the gooks because Big Track had said: "When'ya kill one gook, ten new gooks come runnin' at'cha. The more'ya kill, the more'ya got'ta kill." She feared the rebellious Negroes because her preacher had said: "If the Lord had intended for Negroes to mix with whites, He would not have made them black." The voters of Atoka County believed that racial separateness is God's plan. They expected Sheriff Bascomb to defend God's plan. And Maybelle had lived by God's plan. Not once in her life had she ever spoken to a Negro. No Negro had ever entered a house in which she resided. She had never entered a Negro's house or school or church. She saw Negroes on streets, in stores, on television. Otherwise they were as foreign to her as gooks. (Not one Alabamian in ten ever had a Negro mammy or any sort of Negro servant. The mammies served the romantics and the few.)

But the President of the United States, the Commander-in-Chief of the Army, did not believe that racial separateness is God's plan. He wanted mixing. How was Sheriff Bascomb to remain an Army hero, admired by Presidents, and still please the voters of Atoka County? How was Allen Bascomb to be welcomed to West Point as the son of Big Track and Maybelle?

These questions were causing Maybelle uneasiness; they were also causing her embarrassment. All her life she had said "niggers" as naturally as she said "biskits." But a year ago, at the dinner table, her son had said: "Mama, I don't think you should say 'niggers' any more. It doesn't sound right. Negroes are just people like everybody else. Maybe Dad has to say 'niggers' in his work. The voters might not like it if he quit saying 'niggers.' But, Mama, I wish you'd start saying 'Nee-grows.'"

Secretly Maybelle cried over that. Why would her son for whom she worked, prayed and planned, embarrass her? She began practicing "Nee-grow" when she was alone, cooking and washing dishes. She learned to say it, and now, haltingly, she said it. Her son had asked her to change, so she changed. For she was not devoted to maintaining the Southern way of life. Only to re-electing her husband and sending her son to West Point and her daughters to the university.

Maybelle felt uneasy when she learned that Allen, at the school library, was reading national magazines like *Look* and *Life* and *Time* and *The Saturday Evening Post*. What she knew about these magazines was that Governor Wallace cursed them every time he appeared on television. So they were hated by most of the voters in Atoka County. When she asked Allen about his reading he said: "Mama, at West Point they read those magazines. So don't you think I should begin reading them?"

Maybelle sighed. "I guess that's right," she said. "But make sure the other students don't see'ya readin' 'em."

Whenever Maybelle saw a Negro face on television she felt apprehensive. She couldn't keep from counting the Negro faces on a baseball or football team, and she couldn't understand when Allen, even Big Track, seemed to be pulling for a Negro to get a hit or score a touchdown. She was startled by the first Negro face she saw in a TV commercial. She liked for her children to watch westerns because there were no Negroes and all the colored faces were evil. She liked Ben Casey and Doctor Kildare because they almost never had Negro patients. She liked Lawrence Welk because if a Negro ever appeared he tap-danced or picked the banjo, which seemed natural. She was dismayed when all three of her children began liking *Mister Novak,* which was about a school where white and Negro children mixed and where one of the teachers was a Negro man.

What most confused Maybelle was the TV war reports which showed Negro sergeants in the fighting army. Of one fact about Negroes she had been certain. No Negro can ever become a dependable front-line soldier. Negroes run. Every Negro shows the "rabbit blood" in him when guns begin firing. The Negro doesn't live who isn't afraid of the dark, and whole platoons of Negro soldiers will vanish at night if the enemy arches a flare in their direction. So how could a Negro be a sergeant in a jungle battle against gooks? For Maybelle this had to be confusing. How could she not be confused at the sight of Negroes giving orders to white men in battle?

As she waited for Big Track to come home, of immediate concern to Maybelle was information she had received while he and Allen were gone to Mobile. She, like everyone else, knew of the conflict between Butt Cut and Breck Stancill over Butt Cut's billboard activity. She had heard that several white football players had begun helping Breck tear down the clippings. Then on Saturday a teacher at the high school told her that the leader of this white student revolt against Butt Cut was Allen Bascomb. Maybelle hadn't mentioned it to Allen. She wanted first to discuss it with Big Track. But not tonight. Whenever Big Track reached home after 10 P.M. she never burdened him with a new problem.

When she heard Big Track turn into the driveway, about 2 A.M., she went to the kitchen door and opened it for him. "You must be mighty tired," she said.

"Yeah, honey, I shore am," he said. "I had a long trip and a long day. I'm shore glad'ta git home."

She helped him undress, drew water for him into the outsized bathtub, and sponged his massive back. While he completed his bath she fixed his bowl of strawberry pie and his glass of cold milk. Then, sitting in the bedroom, in his pajamas and big, bare feet, he ate his pie, drank his milk, and told her what had happened.

"You reckon I done right, honey?" he asked.

Maybelle's uneasiness had grown as she listened. The more she heard, the more she feared Loretta Sykes. But she never evinced fear to Big Track. So she answered: "I don't see what else you could'a done. You didn't hurt nobody. You helped the girl. I don't see how nobody could blame you. You sure Breck didn't blame'ya none?"

"He didn't blame me a bit. Not at the hospital and not when I seen him out there side'a the road. He seemed real friendly. He told the doc I was the best sheriff the county'd ever had. He asked me'ta shut this case up and let it die, and I told him he could count on me."

"That's good," said Maybelle. "I ain't never wanted you to get crossed up with Breck. We got too much'ta thank him for." She wanted to relate how Allen was now supporting Breck against Butt Cut. Instead she said: "They shouldn't'a done it to the girl. They sure shouldn't'a done it in the jail. But they figured they was doing right. And I guess something like that don't shame a Negro girl like it would if she was white."

Big Track thought of telling Maybelle that Loretta had been a virgin. But he didn't. He let Maybelle keep talking.

"One thing I'm thankful for," she said. "You haven't had to kill no agitator. And you haven't had'ta turn'ya head while they kill one. You had'ta turn'ya head and let 'em kill Willie Washington. But he wasn't no agitator and he deserved killing. I hope'ya don't have'ta turn'ya head and let 'em kill one'a these agitators who ain't done nothing but provoke folks. I don't think provokin' is enough'ta kill a agitator for. Provokin' makes folks mad, and maybe it's cause for cussin' and fist fightin'. But it ain't proper cause for killin'."

"You don't have'ta worry none about that," said Big Track.

"We ain't gonna have no killin' fer provokin'. They done had plenty'a that in Mississippi, and in the Birmingham church, and down around Selma. It ain't done nothin' but harm. So we ain't gonna have it. Hardy Riddle's against it and I'm against it. So we ain't gonna have it."

"We just can't afford'ta have it, Track," said Maybelle. "What they got'ta remember is that you ain't like other sheriffs. A lot'a people look up'ta you, even from 'way off. You got'ta think about what the President thinks and what the Army thinks. We got'ta do right for the sake of everything we got and everything we want for our kids."

"You got nothing to worry about, honey," repeated Big Track. "But one little thing sort'a puzzles me. The TV said the FBI boys were coming in here'ta help me. That was four hours ago and they ain't showed up yet. I been looking out fer 'em since midnight."

"Well, don't worry," said Maybelle. "Maybe they'll decide you don't need help. So maybe they won't come."

"They'll come," said Big Track.

When Big Track crawled into their standard-sized double bed he all but filled it. But Maybelle, naked, knew how to slip into his bearlike embrace. The room was dark except for the glow of the street light through the drawn curtain. His big hands moved possessively over her smooth, firm, familiar body, to her breasts, thighs and buttocks, as his mouth found hers. Her hand massaged his genitals. When he was ready, she turned on her side, her back to him, and raised her knees in invitation. He then took her like a big man can best take a little woman at 2:30 A.M. when he's tired and when, during his act, he wants one hand active on her breasts and the other active in her crotch.

When he had had his comfort, and felt her orgasmic spasms, Big Track lazily retreated, sprawled, and fell almost instantly to sleep. Maybelle found the position in which she felt most secure: her blond head on his chest and her right hand on his genitals. Then she, too, fell asleep.

CLAY WILBANKS

In ALABAMA, each year from 1935 to 1965, about 100,000 acres of cleared land were reforested. By 1965 two-thirds of the state's land area was in forests; and despite an accompanying growth of the lumber and paper industries, each year 20 per cent more timber was grown in the state than was cut. Among the states in the union Alabama became second (to Georgia) in tree farming. This same process of turning from cotton to trees went on in all the states of the Southeast; and that is how the Negro ghettos grew in the northern and western cities. People, some of them whites but most of them Negroes, were displaced by trees, pastures and mechanization; and the displaced Negroes, sons of slaves who by law could not be taught to read, "went Greyhound" to urban Promised Lands where only the lettered and the skilled can find milk and honey.

Since Atoka County was entirely agrarian in 1935, reforestation proceeded even faster there than in the state at large. A man could watch the frontier experience being reversed. In 1815 when Fowler Stancill arrived he found 384,000 acres of forest. Not one acre had ever been cleared. (The Indians lacked tools to fell trees. They cleared land for corn by "girdling" trees and waiting for them to die and be felled by the wind.) Then Fowler Stancill, his slaves, and those who quickly joined him, cleared 190,000 acres—half the county; and by 1855 they were growing each year 25,000 bales of cotton, 800,000 bushels of corn, and 85,000 bushels of wheat. These figures are from the first history of the county, published by the newspaper in 1855. Here are other excerpts from that history:

> MANUFACTORIES—We have nothing in this county worthy of the name of manufactories, unless producing the raw staple may be so considered. A few small tanner-

ies and one or two waterpower wool-carding machines constitute the sum total under this head.

CHARACTER OF THE INHABITANTS—Atoka County is decidedly a religious community. We have many professors of religion, hospitable and social, free and easy. There are few men of highly cultivated minds, but most of the leading characters are men of ordinary education, plain, yet intelligent; many good business men, some connected with Mobile houses. The preachers of the gospel are not men of cultivated minds, but many of them are respectable notwithstanding. The numerous schools now springing up in this county have begun to raise the standard of intelligence among the youth. Atoka sends more than her quota to the State University annually, and one of her sons is now a professor there. If our people excel in anything, it is in being a peaceable, law-abiding community, when let alone by demagogues. The prevailing occupation, it scarcely need be remarked, is agriculture; corn and cotton; more cotton to purchase more land and Negroes to raise more cotton.

ANTIQUITIES—Atoka County was neutral ground between the Creeks, the Choctaws and the Chickasaws, but I know of no mounds, graves or monuments of the aborigines in her borders. Both De Soto and Bienville, with their warriors, visited Atoka, or the territory now so called.

LOCAL DISEASES—The local diseases are those arising chiefly from miasma—intermittent and remittent fevers; certain forms of neuralgia and typhoid fever also seem local, and to some extent produced by miasma; in summer, fever, in winter, pneumonia; the latter being connected frequently with remittent fever, the result, perhaps, of miasma imbibed the previous summer. In 1851-52-53-54 pneumonia assumed an epidemic character, and in the summers following epidemic dysentery prevailed and was very fatal. The chief local cause of disease is miasma, arising from the extensive creek bottoms, pools and ponds, filled with decaying vegetable matter, interrupted by rafts, causing frequent overflows in the wide swamps, which dry up in summer, except in pools where the water becomes stagnant. The planters who own the high ground in the county usually live on it, with their slaves, to partially escape the miasma and enjoy the sweeter free-stone water.

POPULATION—According to the latest census (1855) the county now has 9,167 white inhabitants, 42 free Negroes, and 9,236 slaves, making a total of 18,445. The slaves are owned by 86 slaveholders, some of whom own one to three slaves. Our largest slaveholders are our first settler, Fowler Stancill, and his son Landers Stancill. Together the Stancills own 718 slaves.

Thus Atoka County had three thousand fewer inhabitants in 1965 than it had in 1855. It had two thousand more whites, but it had five thousand fewer Negroes. This means that after 1855 the county became a nursery for emigrants, both white and Negro. The natural increase emigrated. When a father and mother produced five sons, four sons went west or north and one stayed at home. Sometimes no son stayed at home, or daughters, and families petered out. The most dramatic movements were in 1861-70, when many white men went to war, when some slaves ran off, and when the remaining slaves became serfs. After 1870 the Negro emigration slowed, and their number in the county increased each year until it reached 14,000 in 1916. But with the First World War the black movement toward the northern cities accelerated, and each year thereafter all the natural increase and some of the brood stock among the Negroes moved northward and westward.

Emigration and the wars affected the Stancill family much as they did the Negroes. In 1860, at sixty-seven, Fowler Stancill died. He had sired six sons, five of whom had gone to Texas or California. Only Landers remained. When, in 1861, one week before Alabama seceded, Landers Stancill was hanged, his wife, his two daughters, and two of his three sons fled north with $68,000 in gold to escape death or persecution. All remaining Stancill property, including 13,000 acres and 761 slaves, was confiscated by the Confederate States of America. But the youngest son of Landers Stancill, Philip, born in 1845, went to the woods and eluded the Confederate military police for four years. He had $6,000 in gold buried in a cave on Stancill's Mountain. When the war ended he killed two of his father's murderers, hired four others killed, and spent his life recovering the 13,000 acres on which still lived many of the former Stancill slaves, their children and grandchildren.

But Philip Stancill didn't become rich. His wealth was in poor land, poor Negroes, and revenge. He enjoyed taunting the ruined Secessionists and being hated by them. He announced that when he had found and killed all his father's murderers he'd start looking for their sons and grandsons. All the children of his first marriage left Atoka County as soon as they were old enough. In 1890 Philip made a second marriage and built the home in Ellenton where, in 1895, his wife bore Harvey Stancill. Philip died in 1912. Harvey went off to France in the First War and returned to Atoka County only in body, never in spirit. In 1920 he brought a Mobile beauty to Ellenton as his wife. He then stayed drunk for twenty years, presiding over the piecemeal sale of most of the 13,000 acres. He sired two daughters and one son, Breck, in 1924; and each year the Atoka Lumber Company acquired more Stancill acres, drove off the Negroes, bulldozed away the shacks, and planted the acres in pine trees.

No two Americans greeted the Second World War quite as gratefully as did Harvey Stancill and his wife. The war liberated him at forty-six and her at forty. Their three children left, and Harvey went off as a major in the Quartermaster Corps. In 1945, while celebrating victory and his fiftieth birthday in Paris, he died of a stroke in the act of copulating with a French woman. Within an hour after she learned of his death, his wife sold the Ellenton house to Hardy Riddle; and next day she shook the dust of Atoka County from her feet and went to Miami Beach, where she promptly married a retired Jewish millionaire.

On the morning of June 3, 1946, First Lieutenant Breck Stancill, twenty-two, USMCR, walked out of the Navy Hospital at Bethesda, Maryland. He wore a new tan linen suit, two-tone brown and white shoes, and a straw hat. He carried an aluminum walking stick, and an orderly carried his Valpac and placed it in a taxicab. The lieutenant had spent fifteen months in four different hospitals, had survived five operations, and had learned to walk on an aluminum leg. Now he was sound, free of Japanese steel, and ready to resume civilian life.

The taxicab took him to the airport, from which he flew to Birmingham, then took a bus to Ellenton. He stepped off the bus at dusk. He had been gone almost exactly four years. He had graduated from high school on May 28, 1942, and enlisted in the Marine Corps next day. He was met at the bus by Hardy Riddle because the sole purpose of his return was to sell the last three thousand acres of Stancill land to the lumber company. He expected to be in Atoka County no more than four days. Then he was flying to Albuquerque to enter the University of New Mexico under the GI Bill.

"Welcome home, Breck," said Hardy. "You look great."

"Thanks, Hardy," Breck said. "But I guess it isn't home any longer. The Stancills finally petered out in Atoka County."

"Nonsense," said Hardy. "This will always be your real home. I wish you'd change your mind and not go to the motel. We'd like for you to stay with us at the old house. We've remodeled it. But it's still the Stancill house, just like Philip built it in 1890, and just like it was when you were born in it. Why don't you change your mind and spend your four days here with us?"

"That's kind of you," said Breck. "But I don't want to trouble your wife. I'll stay at the motel."

En route to the motel Hardy said: "I guess your mother wrote you about it. She sold me all the furniture, but she packed your books and clothes and all the other things in trunks and boxes. The other things are keepsakes, I guess, like old guns and newspapers and letters and pictures. I've got it all for you at the warehouse. You may want to look through it while you're here and discard some of it. Then I'll ship what you want of it wherever you say. Or I'll just keep it for you indefinitely."

"Yes, Mother told me," said Breck. "She visited me last month in the hospital. I'll want to look through everything."

"That'll be a big job. You must have a ton of books. You must have read a lot when you were coming up."

"Yes, we read a lot. My mother started reading to me when I was three or four. Then we read a lot to each other."

"Well, all the books are waiting for you," said Hardy. "Right there in the warehouse."

"There is one favor you might do for me," said Breck. "Can you lend me a horse tomorrow?"

"Sure. Glad to do it." Then, in delayed surprise, Hardy asked: "Can you still ride?"

"I think so," answered Breck dryly. "I think there's enough left of me to straddle a horse."

"I'll send one over first thing in the morning. In fact I'll do you a real favor. I'll send you my wife's horse. A big palomino named Pal. He ought to be a good one. I paid twelve hundred dollars for him."

Next morning in faded khakis and tan Marine field shoes Breck rode east on the palomino, toward Stancill's Mountain. At the edge of town he left the black-topped highway for dirt roads and paths he had known all his life. Two miles from town he entered the bottomlands which were part of the old 13,000 Stancill acres. Fields which for a century after 1820-30 were planted in cotton and corn were now in pine trees. A loblolly pine seedling can be twelve feet high in six years. In twelve years it can be thirty feet high, five inches in diameter, and can be harvested for pulpwood or left to grow another twenty years for sawlogs. By the height of the trees in any former cotton field Breck could tell which year his father sold that field to the lumber company. From the time Breck was ten until he left for the war he spent many of his outdoor hours watching the company foresters plant the seedlings, thin the shoulder-high trees, prune the higher trees until their boles were clean up to two-thirds of their height, and plow the six-foot-wide furrows which were firebreaks and had to be kept free of flammable material like grass, leaves and wood.

On the slopes as he approached the mountain Breck found stands of shortleaf pine. Loblolly is the fastest-growing pine but it needs moist soil. Shortleaf is better suited to slopes. But shortleaf is less resistant to disease and insects. It needs more care. So Breck looked for signs of care, found them, and approved them. There was no underbrush, no rotting logs to shelter beetles, and when he looked up Breck could see three or four feet of blue sky separating the crown edges. Healthy pine trees need room to grow, and they must not be over-topped by worthless oak and hickory.

When he was growing up Breck had felt sad each time he learned that his father had sold another thousand acres of Stancill land. It didn't seem fair to Fowler Stancill who had cleared it; to Landers Stancill who had lost it, along with his life; or to Philip Stancill who had regained it. Why didn't Harvey Stancill quit drinking whiskey, quit selling land, and plant the trees himself? Now Breck thought: Well, my father didn't want responsibility. He was the son of a young mother and a hard, fifty-year-old father. And his war, unlike mine, was a war of hope, and hope died. So maybe he couldn't have been anything but what he was. In any case he's dead now, and I must give the company credit. They practice first-class forestry. They have improved the land.

Breck and the palomino stood on a slope, looking back across the bottomland toward Ellenton. Breck could see the courthouse clock, the water tower, the church steeples, the lumber company's smokestack. Suddenly he noticed what was missing. People. He had ridden back roads and paths for an hour without passing a shack. Or hearing a dog barking. Or a Negro singing. The people were gone. Not only had the Negroes moved to Chicago but the whites had moved to the highway, or to Ellenton, or to California, or to the industries of the Tennessee River Valley. The countryside was vacant. For old land to be improved did people have to leave?

Breck soon found people. He found them as he rode on up the mountain and onto land which didn't belong to an efficient company but to him. He heard dogs barking. He heard an old man singing "You're As Welcome As the Flowers in May." And in the woods only Nature's forestry was being practiced. The underbrush was dense. Rotting logs harbored beetles. Mutilated and half-rotten old oaks and hickorys overtopped young pines which had been neither thinned nor pruned. The old oaks and hickorys were worthless, but they were essential to deer, squirrels and birds. So was the underbrush essential to quail, foxes and wild turkeys. There is no food or shelter for wildlife in a tidy and profitable stand of shortleaf pine.

Breck made several stops among the sixty or more rotting shacks which were strung out along the graveled mountain road. Each shack housed from one to four Negroes, and around it were two or three cleared acres on which grew stunted cotton, a garden, perhaps a patch of berries. A few milk cows grazed in small pastures or stood chewing cuds at tiny, decaying barns. Most of the Negroes were old, the unemployable residue of decades of slavery and serfdom. But there were a few small children, even babies, whose mothers had made roundtrips to Chicago.

Each time Breck stopped, the Negroes gathered from the nearby shacks to welcome him home from the war, to insist that he climb off his horse and demonstrate that he could walk, to then insist that he pull up his pants and let them thump his artificial leg, and to wonder what in the world would become of them if he ever sold the mountain to the lumber company.

Most of the older Negroes didn't worry about the mountain being sold, and they told Breck why.

"You couldn't nevah sell the mountain, Mistah Breck. That's why yo' daddy left it to'ya. Yo' daddy always said he might sell everything else, but he'd nevah sell the mountain."

"Don't nevah let nobody tell'ya that yo' daddy wasn't a good man, Mistah Breck. Maybe he nevah drew many sober breaths, and maybe he lifted more'n his share'a skirts. But he was good. God rest his soul 'way ovah yondah 'cross the water."

"I 'member yo' old granddaddy, Mistah Breck. Old Mistah Philip. He was a piss-cutter. He'd turn ovah in his grave if you evah sold the mountain."

"The graveyard's up here, Mistah Breck. A mountain with a graveyard on it can't nevah be sold!"

"And don't you evah fergit, Mistah Breck, that yo' old great-granddaddy is buried up here som'ers. The Lord only knows where, but he's buried on this mountain. And so's Old Ab."

The story of Landers Stancill's burial was known to every Negro who ever worked for the Stancills. On that terrible night when Landers Stancill was seized in Ellenton and then hanged on the mountain, his family had to run. That slave boy who walked from New Orleans with Fowler Stancill in 1815 was still living. His name was Absalom, and by 1861 he was called Old Ab. Sometime after midnight, while all the other Stancill slaves hid in terror, Old Ab hitched up a one-mule wagon and drove to where the body was hanging. He cut it down, and before daylight he buried it secretly so that the grave could not be desecrated. The legend said that the burial was in one of several caves on the mountain. But no one ever knew which one because Old Ab never told; and in 1862 he was murdered by Secessionists for refusing to tell them where Philip Stancill was hiding.

At the spot where Old Ab cut down the body, Breck stopped the palomino and reflected. He was alone, among the old trees, and impulsively he recited aloud the portions of his great-grandfather's speech which caused the Secessionists to hang him.

> Before the bloodbath begins, let this be said. I am the son of a father who rode proudly into this county with Andrew Jackson. My father, like Jackson, fought all his life for the Union. How can I do less?
>
> I take no pride in being a slaveholder. My pride is in being a free American planter. I own slaves because I am a planter, and the available laborers are slaves. But human slavery is evil, just as Jefferson and Madison so pronounced it a century ago. Ten thousand preachers can stand in pulpits and affirm that slavery is divinely ordained, and it will still be a lie.
>
> Slavery has been perpetuated in the South not only or even chiefly by the few slaveholders. Slavery has been perpetuated, and the South is being led to destruction, by demagogues elected by white men who do not own slaves but who cannot abide the thought of living in a nation where Negroes are free.
>
> Both my late father and I have advocated education and gradual emancipation for Negroes. As a planter I do not fear the prospect of dealing with free Negro labor. As an American I am not afraid of living in a community where Negroes enjoy every right granted to every man by the Constitution of the United States.

He must have known that poor white men might hang him for saying that, thought Breck. Then why did he say it? Or why hadn't he sold out and gone west with his brothers in the 1850s?

Breck stopped at the Negro church and cemetery. The Stancill's Mountain Baptist Church. First built by Fowler Stancill, then rebuilt by Philip Stancill, and reroofed in 1925 by Harvey Stancill. Perhaps as many as two thousand burials had been made in the cemetery. The oldest known markers were for slave children who died in 1819, the year Alabama became a state in the Union. Old Ab's grave was there, and it was still tended. But most of the pre-1910 area was now wooded over, though stones could still be found among the trees and underbrush. Breck looked at the new stones, for those who had died while he was gone, and tried to remember which ones he had known. Every inscription expressed Hope of Heaven and anticipation of the Great Gittin'-Up Mawnin'.

The highest portion of the mountain was its northern end. There was no peak, only a wooded plateau, about three hundred acres in extent, and in this woodland there were several two- and three-acre clearings for shacks. From the plateau the mountain dropped off sharply on three sides: steep, wooded slopes broken by bluffs with sheer drops of up to sixty feet. Thus the mountain, when viewed from Ellenton, was wedge-shaped: thin and low on its south end, thick and high on its north end. The gravel road didn't cross the mountain. It ran south to north, from the south end where it met the black-topped highway, to the north end where it ended at an overlook on the high northern rim of the plateau.

Before he reached the plateau Breck turned off the road a few yards and found a "blowing" spring from which issued a constant blast of cold air and a stream of clear, cold water. He dismounted, drank, watered the horse, and sat down in the shade to eat the lunch which Hardy Riddle's wife had prepared. "The lunch is coming in the saddlebag with my horse," she had telephoned him. As he ate the fried chicken, pickles, potato salad and fruit, and drank the thermos of iced tea, Breck noticed how good he felt. He loved animals, forests, peace and simplicity. Two chipmunks ventured out to see him, then a doe and her fawn. Squirrels played in the tree over his head. He asked himself: Do I feel like I've come home? He didn't want to feel that way because he didn't want to be trapped into staying. He knew how unhappy his parents had been. He knew that the wise Stancills were the ones who had left Atoka County when they were twenty-two, not the ones who stayed.

After his lunch Breck rode up on the plateau, heading for the "Taj Mahal." In 1937 his father built a log cottage for a woman he had found in New Orleans. She lived in the cottage until the war began. Then she, too, left the county. Her name was Martha Hinkle. Breck never spoke to her: he couldn't speak to her without being disloyal to his mother. But when he was fourteen and fifteen he sometimes sat in the woods, without Martha Hinkle knowing he was there, and watched her work. She worked determinedly at painting. One of the gossips in Ellenton recalled that the Taj Mahal in India was built to honor a woman. So the gossips, and finally everybody, including Martha Hinkle and Harvey Stancill, called the log cottage the Taj Mahal or, more often, "Harvey's Taj."

From one source or another the gossips assembled some of Martha Hinkle's story. She was a tall, thin, long-haired Mississippi school teacher who yearned to paint. In 1935 she quit teaching and went to New Orleans. Her paintings wouldn't provide food and shelter. So when her savings vanished, to continue painting she turned to genteel whoring. A hotel bell captain became her agent. For the inflated price of thirty dollars, of which ten dollars went to her agent, Martha would visit a man's room and "paint his picture." After she painted Harvey Stancill's picture he made her an offer. Adequately but inexpensively he would maintain her in return for his visiting her twice a week. When he further agreed to limit each visit to two hours, she accepted. This arrangement worked until another war came to divert Harvey Stancill. Martha Hinkle liked the arrangement, not because she liked Harvey but because she valued him. The man who would provide her food and shelter for the least number of hours of her time was the man Martha Hinkle valued most in all the world.

Before he reached the Taj Mahal Breck stopped at a shack. A worn Negro woman in her thirties came out.

"Are you Susan Sykes?" he asked.

"Yassuh, I is, Mistah Breck."

"Mr. Riddle told me you have a key to the cottage."

"Yassuh, I got it. I been cleaning that place once a month ever since yo' daddy left for the war. The woman went off the week befo' yo' daddy did. Everything up there's nice and clean. But there ain't been nobody but me in it fo' might nigh five years."

While Susan Sykes was inside, getting the key, a three-year-old girl stood on the porch and eyed Breck curiously. She was Loretta Sykes.

Susan Sykes handed the key up to Breck as he sat on the horse. She said: "Now that you done growed up, Mistah Breck, you sho' does favor yo' daddy. He was a good man. I sho' felt lonesome and mighty low when I hear'd he'd done died 'way ovah yondah 'cross the water."

"Thank you, Susan," Breck said.

The cottage stood at the end of the road, on the northern rim of the plateau, and from its front porch you could look north for twenty miles. The walls were of pine poles, each about five inches in diameter. Before their emplacement the poles had first been barked, then soaked in a preservative

which turned them Turkish-tobacco-brown. Next they were
shellacked. When they were notched and in place, the cracks
were filled with off-white mortar. The high-pitched roof was
of cedar shakes. So the cottage looked brown-and-white
striped, topped by the weathered cedar-red of the roof, and
overtopped by tall pines.

Breck had never been inside. Now he unlocked the front
door and entered, uneasily, wondering if he might be committing an impropriety against his father. He wondered if perhaps he shouldn't burn down the cottage without inspecting it.
It had been a shameful place: some cultures prescribe such
burnings. The main room was twenty-four by thirty feet, with
a cathedral ceiling supported by visible, shellacked poles.
Glass filled much of the end facing the overlook, and a sand-
stone fireplace filled much of the opposite end. On each side
of the fireplace hung a painting: his father and a self-portrait
of the artist.

"Good Lord!" exclaimed Breck audibly. In the painting his
father wore a buckskin hunting coat and looked like an empire builder. He was strong, proud, fulfilled; not weak,
ashamed, bored. Martha Hinkle was all black and red: black
eyes and long, loose, unadorned black hair framing the thin,
burning red face of an ascetic.

Off the main room, to the left, was a kitchen and storage
room; to the right was a bedroom and bath. Water for the
plumbing came from a well in which there was an electric
pressure pump. All the furniture had been made of cedar by
local craftsmen. The polished pine board floor was covered in
several places by red-and-yellow hooked rugs. In the storage
room Breck found fifty or more unframed pantings. He examined some of them and felt sorry that so much effort had not
been enough to make them valuable.

Breck went outside, mounted the palomino, and rode slowly around the immediate area. Two hundred yards south of
the cottage was a three-acre clearing and a shack which before 1942 was occupied by a white tenant. Now this shack,
too, was vacant. Breck inspected it, then rode back to the cottage and sat there on the horse, thinking. He could feel the
old trap of land ownership closing on him.

This land, he thought, has never belonged to anyone except
the United States and the Stancills. Why shouldn't it continue
to belong to me? I love forests; I own one; why don't I keep it?
I like solitude; I own a place for solitude; why don't I enjoy

it? Why should I sell this land and buy an apartment house in California? What do I remember about California except restless, rootless people and my lonely liberties in San Diego? New Mexico? Why should a man live in a desert and breathe dust when he can live where sixty inches of rain falls every year? Why shouldn't I live in this cottage? The copulating ghosts of my father and his woman won't bother me. I can beautify this cottage, move my books and keepsakes into it, make it into a home.

Ever since he entered high school Breck had assumed he would go to college. His mother expected him to go. Suppose that now, with the capacity, the money, and the opportunity to go, he decided not to go? Wouldn't he regret it for the rest of his life? Well, I've lost four years to the war, he thought. Why can't I educate myself? I have Shakespeare's plays, the Federalist essays, *The Revolt of the Masses, The Education of Henry Adams, Democracy in America, The American Commonwealth, The Decline and Fall of the Roman Empire, Democratic Ideals and Reality,* and the poems of Yeats and Blake. Isn't that a fair start? I want to be a woodsman and a conservationist. I can study with the foresters at the lumber company. They have college degrees.

The most difficult question Breck asked himself was: Do I want to hide in the woods because I'm mutilated? Am I seeking solitude because I've seen a girl shudder at the sight of a naked one-legged man?

Breck considered all these questions as he rode down the mountain and back to Ellenton. Next morning he was in Hardy Riddle's office. "I'm going to back out on you, Hardy," he said. "I'm keeping the mountain. I'm going to live in the Taj Mahal."

"That doesn't surprise me much," said Hardy. "While she was fixing your lunch yesterday morning my wife predicted that you'd decide to stay."

"Maybe it was the lunch that changed my mind."

"Whatever it was, I'm glad," said Hardy. "You belong in this county. You can keep the Stancills from petering out. And what the hell, the company'd rather you grew the trees for us than for us to have to invest our money and grow them."

Then Hardy asked Breck to cooperate with him in solving one problem. "Times are changing," he said. "Our county now has a chance to become something besides a goddam

poorhouse. We're swapping Negroes for Yankees and making·
progress. But we still have one problem. There's just no place
here any longer for Negro sharecroppers and field hands. And
there's damn sure no place for Negroes who don't work at all!
That includes about two hundred on Stancill's Mountain.
During the last ten years everybody has cooperated in pushing
Negroes out. Everybody but Harvey Stancill. Now, Breck, I
don't have to tell you how your daddy was. He was good-
hearted. But he didn't give a goddam about improving the
county! He'd sell land to us and we'd improve it. We'd give
the Negroes six months to get off, then we'd send in the
bulldozers. Most of the Negroes would go to Chicago, but
some of them would go crying to Harvey. You know how Negroes will impose on a good-hearted white man. Harvey'd let
them move in up on the mountain. He'd give them three or
four acres to grow beans on, even a little cotton. And he'd
never charge the Negro a red cent! He gave it all to them and
he still had to pay the taxes!"

"I understand, Hardy," said Breck. "Of course that must
change. For the Negroes' sake it must change, as well as for
the county's."

"Hell, it must change for your sake, Breck. You've got at
least sixty shacks up there now. Around each shack is three or
four unproductive acres. That's two hundred acres that should
be in trees. At five dollars per acre per year that's a thousand
dollars a year. In the last twenty years those Negroes have
cost twenty thousand dollars that you'd have right now in tree
value if the Negroes had been pushed off."

"I know," repeated Breck. "It must change. It will
change."

"It's got to change. We don't want to *demand* anything of
you. 'Demand' is not a word that friends use to each other.
But we must urge you. Because those Negroes are costing the
county money. We have to give the old ones fifty-five dollars
a month; we have to bus the young ones to town and educate
them. When the young ones are educated they run to Chicago. So your Negroes are a dead loss to you and to the county.
They've got to go!"

"I'll help," Breck said. "I can't run the old ones off. But I'll
run the young ones off so there won't be another generation."

"That's the way to do it," said Hardy. "When an old one is
about to die, you call me, and, at no expense to you, we'll
stand by to send the bulldozer. The first hour the shack is

empty the bulldozer will smash it, the barn and the privy. The crane will lift everything onto the truck, and by night the bulldozer will have those four acres ready for you to plant in trees. But if you leave the vacant shack standing there, hell, some Negro back from Chicago will move in without telling you. Sure they come *back* from Chicago! Even young ones! Up there it's root hog or die. The rent comes due every week, and those Jews in Chicago run a Negro back to Alabama the minute he can't pay his rent. So the way to protect yourself and the county is to bulldoze the shack the minute you can get it empty."

"I understand," said Breck. "I'll cooperate."

On Monday, April 12, 1965, Breck was up at sunrise fixing his breakfast. In nineteen years he had reduced the sixty shacks to forty, and the two hundred Negroes to about one hundred. Hardy Riddle said that "by and large Breck's done a good job." But others said: "Breck ain't no better at runnin' niggers off than Harvey was." The Ku Klux stood ready, with whips, fire and dynamite, to help Breck run the Negroes off, but he resisted Ku Klux help.

Except for the 150 acres still blighted by the primitive existence of the Negroes, Breck had converted his inheritance into a model tree farm on which he netted ten thousand dollars a year. That is, it was a model for those farmers who compromise between profits and protection of wildlife. By destroying all food and cover for wildlife and growing only resinous trees, Breck could have made more money. Instead he allowed many hardwoods to overtop his pines; and on some acres he encouraged a moderately heavy undergrowth. He even planted a few patches of grain. This gave him less marketable timber, but it gave him deer, squirrels, foxes, wild turkey, quail, and thousands of song birds. His own home, the Taj Mahal, had been enlarged and made as comfortable, book-filled and gadget-assisted as any home. It was even air-conditioned: by a General Electric heat pump.

After breakfast Breck followed his usual workday routine. He saddled his palomino, put him in the horse trailer, and hooked the trailer to the Chevrolet pickup. In the truck were pine seedlings and tools for planting, thinning, pruning, clearing underbrush, poisoning insects, and marking trees for harvest. He also carried his lunch and a thermos of water. His Irish setter jumped into the seat with him, and he drove toward the selected work area. Sometimes he used two or three old Negroes who could still work to help him plant or clear. More often he worked alone. He spent much of his time on the horse, riding firebreaks, looking for insects or disease, or marking trees to be harvested by the company gangs with their labor-saving powered tools.

About 4 P.M. Breck was on the east slope of the mountain pruning five-year-old trees. Because of the noise of the power saw he didn't realize anyone was approaching until a man was within twenty feet of him. Breck cut off the motor.

"Mr. Stancill?" the man asked.

"Yes, I'm Breck Stancill."

"I hope I didn't startle you."

"Not seriously. My dog should have told me you were coming. I suppose he's looking for quail."

"My name is Clay Wilbanks. I'm an agent for the Federal Bureau of Investigation. Here are my credentials."

Breck glanced at the photo and noted that Wilbanks, like himself, was born in 1924. Wilbanks was tanned and wiry, and he wore faded khakis, GI shoes, and a hunting cap.

"I've never thought of FBI agents as woodsmen," Breck said.

"Oh, yes," said Wilbanks, "we have to be woodsmen, too. Lately I've spent a lot of time in the woods, working on cases involving the Ku Klux Klan."

Breck looked at him more closely, then asked: "What is it you want from me?"

"Well, first," began Wilbanks, "let me say that I didn't drive up to your house, and I have contacted you in the woods so that we can talk without anyone knowing we have met. Two hours ago my partner let me out of a car on the road east of here. Since then I've been circling and listening, looking for you. I feel sure no one has seen me."

"That's an impressive amount of trouble for a man to go to," said Breck. "My pickup is about a hundred yards from here. On it I think we can find two camp stools and a jug of water. I suggest we go and sit down."

When they were seated Wilbanks said: "I believe you are aware of the crime committed here last night?"

"You mean the assault on Loretta Sykes? Yes, I'm aware of it."

"And I assume you know that racial demonstrations began

this morning in Ellenton? And that they are likely to continue for a week or more?"

"I've heard that they might begin."

"Well, they began," said Wilbanks. "I was at the court-house between eight and eleven A.M. There were about a hundred demonstrators. The leaders are one of Dr. King's men and a Presbyterian ministerial student. About twenty of the demonstrators are outsiders. About eighty are teenagers from the Ellenton Negro school."

"Anybody hurt?"

"Not up to the time I left. Big Track had the demonstrators roped off near one of the courthouse entrances. They stood there praying, singing, with their signs asking for integrated washrooms and drinking fountains in the courthouse and for jobs in the Ellenton supermarkets and variety stores. The whites stood across the street jeering and cussing. But nobody was throwing anything. The television cameras are there. So the networks will start showing it this evening. Big Track will be the star of the TV show. If the demonstrators hold out for two weeks, Big Track may get more publicity than Bull Connor or Jim Clark or even George Wallace."

"That follows," said Breck. "Big Track's a national hero. So of course they'll keep the cameras on him."

"Big Track is also either lucky or smart."

"In what way?"

"In having Loretta Sykes alive. She wasn't murdered. She can talk. So he's using her."

"How?"

"Well," said Wilbanks, "you have noticed that in other places in Alabama and Mississippi, where there have been demonstrations there have been atrocities. Usually one or more murders. Like Medgar Evers. Or the children in the Birmingham church. Or Reverend Reeb and Mrs. Liuzzo around Selma. Or the three in Neshoba County. At every place the Ku Klux have accused Negroes and outsiders of the crimes. Then came the truth: the Ku Klux or other white racists had done it. Last night here in Atoka County we had the atrocity. Within an hour Big Track accused Negroes and outsiders. And here comes the difference. This morning Big Track went to the hospital and recorded Loretta Sykes saying it was Negroes and outsiders. She says they grabbed her off the street in Ellenton at seven-fifteen last night and assaulted her because she wouldn't agree to help them. Big Track has given the re-

cording to TV. So now Big Track has the demonstrators at a
big propaganda disadvantage. He calls them rapists, and says
he's going to arrest some of them. And suddenly he's the national hero of racists everywhere. He's receiving a flood of
telephoned and telegraphed congratulations. He's the first
sheriff to prove that the Negroes and the outsiders are the
ones who commit the atrocities. And he could never have
done it if Loretta Sykes had been dead."

Breck Stancill and Clay Wilbanks sat there in the woods
looking at one another. The sun was sinking, so its light
filtered through the tree tops in broken beams. The two men
resembled one another in dress and manner. Breck was a little
heavier. His face was not as bony, and his hair was lighter
and grayer at the temples. Breck asked: "What did Loretta
Sykes tell the FBI?"

"Nothing," replied Wilbanks. "She told us she had told the
sheriff all there was to tell."

After another pause Breck asked: "Mr. Wilbanks, where do
you come from?"

"I was born in Pontotoc, Mississippi," he said. "I was a platoon leader in the Fifth Marine Division at Jwo Jima. After
the war I graduated from the Ole Miss Law School. I've been
an FBI agent for twelve years, assigned to Mississippi and
Alabama."

"That practically makes us cousins, doesn't it?"

"Yes," said Wilbanks. "It makes us such close kin that if I
had been in your place last night, and if I had been thinking
of what was best for Loretta Sykes, I'd have told her to tell
Big Track whatever he wanted to hear. And I'd have told her
to tell the FBI nothing."

Breck grunted. Then he said slowly: "Since we are old Gy-
rene buddies, both trained in jungle fighting, I'll ask you this.
When you approached me a few minutes ago, how close did
you get to me before I knew you were in these woods?"

"Twenty feet," said Wilbanks. "And if I were blind in one
eye and couldn't see good out of the other, I couldn't have
missed your back with a double-barreled shotgun loaded with
buckshot."

"Do you know how easy it is to set fire to a woods? Have
you ever watched wildlife fleeing a forest fire? Have you ever
studied what fire can do to a model three-thousand-acre tree
farm?"

"I understand forest fire."

"You mean you have a detached understanding of forest fire. From your safe distance the fire looks terrible, but it also looks beautiful. The red glare against the night sky, the exploding brands, the shooting Roman candles. But if you've planted those trees with your own hand and nursed them for fifteen years, you bleed as you watch them burn. It's almost like watching your Marine buddies being slaughtered in a trap while you're pinned down and can't help them."

"I know about your trees," said Wilbanks. "You give each tree tender, loving care. You call every deer, fox and squirrel by its name. I also know about your house. Did you notice that helicopter over here about three hours ago?"

"I saw the Forest Service helicopter."

"My partner and I were flying with the Forest Service. We mapped the place where Big Track said the rape was committed. So we also mapped your place. That gravel road leaves the highway and snakes three miles up the spine of this mountain to your house. Nobody lives between you and the highway except Negroes and Nancy Poteet, the rape victim of Willie Washington. With her two babies Nancy lives just two hundred yards south of you. Then there's the Taj Mahal sitting up there defiantly on the rim. One Molotov cocktail against its high-pitched cedar roof would light a bonfire which everybody in Atoka County could watch. So as one old jungle fighter to another, I'd say you've pitched camp in the worst terrain for one man to try to defend I ever saw."

"Then why did you sneak up here to see me?" demanded Breck. "Your precaution proves that you know you are jeopardizing me. If Loretta Sykes or I know anything, what can we accomplish by telling it to you? Where were you when she was falsely arrested, then raped? You're only an investigator, not a policeman. Can you punish a rapist? Can you even make an arrest? Since you can't help us, why must you jeopardize us?"

"I can answer those questions," said Wilbanks. "First, we *are* helping you. There is a dangerous Ku Klux Klan organization in this county. It has forty-seven members. One member is our informer. We have watched this Klan for three years. Watching is a form of fighting. You watch to get ready for a showdown fight."

"Then why hasn't your informer told you what happened to Loretta Sykes?"

"He doesn't know. He's not a member of the Action Squad.

Of those forty-seven members only nine are members of the
Action Squad. The other thirty-eight members never know
what the Action Squad is planning or doing. It's that way in
all Klan groups. This Ellenton Action Squad lynched Willie
Washington. I know that. I suspect that it also directed the
rape of Loretta Sykes. All I ask of you is that you save us
time by confirming my suspicions. You talk to Loretta and
you tell me all she knows about what happened."

"I won't do that, Wilbanks!" snapped Breck. "If I go one
inch with you, you'll insist that I go a mile. You won't stop
until you've got me burned out and probably dead. The sys-
tem doesn't allow you to consider my safety. You know that;
I know it. You say you know that this Action Squad lynched
Willie Washington. Then why haven't you arrested the
lynchers? Why are they free to assault Loretta Sykes? You
haven't arrested them because no jury in Atoka County will
convict them. If you knew the identity of these rapists, would
you arrest them? You know goddam well you wouldn't. Because you can never punish them. So you are asking me to
join you in a battle in which you fight from a protected position. You take no risks. The United States of America stands
behind you. I take all the risks. I fight from the exposed position of Stancill's Mountain. Who'll stand watch for me while I
sleep? You want to enlist me in a battle in which I have everything to lose and nothing to gain."

"Hell, Breck, you're not making sense!" said Wilbanks.
"I'm not trying to enlist you. You've already volunteered. I'm
not jeopardizing you. You've already jeopardized yourself.
Why the hell did I come to see you? Here's why. One month
after Willie Washington was lynched you began jerking Butt
Cut's Ku Klux clippings off bulletin boards. When the Ku
Klux began harassing Nancy Poteet you moved her up here
with you! Hell, you moved her into the same shack where you
once allowed Big Track and Maybelle to live. By both those
actions you provoked Klansmen and jeopardized yourself. So
who are you to complain of jeopardy? You're already in
jeopardy!"

"But there are degrees of jeopardy," insisted Breck. "My
provocations have been calculated. I have acted from my
knowledge of individuals. I know Big Track and Butt Cut and
Hardy Riddle and Vernon Hodo. I know them well. These
acts you mention have been limited acts with which a man
can define a position and still stop short of violence. I can

provoke Klansmen and still not provoke them enough to use the faggot and the shotgun. But if I cooperate with you, then you'll be calculating my risks. There's a difference, and you've been trained to understand it."

The two men sat looking at one another for several minutes. The sun was going down. "Well, that's that, Clay," said Breck. "I'm not going to cooperate with you. I'm sorry. I don't know all that happened to Loretta Sykes and I doubt that I shall ever ask her. I want her to go back to Chicago and forget it. But I don't meet an old Marine buddy every day. So here's what I suggest. There's nobody at my house. My cook is nursing Loretta's mother. And it's dark enough so nobody can see you in my pickup. So let's drive to my house where I'll give you a drink and cook you a steak. Then I'll drive you to the highway and put you out near a telephone where you can call your partner to pick you up."

"That sounds good, Breck," said Clay Wilbanks.

NANCY POTEET

AMONG NEGRO wage earners in Atoka County the best paid were the 105 men who worked for the Atoka Lumber Company. They were paid well because the company was engaged in interstate commerce, so all of its employees were protected by the Federal Minimum Wage Law. The highest paid of the company's Negro workers were the members of four ten-man gangs which harvested trees. The company employed eight such harvest gangs: four white gangs, four black gangs. These eight gangs were supervised by Vernon Hodo. They harvested both sawtimber and pulpwood. With their power saws, forklifts, skidders and hydraulic loaders they could harvest trees faster than could Paul Bunyan with his mighty axe and blue ox.

Twenty-three-year-old Willie Washington was a sawman in one of the black gangs. With his one-man, hand-held power saw he could trim the limbs from the bole of a tree "almost before it hits the ground." Willie was lithe and quick. He was a brash driving-man. No sawman could match Willie. He was proud, bellicose, and as "greasy black" as his Nigerian forebears. Every Saturday at noon he drew sixty-two dollars.

In the Ellenton "niggertown" where he lived with his mother Willie was a problem. He was a sexual menace to wives. He didn't want his comfort from single women; he wanted it from wives. He wanted sex to be a contest, not only between him and the female, but also between him and her husband. To the young, wifeless Negro males who drank his whiskey on Saturday night, and gambled with him, and looked up to him, Willie often explained: "Man, when I's fuckin' a single gal, no matter how good a piece she is or how strong I's pourin' it to her, I keep feelin' I ain't doin' no more'n single-fuckin'. I knows I ain't fuckin' nobody but her! But when I's fuckin' a married lady, man, I's double-fuckin'! It's twice as good 'cause I can feel myself fuckin' *him* while I's fuckin' *her*.

And, man, when I finally turns that lady a-loose, when that sad cat gits back in there, he's gonna find out that Old Willie's done made some changes!"

Willie's aggressions had caused the Ellenton city police to hurry to Niggertown more than once to stop fights and prevent murder. They had arrested Willie as a chronic troublemaker. But they never could punish him because Vernon Hodo would make bond for him and persuade Hardy Riddle to get the charges dropped. Vernon liked Willie. Vernon often amused the Ku Klux with stories about Willie.

"Hell," Vernon would chuckle with the Klansmen, "that nigger wife-pussy that Willie gets is what makes him the best sawman I got. Let Willie blacksnake a couple of nigger wives on Saturday night and Sunday, and on Monday he's rarin' to go. The week after he blacksnaked that new nigger preacher's wife, Willie was a one-man gang in the woods. He felt like he could drive that chain saw through the whole fuckin' world!"

Vernon's accounts of Willie's wife-topping were almost as amusing to Ku Klux as the shows Lightning Rod put on in the woods when a Negro girl was flung into a ring with him.

A little after midnight on Sunday morning, January 19, 1964, Willie was driving toward Ellenton. With him in his car were three other Negro males, all younger than he. They had spent Saturday evening drinking and playing *tunk* and *skin* in Negro "jukes" along the highway. They planned one more stop, at a Negro whorehouse, then they were going home. Cold, light rain was falling. About four miles from Ellenton the highway ran through a lonely creek bottom. There, in his lights, Willie saw a car parked on the shoulder of the road. He guessed it had been abandoned. He slowed, then moved very slowly past the parked car while his companions examined it with a flashlight. They were looking to see if the tires were worth stealing. When the flashlight revealed a young white woman and a small child sitting in the front seat, Willie increased speed and drove on.

Almost at once, before he had traveled half a mile, Willie overtook a young white man who was walking rapidly, almost running, toward Ellenton. The young man waved, shouted, pleading for a lift. Instead of playing the Good Samaritan, Willie speeded up, guessed what had happened and laughed.

"Well, looky there!" said Willie. "Ain't that too bad! Daddy's old car done broke down in the rain. And won't nobody stop to help him. Not on this road this time'a night! So pore

Daddy's got to go joggin' four miles to Ellenton and leave little Mama and the baby just settin' there all huddled up and
scared on the side'a the road. Now ain't that a cryin' shame!"

The mother in the stalled car was Nancy Poteet: twenty-
two, thin, modest, blond, and four months pregnant. The
child was her three-year-old girl. The father jogging toward
the all-night service station was Bobby Poteet: twenty-four, a
meat cutter for the A&P supermarket in Ellenton. Nancy was
reared in an orphanage in Kansas, and she was working as a
practical nurse when she met Bobby. They were proud of
each other, proud of their child, and proud that Nancy was
pregnant again. They were members of the poor-white West
Ellenton Baptist Church where Bobby sang in the choir. At
eight o'clock that evening, after the supermarket closed, they
had driven thirty miles to see Bobby's sick mother. They waited later than they should have to start back. When the car's
engine failed, Bobby first tried to fix it. Then he tried for
twenty minutes to flag down a passing car. When no one
would stop, and when cars began passing infrequently, Bobby
faced a hard choice. Unless his family was to spend a freezing
night in the car, either he or all three of them had to travel
afoot in the cold rain. Rather than subject his pregnant wife
and child to such a walk, he fearfully chose to lock them in
the car and leave them for perhaps forty minutes while he ran
for help.

Had Willie Washington not seen the husband in trouble as
well as the wife, he might have ignored Nancy Poteet. But the
opportunity to victimize both a husband and wife was too attractive for Willie. He was like those Russian soldiers who
enjoyed gang-raping a German wife only if her husband could
be compelled to watch. Willie pulled into a side road to turn
around.

"We ain't goin' to no whorehouse," he said. "We's goin'
back and git on little Mama."

His companions revolted. "The hell we is!" they chorused.
"You done gone crazy, Willie! You want to git us all killed?"

Willie jerked the car into the highway, raced for Niggertown, and discharged his chicken-hearted companions. Then
he raced toward Nancy. He met Bobby Poteet, still jogging
through the rain, still almost two miles from help.

"You sho' better run, Daddy," Willie said aloud to himself.
"You better run faster. 'Cause while you're runnin' Old Willie's gonna be on yo' nest. And when Daddy gits back on little

Mama, he's gonna find that Old Willie's done made some changes!"

Willie drove past the stalled car, turned around, and stopped his car at the rear of the stalled car, leaving his headlights on. From under a seat he got a hammer and a .38 Smith & Wesson revolver. He walked to the right side of the stalled car, where Nancy was sitting. She could see him clearly.

"Yo'all need some help?" he shouted.

"No, thank you," Nancy shouted back. "My husband will be here any minute."

Willie showed her the gun. "Open the door," he demanded. She hugged the child and shook her head. Willie swung the hammer while Nancy shielded the child and her own eyes from the shattering glass. Willie reached in. He cut his left hand on glass as he opened the door.

Since Nancy, though terrified, was thinking first of the child, she followed Willie's orders. She got into his car and sat between him and the crying child. As he raced off, Willie said: "I'm from Chicago. I done robbed a bank and killed two white men today. So killin' yo' kid won't make no mind to me. So you better do's what I tells'ya, little Mama, and do's it so's I likes it."

"Why do you want to harm me?" asked Nancy. "I've never harmed you. You don't know me."

"I'm gonna know you, little Mama," said Willie. "I'm gonna know you good. You gonna know me."

Willie turned off the highway, onto a red clay logging road. He stopped briefly while he wound a handkerchief around his bleeding left hand.

"What about my little girl?" asked Nancy. "You're scaring her to death."

"She'll git over it," said Willie. "Iffen I ain't got'ta kill her. She's just gonna see her mama git fucked. Ever' little girl sees her mama git fucked. Little boys, too."

"But I'm pregnant," insisted Nancy. "You don't want a pregnant woman."

"I been told that befo'," said Willie. "By wives a-tryin'ta keep me off. It ain't never kept me off yit. It ain't gonna keep me off'a you."

Willie turned into the woods, stopped, switched off the lights. He held the pistol in his right hand, the flashlight in his left. He put his right arm behind Nancy and turned the flashlight so she could see the pistol against the child's head.

"Now, little Mama, you git busy pleasin' Old Willie," he said. "You pull up that nice blue skirt and shuck off them silk pants. Then you open my britches and take out Mister Man. Then you slip right out on the edge of the seat so I can git down in there on my knees and find things just right. Then you put Mister Man where he belongs and go to work for him. And be sho' you don't pull back none when Mister Man goes all the way home."

When Nancy hesitated she heard the click of the pistol cocking. Trembling, she began doing what he said. As he went inside her Willie dropped the flashlight and savaged her in darkness. She held the crying child tightly by the hand.

"Now git out," ordered Willie. For the first time he began thinking of safety. Another rapist might have killed Nancy. But Willie wanted only to rape, not to kill. For Willie to feel that he had satisfactorily victimized the husband, the wife had to live. "Don't make me no trouble," said Willie. "If'ya does I'll come back from Chicago and kill'ya kid." He drove off.

Carrying the child in the rain and darkness, Nancy began walking to the highway. She slipped in the red mud. She stumbled into mud holes. But in ten minutes she reached the highway where a truck driver quickly picked her up and delivered her to the service station in Ellenton.

So fast had it all happened that Nancy reached the service station just as Bobby and a repairman were preparing to leave in a tow truck. The time was 1:10 A.M. Nancy told Bobby what had happened, and the tow truck rushed her to the Atoka Hospital.

Meanwhile, in Niggertown two of Willie's companions, to protect themselves, had told their mothers what Willie might be doing. The mothers, who didn't like Willie, knew the danger. Their sons had been seen with Willie. If there was a rape, would a lynch mob bother to believe that his companions had left Willie before the rape? At 12:55 A.M. one of the mothers telephoned Sheriff Bascomb, told him what might be happening, and assured him that her son was at home. So Big Track was dressed and leaving his house when the service station manager reported the rape. Big Track hurried to the hospital and talked to Nancy in the Emergency Room.

Nancy described the rapist and added: "He called hisself Old Willie. He cut his left hand on the glass, and it was bleeding pretty bad. This blood on my blouse and skirt is his.

And hanging down from his rear-view mirror was some kind'a little doll."

At 1:50 A.M. when Willie returned home Big Track was hiding in the house. As Willie opened the door Big Track rammed the .45 automatic in his stomach and grabbed his collar.

"You black s'nuvabitch, gimme that gun!" Big Track got Willie's pistol and said: "Show me your left hand." Willie displayed his cut hand, still wrapped in the bloody handkerchief. Then Big Track asked: "In that old car o' yours, is there some kind'a doll hanging from the rear-view mirror?"

"Yeah," said Willie. "It's one'a them grass-skirted hula girls."

"I'd shoot'ya right where'ya stand," said Big Track, "but shootin's too good for'ya. Come on!"

After jailing Willie, Big Track returned to the hospital for Dr. Parker's report. "How bad's she tore up, Doc?" he asked.

"She isn't torn up at all," replied the doctor. "Nancy's fine. She's ready to leave the hospital."

"But she's been raped, ain't she?"

"That's a legal, not a medical, question. Certainly Nancy has engaged in, or been subjected to, coitus during the last hour or so. I removed fresh sperm from her vagina. I also treated her for possible venereal infection. She has been excited, probably terrified. But she didn't panic or become hysterical. Her pulse rate is now about normal. She's four months pregnant, but she isn't going to miscarry. In short, she's thin, but she is a healthy, vigorous young woman; and thank God, she's suffered no lasting physical damage."

"But good Lord, Doc!" said Big Track, "that black s'nuvabitch tore into her!"

"From evidence other than medical I'm convinced he did," said the doctor. "I'm convinced it was forcible assault against her will, which is rape. Rape is a grave crime against society and against a human personality. In this state it is, and probably should be, a capital crime. But, as I say, that is a question to be decided in a court of law. My responsibility is the medical facts. A healthy, normal, young woman is built to survive being torn into. Hell, the human vagina may be the most durable piece of equipment ever devised by Nature or the Creator. It can survive an incredible amount of lunging, thrusting, pounding and stretching."

Big Track was becoming confused and irritated. "But, Doc," he said, "this girl has been blacksnaked!"

"So it appears," the doctor said. "A blacksnake is a penis which the vagina is designed to handle. The normal blacksnake is no larger or more fearsome or more damaging than the normal white snake. It is also my supposition that Nancy, having a head on her shoulders, did what she could to tame the snake, so that she and her child could escape with a minimum of damage."

"Doc," said Big Track, "if you're saying what it sounds to me like you're saying, then goddam, you better drop'ya voice and make sure nobody hears it but me and you."

"I'm not making a public speech," said the doctor. "I'm speaking as a physician to the sheriff of Atoka County. I'm not saying that Nancy Poteet relaxed and enjoyed it. I'm saying that thank God she didn't panic and get herself and her child killed."

Big Track reflected, then said: "But, Doc, don't you think that, just to make it look right, you ought'a keep her here in the hospital, at least for the rest'a the night? You ought'a kind'a observe her, or treat her for shock, or something?"

"No, I don't think that," said the doctor. "Nancy has worked in hospitals. She doesn't pamper herself. I've known her for four years. I delivered her little girl. She's a good woman and a good mother. Right now she's feeling relieved and thankful, like you'd feel if you had just survived a cyclone. She wants to show you the scenes of the crime, to help you prepare the evidence for a quick trial. You need to move fast and make sure the stupid Ku Klux don't commit a graver crime. And Nancy needs to be at home with her husband and child."

Nancy and Bobby Poteet went with Big Track to the stalled car. They examined the smashed window, Willie's tire marks on the rain-softened shoulder of the road, and Nancy's heel marks where she got out of the stalled car and into Willie's car. Nancy found the road where Willie turned off the highway, then she found the rape scene. Nancy's heel marks were there; and since she was carrying the child over wet red clay, Big Track easily followed her heel marks to the highway where the truck driver picked her up. At the jail when Nancy looked at Willie she didn't scream or weep or tremble. She said: "Certainly he's the man." Then Big Track took Nancy and Bobby home.

About 4 A.M. Big Track got back to the jail. Hattie and Butt Cut were taking turns talking to reporters on the telephone. Hattie told Big Track that Hardy Riddle wanted to see him. Big Track drove to Hardy's house, and Hardy met him on the driveway. "Is there any doubt in the world that Willie did it?" Hardy asked.

"None a'tall."

"Well, Track," said Hardy, "Vernon's been up here. He and his boys are waiting down in the lumberyard. He thinks they ought to take Willie out. I'm inclined to agree. What do you think?"

"I don't know," said Big Track, chewing on his cigar. "Any other time I'd be hard set against it. But in this case I might say 'yes.' The victim is a nice-looking little yellow-headed gal. Good wife and mother and Baptist. But she's a cool cucumber. She didn't fight the nigger. So a jury wouldn't like her. The crowd wouldn't like her. The jury thinks a little white gal who's been blacksnaked ought to feel so ashamed that she don't like'ta show her face. If she ain't dead she at least ought to be tore up, cryin' and tremblin' from the shame of it. Th' crowd thinks the same way. But, hell, this gal stayed ᶜ ᵒ ʳ even while that s'nuvabitch was pourin' the blacksnake to her. Since Willie was holding a .38 in his right hand and a flashlight in his left, and his left hand was cut and bandaged, some folks might decide that she put it in for him. And right this minute this gal don't act like she's 'shamed o' nothin'! Of course any jury's gonna give Willie the chair. No doubt about that. But life's gonna be mighty tough for Nancy Poteet from here on, 'specially if she can't show more shame. A trial sho' wouldn't help her none. Then, what the hell, Skipper, you and Vernon always took up for Willie in his nigger-wife-gigging. If we have a trial, Huntley and Brinkley might say that the Atoka Lumber Company was to blame for the rape."

"I've thought of that," Hardy said. "I don't like lynching. It creates a bad image. But I think it may be best for the county and for everybody if we just get this over with. A lynching will last one day on TV. But if we drag on and have a trial, hell, the agitators will be in here yelling about Negroes on juries, and we'll be the TV rape capital of the world for a whole goddam month."

At 5 A.M. Big Track was investigating a reported burglary at a crossroads store three miles from the jail. Butt Cut, inside the jail, noted that it was time for him to unlock the front

door to see if the rain had stopped. As he stepped outside he
felt a shotgun in his ribs. So he and Hattie were compelled to
deliver Willie Washington, with cuffs on his wrists and ankles,
to seven masked Ku Klux who sped away in two cars which
had no license plates.

The stalled car in which Nancy was sitting when Willie dis-
covered her had been towed away. But at the spot where the
car had stood, on the shoulder of the highway, Willie was
tossed out. Flashlights illuminated him. Vernon Hodo looked
down at Willie and said: "Goddam, Willie, I always took up fer
you. You was the best sawman I had. What'd'jah have'ta go
put that black peg in a white hole fer?"

Like a troubled master compelled to kill his dog because
he's caught him sucking eggs, Vernon raised his 12-gauge automatic shotgun and fired three loads of double-aught buckshot into Willie. Five other Klansmen, in turn, each fired three
shots. The seventh member of the Action Squad didn't fire.
He was the Reverend Mark Alverson. As the Klan Kludd, or
chaplain, he didn't bear arms.

"After being raped," said Breck Stancill to Clay Wilbanks,
"Nancy Poteet became an outcast. Like a leper."

"You must have known she would," said Wilbanks. He had
eaten his steak, and before the open fire he was sipping Jack
Daniels. "I followed the case. I wasn't surprised because I
know that Ku Klux can't tolerate the sight of a white woman
who has been raped by a Negro. They must drive her out.
Perhaps murder her."

"I suppose I have always understood that," said Breck.
"But when I heard that it was actually happening here in
1964 I was surprised. So I read *The Clansman* again; and
when the Ku Klux showed *Birth of a Nation* at the Ellenton
drive-in, I went to see it." Breck walked to a bookshelf and
picked up a copy of *The Clansman*. "I had to be reminded
that to Klansmen, whenever a white girl comes to her senses
after being raped by a Negro, she must commit suicide at
once. Here is the rape scene in *The Clansman:*

> The door flew open with a crash, and four black
> brutes leaped into the room, Gus in the lead, with a re-
> volver in his hand, his yellow teeth grinning through his
> thick lips. "Scream, now, an' I blow yer brains out," he
> growled.

Blanched with horror, the mother sprang before Marion with a shivering cry: "What do you want?"

"Not you," said Gus, closing the blinds and handing a rope to another brute. "Tie de ole one ter de bedpost."

The mother screamed. A blow from a black fist in her mouth, and the rope was tied.

With the strength of despair she tore at the cords, half rising to her feet, while with mortal anguish she gasped: "For God's sake, spare my baby! Do as you will with me, and kill me—do not touch her!"

Again the huge fist swept her to the floor.

Marion staggered against the wall, her face white, her delicate lips trembling with the chill of a fear colder than death.

"We have no money—the deed has not been delivered," she pleaded, a sudden glimmer of hope flashing in her blue eyes.

Gus stepped closer, with an ugly leer, his flat nose dilated, his sinister bead-eyes wide apart gleaming ape-like, as he laughed: "We ain't atter money!"

The girl uttered a cry, long, tremulous, heart-rending, piteous. A single tiger-spring, and the black claws of the beast sank into the soft white throat and she was still.

It was three o'clock before Marion regained consciousness, crawled to her mother, and crouched in dumb convulsions in her arms.

"What can we do, my darling?" the mother asked at last.

"Die! Thank God, we have the strength left!"

"Yes, my love," was the faint answer.

"No one must ever know. We will hide quickly every trace of the crime. They will think we strolled to Lover's Leap and fell over the cliff, and my name will always be sweet and clean—you understand—come, we must hurry."

With swift hands, her blue eyes shining with a strange light, the girl removed the shreds of torn clothes, bathed, and put on the dress of spotless white she wore the night Ben Cameron kissed her and called her a heroine.

The mother cleaned and swept the room, piled the torn clothes and cord in the fireplace and burned them, dressed herself as if for a walk, softly closed the doors,

and hurried with her daughter along the old pathway
through the moonlit woods.

"Now note," said Breck, "that the victim of that rape, who
was seventeen, was physically strong at 3 A.M. when she regained consciousness. She was as strong as Nancy Poteet was.
She didn't need hospitalization. She wasn't even bleeding, as
Loretta Sykes was. She was strong enough to bathe, dress, and
go hurrying through the woods with her mother, who was
thirty-five. Yet daughter and mother agreed that suicide was
necessary."

"Don't forget," said Wilbanks, "that the readers of that
scene favored suicide. And the readers included Woodrow
Wilson who called *The Clansman* a great novel and *Birth of a
Nation* a great film."

"Here is the suicide scene," said Breck.

On the brink of the precipice, the mother trembled,
paused, drew back and gasped. "Are you not afraid, my
dear?"

"No, death is sweet, now," said the girl. "I fear only
the pity of those we love."

"Is there no other way? We might go among strangers," pleaded the mother.

"We could not escape ourselves! The thought of life is
torture. Only those who hate me could wish that I live.
The grave will be soft and cool, the light of day a
burning shame."

"Come back to the seat a moment—let me tell you my
love again," urged the mother. "Life still is dear while I
hold your hand."

As they sat in brooding anguish, floating up from the
river valley came the music of a banjo in a negro cabin,
mingled with vulgar shout and song and dance. A verse
of the ribald senseless lay of the player echoed above the
banjo's pert refrain:

"Chicken in de bread tray, pickin' up dough;
Granny, will your dog bite? No, chile, no!"

The mother shivered and drew Marion closer. "Oh,
dear! Oh, dear! has it come to this—all my hopes of your
beautiful life!"

The girl lifted her head and kissed the quivering lips.

"With what loving wonder we saw you grow," the mother sighed, "from a tottering babe on to the hour we watched the mystic light of maidenhood dawn in your blue eyes—and all to end in this hideous, leprous shame! —No!—No!—I will not have it! It's only a horrible dream! God is not dead!"

The young mother sank to her knees and buried her face in Marion's lap in a hopeless paroxysm of grief.

The girl bent, kissed the curling hair and smoothed it with her soft hand.

A sparrow chirped in the tree above, a wren twittered in a bush, and down on the river's bank a mocking-bird softly waked his mate with a note of thrilling sweetness.

"The morning is coming, dearest; we must go," said Marion. "This shame I can never forget, nor will the world forget. Death is the only way."

They walked to the brink, and the mother's arms stole round the girl. "Oh, my baby, my beautiful darling, life of my life, heart of my heart, soul of my soul!"

They stood for a moment, as if listening to the music of the falls, looking out over the valley faintly outlining itself in the dawn. The first far-away streaks of blue light on the mountain ranges, defining distance, slowly appeared. A fresh motionless day brooded over the world as the amorous stir of the spirit of morning rose from the moist earth of the fields below.

A bright star still shone in the sky, and the face of the mother gazed on it intently. Did the Woman-spirit, the burning focus of the fiercest desire to live and will, catch in this supreme moment the star's Divine speech before which all human passions sink into silence? Perhaps, for she smiled. The daughter answered with a smile; and then hand in hand, they stepped from the cliff into the mists and on through the opal gates of Death.

"Nancy Poteet couldn't afford that sort of conduct," said Breck, shelving the book. "She had a three-year-old daughter to consider. Also a husband and an unborn child. She couldn't afford to believe that she had suffered a 'leprous' shame. She decided not to act like a leper, and not to let anyone treat her like a leper. Did the FBI receive a report on what happened at the West Ellenton Baptist Church?"

"None that I recall," said Wilbanks.

"Well, since it was Sunday, ten hours after the rape and six hours after the lynching Nancy bathed and dressed herself and her child, and, with her husband, she went to church as she was accustomed to doing. For her family's sake she wanted to carry on as though nothing catastrophic had happened. Bobby Poteet sat in the choir and joined in singing 'Bringing in the Sheaves' and 'What a Friend We Have in Jesus.' Nancy sat in the congregation. All that she and Bobby needed were a few pats on the back, a few kind words. With their presence they were pleading for help. But they didn't get it. The church members were too shocked, too confused, too sickened to comfort Nancy and Bobby. I say 'sickened' because one woman, sitting near Nancy, vomited during the sermon and had to be assisted out. The 'nigger odor' which she smelled on Nancy had turned the woman's stomach. Several other women smelled the odor, but by holding perfumed handkerchiefs to their noses they managed not to throw up. To her fellow Christians Nancy had become loathsome . . . leprous . . . an Untouchable."

Clay Wilbanks sipped his whiskey. "Why didn't that preacher do something?" he asked. "Why didn't he make some gesture which might have helped dispel that nigger odor?"

"Bobby Poteet went to him next day and asked him why," said Breck. "The preacher said he would have helped if Nancy had stayed away from the church for two or three weeks and given people time to get over the shock. The preacher said Nancy acted unwisely in coming to the church 'so soon after she had been in that nigger's foul embrace.'"

"It was the husband that I sympathized with," said Wilbanks. "That poor bastard! I could just see him, working in the A&P, trying to cut pork chops for a housewife, with him knowing that she was watching him, wanting to ask him how he liked screwing a wife who's been screwed by a nigger. The poor bastard! And him lying in bed with his wife at night, listening to high school kids drive by yelling 'nigger fucker' and 'nigger pussy.' And that Chicago Negro paper calling Nancy a slut and saying she had been giving it to Willie for weeks. We counted a hundred and fourteen copies of that paper in the mails: Chicago Negroes, who thought it was true, mailing it to 'Nancy's Husband, Ellenton, Alabama.' The poor bastard! I had a bet with my partner on how long the poor bastard could take it. I said he'd run in three weeks. My partner said four. I won."

"They considered running away together," said Breck. "But they couldn't run, or do anything else together again, until they answered the question which haunted them both. Were they still mates? Could he ever raise a hard for her again? They both believed he could; then they began to doubt; then they knew he never could. Nancy told me how he kept trying, and how he cursed himself and wept. She had become leprous to him. He could do nothing but break and run. She'll never hear from him again. His whole family turned on her when he ran."

"How did you get involved?" asked Wilbanks.

Breck sighed. "Oh Lord," he said, "that's a good question. It was a month after the rape and lynching. I was eating supper when Dr. Parker stopped here at my house. He came in for a cup of coffee. He was pissed off. He told me some of what was being done to Nancy. He denounced it as voodooism, medievalism. He said *we* had to help her. 'Now stop right there, Doc,' I said. '*You* know Nancy Poteet. I don't. *You* want to help her. Okay, I'll help you help her. I happen to have two hundred dollars. You take it. You put two hundred with it, and you ship Nancy and her child off to the Catholic Church, or the Salvation Army, or the Great Society, or whoever is in the business of giving shelter to little pregnant mothers who are outcasts. Obviously there is no point in trying to keep her in Atoka County.'"

"The doctor didn't like that, I guess?"

"It wasn't what he had in mind. He told me he had delivered Nancy's first child; that she was five months pregnant; that he wanted to care for her and see that, with all her troubles, she didn't miscarry; and he wanted to deliver the second child. So he wanted to keep her near him, and protect her, until her baby came and she was able to travel. He had found out that my 'white' shack, where Big Track once lived, was vacant. No Negroes have ever lived in it. At his expense the doc wanted me to repair the shack, install a bathroom in it, and let Nancy live there for five or six months."

"Why did you agree?"

"Well, the doc is my friend. Over the years I have talked him into helping me help a few people—including Big Track and Maybelle. We argued for an hour, and I made the mistake of taking a couple of convivial drinks. 'Doc, what the hell,' I said, 'all you really want to do is to defy witch-burners. You despise Ku Klux, so you want to protect Nancy Poteet

from Ku Klux. But you want me to do all the defying and
protecting. And I may already be doing all the defying and
protecting I can get away with. You know the Ku Klux don't
like my sheltering these Negro relief clients. If I also shelter
Nancy Poteet, that could be the straw which gets me burned
out!' The doc came back with that nonsense which is always
thrown at ex-Marines. We are supposed to be perpetually defiant and protective. 'Oh, hell, Breck,' he said, 'the Ku Klux
are scared of you. You killed as many gooks as Big Track.
You break necks with your bare hands. Even without your tin
leg you can hop around and disarm a berserk Negro. When
Nancy gets up here, for the Ku Klux she'll be out of sight and
out of mind. Nobody'll be yelling obscenities at her, or smell-
ing nigger odor on her, or looking at her like she makes a
habit of laying for niggers. Nobody comes up here—except
me, and a woman now and then to spend a Sunday with you.'
I let him talk me into it—and it was a mistake."

"You mean you are sorry you allowed the doctor to move
Nancy up here?"

"Sure, I'm sorry," answered Breck. "Because how am I ever
going to get rid of her? Once she and her child moved up
here, they lived within two hundred yards of me. They became the only neighbors I have—the only white neighbors.
She was pitifully lonely, her belly getting big as a barrel. Her
child was pretty and intelligent, with no other child to play
with. I had to bring food to them. Their only visitors were Dr.
Parker and me. So I had to begin sitting and talking with her.
I had to put the little girl on my horse. I had to find a small
dog for her to play with. You can't live close to lepers without
getting involved in the tragedy of their lives. You get mad. At
the man who raped the mother in the presence of the child.
At the men and women who were not content to lynch the
rapist, but who then had to make a leper out of his victim.
Then you get uneasy. Before I could lie down to sleep, I
found myself walking out in my yard, looking toward Nancy's
shack, listening, assuming guard duty. Sometimes I wake up
during the night—I still do—listening. Maybe I'd get up and
get my gun and circle Nancy's shack. Until Nancy and her
child moved here, I hadn't picked up a gun against the possi-
bility of a human intruder since Iwo Jima. So am I sorry I let
myself become involved with Nancy and her children? Certainly I am."

"After Nancy moved up here, when you found yourself

getting mad, is that when you started ripping Butt Cut's clippings off of bulletin boards?"

"Yes. And that was another mistake. One day I noticed a clipping on the board in the courthouse. I didn't know who had put it there. It had quotations from *The Clansman*. On an impulse I ripped it down. Several people saw me. Then I learned that Butt Cut, with Hardy Riddle's approval, was putting up such clippings all over the county. My witnesses broadcast the word that I was tearing the clippings down. So I had to continue. I couldn't enter the area of a bulletin board without folks stopping to see if I dared to demolish another clipping. Then came the Barbershop Showdown. There I was, getting a haircut. Hardy Riddle was in the next chair. Several other men were sitting around. Big Track and Butt Cut came in. We were all talking, being old buddies. But up there in front of everybody was another one of those goddam Ku Klux clippings! It was my move. If I performed my act before that crowd, Butt Cut almost *had* to hit me. And if he tried to hit me, I wasn't sure I was still fast enough and strong enough to break that thick neck of his. But I had to risk it. I got out of that chair and moved to that board just like I was nineteen, moving across a beach, with a grease gun in my hand and a rifle platoon behind me. I jerked down that clipping, tossed it in a wastebucket, and stalked out like I wasn't afraid of a regiment of Butt Cuts. I still don't know how I got away with it. And, of course, I didn't get away with it. Sooner or later Butt Cut must try to hit back."

Clay Wilbanks asked: "Have you heard that Big Track's boy, Allen, has begun imitating you—jerking down the clippings?"

"Yes, I've heard it," said Breck. "I'm going to stop him. He's a fine boy. He wants to go to West Point. He must have Hardy Riddle's support. So he must stop."

"What happened when Nancy's baby was born? I heard that you and the doctor had several varieties of trouble."

"That was ten months ago," said Breck. "We had all sorts of trouble. First, while Nancy was in bed, who was to care for the four-year-old child? The Negro women up here were afraid to get near her. No white woman in the county would keep the little girl. So we decided to let her stay in the hospital room with Nancy. I drove them both to the hospital. The doc thought he could protect them there. But he couldn't protect Nancy from the tongues and stares and covered-up noses of nurses and other patients. Half the women in Ellenton were sure that the baby would 'come black.' Or that it would be blind because Willie had syphilis. While Nancy was in labor doc learned that Ku Klux had asked two nurses to smother the baby if it 'came black.' Or even if it only had kinky hair. When Nancy was moved to the delivery room, everybody in the hospital and most everybody in Ellenton seemed to want a report on the color and condition of the baby the moment it became visible. The hospital switchboard was jammed. The baby was perfect—another little girl who looks like Bobby Poteet."

"How long was Nancy in the hospital?"

"The doc kept her ten days, because she had to be strong enough to care for both children when she came *home*. And that shack was 'home' by then. The four-year-old couldn't be kept in the hospital ten days. She cried to come home to see her dog and her dolls. So I had to keep her here in my home for three days. And I mean *I* had to keep her, because my Negro cook and housekeeper wouldn't enter the house while the child was here. She was too afraid of Ku Klux."

"How is Nancy feeling now?" asked Wilbanks.

"Fine. She's an excellent housekeeper. She has fixed up the shack. She takes good care of her children, plants flowers, looks at television, and bounces around in her stretch pants. The doc and I provide food, clothing, shelter, protection and visits. The Negroes I shelter are on relief, so I don't have to provide much else but shelter. But Doc is afraid to put Nancy on relief: afraid it might increase Ku Klux resentment. So Nancy is fine—a young, healthy, full-breasted, rosy-cheeked, yellow-headed little mother who can look attractive. Her only handicap now is the fear that she can never attract another white man. So what she needs is for some decently lecherous white man to come by some evening, after she has put the children to bed, and look at television with her, and then slap her on the tail and convince her that he wants a piece of it. That would complete her rehabilitation."

Clay Wilbanks smiled. "What about you? Can't you do that?"

Breck shook his head. "Not me. I suppose I'm as decently lecherous as the next man. But my lechery doesn't extend to trapped women. I'm sorry for Nancy, so what I want is for someone to take her off my hands. What about you? As a public servant, couldn't you watch TV with her this evening and give her the assurance she needs? Couldn't the FBI help me find a new home for three young females?"

Wilbanks continued to smile while Breck poured him another drink. Then he quit smiling and said: "You know, Breck, after talking with you for three hours, after drinking your whiskey and eating your cooking, I think I understand a little about you. You've done a good job of living in Atoka County. You've succeeded in living as an independent, fair-minded, humane individual. You have preserved the wildlife on your land when by destroying it you could have made more money. You have encouraged young Negroes to strive, you have helped old Negroes into their graves, when by driving them all off you could have made more money and fewer enemies. You have helped Nancy Poteet and defied Butt Cut. You have correctly calculated your risks, and to this point you have survived. But since you don't watch television, I don't think you realize how much television endangers people like you."

"You mean TV makes my life more dangerous?"

"It sure does. TV brings racial conflict into most every home most every night. This causes every white American who is inclined to fear free Negroes to become a little more afraid. When Lincoln was elected President in November, 1860, what most white Southerners feared was not the abolition of slavery per se, but the prospect of having to live with four million free Negroes. That's why the majority of white people in Alabama panicked. That's why they hanged your great-grandfather: he didn't fear free Negroes. This is why the majority of white people in Alabama today follow a demagogue like Wallace. He feeds their fear of free Negroes. White people don't fear controlled Negroes. But most white people, in Alabama and elsewhere, still fear the prospect of Negroes being free enough to vote, to sit on juries, to get good educations, to join labor unions, and, above all, to move into any homes which they can afford to rent or purchase. TV feeds this fear every night."

"And I suppose," said Breck, "that the people of Atoka County are having their fear fed at this moment?"

"You can be sure they are," said Wilbanks. "Most every white man and most every Negro in this county is watching some of what happened at the courthouse here this morning. And what is the viewer seeing? In essence he is seeing a Negro youth looking up at Big Track, saying: 'Sheriff, I ain't afraid o' you no more. I'se gonna be free.' Now, Breck, that's a frightening prospect to the white people of this county. It will grow more frightening each day the demonstrations continue in Ellenton. From fright comes panic, and what happened to your great-grandfather can happen to you."

"You overlook one point," said Breck. "My great-grandfather was conspicuous. He owned the most land, the best land, and the most slaves. And he spoke out. I'm inconspicuous and silent. I own the poorest land and I don't make speeches or write letters to editors. So surely I stand some chance of being ignored."

"You stand no chance of being ignored," said Wilbanks. "Ku Klux regard as Ku Klux every white person who approves of Ku Klux or who fails to stand publicly against Ku Klux. So to Ku Klux, every white person in this county is a Ku Klux except Dr. Parker and you. The doctor is difficult to attack. You are easy. And who says you don't make speeches! You made a speech every time you jerked down one of Butt Cut's clippings. One word: 'Trash!' Every Ku Klux knows you've called him trash, and you've called everything he believes trash. At the high school Allen Bascomb has been practicing saying 'trash' like you say it. Wait till Big Track hears him!"

"Well," said Breck slowly, "what can I do except carry on? No man accepts the certainty of catastrophe. He gets up in the morning, goes to work, fears the worst, hopes for the best."

"If you see a storm coming, you don't go to work. A storm is going to hit you. To protect yourself you must take one of two actions. You can sell out and leave. If you stay, you must help me. I'm your only ally. Together we can hurt the Klan."

"How? Suppose Loretta Sykes told us that Klansmen raped her? With her unsupported statement we could prove nothing. Then how could we hurt the Klan?"

Clay Wilbanks got up and stood before the fire. "Here's how. Secretly Loretta tells us all she knows. Publicly she stands by her recorded statement to Big Track. In that way she should be safe. Assuming Loretta confirms what I suspect, then the FBI leaves the county. We accept Big Track's story. We encourage the rapists to feel secure and self-satisfied. Meanwhile, secretly, we study each member of the Action Squad. When we decide which man is weakest, *you* approach him, seeking a deal. He might run from me. But he'll know you, and you can get him into a graveyard at midnight and discuss a deal. You offer him money—lots of FBI money. You offer him a protected new life in California or Canada or Australia. Maybe you start with his wife, and whet her appetite for money and a new life. We do whatever is necessary to get a sworn statement from a Klansman identifying all other guilty Klansmen."

"It wouldn't be enough," said Breck. "Even if we could obtain such a statement, no jury in this county would convict the Klansmen. What juror could afford the risk of voting guilty?"

"That's the beauty of this case," said Wilbanks. "A guilty verdict isn't necessary. Truth alone will be enough to hurt the Klan in Alabama and wherever else the Klan is strong. Because in this case the Klansmen made a mistake. They committed a filthy, disgusting, bestial crime—not a clean, manly, noble crime like murder. When they lynched Willie Washington, they had much public approval. For Willie had committed the bestial crime. But when Klansmen are exposed as the rapists of Loretta Sykes, they will not even have local approval. Because now it is Klansmen who have committed the disgusting, bestial crime—against an innocent."

"But is Loretta innocent?" asked Breck. "She is called a civil rights worker. To most of the white people of Alabama she is therefore a hated agitator, not a sympathy-deserving victim of brutality."

"Think faster, Breck," said Wilbanks. "That's part of the mistake made here. Remember how the Marines taught us to exploit enemy mistakes? *Once* Loretta was an agitator. *Now* she isn't. Butt Cut investigated her and washed her whiter than snow. Loretta has two character witnesses: Butt Cut and Big Track. They say she's a 'good nigger' who was nursing her dying mother when she was assaulted by bestial agitators for refusing to become an agitator. The Klansmen are refining their tactics. Heretofore they have called their murder victims agitators, whores and Communists. In Loretta's case they are calling agitators 'bestial rapists.' To emphasize the bestiality of the rape, the Ku Klux must emphasize the innocence of the victim. For accusing agitators of bestial rape, Big Track is being congratulated, not only by white people in Atoka County, but also by white people throughout the state and nation. Now—what happens when you and I reveal that the beasts who raped the innocent Loretta were not agitators but Ku Klux Klansmen?"

Breck Stancill didn't reply. He gazed into the fire, thinking. Clay Wilbanks added: "This is a Klan mistake we must exploit, Breck. We couldn't have hurt the Klan by identifying the lynchers of Willie Washington. But we can damn sure hurt the Klan by identifying the rapists of Loretta Sykes."

Breck continued to gaze into the fire. Then he said: "Let's go, Clay. I'll drive you out to a telephone. We can talk some more as we drive. You came in here to recruit me. I've been recruited before. So I don't recruit so easily any more."

"I didn't come to recruit you. I came to join you."

"Yeah, so you've said. So a Marine Corps recruiter said to me twenty-four years ago. You came to recruit me. Let's go."

In the Chevrolet pickup Breck Stancill and Clay Wilbanks drove down the forested spine of the mountain. They passed Nancy Poteet's shack, then, one by one, the shacks of the Negroes. In every shack a light was burning: it was Monday night and Nancy and the Negroes were watching Ben Casey work miracles.

"Clay," said Breck, "a tree takes thirty years to grow into sawtimber, fourteen years to grow into pulpwood. So a tree farmer learns to take the long view. And from the long view nothing looks so ridiculous as an individual effort to change the nature of man. You came in here to tell me that the rape of a Negro girl named Loretta Sykes is significant. That if I'll publicly identify the rapists I'll open the eyes and thereby change the nature of a few men. You tell me that here is the ditch worth dying in, and you expect me to believe it."

"No, I don't expect you to believe that," said Wilbanks. "That isn't what I've said. I didn't say that the rape of Loretta Sykes is significant. Rape is a common crime, becoming more common every year. Most Americans don't believe reports of rape, so most rape victims don't make reports. I said that the Ku Klux Klan made a mistake in raping Loretta, and that Big Track compounded the mistake. I said that you can exploit this mistake and thereby hurt the Klan. I believe you'll do it. You won't do it because you hope to change the nature of man. You'll do it because you're a fighter, and not to fight would change your nature. The FBI alone can't fight the Ku Klux Klan. The FBI can only look for a fighter and help him fight."

"And the fighter always loses in the end."

"That's right," said Wilbanks. "He suffers disillusion and

death. Cussedness takes over until another fighter comes along."

After a moment Breck said: "The trouble with my fighting here is that I have to fight my friends—men who are not one hundred per cent evil but are only ten or twenty per cent evil. Why don't you recruit me to go to Vietnam? That would be easier. Here I have to move against men who have shared whiskey and food with me, who have helped me put out fire. Take Hardy Riddle. I remember when he came back in 1936 as an all-American football hero. I was twelve then, so I thought he was great. I remember when he began working for the lumber company. He was kind to my father. He helped my mother while she was alone in Ellenton during the war. He has done a lot to develop Atoka County. For fifteen years after the war he and his wife lived in the old house where I was born. I've had Sunday dinner with them many times. Hell, Hardy's present woman is one I used to have. How much closer can two men get?"

"That's why the Klan has always been so hard to fight," said Wilbanks. "It has so many members and supporters who are otherwise good. That's why, in fighting it, the Federal Government several times has had to resort to martial law. Riddle, in most ways, is a good man. But if he hadn't approved the Klan's being organized here in 1962, it would not have been organized."

"I told him then that he'd be sorry. He was influenced by people in Montgomery. They foresaw race trouble, and Hardy came to see the Klan as a possible 'useful adjunct to police power.' He thought it might help scare off agitators and labor organizers."

"That makes him a party to one lynching, one rape, fifty cross-burnings, a dozen dynamitings, and several whippings."

"I suppose it does," said Breck. "I don't know how much Vernon Hodo tells Hardy. I can see Hardy agreeing that Willie should be lynched. I can't see him approving a rape."

"How do you stand with Vernon Hodo?" asked Wilbanks.

"We're friends. His crews have harvested my timber for eighteen years. He's helped me put out fires. Once, when I fell and broke my arm, his men did my work for two months and he charged me nothing. His wife is German. When she makes wine she sends me some. She cooks pastries and ham hocks and sauerkraut. Because I live alone, people think the kindest thing they can do for me is to ask me to eat with them. I've eaten with Vernon and his family many times. Every year, in deer season, we kill a number of bucks to keep the herd from becoming too large. I have more deer on my land than the company has, and more good shooting stands. So every year I let Vernon kill two bucks on my land. Last year I let him kill three, so he could give one to that preacher he has with him in the Klan."

"The Reverend Mark Alverson," said Wilbanks. "We have a line on the reverend. A morbid nigger-hater."

"I don't know him," said Breck. "I know his wife. She's head of the bird watchers in Ellenton. Twice a year they come out here before daylight and spend the morning counting the different species of birds. Mrs. Alverson seems like a pleasant soul."

"I guess the reverend is pleasant, too," said Wilbanks, "except when he's thinking about Negroes and Communists. He regards them all as soldiers of the Antichrist, and he'd like to see them dead and in Hell."

"Vernon Hodo isn't that way," said Breck. "He takes pride in his Negro work gangs. Like a horse trainer takes pride in his horse. But Vernon can't associate Negroes with humanity. He could shoot Willie Washington like he'd shoot a dog that was causing trouble. As for the rape of a Negro female, Vernon might chuckle at it, or he might watch it as indifferently as he'd watch a bull service a heifer. That cruelty, or indignity, or shame, or injustice was being inflcted wouldn't occur to him."

At the highway Breck turned left, or east, away from Ellenton, and drove toward a Negro juke joint. "What bothers me most," he said, "is that while I might want to hurt the Klan, I don't want to hurt Big Track. You know the relation I have with Nancy Poteet and her children. Well, from 1947 to 1953 I had a similar relation with Maybelle Bascomb, her son, and Big Track. Maybelle and Big Track moved into that shack, almost in my back yard, when they were semiliterate teenagers in trouble. They lived there for six years! Maybelle and Allen were there while Big Track was in the Army. I brought Maybelle the news that Big Track had won the Medal of Honor. I helped her get ready to go to Washington, I told her what to wear, and I drove her and Allen to the airport at Tuscaloosa. Maybelle has cooked for me when my Negro cooks were sick. I've shared loneliness with her; in the middle of the night I have rushed her child to the hospital when he had the colic. I put Allen on his first horse. I taught him to shoot. Hell, even now he thinks of the mountain as home. He borrows books from me. He tells me things he can't tell his father or mother. He brought his girl to see me, and about twice a week he brings her up here and parks, about a hundred yards from my house, along the overlook. He flashes his lights a certain way so I'll know it's him. Now, in this position, how can I risk hurting Maybelle, Allen and Big Track Bascomb?"

"Men sometimes have to fight their brothers, Breck," said Wilbanks. "Fathers have to fight sons. Big Track thinks like a Ku Klux, doesn't he?"

"Not entirely. He can come nearer giving a Negro his due than most men. Here's an illustration. Last September 1964 Sergeant York died. Since he was the most famous of the semiliterate Anglo-Saxon heroes, the surviving heroes gathered for his funeral. Hundreds of aging mighty men of battle, all wearing their Legion caps on balding and graying heads, all showing their Purple Hearts, their Silver Stars, their Navy Crosses, their Medals of Honor for slaying the enemy in three wars. Four of us, led by Big Track, were sent to represent our Legion post. We gathered up there in the Cumberlands where no Negro lives now, or has ever lived. Well, you know what we all believe from birth. That every battle from King's Mountain to New Orleans to the Argonne to Omaha Beach to Iwo Jima to Pork Chop Hill was won by lean and leathery Anglo-Saxons! Sons of Old Hickory, Daniel Boone, Sam Houston and Davy Crockett! 'Who ever heard of a damn nigger on a firing line, or in a night patrol with close killing to be done! Alvin York, in the Eighty-second Division, didn't go into battle flanked by niggers! Neither did you nor I nor Big Track! Running is a nigger's nature! He's got rabbit blood! A nigger's just natchelly so scared o' the dark that he's got to bug out at the first flare!' "

Clay Wilbanks chuckled. "Then the old heroes saw the New Army?"

"We sure did," said Breck. "The Eighty-second Airborne had come to bury the Old Sergeant: band, honor guard, color guard, ushers, firing squad, buglers. A backwoods version of the Kennedy funeral. Except the ten thousand spectators, spread over a sunlit hillside, were all white, and every fourth man in the Eighty-second was black! The drum major was black. He led the band in 'What A Friend We Have In Jesus.' The corporal who carried the standard of Sergeant York's

regiment, the 325th Infantry, was black. There he stood, before all the old heroes, a Negro, bearing a standard with battle
streamers for St. Mihiel, Meuse-Argonne, Lorraine, Sicily,
Naples-Foggia, Normandy, Rhineland, Ardennes-Alsace and
Central Europe. Old heroes said: 'Wasn't no damn nigger in
none o' them battles! I was there! So what's a nigger doing
carrying the standard of the 325th!' The bugler who blew
Taps was a Negro. An old hero said: 'I've seen signs and
wonders in my time. But I never thought I'd see a nigger blow
Taps over Alvin York!' "

"What did Big Track say?"

"I'm coming to that. After the funeral some of us gathered
in a motel for a drink before we left. A young captain from
the Eighty-second was there. He was a Georgian, and he had
been in Vietnam. He made a short speech and told the heroes
that Negroes are making good soldiers in Vietnam. He was
heckled with remarks like 'Yeah, now we know why the
Army's always gittin' ambushed in Vietnam. You're usin' niggers as perimeter guards at night. The niggers are bugging out
and letting the gooks cut your throats while you sleep!' I said
a few words, like 'If we want Negroes to fight we must give
them more to fight for; a Negro who carries the standard of
the 325th isn't likely to disgrace the regiment; and Negroes
privileged to help bury a hero will know that they must help
fill his shoes.' But Big Track was more effective. He was the
youngest Medal of Honor winner present, and he said: 'Let's
give the nigger his due. I know niggers who'll fight. I watch
some of 'em on the Baltimore Colts and other teams. I know
niggers I could train and lead into battle and I wouldn't be a
damn bit scared o' being left by myself on a firing line.' "

"Did Big Track say that?"

"He sure did. He's not a Ku Klux at heart."

Wilbanks knew that Breck had thrown him on the defensive. He said: "Big Track is the worst sort of Ku Klux. He's a
party to every crime they've committed."

"You mean he's a member? I figured he was outside of it."

"He doesn't wear the sheet," said Wilbanks. "He does
what's worse. A long time ago Klan organizers learned what
the Communist Party learned later: that they had to leave
their members who were public officials free to deny they
were members. Big Track is such a member of the Klan.
There is no record of his membership. But here is the oath

that he swore in March, 1962. You may want to listen carefully:

> I most solemnly swear that I will forever keep sacredly secret all my knowledge of the acts and proceedings of the Ku Klux Klan.
>
> I most sacredly vow and most positively swear that I will die before I ever give evidence against any member of the Ku Klux Klan.
>
> I most sacredly vow and most positively swear that I will never yield to bribery, flattery, threats, passion, punishment, persecution, persuasion, or any other enticement whatever coming from or offered by any person or persons, male or female, for the purpose of obtaining from me any secret or secret information of the Ku Klux Klan. I will die rather than divulge the same, so help me God.

Breck pulled to the side of the road and stopped. "Are you sure," he asked, "that Big Track swore that oath?"

"I have his voice on tape," said Wilbanks. "He was in his re-election campaign. The Democratic primary. The newly organized Klan controlled three hundred votes. Had the Klan taken those votes away from Big Track and given them to his opponent, Big Track would have lost. So he gave the Klan his soul."

"That jolts me," said Breck. "I never thought that Big Track would subject himself to Klan discipline. A Medal of Honor winner! Now he's a traitor. His allegiance is not to Atoka County, or Alabama, or the United States. It's to the Ku Klux Klan."

"That's the way it is," said Wilbanks. "The High Sheriff of Atoka County is chained, handcuffed and manacled. He can't seek, present or divulge evidence against a Klansman. He's the sworn protector of Klansmen in whatever crimes they decide to commit."

Breck turned back into the highway and continued driving east. Ahead he saw the Negro juke. "There's a telephone in that juke," he said. "You want me to drop you there?"

"No," said Wilbanks. "Let me out here. I'll wait in the woods. You go to the telephone and call this number collect." He gave Breck a card with a telephone number on it. "Tell whoever answers that a man is out of gas on this highway at this point."

Again Breck stopped. "Clay," he said, "this is all very disturbing. I'll sleep on it. Tomorrow I'll go to the hospital and see Loretta. She'll probably come back to her mother's shack. If I have any information for you, how do I communicate with you?"

"Just call that number. Tell whoever answers who you are. Then state a time. Like: 'I'm Breck Stancill. The time is eight o'clock tonight.' Then, driving slowly, you approach this spot from either direction at the stated time. If no car is in sight, flash your lights twice: dim-bright, dim-bright. You'll see me step out on the highway. Pick me up and we can talk."

"I understand," said Breck.

Clay Wilbanks got out and hurried into the woods. Breck drove on. He made the telephone call, then drove back up the mountain. Excepting the one where Susan Sykes was dying, all the shacks were dark. Ben Casey had worked his weekly miracle, and the Negroes and Nancy Poteet had gone to bed.

JOSH

AT 9 A.M. on Tuesday, April 13, 1965, the city of Ellenton, Alabama, was suffering from a disorder. Just as a man can be convulsed by a grain of popcorn in his windpipe, so Ellenton was being convulsed by the knot of agitators in the courthouse square. The agitation was on every mind and tongue, and many white citizens either gathered in the square, or drove through it, to call the agitators black-assed apes, white-niggers, nigger fuckers, and mother fuckers.

The convulsive knot looked like high school students waiting for their bus: in all, sixty-three agitators, forty-seven of whom were local Negroes, from twelve to seventeen, absent without leave from the Ellenton Negro school. The other sixteen were outsiders. The leaders were "Reverend Josh" Franklin and Charles "Big Pecker" Peck. There were two young, white, white-habited Catholic nuns. Of the other twelve outsiders, three were white females, three were Negro females, four were white males, and two were Negro males, all of them eighteen to twenty years old.

They were standing in a marked-off rectangle in the street, next to the courthouse. They were not allowed to stand on the sidewalk, so their asphalt rectangle was bounded on the west by the curb, and on the north, east and south by sawhorses. In this stall, from 9 A.M. to 5 P.M., they were allowed by the sheriff to stand, with these conditions: they were not to return insult for insult, either by gesture or shout; and they were not to hug, kiss, urinate or copulate in the street.

Around this barricaded rectangle Big Track and Butt Cut patrolled. Four state troopers stood by, and from time to time they relieved Big Track and Butt Cut. While Big Track was in his courthouse office he could watch the agitators from a window.

The agitators stood, talked among themselves, sang freedom songs, and waved their placards asking that Negroes be allowed to use all public toilets, to register to vote, and to be considered for employment in supermarkets. Why didn't Big Track disperse them? If he dispersed them, or allowed them to be dispersed, Federal marshals would come and protect them. So he was protecting the agitators in order to keep the marshals out. He also protected the cameramen. But the protection was only from physical attack. Verbal attack was constant.

Breck Stancill stood on the sidewalk, across the street from the courthouse, looking for Big Track. He didn't see him, so he crossed the street, toward the sheriff's office. As he passed the sawhorse barricade, he met Butt Cut and asked him where Big Track was.

"You'll find him in his office," Butt Cut said.

At that instant Josh Franklin, standing behind the sawhorse, raised his voice and asked: "You, sir, are you Mr. Stancill?" Breck turned to him and said "Yes."

"Will you talk to me for a moment?" Josh asked.

Breck looked at the enraged faces across the street. Had Butt Cut not overheard Josh's request, Breck might have ignored it and walked on. But before Butt Cut he preferred not to appear afraid to listen to an agitator. "Yes, I'll talk with you," he said. He and Josh moved out of Butt Cut's hearing, Breck outside the barricade, Josh inside. Watched by all the enraged faces, and by Big Track and Trixie Cunningham from their office window, Breck leaned against a sawhorse and gave his ear to Josh.

"Mr. Stancill, I guess you know that last Saturday night Charles Peck and I climbed your mountain and talked with Loretta Sykes?"

"Yes," said Breck. "Loretta has paid for that visit."

"We didn't realize we'd be exposing her to such risk."

"Why didn't you realize it?" asked Breck. "Among your agitators here this morning I don't see one adult Negro from Atoka County. You know that local Negro adults can't risk helping you."

"But we thought Loretta's situation was different," insisted Josh. "She doesn't live or work in this county. She can't be fired by these white people or her relief money cut off. You're her mother's landlord, and you're the one white man in the county who's said to be tolerant of the Movement. So we thought Loretta could at least talk to us safely, in the dark."

"Well, you were wrong."

"We know that now," said Josh. "We're sorry. But that doesn't make us guilty of rape. Like the sheriff says we are, and like Loretta seems to have told the sheriff. So I'm asking you, sir, to encourage Loretta to tell the truth. She told us that you are a man of courage, that you stand up to the sheriff and the Ku Klux."

Breck looked at this tall, bare-headed, earnest young man, with his clerical collar, his blue jeans, his rough, high-topped shoes, and Breck thought: Good Lord, here's a second effort to recruit me. First the FBI, now the Movement. "Tell me," said Breck, shifting the subject, "is this all you expect to do here for two weeks? Just stand around?"

"Never underestimate standing, Mr. Stancill," said Josh. "Remember Jericho? Violence wasn't needed to bring those walls down. Just a little marching, a little singing, a little horn-blowing. Injustice always crumbles when a few good people stand up to it."

Breck wondered if, along about 1942, he himself had ever sounded like that. He said: "You stand here for the cameras, don't you? Primarily, you are here to produce television film?"

"That's true," said Josh. "Without television there could be no Movement. There could have been no Selma March. Except for television Big Track would crack our heads and disperse us. Before the cameras we stand each day asking that a Negro child be allowed to pee in a public toilet. That a Negro be allowed to vote and to work in a store. People everywhere watch us. They watch Big Track and Governor Wallace and the enraged white mob. The people's white-maned servant, Senator Dirksen, watches. So you can truthfully say that we produce film to soften the great heart of Senator Dirksen."

"That clerical collar you wear," said Breck, "I suppose it attracts the cruelest blows and the harshest obscenities?"

"A clerical collar is supposed to attract blows and obscenity," said Josh. "Mine has caused me to be called a Communist and jailed a few times. It has caused me to be called a mother fucker a few thousand times."

"That doesn't bother you?"

"It saddens me but it doesn't discourage me. Christianity is a religion for revolutionaries. Any time Christians, particularly Presbyterians, go for a decade without hearing themselves called Communists and mother fuckers, the church is losing its reason for being."

"The nuns? How do they react to being called nigger fuckers?"

"Nuns have always been called fuckers of some sort. These nuns stand and pray for those who revile them."

"Well, speaking of fucking . . ." said Breck.

"By all means speak of it," said Josh bitterly. "When white people in Alabama speak of the Movement they can speak of nothing else."

"Well, speaking of it," said Breck, "on the Selma March there must have been no little of it."

"Not a tenth as much as the Ku Klux say," said Josh. "But there was some. So what? In every crusade in history saints have marched with whores, thieves, atheists, and mixed-up young people seeking a sense of participation. Our Blessed Lord didn't shrink from the touch of an adultress. Why should Christians hesitate to march with sinners toward a better world?"

"And you yourself? I understand that while trying to help Negro girls in Alabama you also fuck some of them?"

"A Ku Klux lie! I'm an unmarried ministerial student at McCormick Seminary in Chicago. Any lustful act outside marriage would be against my religion."

"But you hug, kiss and fondle Negro girls?"

"Not lustfully. But I'm a minister to lepers. Every doctor in a leprosarium knows that to help his patients he must touch them freely and often. I live with Negroes. I go to jail with young Negroes. I stand with them, as we are standing now, besieged, under the whip of white abuse. We sing, we dance, we try to encourage one another, and when we win a small victory we celebrate, like cheer leaders at a football game. So, yes, I've hugged and kissed. I've touched freely and often. But this is comradely contact, not the lustful contact which Ku Klux see in their race-sex fantasies."

"Well," said Breck, "in a way that's a pity."

"A pity?"

"Yes, a pity. If you were a fucking man, I know where you could be helpful. Out on my mountain there is a white girl who was raped by Willie Washington."

"I know about Willie. He was a Ku Klux victim."

"This girl was Willie's victim. The rape made her an Untouchable, so she had to withdraw and become dependent on me. She lacks confidence to face the world because she can't believe that any white man will ever want to touch her again.

What she needs most is a white man's love. But without love, she could be helped, and I could be relieved of her, by a white man doing nothing more than decently fucking her. I can't restore her confidence because I can't fuck a girl who needs my help. So when I heard that you had been out on the mountain, and that you can fuck girls you are trying to help, I hoped I might persuade you to help Nancy Poteet and me."

Josh's face clouded. He began to feel angry. "I'm waiting for you to grin, Mr. Stancill," he said. "You're a cynic."

"Am I?" asked Breck. "I've wondered if I were. I think of myself as a realist. You say you are waiting for me to grin. I would grin if I were a cynic. But as a realist I can't afford to grin. All those furious faces across the street are looking at me. I want them to think I'm trying to persuade you to leave."

Josh said: "Outwardly, to protect yourself, you may not be grinning. But inwardly you are grinning at me. You tolerate the Movement only because you know it will fail."

"The Movement won't fail," said Breck, "unless it promises too much. Negroes can become as free as whites. Then God help them! They will find that they still must pay rent, and most of them, like most whites, will still need wars, circuses and tranquilizers."

Josh looked at this one-legged tree farmer, in faded khakis, leaning on a sawhorse and an aluminum walking stick, and he saw him as an enemy. "Not all cynics grin," he said. "Some weep. Maybe you're a weeper. In either case you're our enemy. We can defeat the Ku Klux. They believe in White Men. You may be harder to defeat. You don't believe in men of any color. You don't believe in Man—period."

"When did Christians start believing in Man?"

"You are doing Big Track's work for him," said Josh, ignoring the question. "You are doing what you want the Ku Klux to think you are doing. You are trying to get shut of me. In my heart there is hope for Man. In your heart there is only pity. What's pity worth? Can it spark a crusade? Can it fuel a movement? Pity can only dishearten. If we listened to you, we'd all weep for mankind and surrender to the Ku Klux. So save your breath. I asked you for truth. Will you encourage Loretta Sykes to tell the truth?"

"When did Christians lose their regard for pity?" asked Breck. "But you want an answer, not questions. To soften the great heart of Senator Dirksen you came to the Alabama backwoods to provoke violent reaction. Your provocation already has damaged Loretta Sykes. Now, in the name of truth, you want to further jeopardize Loretta Sykes. So here's my answer. If you can soften Senator Dirksen's great heart only at the expense of Loretta Sykes, then I say fuck Senator Dirksen, fuck truth, and fuck you."

Breck Stancill straightened up to leave. Josh Franklin shook his head in disgust. "One word more, Mr. Stancill," Josh said. "When you reconsider that fuck-you-all speech, you won't be proud of it. Because with that speech you joined the Ku Klux Klan. You know that Ku Klux raped Loretta Sykes. Big Track says agitators raped Loretta Sykes. What do you say? You, the man of courage who stands up to Big Track and the Ku Klux! You say *provocation* raped Loretta Sykes. Now why don't you wear your sheet when you come to town?"

Breck shook his head in disgust. "Don't you want to add two more sentences?" he said. "Don't you want to remind me that to make an omelet one must break eggs? That ends justify means? I don't want to see Loretta Sykes killed. Do you?"

Breck walked away, toward the entrance to the courthouse. Josh walked back to where Charles Peck was standing. "Is he gonna help us?" asked Peck.

"No, he's hopeless," replied Josh. "He says provocation raped Loretta Sykes."

"Old Man Provocation!" said Peck. "He sho' does a heap'a rapin' and killin' down heah in Alabama. A nigger kid wants to pee in a public toilet, so Old Man Provocation just has'ta go and rape him a nigger gal!" Peck raised his voice to the whites across the street. "Step right ovah heah clos'a, you white folks, and let us provoke yuh! Then'ya can go kill'ya a niggah and tell the judge: 'Yo' Honor, we wuz provoked!' "

In the sheriff's office Breck was greeted by Trixie Cunningham. Big Track was on the telephone. "While he's talking, Breck," said Trixie, "let me whisper something to you. I wish you'd leave the county till this is over."

"Why?"

"You just can't realize what people are saying. I started hearing it yesterday. They're saying that these outside agitators are spending the night on Stancill's Mountain!"

"How can anybody say that? I heard that Big Track and the state troopers are to escort the agitators out of the county every afternoon around five-thirty?"

"That's true," said Trixie. "The outsiders are spending every night in Tuscaloosa. I know that. Everybody ought to know it. But they don't know it and they don't want to know it. People will believe anything now. They've gone crazy. I've heard a dozen people say that that fake preacher out there—Josh—that Josh is staying in your cottage with you. And that a whole nest of agitators are staying in shacks on the mountain."

"Well," said Breck, "I don't see how my leaving would help. I'd just be inviting the fire. So what else do you suggest? That I buy time on the radio? That I pass out handbills? Or that I walk around in the square with a sign on my back saying it ain't so?"

"Well, you could'a not done what I just seen'ya doing. You could'a not stood out there just now, before God and everybody, talking to that fake preacher like he was your long lost brother! Now everybody *knows* he's staying with you. Nobody else has talked to him, except to call him a white nigger and a mother you-know-what."

"Oh, hell, Trixie!"

"Don't 'oh, hell' me," she said sternly. "I'm the best friend you got and you know it. There's nothing I won't do for you. *Nothing!* I'm always looking after you. And you need looking after: you do such risky things. Like tearing down little old bits'a nothing that Butt Cut likes'ta paste up. Like letting them old nigger relief-hounds keep living out there on the mountain, eating up good money that the county needs to build better schools with. Like keeping that trashy Nancy Poteet out there with'ya like she was'ya woman. And like last Sunday night, you down here at midnight botherin' yourself about that nigger Loretta."

"What are they saying about Loretta?"

"Well, some of 'em—most of 'em, I guess—are taking Big Track's word that she's a good nigger. But a good many still think she's'a agitator. They think she might'a cooked up this whole agitation in Chicago and brought it in here. She's not making friends at the hospital! The nurses say she don't even talk like a nigger. And she gets flowers wired to her from Montgomery Ward in Chicago! Can you imagine white nurses totin' red roses for a nigger in the Atoka Hospital! Not one of them nurses ever got sent a red rose in her life! Come to think of it, you're the only man who ever sent *me* one!"

Big Track put down the telephone, and he and Breck went

into his private office and closed the door. They stood at the window, looking at the agitators and the yelling white mob. "Ain't that the filthiest bunch'a scum'ya ever seen!" said Big Track. "That goddam fake preacher posin' as a Christian! That impudent, sawed-off nigger with them boots on! Them Red nuns tryin'ta look like the Mother'a Jesus! Them stringy-haired, nigger-fuckin' white whores! I tell'ya Breck this may be more'n I can bear!"

"You're doing a good job protecting them," said Breck. "They have a right to stand and protest. You must protect them in it."

"That's what Hardy says. He says the only way'ta beat 'em is'ta protect 'em. But it's hurtin' me, Breck. And I ain't sure Hardy's right. I always try'ta figure what Harry Truman'd do if he was me. I wish I could phone him right now and ask him what to do. Truman says this scum ain't got no right'ta be down here provokin' trouble. If Truman was in my shoes right now, I bet he'd turn around three times and that scum'd be high-assin' toward the county line."

"Maybe," said Breck. "Truman talks a lot."

Big Track sighed. "I'm losin' next year's election right now. I'm breaking a solemn promise. Just like Wallace promised'ta keep niggers out'a our schools, I promised'ta keep agitators out'a this county. Now these good home folks are comin' up to me saying 'Goddam, Track, 'member what'cha promised? Why don't'cha stomp yer foot and run these piss-ants off? Or git out'a my way and let me run 'em off?' And I ain't got time'ta explain."

"After it's over there'll be time to explain that you did the right thing. Hardy can help you explain."

"They may not listen. To me or Hardy either one. Because they're watchin' me take impudence off'a that nigger, Big Pecker. Yesterday that black s'nuvabitch looked right at me and called me Big Track. 'You call me Mister Sheriff, nigger,' I said. He grinned and talked back: 'Naw, Big Track, I ain't gonna call you Mistah Sheriff. It says Big Track on the ballot, so I'm gonna call you Big Track, Big Track.' That s'nuvabitch said that to me before a crowd of good white men and I stood there and took it. Now, Breck, you know that no sheriff can keep the respect of decent white people if he lets a nigger be impudent to him and he don't cold-cock that s'nuvabitch! That crowd expected me to cold-cock him, and I didn't. So I'm losin' their respect."

"You're doing right, Track," said Breck. "A man can't always be popular if he does right."

"I'm doing what Hardy tells me to." Big Track put his cigar back in his mouth and started chewing on it. "I seen'ya out there talkin' to that fake preacher. What'd he want?"

"He wants me to encourage Loretta Sykes to tell the truth," replied Breck. "I told him Loretta had said all she'd ever say."

Big Track rolled his cigar around in his mouth. "I tell'ya this, Breck. I'm gonna do my best, but my best ain't gonna be good enough'ta protect that fake preacher. The United States Army couldn't keep him living. Our good Christian people just ain't gonna let him come in here shamin' the Christian church like he's doing. They gonna shoot that black shirt and white collar off'a him, and send him straight'ta Hell."

After a moment Breck said: "I hope that doesn't happen. But it brings me to why I came in here. I'm going up to the hospital, and I guess I'll take Loretta Sykes back out on the mountain."

"Yeah, the doc told me he was gonna let her go today."

"You think she'll be safe on the mountain?"

Big Track narrowed his eyes. "She's got'ta look out fer them agitators. She hit agitators pretty hard with her statement."

"Other than agitators," said Breck, "you figure anybody else might want to hurt her?"

"I don't see why. I'm tellin' folks she's a good nigger. God knows I done all I could fer her." Big Track paused, then went on: "But *you* got to be careful, Breck. Hard times are here now. Folks are all worked up. Every day that that scum stands out there bein' impudent to us . . . every night that our good folks see TV tryin'ta make that scum look like Christian martyrs . . . . folks are gonna git more worked up. And you know how you've treated folks, Breck."

"How have I treated folks?"

"Well, now hell, Breck," said Big Track, "you've treated me like a brother. Me and my family's the best friends you got. Ain't nothin' we won't do for you. But you ain't treated folks like you treated us. Folks think you don't give a good goddam what they think. Folks think you just natch'ly take the nigger's part against the white man. Folks know you stood right in the barbershop and grinned and called George Wallace a piss-ant. So you ain't been good to folks, Breck. You hurt folks's feelings. And you know how that works out. As long as there ain't no trouble, folks disremember. Then trouble comes. The shoe pinches. Chickens come home to roost. And folks start rememberin'. All the things a man's done begin'ta add up in folks's mind. So you got'ta lie low and give folks time'ta disremember again."

Breck turned to go. "I'll do what I can. A man's what he is."

"Before'ya go," said Big Track, "le'me ask'ya a personal favor. You know how'ya been pullin' down Butt Cut's little old sayings? I never could figure out why'ya bothered'ta do it. Pasting up them sayings makes Butt Cut feel like he's helpin' folks'ta know things. Then you come along and hurt his feelings! Butt Cut's took it pretty hard. He's wanted'ta call'ya hand, but I said no."

"You want me to quit hurting Butt Cut's feelings?"

"That ain't what I'm askin'ya. You know my boy Allen thinks the world'a you. And I guess you heard that he's started hurtin' Butt Cut's feelings like you do. Allen needs'ta stop it. But if I tell him'ta stop—well, I thought you might tell him? And tell him why?"

"I'll tell him."

Big Track walked to the door with Breck. He didn't want Breck to go. He felt like he needed a long talk with Breck. He felt afraid he hadn't said the right things to Breck. He put his hand on Breck's shoulder and said: "Breck, I ain't never told you this. When I was in Korea maybe I made a good soldier. Truman says I did. If I did it was because I had you with me. I knowed my wife and boy was livin' up there with you, and you was lookin' after 'em. I knowed if one of 'em got sick in the night you'd git the doctor. I couldn'a made it without you, Breck."

"I was glad to help, Track," said Breck. "I'm proud of Allen. I'm proud of Maybelle. I'm proud of you. You're a good man. A good sheriff."

"God knows I'm tryin'ta be," said Big Track. "But this is a hard time'ta be sheriff. And, Breck, I need'ta feel that I got you behind me just like I had'ja when I was killin' gooks in Korea."

Breck said: "I'm behind you, Track. But keep in mind that you're not killing gooks in Atoka County. Your job here is to keep folks from hurting other folks."

In the Chevrolet pickup Breck and Loretta, going home from the hospital, had reached the foot of the mountain. At his request she had told him the story of the rape and of her deal with Big Track. Breck had driven slowly, on a sunny April afternoon, and Loretta, tight-lipped, ashamed, bitter, had told it all.

"Now I'm damaged goods," she said. "I'm merchandise that's been abused in handling. I've been raped on television. From now on people will stare at me, and point at me, and never feel comfortable around me again."

"Stop talking like that," Breck said. "In a few days you can leave here and never come back. You'll forget, and people will forget. How many masked men, would you say, witnessed the rape?"

"Maybe four or five, or more. At first I saw only masks, looking through those little windows. Then they opened the door and walked in and out, looking down at us, joking, like schoolboys watching a wrestling match on a playground. I saw at least four, and others may have stayed out in the hall."

"Did one of them look short and stocky, like Butt Cut?"

"They all looked like white-robed giants to me, since I was flat on the floor, looking up, and they were standing over me, looking down, enjoying what was being done to me, like Romans enjoying a lion eating a Christian."

"You think Hattie Bascomb witnessed the rape?"

"She might have. When I first saw her she was wearing slacks. When she put me in the padded cell she was in a skirt —dressed up. When it was over she was back in slacks. She helped me dress and put me in the car. She might have put on a mask and watched through a window. She would have enjoyed it."

"When did you first see Big Track?"

"When he got in the car to drive me off. He could have been one of the Ku Klux who watched. But I don't believe he was."

As they neared her mother's shack Loretta said: "Don't you think I ought to tell all this to the television reporters? Surely nobody would blame me for breaking a promise I had to make to a sheriff to keep him from killing me? The sheriff and the Ku Klux can't hurt Mama much; and they can't hurt me much more than they already have. And I'm not playing fair with Reverend Josh and Charles Peck."

"You must say nothing, see no one, and stay here on the mountain," said Breck. "Without supporting evidence your story would be ignored. Big Track could produce witnesses who saw you leave the jail at seven-fifteen, and saw you enter a car with Negroes. But after you are back in Chicago the time may come when your story can be helpful. So I'll bring you a recorder and you put it all on tape. Don't let anybody know you are doing it."

Loretta got out of the car at her mother's shack, and Breck drove on up toward his cottage. Nancy Poteet saw him coming, and ran out and waved for him to stop. "It's terrible, Mister Breck!" she said. "They've shot Chrissie!"

Breck jumped out of the car and followed Nancy as fast as he could to a spot about two hundred yards from his cottage. There under a tree, lying on pine needles, they found the russet-red Irish setter. "I heard the shot and I heard Chrissie holler," Nancy said. "I ran to the window, and back in here under these trees I saw a man running with a gun. Then I ran here and found poor Chrissie. I've tried to bandage him and stop the bleeding, but he's dying, Mister Breck!"

Breck knelt and began examining the six-year-old dog. Nancy began to cry. "He looks so pitiful, Mister Breck. Look at his big, soft, brown eyes! He's so beautiful, and he can't understand what's happening to him. Can't you help him, Mister Breck? Can't you do something?"

The dog was conscious, and he licked Breck's hand as Breck felt of him. The shotgun charge had hit him in the upper foreleg, neck and shoulder, breaking his shoulder and damaging, perhaps severing, the spinal cord. The dog had no feeling in his legs and could not move them.

"You better go and stay with Charlene and the baby, Nancy," said Breck. "There is nothing I can do except end his misery and bury him."

"I want to stay here," insisted Nancy. "Charlene is playing with the baby. I want to stay with you, and with poor, beautiful Chrissie. Let me help."

"All right," said Breck. "You stay here with him while I go get what we need. Don't touch him or get too close to him. He might become hysterical and bite you."

Breck went back to the car and drove on to his house. "Goddam them!" he said aloud. "Goddam the man who fired that shot! The cowardly, ignorant, red-necked, Ku Kluxing, Anglo-Saxon s'nuvabitch!" At the house he got a .25-caliber pistol which he had taken from the dead hand of a Japanese captain at Tarawa. Breck called it his "misery ender." The captain, with a mortar fragment in his stomach, had ended his own misery with it; and twice Breck had used it to end the misery of animals who were dying of disease or old age. In 1959 he shot his Irish setter, Christopher the First; and in 1960 he shot his palomino, Prince Dan the First. Breck also picked up the blanket on which Christopher the Second had slept before the fire. Then he went to perform his sad duty.

Nancy was still crying—and disobeying Breck by sitting and stroking the dog's head. "How low down can a man get!" she sobbed. "To hurt another man by shooting his dog! It's the most awful thing I ever saw! It makes you want to die, just to think that people can be so cruel!"

"Get behind a tree, Nancy," said Breck. "And don't watch."

Beside the dog Breck went to his one good knee. His chin trembled and tears came into his eyes as he stroked the beautiful, intelligent creature which he loved. Quickly he placed the pistol's muzzle at the back of the dog's head and fired the bullet through his brain.

Breck stood up, and Nancy came from behind the tree and stood by him. For the first time he touched her: he put his arm around her waist, and she put her arm around him. They stood there for two or three minutes, waiting for the last heart beat, then they wrapped Chrissie in the blanket. Breck picked the body up and carried it, with Nancy at his side, supporting him. They walked past Breck's house, past the stable and tool house, to Breck's animal cemetery. In this cemetery were two graves, each marked with a small bronze plate set in the grass:

In Loving Memory of
CHRISTOPHER
1946-1959

In Loving Memory of
PRINCE DAN
1945-1960

Ordinarily, for a man with one leg, digging a grave is hard work. But in his years of planting trees, Breck, by learning to rock on his metal leg and exert pressure with his good leg, had mastered the dibble, the spadelike device which is used to

open a trench in the earth for a pine seedling. From the tool
house he brought a spade and a grubbing hoe, and in fifteen
minutes he had dug the grave.

"Shouldn't we find a box to bury him in?" asked Nancy.

"No," said Breck. "The blanket is enough. I've helped bury
human friends in nothing more than a mattress cover. I don't
like burial boxes, unless they are simple, homemade pine boxes. Earth is the mother of life. Whenever a man or a dog dies,
what's left should become earth again as rapidly as nature
intended."

Tenderly, they put the body in the grave, curling it in a
sleeping position. Breck covered it with the rich woods dirt.
As he and Nancy carried the tools to the tool house, they
passed the fence where the palomino, the second Prince Dan,
was standing. The horse had watched the burial, and now he
nickered gently and Breck and Nancy stopped and petted
him. "Our pal's gone, Dan," Breck said. "Tomorrow I'll have
to telephone all the breeders of Irish setters and find young
Christopher the Third."

Breck and Nancy walked on into his yard and stood there,
gazing north into the distance, and clinging to one another,
feeling sad, outraged and afraid. "This is just the beginning,
isn't it?" Nancy said. "Next they'll have to shoot Dan or set
the woods afire."

"Maybe not," said Breck. "Maybe this was the work of one
miserable redneck who had to try to hurt some white person
he thinks is taking the Negro's part against him. He couldn't
reach Lyndon Johnson, or Reverend Josh, or one of those
nuns standing at the courthouse. But he could reach me.
Maybe one blow will satisfy him." As he talked Breck noticed
how soft Nancy felt to him. This surprised him: he had
thought she'd feel hard and tough. He noticed how small she
was, in her beige stretch pants, her sky-blue blouse, and her
yellow hair falling down on her shoulders. He said: "Nancy, I
want you to take this pistol and keep it near you."

"I couldn't use it," she said. "I'm afraid of guns."

"Then go back to your children and keep your doors
locked. I have to be gone now for a few minutes, and I'll be
gone for an hour just after dark. But you can count on me
being here—with my eyes open. Don't worry, and don't let
Charlene know you are afraid. She's old enough now to
notice."

Inside his house Breck went to his gun case, replaced the

pistol and selected a carbine. He loaded it and set it for automatic fire. He had it with him in the pickup when he drove off. At the first cluster of Negro shacks several worried old Negroes were waiting in the road to intercept him. They knew the dog had been shot. Breck told them he was in a hurry but to pass the word that he'd return in a few minutes and stop and talk. He drove down to the highway and to the telephone at the Negro juke. He called the number given him by Clay Wilbanks and left this message: "This is Breck Stancill. The time is seven o'clock this evening. Bring me four compressed-air fire whistles and one tape recorder."

As he drove back up the mountain Breck stopped first to see Loretta. She came out in the yard. She had changed into gray slacks and a turtle-necked yellow sweater. "How's your mother?" he asked.

"Much worse. She knows approximately what happened to me. So she wants to die quickly. She feels that every minute she lives keeps me here and subjects me to more risk. We're not giving her glucose, and she refuses to eat. She's bound to go into a coma soon."

"I'm sorry."

"I heard about your dog," said Loretta. "Now the Ku Klux think they have hurt you twice. First by raping a nigger you cared for, and second by shooting a dog you cared for."

"You mean they raped you to hurt me?"

"They thought they were hurting you. If they hadn't thought you cared for me, in some sense, they'd never have thought of raping me. And they wouldn't have enjoyed it so much. Being Ku Klux, they thought your care for me was sensual. Every one of those Kluxers who watched me being raped thought I was your prize piece of brown comfort. They thought they were fouling a nest you liked."

"I didn't think of that," said Breck.

"I didn't think of it at first. Now I've had time to go over it all in my mind. I remember how lasciviously Butt Cut looked at me on Sunday afternoon when we were standing here in this yard. I thought then it was because he thought I had been to bed with Josh or Charles Peck. Now I know it was because he thought I had been in your bed every night since I returned from Chicago and for several years before I went to Chicago. Those Kluxers enjoyed doing it to me because they thought you'd care."

"Butt Cut may have enjoyed thinking that I'd care," said

Breck. "But the chief reason they all wanted to rape you is because you care for yourself. Vernon Hodo and Reverend Mark Alverson wouldn't have bothered to rape an ordinary nigger on a Sunday evening. They wanted to rape you because they thought you'd care about being raped. You care for your hands, your hair, your body, your brain, your personality. That's why they enjoyed watching you stripped, hit, flattened, ravished, and beaten back down into your place."

"I guess they thought of that," said Loretta. "But my caring for myself isn't what they hate most. Other Negroes in this county care for themselves. The teachers get degrees from Columbia University, drive new Chevrolets, and dress stylishly, and the Ku Klux don't rape them. What Ku Klux can't tolerate is the thought of a Negro being cared for by superior white men. That's why the rednecks hated the slaves. Superior white men cared for the slaves. Superior white men despised the rednecks. I think the Ku Klux may try to kill me. They're bound to hate me more today than they did last Sunday, because since they raped me they've seen evidence that I'm still cared for."

"You mean what little I've done for you?"

"That and other evidence. I made new enemies at the hospital. I made enemies Sunday night when you came in to see me. I made more enemies today when you came to the hospital to get me. You don't realize how white people look at you, Mister Breck. You wear faded khakis, and rough, Marine shoes, and a tan work cap, and you plant trees and drive a pickup truck, and you don't think people think you're a big man. But to poor white girls in Atoka County who become nurses and nurses' aides, you're rich and handsome and sexy and educated and superior. You're the biggest man they know except maybe Hardy Riddle and Dr. Parker. You're single, and your father and grandfather were tireless skirt-lifters, white and brown, so white girls speculate endlessly on your sex life. And everybody in and around that hospital saw evidence that you cared for me. They saw evidence that 'Montgomery Ward' cared for me. Red roses were wired to me all the way from Chicago. Dr. Parker made bitter enemies for me by stopping in my room to talk, like he thought I was an interesting person even after I had been raped. How can the poor white folks of this county *not* try to kill an uppity nigger wench who, after she's been damaged by rape, is still cared for by Breckenridge Stancill, Dr. Parker and Montgomery Ward!"

"Maybe Ku Klux don't think quite as much or as clearly as you do," said Breck.

"I hope not," said Loretta. "But I think they may try to hurt you some more. They may not be satisfied with just me and the dog. It's more fun to hurt a man who cares. It's more fun to rape the nigger of a man who'll visit her in the hospital. It's more fun to shoot the dog of a man who'll cry while he's burying the dog. It's more fun to burn the trees of a man who cares about trees in ways that have nothing to do with money. You care, Mister Breck. You care about everything that's living and beautiful and sensitive and striving. So you and I are going to be lucky if we survive what's going on in this county this week."

Loretta stood with her arms folded, leaning against the truck. Breck thought she seemed less depressed and more assured. The thinking and the understanding had helped her, along with the care and her getting away from the hospital and back to the mountain. Her eyes looked luminous and big, and Breck thought she was more attractive than she had ever been. She seemed to relax as she went on: "I think I've come to know you pretty well, Mister Breck. When I was sixteen I very much wanted you to take me sexually. I had read the stories about how the master always deflowered the comely slave girls on the old plantation. And from what everybody said your daddy and your granddaddy wouldn't have overlooked me. So I used to dress up and try to attract your attention, and I used to cry when I saw you drive off after some white woman when I knew you could do better at home. Then I came to understand. You can take a woman only if she means nothing or everything to you, and I fell somewhere between nothing and everything. You cared for me too much to use me and not enough to cherish me."

"Looking back on it," said Breck smiling, "maybe I should have had more of my daddy in me."

"Maybe you should have."

"Well," said Breck, "we'll resume this conversation when we have more time. Right now let's plan to survive. I once helped capture a mountain called Suribachi, so maybe I can defend my own mountain. Tonight about eight I'll bring you a fire whistle. Put it in your north window. If a strange car comes up the mountain, or if you notice any other suspicious movement, pull the trigger and you'll set off an alarm that I can hear. I'll put three more whistles in houses up the road, between your house and mine, and when the whistles blow I'll move fast."

"I know how fast you can move," said Loretta. "While I was in jail I remembered that night when I ran all the way to your house and you broke a speed record getting down here to take that knife away from that man who was trying to kill Mama."

"I may not be that fast now," said Breck. "I'm older. But I ought to be fast enough to deal with Ku Klux."

Between Loretta's house and his house Breck stopped three times to listen to groups of his worried tenants:

"Is dey gonna burn us out, Mistah Breck? Is dey gonna shoot us all down like dawgs?"

"Mistah Breck, yo' ain't gonna let 'em drive you out, is you? Yo' ain't gonna sell de mountain and leave us to be driven 'fore de Philistines?"

"I got mah ole rabbit gun loaded, Mistah Breck. Yo' wants me'ta stand guard ovah Prince Dan? Dem Ku Klux'll sho' try'ta shoot dat purty horse!"

"Don't let 'em drive us out, Mistah Breck! We ain't got no place in dis whole wicked world'ta go!"

To all of them Breck replied calmly: "Let's keep our shirts on. Nobody will be driven out, and there won't be any fire. Remember that my land is surrounded by other folks' land, and fire spreads. Nobody can fire my woods without firing other folks' woods. What we must do now is lie low. Play possum. Don't go to town: you can see Big Track and the agitators on Huntley-Brinkley. Stay in your houses. When night comes, black out, like you've always done when trouble comes. Load your guns but don't use them unless somebody actually tries to fire your house or dynamite it. Don't get out of your house with a gun in your hand. The Ku Klux have more guns than you have, and they'll use your gun as an excuse for killing you. Now tonight we'll try something different. Don't let it scare you. In several of your homes I'll place a little machine that is a fire alarm. When a trigger is pulled the machine whistles and blows like an old steam railroad engine. If any Ku Klux come up here, the whistles will blow, and I'll meet them with one of those fast-shooting guns like you see on *Combat*. You just sit tight in your homes. Don't worry. Don't shoot one of your neighbors. Above all, don't shoot me.

When I was in the Marines I worried more about being shot
by a trigger-happy Marine than I did about being shot by a
Jap."

At 7 P.M. Breck picked up Clay Wilbanks. "I've got the tape
recorder and the first whistles in a car up ahead," said Wilbanks. "Just drive on and the car will fall in behind us and we
can stop and make the transfer."

"They shot my Irish setter about one P.M.," said Breck. "I
had to finish killing him."

"That doesn't surprise me. Surely you expected it?"

"No, I didn't expect it. Even when I know such blows may
come, I still can't expect them."

"Are you ready to help me?"

"In a limited way. I'm going to give you some information.
But you must handle it in a way that will indicate I didn't help
you get it."

"If that's the way you want it."

"It's the way it has to be. I can't live in this county if I'm
ever suspected of collaborating with you."

"All right. We'll do it your way."

"I brought Loretta home from the hospital today," said
Breck. "She told me the story. They raped her in the jail about
eight P.M. Sunday. They put Lightning Rod in a padded cell
with her, and several robed-and-masked figures watched the
rape."

"Who's Lightning Rod?"

"A big, feeble-minded Negro who has been used for rape
shows for years. He can't speak."

"If they raped her at eight," said Wilbanks, "Big Track
wasn't there. We've learned that he didn't get back from Mobile until nine."

"Loretta doesn't think she saw him until after nine—after
Hattie had helped her dress and put her in a car. Big Track
drove off with her, apparently intending to kill her. Instead he
offered to deliver her to the hospital if she'd promise not to
accuse the Ku Klux and not to tell anyone that the rape was
committed in the jail."

"Two questions occur at once," said Wilbanks. "One: why
did the Ku Klux, including Butt Cut, feel free to commit the
crime in Big Track's jail? Answer: they had Big Track hog-
tied. Ku Klux prefer to commit their crimes in jail; it discour-
ages criticism by reminding their possible critics that Ku Klux

control the law. Question two: why didn't Big Track kill her? Why did he choose to risk her talking to the FBI? Answer: he was taking risks either way. Not killing her seemed the lesser risk."

"He didn't want to kill her," said Breck. "He's not a cold-blooded killer."

"Well . . . maybe he isn't," conceded Wilbanks. "I can guess who some of the witnesses were. Butt Cut certainly. Probably Vernon Hodo and Reverend Mark Alverson. We've already checked and found that the reverend failed to show in his pulpit Sunday evening. The other two or three could have been any of six other members of that Action Squad. We'll start checking their lives tonight, seeing which one wants you to give him a rich, new life in Australia. Now when can I see Loretta and get her signature on a sworn statement? Hell, we might decide to arrest Big Track on no more than her statement that she was raped in jail!"

"You can slow down right there," said Breck. "You aren't going to arrest anybody. Not now. You aren't going to get any statement from Loretta. Not in Alabama. Tonight I'll take your recorder to her and let her record the story while it's fresh in her mind. Tomorrow I'll give you back the recorder, but I'll keep the tape. As soon as her mother goes into a coma I think I can persuade Loretta to leave. Once she's safe in Chicago, you can go there, pick up the tape, get her signature, then both you and she can announce that you persuaded her to reveal the truth after she left Alabama. As for buying a confession from a rapist, you can do that, not me."

Clay Wilbanks felt exasperated. "Goddam, Breck," he said, "don't you realize the enormity of the crime you have just described? You can't hold back now. This is no mere individual crime: police participation makes it a state crime! No matter what it costs him, every man who respects himself must fight crime in which sworn public protectors participate. Remember the Dreyfus Case? No citizen is secure where police join Ku Klux in committing rape in jail!"

"Don't lecture me, Clay," said Breck. "This is a state crime but the state can't punish the criminals. Even if you buy a confession, arrest the criminals, and exhibit them on television, they still go free and I have to live with them."

Wilbanks backed off. "Okay, Breck," he said. "My car is behind us. Pull into a side road and we'll give you the recorder and the alarms. But let's consider one other move. How about me sending men to guard Loretta? We'd be tipping off Big Track that she has talked to us, but we'd be making sure they don't kill her before we get her signed statement."

"That's a good idea," said Breck. "You should guard Loretta. But not on my land. Why don't you arrest her as a material witness, bring an ambulance, and move her and her mother out of the state?"

"Yeah, we could do that," said Wilbanks, thinking. "We could announce that we had to move her off your land because you had ordered her not to talk to us. We could charge you with obstructing justice. In that way we could safeguard her and make it look like you're collaborating with Big Track and the Klan."

Breck reflected. "Now, you're making sense," he said. "Will you do it?"

"I feel sure we will," said Wilbanks. "But we can't act tonight. Now that I know the story I'll have to go over it with other people in the Justice Department. What they'll want most is the confession identifying all guilty parties. Loretta's statement is important, but it's limited: she doesn't know who was behind the masks. So we'll have to estimate just how much our guarding and moving Loretta might jeopardize our chances to get the confession. We can't act until we weigh all factors."

"How long will that take?"

"Not long. Maybe twenty-four hours. Maybe forty-eight. You know how bureaucracy works."

"Yeah, I know," said Breck. "I've been trying to remind you how bureaucracy works. Just give me the recorder and the five whistles, and I'll try to keep Loretta alive while you bureaucrats weigh all factors."

Driving back up the mountain Breck stopped and gave Loretta the tape recorder and one of the whistles. Between Loretta's house and Nancy Poteet's house, not a light was visible. Every Negro's shack was blacked out. About halfway between Loretta and Nancy, Breck stopped at a shack in which lived a Negro woman named Lenore Roundtree. Breck called to her and walked up on her porch, carrying a flashlight. She opened the door.

"Mistah Breck," she said, "a car passed heah goin' up'ta yo' house 'bout twenty minutes ago. It ain't come back down yit. It might be the High Sheriff's boy."

"Loretta told me," said Breck. "I'm sure it's Allen Bascomb. He's all right." Then Breck showed her the fire alarm which was a quart-sized metal canister of compressed air. Atop the canister was a trigger-controlled whistle or horn. You could hold it and blow it in short, repeated blasts; or after starting it blowing, you could lock the trigger in a slot and walk away from it, and it would blow continuously for three minutes before exhausting its air supply. The steam-whistle sound, on a wooded mountain with no competing noises, would waken a normal adult two miles away.

"Lenore," said Breck, "here is one of the fire whistles you heard me mention. I want to put it in your house, and I want you to operate it for us."

"I'se afeard, Mistah Breck," she said. "I got high blood, and I might git so scairt I'd jest keel over and couldn't pull de trigger."

"No, you won't get that scared," said Breck. "Your hearing is still good, isn't it? And you've still got good eyesight?"

"Oh, yassuh. I can still thread a needle and hear a pin drop. And I sleeps with one eye open."

"Then you're the lookout we need. Just put this in your north window and keep your eyes and ears open. If you hear another whistle blow, you blow yours. If you don't hear another whistle, but you see somebody who doesn't belong up here, just haul off and blow like Old Gabe blowing on Judgment Day."

"If you says so, Mistah Breck, I'll try."

Breck's next stop was at Nancy's house. She had put the children to bed, and, in her blue pajamas, she was sewing and looking at Red Skelton. Breck placed the alarm in her bedroom window and showed her how to use it. "Can't you stay for a cup of coffee?" Nancy asked.

"Not now," said Breck. "I have to talk to Allen Bascomb."

Nancy smiled. "He's out there parked with his cheerleader, Billie Jean," she said. "He stopped here and asked me where you were. He's mighty anxious to see you. But I don't think he'd mind waiting a while. I imagine he's busy, don't you?"

"Yeah, I imagine he is," said Breck, smiling. "It's springtime and the sap's rising." On that note Nancy's eyes met Breck's. He considered her, reflected briefly, then added: "Suppose we have the coffee in about an hour? I'll talk with Allen and look around a little. Then I'll come back."

"I'll keep the coffee hot."

A few minutes after Breck reached his house Allen drove into the yard, entered the house, and spoke to Breck. "I've come to stay with you and help you," he said. "I brought my gun."

"You what?"

"I brought my gun. I've come to spend the night with you. I'll drive Billie Jean home after a while, then I'll come back. You and I can take turns standing guard. They killed Chrissie. If they come back to do any more killing or burning, you and I can handle 'em."

"Have you told your mother and dad?"

"Not yet. Dad doesn't get home till ten-thirty or eleven. I'll tell them when I drive Billie Jean home. They'll both want me to stay with you. You're the best friend we have. Dad's tied down guarding the demonstrators, so it's up to me to help you."

"Well," said Breck, "first—would Billie Jean like to come in and listen to records while you and I talk a few minutes?"

"She said she'd just sit in the car. The radio's on."

Breck and Allen sat before the fire and Breck said: "Al, I appreciate your offer to help me. But I'll have to refuse it."

"You don't want my help?"

"Not your armed help. I don't think I need armed help, so I don't want folks hearing that I'm accepting it. I intend to stay calm, not rattle any sabers, and hope I'm right in thinking I don't need help."

"I see what you mean," said Allen. "But I'm afraid you do need help. The Ku Klux have phonograph records out now. Kids play them at school. Today they were playing one called 'Run Them Niggers North.' I heard kids saying that the time's come to run 'them old nigger relief-hounds' off Stancill's Mountain."

"Talk's one thing," said Breck. "Action is something else."

"But they keep harping on how you've let these Negroes continue to live here. They say if you had run them all north twenty years ago, then we could have had a new football stadium and higher pay for teachers. Now they're saying that you made Loretta into an uppity agitator. This afternoon I heard that this morning you 'joined the agitators' and 'stood with them' at the courthouse."

"More talk," said Breck. "Even if I did need armed help, you're not the one to give it to me. You must think of your dad. I only have to be tolerated by folks. He has to be approved. You must help him be approved."

"I try. I wish he wasn't in politics."

"But he is. He lives by re-election. Every Christmas he sends your picture to every voter. So you must never displease voters. And that brings me to a question. I hear you've taken up my habit of pulling down Butt Cut's efforts to inform public opinion?"

"Yes, I have," said Allen. "Folks think Butt Cut's pasting up those clippings because Dad tells him to. That's a lie! Dad is no Ku Klux! He roots for Willie Mays and Lenny Moore. He thinks Negroes are making good soldiers in Vietnam. So I have to jerk down those clippings to show folks that Dad is not like Butt Cut."

"That's a good reason," said Breck. "But you're forgetting you want to go to West Point."

"To go to West Point do I have to give up all my freedom?"

"You have to give up part of it. There are two freedoms which West Pointers can't afford. Controversy and sex."

"I'm beginning to realize what that means," said Allen. "On our trip to Mobile Dad talked to me about sex. He's afraid I'm going to knock up Billie Jean and knock myself out of West Point."

Breck smiled. "Well," he said, "that's reasonable fear, isn't it?"

"I don't know," said Allen. "I just don't know what to do. Billie Jean's seventeen and I'll soon be eighteen. We're in love. She wants us to start going all the way. She thinks that's best for both of us. She doesn't want me starting with some older woman. Dad thinks she's wrong. He wants me to save Billie Jean until I finish West Point and marry her, and now he wants to get me an older woman. What do you think I ought to do?"

"Lord, don't ask me," said Breck.

"What did you do when you were my age?"

"I didn't start with any maiden. My mother made me shy of maidens. She raised me to be ashamed of all my father's skirtlifting. So I started with camp followers in San Diego and whores in Honolulu. I know nothing about maidens. All the women I've known were experienced operators when I arrived."

Allen felt surprised. He had never guessed it was that way with Breck.

"Here's the only advice I can give," said Breck. "If you aren't going to do what your dad says, then you and Billie Jean should go see Dr. Parker and do what he says." Breck got up and got his hat. He said: "Al, I'm going out and look around for a while. Why don't you bring Billie Jean in and play the records and watch the fire and drink Cokes or coffee? I'll be gone an hour or so."

Breck went out the back door, got the carbine from his truck, and walked toward the barn. The moon was out, and in his jerky gait he walked slowly around the barn and tool shed. He patted his horse and stood again where he had buried his dog. Then he walked toward Nancy's house.

As he walked, Breck thought: I suppose every man has nights when his life seems inexplicable. I remember standing on street corners in San Diego, and Honolulu, and San Francisco, in jungles and on beaches, wondering how I got there. Tonight I wonder how my great-great-grandfather ever happened to claim this particular mountain and why there has been so goddam much trouble here. I wonder why folks hate me enough to kill my dog, and rape my nigger, and may try to kill me, just as they killed my great-grandfather. I wonder why I'm walking down this road to fuck a little blond, leprous mother. Don't I know she was fucked by Willie Washington? Don't I know Ku Klux will loathe me for taking a nigger's leavings? What about my having felt so sorry for Nancy that I couldn't fuck her? That stopped me before; why isn't it stopping me now? Is it because I figure that Nancy now has reason to feel as sorry for me as I feel for her? Have my balls been tickled by the presence of young lovers who are going all the way, if not tonight then tomorrow night? Am I fucking Nancy because I'm sorry I didn't fuck Loretta when she was sixteen, as my father and grandfather would have done? Or is it the old, simple story: I'm ready to fuck because I'm ready to fight? I've got a hard on because I've got a fast-shooting gun in my hand and I'm ready to kill some s'nuvabitch? I'm horny because the smell of gunpowder has always been the most potent aphrodisiac in the whole fucking world?

When Breck Stancill crawled out of Nancy's bed, strapped on his tin leg, and walked back home, she had been rehabilitated. She knew she wasn't a leper any more.

TAG

AT 8:15 A.M., Wednesday, April 14, 1965, the Reverend Mark Alverson and his wife Euba were at their breakfast table. Their children had left for school, and the reverend was reading the Birmingham *Post-Herald*. Euba Alverson, in a pink housecoat, was sipping coffee. She was pleasant, round-faced, and her black hair was beginning to gray.

"Mark," she said, "I never mention your Ku Klux activities."

"You must not," he said. "Except for our public meetings our activities must never be mentioned. We are an invisible empire—secret, Christian, patriotic."

"I shan't mention activities. I only want to ask you to help Breck Stancill."

The reverend lowered his paper. "Why does he need help?"

"His dog was shot yesterday. Pressure is being put on him to run his niggers north. I want you to help him."

"Why do you want him helped?"

"Because he's a good man."

Reverend Alverson put aside the paper and said: "That's a strange judgment for you to make, Euba. A Christian wife and mother saying Breck Stancill is good!"

"I say it because I believe it," said Euba Alverson firmly.

"Well, let's see how good he is," said the preacher. "Is he godly? We godly men stand at the final battle: Armageddon. Our God has been banished from the schools of once-godly America. Our Communist enemies are within our gates. Where stands Mr. Stancill? With godly men? No, he's ungodly. When godly men are on our knees worshipping God, he is on his horse worshipping trees."

"A man doesn't have to be godly to be good."

"No? Then let's ask a further question. Is Mr. Stancill moral? He lives in a house built for immoral purpose. What dreams does he dream, lying in a bed in which his father clasped a New Orleans whore? He himself lies with whores, white and nigger alike. He partakes of white flesh which was defiled by a black beast. Is this the man you would stand before our children and call good? A violent, ungodly, immoral, defiant man from a violent, ungodly, immoral, defiant family!"

Euba Alverson resisted her husband's logic. "You may laugh at why I think he's good," she said. "But Our Lord wouldn't laugh. I'm a bird watcher. I feel close to God when I'm in the woods counting birds. I worry because birds are leaving this county. Pine trees offer them no food and little shelter, and everybody wants more pine trees. The only place where birds are still plentiful is Stancill's Mountain. Take yellowhammers. They are beautiful birds. But they need a worthless, half-rotten, old oak tree to live in. And the only tree farmer who spares old oak trees is Breck Stancill. He lets the old trees stand there, overtopping his young pines, spoiling the symmetry of his forest, costing him money, all for the sake of yellowhammers. Will a Lord of Creation whose eye is on the sparrow turn his face against a man who cares for yellowhammers?"

Reverend Alverson smiled at his wife. "That's a nursery tale to tell children," he said.

"Then listen to one more tale. From his living room Breck Stancill can look for twenty miles across Northwest Alabama. Because moisture sometimes clouded his windows, he removed the old glass and installed thermopane so the glass would always be clear. But the new glass was so clear that birds couldn't see it, and several broke their necks against it. So to warn the birds he built a partial lattice before the glass. He sacrificed part of his magnificent view so as not to endanger the birds. I say only a good man would do that, and from my heart I ask you to help him."

"What about his niggers?" the preacher asked. "He not only allows worthless trees to stand, he also allows worthless niggers to stay, and listen to agitators, and cause trouble, and eat up public money. You want me to help him turn the county over to niggers and agitators?"

"I don't know about that."

"Well, you see, that's the point. You can quit worrying about Stancill and the birds. They are in no danger. For your sake I'll do what little I can to protect them. But Stancill can't continue to offend godly men by allowing worthless niggers to threaten our safety and devour our substance. Let's say that he can keep his yellowhammers but not his Black Birds. That's fair, isn't it?"

Reverend Alverson, feeling satisfied, returned to his newspaper. His wife was not satisfied. She wanted to ask him about conduct which puzzled her. For years they had not had sexual intercourse on Sunday. But last Sunday evening Ku Klux activities had kept the reverend from his pulpit, and when he reached home and bed he had savagely tended to her. She had wondered why. Now, suddenly, she knew why. But the knowledge repelled her, so she dismissed it, got up, and went about her work.

An hour later Loretta saw a station wagon coming up the mountain. She was about to blow the whistle when she noticed lettering on the car which indicated that it carried a TV cameraman and reporter. The car sped on to Breck's house and found him in the yard. The TV men introduced themselves.

"What can I do for you, gentlemen?" Breck asked warily. He knew they were dangerous, but he hoped to be agreeable and not antagonize them.

"We wanted to meet you and talk a little," replied the reporter. "We intended to meet you yesterday when you came to the hospital for Loretta. We missed you because we were interviewing Vernon Hodo."

Breck's jaw tightened. What would he have done had they pointed a camera at him and Loretta at the hospital?

"I've been hearing the Stancill legends," the reporter continued, hoping he was breaking ice. "Particularly about you and the Ku Klux."

After a stage wait Breck said: "People talk."

"Yeah, don't they?" The reporter cleared his throat. "I was wondering if you'd help me by answering a few questions before the camera?"

"Like what?"

"Like why you tear down Butt Cut's clippings. What really happened to Loretta last Sunday night. How Nancy is feeling a year after her rape. Why you allow Negro reliefers to live on your land. Who shot your dog. And do you expect any more trouble."

"What purpose would be served by my trying to answer such questions?"

"Noblest purpose on earth. Truth. Free expression of opinion. You'd be helping me inform the American people."

"That sounds impressive," said Breck. "But you can inform the people without my help."

"You mean you're afraid to speak out?"

"I mean I can't think of a word to speak that would be helpful."

"Does that mean you refuse to help me in any way?"

"It means I won't talk for television. Neither will Loretta nor Nancy. Otherwise we welcome you and want to help you. We've always welcomed peaceful visitors to Stancill's Mountain. Lovers, sightseers, picnickers, bird watchers, a few hunters in season, even people with cameras."

"Then here's another request," said the reporter. "Vernon says he likes you: that the only thing Ku Klux don't like about you is your nigger relief-hounds. So will you let me take the camera inside one of your Negro shacks? I want my viewers to know a typical relief-hound on Stancill's Mountain. The world can see how pitifully these old Negroes live in poverty."

"I'll agree to that," said Breck, "if you correctly answer this question. When you showed your pictures of my typical relief-hound, what would a Ku Klux Klansman see?"

"Well," answered the reporter, "he'd see some of what everybody else sees. He'd see old Negroes living in poverty. Maybe he'd understand a little about why you haven't driven them north. Maybe he'd feel so superior to your Negroes that he'd feel less resentful of you. Certainly he wouldn't hate you any more than he does already."

"You flunked the test," said Breck. "There are more white relief-hounds in this county than Negro. The whites, along with their sons and daughters, are Ku Klux. In your pictures they'd see that my Negro relief-hounds get more given to them than the white relief-hounds get from their landlords. I give my Negroes free rent, land for vegetables, wood to burn, poison to kill rats, plastic to turn rain and cold, a church and a graveyard. They have electricity and TV and the same fifty-five dollars a month which white reliefers receive. Except the white reliefers pay rent and get only contempt from their landlords. So if I allowed you inside a Negro shack, you'd only do harm. You'd put more hate for me and for Negroes in Ku Klux hearts, and more arson in Ku Klux minds."

The reporter reflected, then chuckled. "I never thought of it that way," he said. "Why do you give the Negroes so much?"

"It isn't much," said Breck. "Maybe there's some feeling of obligation. My great-great-grandfather brought the first Negro into this county. It takes time to move from slavery to peonage to freedom. The real truth is that all us Stancills have liked Negroes more than we like poor white men. We've cared for Negroes; we haven't cared for poor whites. The Ku Klux have cause to hate me and my Negroes. They hate a nigger-lover, and just as savagely they hate the nigger who is loved."

"It's strange that you've risked telling me that," the reporter said. "It's almost like a confession of guilt."

"I've risked nothing," said Breck. "What I've told you is real truth. So you can't use it. Real truth embarrasses most everybody. So I'm sure real truth is seldom allowed on television."

It was the reporter's turn to feel guilty. Screwing up his courage, he said: "Mr. Stancill, you've been honest with me, so I hate like hell to tell you this. We couldn't report the conflict in this county without covering you. And we guessed you wouldn't talk or let us make pictures. So we've assembled photos of you and Loretta and Nancy. We got them from the Marine Corps, from people in Chicago, from the local schools and newspaper. We have some motion picture footage of Nancy—made at the time of the lynching. We have interiors of Negro shacks we thought were like yours. Tonight on the network we're going to try to tell your story. There's nothing I can do to prevent it. There's nothing you can do. We thought it would explain things, and might even help you."

Breck's shoulders sagged. "That's a shame," he said. "A goddam, stupid shame! There's no way you can show those pictures, or even mention names, without provoking hate and increasing danger to innocent people who have the right to be let alone."

"I understand that now. I'm sorry."

"Is it too late to make changes?"

"No," said the reporter. "There's still a little time. It's a quarter to ten. I have to be in Birmingham at two P.M. to process film and edit narration."

"Then I'll offer you a deal," said Breck. "I don't want my Marine pictures used. They were made when I was striving for noble purpose. So I look belligerent. Belligerence provokes belligerence. Now that I'm only trying to survive and help survive, I don't look belligerent."

"Why don't we shoot some footage of you right now?"

"All right. You can also have new film of Nancy and Loretta. You can photograph some of the Negroes if you'll show only their faces and not mention what I give them."

"Wonderful." The cameraman hurried to the station wagon for the camera. "Will you ride your horse for us?" asked the reporter.

"No, I can't," said Breck. "If I had a poor, trashy horse, I'd show your viewers how a one-legged man mounts and rides. But Prince Dan is a magnificent, expensive, pure-blooded palomino. He looks proud, aristocratic, cared for. At the sight of him every Ku Klux would want to kill him. Just as they killed my dog because he was beautiful, intelligent, expensive and cared for. You can photograph me planting a tree and using that Chevrolet pickup. And please mention that it's the only automobile I own."

"That'll be perfect."

"There's one provision you may not like," said Breck. "While you're photographing the Negroes, I'll have Nancy and Loretta change clothes. At this minute they're probably in slacks or stretch pants, with tight blouses or sweaters. They both are blessed with luxurious teats. Ku Klux think only of fucking, especially when they see women they think are mine and who have been raped. So I'll have Loretta and Nancy lash down their teats, put on flat heels and droopy dresses, and try to look sexless."

"I get it," said the reporter. "How did you happen to think of it?"

"It's as old as history. Sabine women lashed down their teats and wore formless dress, trying not to be noticed by barbarians. So did women in Berlin and Vienna, Hongkong and Singapore."

At 4:30 P.M. Hardy Riddle and Vernon Hodo sat in conference in Hardy's office at the Atoka Lumber Company. Hardy said: "I hear you're going to be on TV?"

"Yeah, Skipper," said Vernon. "I let 'em interview me. They're gonna show it to the whole country tonight at six-thirty. Everybody in the county'll be looking. Most everybody in Alabama, I guess. And I've invited all the TV boys to our big public cross-burning and speaking this coming Saturday night."

"What'd you say in the interview?"

"Nothing that we ain't been over and you said was right. I talked about God and how we got to put Him back in the schools. I said every red-blooded, God-fearing, right-thinking, conservative American ought to join the Klan or pray for it and help save Constitutional government and free enterprise from the Communist-beatnik-liberal-scum. I called the demonstrators at the courthouse atheists, Communists and fornicators. Wolves in sheep's clothing."

"What'd you say about violence?" asked Hardy.

"I came out hard against it. I said the Klan stands shoulder-to-shoulder with every sheriff and policeman in the country, fighting violence, trying to stop looting and raping and breaking our laws. I blamed Earl Warren for starting the law-breaking."

"Did you put in a plug for George?"

"Sure, I never forget our governor. I called him the Great Leader of the White Man's Cause, and said he'd be President in spite of all the Communist-beatnik-liberal-scum that spit on him."

"Did you say the Klan was standing shoulder-to-shoulder with Big Track?"

"I hedged on Track," said Vernon. "I said he was doing what he thought was right in protecting that scum at the courthouse. You're crucifying Track, Skipper, making him protect that scum. He's getting criticism."

"We'll build him up again," said Hardy. "The demonstrations will stop Friday."

"What you giving the niggers?"

"On Friday afternoon we'll let them *integrate* the courthouse. The walls of Jericho will come tumbling down, and they can all go in and piss in the white toilets. They can piss for freedom! They can tear down the White and Colored signs. We'll agree to let *qualified* Negroes register to vote and serve on juries. In the schools they'll win Freedom of Choice. Next fall any Negro can choose which school he goes to. After pissing in the courthouse they can dance in the street. Then Josh and Big Pecker and the TV boys can carry Freedom Now to some other backwoods county."

Vernon grinned. "That'll be a Great Victory! On Monday if one of them coons drags his ass inside that courthouse he'll piss right back down in the basement where he's supposed to piss. And I can see a nigger *choosing* to go to a white school in this county!"

"Be careful with that sort of talk," said Hardy. "On Friday, while the celebrating's going on, you lather up and tell the TV boys that white men have been sold out by the county officials. At your Klan meeting on Saturday you yell that bankers and merchants have betrayed the Southern way of life."

"I get'cha, Skipper," said Vernon, still grinning. "Now what are we gonna give white men? I've had a tough time this week, holding back Kluxers. They've had a hard on to Klux! They've wanted to shoot Josh even while Big Track was escorting him to Tuscaloosa. The brakes must come off a little. We got to run some niggers north. If niggers are gonna vote here, they got to get scarcer. Every nigger we don't need, his black ass is going to Chicago or get singed."

"You know what you can do and can't do."

Vernon lowered his voice. "What about the mountain?"

"Stay away from there," said Hardy. "Breck's a producer for this company. You've already torn down that girl and shot his dog."

"The dog wasn't planned," said Vernon. "One of the boys just hated the sight of that Irish setter."

"Has the girl gone back to Chicago?"

"If she hasn't, she better get going. We used her very effectively. The niggers know we let Lightning Rod tear her down. But we wanted the niggers to see her running north next morning. Doc stopped her. Now that she's out of the hospital, if she don't run, what Lightning Rod left of her ass is gonna get singed."

"Make sure nobody runs into Breck!"

"Nobody needs to run into Breck. He can't run. He can't sneak up behind anybody. At night his horse is in the barn. All he can do is drive along that road where you can see him. A man can sneak through the woods and singe a black ass without running into Breck."

"I'll hurt any man who hurts Breck," said Hardy. "So will Big Track."

"Nobody's gonna get hurt. We're gonna do Breck a favor. For twenty years he's been trying to get rid of nigger shacks. He's got rid of about one a year, and he's got forty left. We'll help him move faster."

"I didn't hear you say that," said Hardy. "But you hear me! This is a dry April. If any burning's done of that mountain, you better see that nothing burns but a nigger shack!"

As Vernon was leaving the office he said: "Skipper, I'm

going on home now. We're having a little party at my house.
Folks coming in to watch me on TV. My wife's breaking out
her best wine."

"I'll go home in time to see you," said Hardy.

Hardy didn't go home to watch the telecast. He drove his
Thunderbird into Trixie Cunningham's back yard and went in
her back door. She met him in a gold negligee. He never wasted time in preliminaries with her. Usually he came in, ran his
all-American-linebacker hands over her, slapped her on the
tail, and began pulling off his clothes. But this time he said:
"Let's wait till after the news. Get me a drink and let's watch
Vernon stand up for Alabama and the Ku Klux."

Trixie didn't like being postponed for Ku Klux, but she
turned on the TV, got the drink, and sat so Hardy could keep
his right hand between her thighs while he drank with his left
and waited for Chet Huntley to finish the Vietnam report.
Hardy liked to feel inside Trixie's thighs. He liked her because
she was literate but lusty, fastidious but earthy; and she knew
how to arouse an important man, then keep him from spending himself too fast.

Hattie Bascomb had finished feeding her twelve prisoners,
and she was in her own cell, sipping a toddy, with the TV on.
She always felt blue at dusk, and tonight she felt awfully blue
because for a week there had been no white female in the jail
from whom she could take comfort. Hattie was uncared for.
Her father had used her until he died, now her brother used
her and never invited her to his home. She had never been
asked how she felt by anyone who wanted an answer. She had
never been welcomed. She had been grasped but never em-
braced. Even when she sat in the Baptist choir she knew she
was tolerated, not included. Except when a woman was with
her she always looked at the TV evening news. On Monday
and Tuesday evenings she had seen Big Track, Josh, Big
Pecker, Butt Cut and outraged citizens. Tonight she expected
to see Vernon Hodo.

Big Track and Butt Cut were in the Wildcat, returning
from Tuscaloosa after escorting the demonstrators. Big Track
had hoped to get home in time for the newscast, but when he
saw he couldn't he stopped at Awful Annie's, the motel-beer-
joint-whorehouse four miles south of Ellenton. He and Butt
Cut went into one of the motel rooms and turned on the TV.

Maybelle was at home, with Allen, worrying about how the criticism of Big Track might hurt her family.

In his yard on the south edge of Ellenton Tag Taggart was working on the engine of a 1959 Ford. His twenty-six-year-old wife was inside the unpainted, four-room house, fixing supper for Tag, their four children, and her sister who was a nurse's aide at the Atoka Hospital. At 6:25, when his wife called him, Tag quit work, washed his grimy hands in kerosene, shook them dry and went in. Every Klansman had been ordered to watch Vernon on TV.

However, at Vernon's $10,000 home on the north edge of Ellenton, none of the guests were Klansmen. The six men who, with their wives, had come to drink, eat and watch Vernon on TV were his peers. They, too, owned homes. They owned small businesses or were foremen in large businesses. So they preferred to be Klan helpers, not Klan members. They wanted one of their number to command the Klan, but they didn't choose to fill the ranks. When a rifle platoon has one officer to command sixty-four enlisted men, its requirement for officers is filled. The Atoka County Ku Klux Klan needed only one foreman and one preacher to lead forty-five laborers who were between eighteen and thirty-eight, who did not own homes, and who earned between $2,500 and $4,500 a year.

One of Vernon's guests was Ellenton's only florist. He had filled the telegraphed order from Chicago for the roses delivered to Loretta in the hospital.

In a downtown motel in Birmingham Clay Wilbanks and his partner were drinking bourbon, with the TV on. Wilbanks felt impatient. At 9 A.M. he had filed his report on how Loretta Sykes was raped, along with his recommendation that she be arrested at once as a material witness. He had waited all afternoon for orders. He was still waiting.

In a Negro motel in Tuscaloosa Josh Franklin and Charles Peck were sipping scotch, waiting for the news. Josh asked: "How much longer you think the TV boys will stay with us in Ellenton?"

"Another day or two," said Peck. "So by Friday we better accept concessions from the Ellenton Power Structure, celebrate victory, and get out of here. When the cameras go we go."

In a shack on the edge of the lumberyard two old Negro women relief-hounds were glued to their TV set, waiting for the third installment of the Ellenton story. With them was Lightning Rod. The old women liked to watch Lightning Rod watch TV. Watching Lightning Rod watch TV was often more fun for them than watching TV. He would grin when they could see nothing to grin at. He would scowl when they could see nothing to scowl at. And sometimes when they laughed at something on TV, he would look at them like he was ashamed of them.

Loretta switched off the tape recorder. She had recorded her recollections of every word and action on Sunday, from the time Butt Cut appeared at the house until Big Track delivered her to the hospital. She glanced toward her mother, who was now conscious only at intervals. Then, fearfully, she switched on the TV. In every blacked-out shack on the mountain a TV screen glowed.

Since he didn't own a TV set, Breck had walked down to Nancy's house. She was busy, because it was the time when she fed, bathed and bedded first the ten-month-old child, then the four-year-old. The house was noisy, and Nancy hoped Breck could hear as well as see. What Breck heard was this:

Here in the Courthouse Square at Ellenton, Alabama, is a familiar conflict. It's between these outside agitators who want new rights for Negroes, and these home folks who want Negroes to stay in their place.

Five miles from the courthouse, on this mountain, is an unfamiliar conflict. It's between the Ku Klux Klan and this man.

His name is Breck Stancill. He's a tree farmer, with three thousand acres of land owned by his family since 1815. He's a much-decorated ex-Marine. He lost a leg on Iwo Jima. He's an American Legionnaire.

So Breck Stancill is no outsider, or agitator, or beatnik. He's not even accused of being a liberal. His conflict with the Klan is over these old Negroes. They are the unemployable residue of generations of slavery and peonage. They are welfare clients, and they live here on Stancill's Mountain in these old shacks. They worship at this old church, and they want to be buried in this old cemetery.

Breck Stancill wants the Negroes to live out their lives here. The Ku Klux insist that they leave.

Recently the conflict has sharpened. Mr. Stancill publicly

expressed contempt for Governor Wallace, whom the Ku Klux call The Great Leader of the White Man's Cause. The Ku Klux continually put up posters which call Negroes beasts. Mr. Stancill tears down the posters and calls either the posters or the Ku Klux "trash."

Memories feed the conflict. On this mountain in 1861 Mr. Stancill's great-grandfather, the county's largest slaveholder, was hanged by Secessionists because he said he wasn't afraid to live in a nation where Negroes were educated and free.

This young white mother is part of the conflict. She is Nancy Poteet. After being raped by a Negro, who was then lynched by the Klan, she was persecuted by Klansmen. Mr. Stancill gave her sanctuary.

This young Negro woman became part of the conflict. She is Loretta Sykes. She lives in Chicago, in this modern apartment building. She earns $105 a week at Montgomery Ward. But she was born here on Stancill's Mountain, in this shack, where her mother is dying of cancer. Last week when she came home to help her mother, she was jailed as a suspected agitator, then raped by unidentified assailants under circumstances still in doubt.

Breck Stancill courteously declines to discuss his perilous position. His prize-winning Irish setter was shot to death yesterday. But today this reporter found Mr. Stancill planting pine seedlings, assuming that he and Loretta and Nancy and the old Negroes will be allowed to live and die in peace.

The conflict at the courthouse will end this week, with meaningless concessions by the townspeople and a meaningless victory for the agitators. But no one knows when or how the conflict on Stancill's Mountain will end.

Hardy Riddle took his hand off Trixie's thigh and reached for the telephone. Because of the anger and embarrassment at Vernon Hodo's house, the telephone rang eight times before Vernon answered. Hardy said: "Now listen, Vernon! I know you're sore because they didn't put you on TV like they promised. I'm sure your Kluxers have all got hards on, rarin' to Klux! But you've got to cool them off. Too many eyes will be watching that place tonight. I know, I know! But you've been riding herd on work gangs for twenty years. You can hold those bucks. I'll check with you later."

As he got up Hardy said to Trixie: "I must run, honey. Keep it warm till I get back."

"When will that be?"

"Maybe tomorrow. I'll call you."

Trixie always hated being made to feel insignificant. Now she hated Hardy for being able to leave without getting what he had come for. And she hated Breck for not having married her. If he'd had sense enough to marry me, she thought, he wouldn't be in the silly fix he's in! Because there wouldn't be any stinking old nigger relief-hounds on his mountain, and there wouldn't be any Nancy or Loretta. I'd have seen to that! There'd just be me and him and our family and our servants. And I wouldn't be at the beck and call of Hardy Riddle!

Hattie Bascomb reacted oddly. The news that Loretta was paid $105 a week choked Hattie with hate and shame. Big Track paid Hattie bed and fatback and fifty cash dollars a month. But the sight of Breck Stancill in his pickup truck reminded Hattie of the one time in her life when she was treated like somebody. It was Christmas 1951, when she was eighteen. Big Track was in Korea, and Hattie was tied down with their bedridden father. The money she had saved for a dress had gone to cocksuckers. Hattie felt like the lowest-down piece of white trash in Alabama. Then a pickup truck stopped, and Breck got out with a food basket and two packages. One package was a new dress he had bought in Birmingham. The other package was two dresses once worn by his mother or his sisters.

"I thought you might be able to use these," he said. "Go put on the new dress so I can see if it fits. Then we'll sit here by the fire while you tell me how you're getting along. You deserve a lot of credit for looking after your father."

Hattie hated Breck for caring for Negroes. But she wished he would bring her another dress and sit and listen to her tell how she was getting along.

As Big Track switched off the TV, Butt Cut said: "Where'ya stand now, Track?"

"Let's get going," said Big Track.

In the car Butt Cut said: "That one-legged s'nuvabitch has been spittin' in our faces for a year. Now he's done his spittin' before everybody. Maybe you're gonna take it. But I ain't. A lot'a good men ain't."

"I didn't see him doing no spittin' on TV," said Big Track. "He didn't say nothing. He just planted trees and drove his pickup. Them two gals didn't say nothing. They just walked around in old Mother Hubbards. Them old niggers just stood there. Nobody said nothing. Except the TV."

"Breck was sayin' what the TV said," said Butt Cut. "They couldn't't'a took them pictures without his say so."

That was what irritated Big Track. Goddam it, he thought, I told Breck to lie low. He said he would. Then why didn't he take his shotgun and run the TV camera off? Why didn't he help me by keeping quiet, instead of going on TV and provoking Ku Klux?

Tag Taggart was so provoked that he was raring to Klux. He told his wife and sister-in-law: "When a man calls me trash on TV, I can't do nothing else but git my gun and go after him."

Every Klansman felt provoked on learning that Loretta was paid $105 a week. Except for Vernon, Big Track and Reverend Alverson, no Klansman in Atoka County had ever earned so much. Moreover, the Klansmen blamed Breck for Loretta's earning power. "He ain't never helped no white girl git that kind'a money!"

Vernon's first reaction to the newscast was surprise. The TV reporter and cameraman had worked three hours with him. He had gone with them to the courthouse square so that while he talked they could photograph him with the angry crowd as a background. They had assured him that he would appear tonight. Why had they wasted their time? Why had they lied to him? He didn't know that out of every ten men who are photographed for TV, only one may appear: and reporters and cameramen don't decide which one. Recovering from his surprise, Vernon got mad. He had been shamed before his wife, his peers and his Kluxers. He told his guests: "I should'a remembered what our governor always says. The TV won't ever do nothing to make Alabama look good. They do everything they can to make Alabama look bad." Then Vernon answered Hardy's call, and he kept answering calls until he told his Kluxers to pass the word that they would meet secretly in the woods back of the Cane Creek Church at 9 P.M.

Clay Wilbanks said to his partner: "That broadcast can't mean anything but more trouble. Let's go."

The partner said: "Shouldn't we wait for the warrant for Loretta's arrest? Without it what can we do? We can't arrest anybody. We're not bodyguards."

"We can do some more investigating," said Wilbanks.

Charles Peck said after the newscast: "Tonight, folks, instead of presenting the struggle for first-class citizenship, we have shown you how Old Massa is still protecting his good niggers from Ku Klux, so they can all go to Hebben together on that Great Gittin'-Up Mawning."

"Somebody in New York should have killed that story," said Josh Franklin. "It can't help the Movement. Look how that reporter was discouraged by Stancill. Until now he has supported us. Then he meets Stancill. What happens? He comes down from the mountain saying that the struggle in the courthouse square will end in meaningless victory. How will that affect Senator Dirksen?"

Peck replied: "It'll give Dirksen another excuse to say legislation can't change the human heart. But note this. Stancill accused us of provoking the rape of Loretta. Now he's doing the provoking. The Kluxers have been wanting to castrate you and me. Now they want to castrate him."

"That would be a useless diversion," said Josh. "Even if Stancill provokes violence, he can't be helpful. Because he wants too little. The essential conflict is between the Movement and the Power Structure, not between Stancill and the Klan. The Movement demands freedom now for black men. Stancill asks only pity for Old Black Joe."

"If you listen close you'll hear him asking for more than that," said Peck. "He's also asking for a fair shake for Old Black Joe's grandchillun. You don't understand Stancill, Josh. You're an outsider and a liberal. He and I are Southerners and conservatives. I like a conservative who really likes Negroes better than I like a liberal who tries to like Negroes."

Loretta knew that the newscast raised the odds against her survival. She wished she could run. But she looked at the withered face on the pillow and thought: There is the only creature who has ever loved me. How could I live with myself if I ran before she died?

When the newscast ended, Nancy said bitterly: "That's what I call sicking the dogs on a man! TV added up all your sins, Breck, from your great-grandfather down to me, and showed the Kluxers that you are their number-one enemy. Now they must try to hurt you again!"

"Don't worry," said Breck, preparing to leave. "Just blow the whistle if you see or hear anything."

"Will you come back . . . to me . . . like last night?"

"If I can."

Breck walked toward his house and thought: Now I suppose they must try to do more than shoot my dog. If they could have whipped or shot an outside agitator, shooting my dog might have satisfied my account with them. Or if my opposition to them had not been publicized, perhaps they could have restrained themselves, or been restrained by Hardy, Vernon or Big Track. But now they know that outsiders know that I oppose them. So they probably can't restrain themselves, or be restrained by Hardy, Vernon or Big Track.

As he ate supper Breck thought: How, where and when are they likely to strike? If they hate me enough to ambush me in daylight, there is no defense. So I can forget that: if it comes it comes. They may try to fire my house or barn and shoot me as I run out. So I must stay outside, hiding, watching for them, hoping to drive them off without having to kill one of them. They may fire my forest. That's easy to do, but unlikely. Hardy and Vernon will issue orders against forest fire. They may attack any or all of forty-one other dwellings, stretched along two miles of winding road. Each group of two or three dwellings stands in a clearing, with woods less than a hundred yards away. In a few seconds a Kluxer can run out of the woods, fire or dynamite a dwelling, and run back into the woods. Their weapons will be shotguns, dynamite and fire bottles. Anybody can make and use a fire bottle. Fill a bottle with gasoline and insert a rag for a wick. Cork the bottle with pine needles. Light the wick, smash the bottle against a shack, and occupants must run for their lives.

I'll operate on these assumptions, thought Breck. They'll come afoot, not in cars. They know I can patrol the road, so they will avoid the road and attack from the woods. They know I can move fast only if I'm in the truck or on the horse. Therefore they will assume that I can't surprise them: that they can see or hear me coming, since a horse can't move quietly through woods. So they will come at night, stealthily, through the woods.

Breck went to the barn, saddled the horse, and put him in the trailer. He hooked the trailer to the truck. In the truck he placed the carbine, a pistol, an automatic shotgun, a searchlight, a blanket, a thermos of coffee and a bottle of whiskey. He drove down the road, past the shacks, to a point near his south property line. There he backed the truck into the woods, unhooked the trailer, and took the horse out and tied him to a tree. Then, in the truck, Breck went to Loretta's shack and picked up the recorder and the tapes on which she had recorded her story. He put the recorder in the back of the truck and locked the tapes in the glove compartment.

Breck told Loretta: "If a car comes up the mountain tonight with its lights on, I think we can assume it's friendly. So don't blow the whistle. Watch for men on foot coming out of the woods. The moon will be up by ten. If they come before ten, they may be using flashlights and you can see them. If they come after ten, you can see them in the moonlight. If you see such men, blow the whistle, then lie down on the floor. The whistle alone may scare them off. If it doesn't, I'll be here before they can hurt you."

Breck drove back to where the horse was tied. He positioned the truck so that it could not be seen from the road. Sitting in the truck he could look off and down for a mile and see the lights of cars on the highway. He could see the lights of any car that turned off the highway and either stopped or continued up the mountain road. The truck stood about three hundred yards south of Loretta's shack. Behind the truck, and also hidden, was the horse. At intervals during the night Breck planned to mount the horse and ride through the woods, stopping frequently, listening for walking men. He would return to the truck to rest, listen and watch.

A few minutes after eight Breck saw car lights leave the highway and start up the mountain. With the searchlight and shotgun he walked out to the road. As the car approached him, he threw the light on it and recognized Hardy Riddle's Thunderbird. Hardy stopped and cut off his engine. "Get in, Breck, and let's talk," he said. Breck walked around the car and got in.

"This is goddam nonsense!" said Hardy. "A man like you having to guard your property!"

"Yes, it's hard to believe," said Breck. "It disgusts me."

"We've got to stop it."

"Just tell me how."

"Well, first," said Hardy, "how did that TV show come about? Surely you didn't encourage it?"

"I tried to prevent it. When I found I couldn't, I gave them pictures that were less inflammatory than the ones they already had."

"It came at a bad time. Vernon thought he'd be the show tonight. He had ordered his Kluxers to watch, and he was giving a party. Then the TV ignored him, and the Kluxers heard you call them trash before the whole country!"

"Surely Vernon can understand that I didn't want to be on TV."

"Maybe we can make him understand," said Hardy. "But a Grand Cyclops who has just been ignored doesn't understand easy."

"You can make him understand. You have influence with Kluxers."

"I may have influence but not control. I'm not responsible for what they do."

"Aren't you? An organized Klan is in this county because you thought it might be a useful adjunct to police power. Doesn't that make you responsible?"

"Let's not revive old arguments, Breck. I'm here to help you."

"All right, tell me how to get a night's sleep."

"Well, obviously," said Hardy, "I must pass some words. I must cool the Kluxers off so they won't bother you. The question is: What words do I pass?"

"Tell them to disband. Tell them that in 1962 you thought they might prove useful against outsiders. But by 1965, when the outsiders arrived, you had decided not to use Klansmen to disperse them. Instead you used your police to protect the demonstrators from your Klansmen. Tell your Klansmen that if they don't disband your police will arrest them as criminals."

"Don't waste time," said Hardy. "Be practical."

"Then tell your Klansmen to file their complaints against me in court."

"You haven't broken any law."

"Then why am I guarding my property?"

"You know why," said Hardy. "Because you're a Stancill. The rest of us try to get along. You have to live against the grain. You want poor white men to tolerate you when you take the Negro's part against them. You want a Kluxer to let you sleep when he knows that you despise him for being a Kluxer. Now cool off and help me figure out what word I can pass that will relieve a killing situation between you and the Klan. You want to orphan some ragged-assed kids tonight?"

"No," said Breck. "So I suggest that I go with you now. Call the Kluxers together. You can stand with me while I answer their complaints. If they want to hide their faces, tell them to wear their masks."

That suggestion surprised Hardy. He said: "What the hell would you say to them? Would you ask their forgiveness for calling their Great Governor a piss-ant? For jerking down Klan doctrine as posted by Butt Cut? For letting nigger relief-hounds gobble up public money? For sheltering the likes of Nancy and Loretta? Would you promise to run them niggers north, vote for Wallace, and purchase a sixteen-millimeter print of *Birth of a Nation?*"

"I'd listen to them. I'd tell them how I feel. I'd ask them to tolerate me so that we don't have to kill one another."

"You'd make it worse," said Hardy. "Hell, you might get us both castrated. Between you and me I may have made a mistake when I let the Klan come in here. But I didn't know what was coming. Wallace was yelling that he'd stand in schoolhouse doors. Bull Connor was repelling invaders at the state line. I thought we might need a Klan to keep out agitators and union organizers. Maybe I was wrong. But at least I've kept this Klan from committing any serious crime. And that's why I'm here right now, trying to relieve this killing situation between you and the Klan. Come on, help me!"

In saying that the Klan had committed no serious crime, Hardy was testing Breck. He wanted to see if Breck would accuse the Klan of raping Loretta and thereby accuse Big Track of complicity. Such an accusation would worsen the killing situation between Breck and the Klan and would precipitate a killing situation between Breck and Big Track. Hardy remembered Big Track saying on Sunday night: *If Breck ever learns the truth about the rape, I figure he'll see that nobody else learns it. I know Breck Stancill purty well. Sure, he hates Ku Klux. But Breck knows how far'ta go. He knows what a killin' situation is. And he don't want'ta have'ta kill nobody, and he don't want nobody'ta have'ta kill him. He's laid by in the killin' business. So I figure when Breck eases up close'ta a killin' situation, he's bound'ta back off and live and let live.* Now Hardy was deciding if Big Track's judgment was correct.

Breck passed the test. He didn't mention the rape. He said only: "I don't see how I can help you, Hardy. You've rejected every suggestion I've made. How do you think I can help?"

Hardy breathed easier. He was convinced that Breck would never make an issue of the rape, and that he would back off from every killing situation. So Hardy said: "Here's how you can help. I'll go and pass the word that you want to get along. That you acknowledge the South's debt to the Christians and patriots in the Klan. That by next Saturday night Loretta and Nancy will be gone. That tomorrow afternoon Big Track will serve your eviction notices on the relief-hounds. That come May 15, 1965, Stancill's Mountain will at last be clear of troublemakers. That's how you can help."

"You think I'll agree to that?" asked Breck.

"I'm not asking you to agree. I'll do the talking. You stay here and say nothing. Then next week, when the demonstrators and the cameras are gone and the county is peaceful, you start trying to cooperate. Loretta will be leaving anyhow. Nancy should never have stayed here after Willie blacksnaked her. She's a burden Doc shifted onto you. And it's no sin to evict Negroes. I do it. Somebody has to think of the good of the county."

When Breck said nothing Hardy continued: "Now, Breck, go home and go to bed. I'll keep the peace. Just remember this! You've been on TV now, so a lot of meddlers will be trying to get in touch with you. If you make me out a liar, then the blood's on your head. If you orphan any ragged-assed kids, you'll be to blame. Not me. It'll be that blind Stancill stubbornness that causes the blood to flow and the fires to burn."

Breck said: "Hardy, if I agree to stand mute while you do all this talking, will you have Big Track find two men who are not Klansmen and deputize them to guard my Negro shacks tonight?"

Hardy was puzzled. "I don't get what you mean," he said. "You don't need guards. Nobody is coming up here."

"Here's what I mean," said Breck. "Because of the threat of Federal intervention, you are now having your police protect the outside demonstrators against your Klansmen. If you don't protect the outsiders, the Federal Government will, so you reluctantly provide protection to keep out the federals. Why not do as much for peaceful citizens of this county? When you send word to your Klansmen tonight, why not tell them that if they go to Stancill's Mountain with guns they will be arrested by sheriff's deputies for armed trespass against the peace and dignity of Atoka County?"

"That doesn't make sense," said Hardy. "To keep Klansmen from attacking you I need to calm them, not inflame them. And Big Track couldn't find men who would be willing to be deputized to guard Negro shacks against the Klan. I'm already hurting Track by making him guard the demonstrators against Klansmen. If I also force him to guard your Negroes against Klansmen, I'll cut his political throat."

"Why can't he find men to serve as deputies against the Klan?"

"Because they are afraid to."

"That saddens me," said Breck. "Men are afraid to oppose the Klan because they know the police are Klansmen. Jurors know this and are afraid to convict Klansmen. So we have a Klan-ridden society. Forty criminals dominating sixteen thousand so-called free people! Doesn't that sadden you, Hardy?"

"No, it doesn't sadden me," said Hardy. "I'm not a sad man like you are. I'm a practical man. A builder. I don't think of Klansmen as criminals."

"But they are! A Klan's reason for being is to threaten use of illegal force. So a Klan's existence is a crime."

"I won't argue with you any longer," said Hardy. "You leave the Klan to me. You go home and read your books."

"Then let me make one more request," said Breck. "Since Stancill's Mountain won't have legal protection, I want you to tell your Kluxers that if they come up here they must kill me or be killed. A one-legged man can't afford to fire warning shots at armed trespassers in the woods at night. They have too many advantages. So I must kill them on sight. Tell them that, Hardy."

"I won't tell them that," said Hardy. "I can't calm them if you threaten them. Nobody is coming up here. And even if a man got drunk and came up here, you wouldn't kill him for just setting fire to a worthless shack. You're not that heartless."

After Breck got out of the car, he said: "Hardy, why shouldn't your Kluxers come up here and celebrate? You'll tell them they've won a victory over me. So they are right and I'm wrong. They are good; I'm evil. They don't fear the law. They feel, as you do, that they don't have to fear me. So why shouldn't your good Christians and patriots celebrate victory by burning out a few Negroes and watching them run?"

"Here's why," said Hardy. "Half of them work for me. The others work for men who borrow money at my bank. When I speak they listen."

"I hope they do," said Breck.

While Breck and Hardy were talking in the Thunderbird, Big Track and Allen Bascomb were in the Wildcat on their way to Stancill's Mountain. "The way I see it, Dad," said Allen, "when I began pulling down Butt Cut's clippings I involved myself in the conflict between Breck and the Klan. The demonstrations plus tonight's TV broadcast have caused that conflict to become a killing situation. And if I don't stand with Breck against the Klan now, then I don't deserve to go to West Point."

"You're tryin'ta take too much on yo'self, son," said Big Track. "You ain't of age yet."

"I'm old enough to enlist in the Marines," said Allen. "Half the Americans who died on Iwo Jima hadn't reached their eighteenth birthdays. So I'm old enough to fight the Klan."

Big Track chewed hard on his cigar. He felt uncertain and afraid. Frustrated and damaged by the demonstrations, he now had to face this situation between Breck and the Klan. What could he do? Klansmen didn't fear him: he was one of them. He couldn't arrest them: he was sworn to protect them. Yet Allen was determined to help Breck; and Maybelle, after viewing the telecast, was saying that their only hope was to stop the conflict.

"If you fight the Klan, son," said Big Track, "you won't get appointed to West Point. Our congressman ain't gonna make no appointments the Klan don't like."

"We're not dependent on our congressman," insisted Allen. "The President also appoints men to West Point. He admires men who fight Ku Klux. The son of Big Track Bascomb doesn't have to depend on how one little congressman acts."

Such talk by Allen made Big Track feel proud. It also made him feel uneasy. He thought: The boy just ain't learned yet what all a man's got to do to get along in this world. I hope he don't never have'ta learn. That's why I want him to go to West Point. He can start high up on the ladder and climb on up automatically. To get along and get ahead he won't never have'ta do things he don't like.

"I've been thinking some more about me and West Point," said Allen. "I'm not so sure I want to go. There's a big future for young men in pine trees in Alabama. I love the woods and animals, peace and quiet. I might want to live close to my family, and not travel so much, like a soldier does. So I might decide to go to the university and study forestry and be a tree farmer like Breck. What do you think about that, Dad?"

"I want'cha to go to West Point, son. I want'cha to get away from situations like the one we're facin' right now."

"You're not worried, are you?"

"No, I'm not much worried," said Big Track. "I figure we can head off a killing. There ain't nobody in the Klan that really wants'ta kill Breck, and he don't want to kill nobody. But I wish you wasn't so dead set on stayin' out here on the mountain. Your mama's gonna get mighty uneasy about you bein' up here all night."

"There's no reason for her to feel uneasy," said Allen. "You know that. I can move like a rabbit in the woods. Breck and I could stand off a hundred Ku Klux. And the three of us, Dad—you and I and Breck—I'll bet we could stand off all the Ku Klux in Alabama!"

"I guess we could, son," said Big Track. "But it ain't just a matter'a standin' 'em off. You got'ta not kill one. Killin' Ku Klux ain't like killin' gooks. Ku Klux are God-fearin' white men who figure they're in the right. Folks on the sidelines mostly figure the same way. No matter what a Ku Klux's doing, if you kill him folks'll say you was in the wrong."

"That's not right," said Allen. "Fifty good citizens should be out here now, standing up for Breck and calling the Ku Klux wrong. Then there wouldn't be any danger of anybody getting hurt."

"Well, it ain't gonna be that way. So I want you to be extra careful, son. Keep your head down. Don't let nobody get a shot at'cha. Don't shoot to kill nobody unless he's got'cha cornered and keeps coming."

As he approached the turn-off to the mountain, Big Track saw Hardy's Thunderbird turn into the highway from the mountain road. The two cars met but didn't stop. Big Track thought: Hardy's running to stop Vernon. The question will be: can Vernon stop the others? There'll be a few hotheads, and unless Vernon threatens 'em hard with Klan discipline they may try'ta do a little Kluxing on their own. Like they done with Breck's dog. I'll have'ta try'ta catch 'em before they get on Breck's land and talk 'em out of it.

When Breck flashed his light on the Wildcat, Big Track stopped and said: "I brought you a new recruit, Breck."

Breck looked inside the car and saw Allen and said: "I see you have. He looks like a good man to have with you in a fight. But I turned him down last night. I'll have to turn him down again."

"He says he won't take turnin' down," said Big Track. "Me and his mama tried to talk him out of it. But he says he's old enough to join the Marines so he's old enough to fight Ku Klux. He says he ain't gonna let you turn him down tonight."

Breck hesitated, then said: "Well, thanks, Al. I appreciate you wanting to help me. But what about it, Track? You know what I'm up against. Are you willing for him to stay?"

"I ain't gonna handcuff him to keep him from staying. I'm between a rock and a hard place. I want'a help you but I can't stay up here all the time myself. I got'ta try'ta catch these hotheads and talk 'em out'a coming up here. Looks like you and Al could sort'a guard each other, and lie low, and not get hurt, and not hurt nobody, till we get this county quieted down again."

"Well, if Al's going to stay," said Breck, "I want you and him both to hear from me just what the situation is. Hardy has just left here, going back to pass the word that I'm willing to do much of what the Kluxers want me to do. So Hardy, Vernon and you, Track, will all be trying to stop them. If all of you fail, then I must try to intercept them here in the woods. What they'll do when I try to turn them back, I don't know. Maybe they'll run. Maybe they'll scatter and try to surround me and kill me. There are men in the Klan who know this mountain almost as well as I do. They work in the company's woods gangs, and they have cut timber up here many times. They know every foot path, logging road and firebreak. They are tough, experienced woodsmen. If they come up here, nobody can predict how such tough, likkered-up, nigger-hating white men will act in the woods at night when they are Kluxing, when they think they have the law with them, and when they think they are standing up for God, Alabama, and the Southern way of life. So, Track, I can't guarantee Allen's safety. I want you and him both to understand that. I want you to tell Maybelle."

"Hell, I understand it, Breck," said Big Track. "Allen thinks he does. He don't. But if he's gonna be a soldier he has to start learning how not'ta get killed in the woods at night."

When Big Track was gone, Breck showed Allen where the truck and horse were hidden. Then, leaving the horse, Breck and Allen got in the truck and headed for Breck's house. As they drove past the blacked-out Negro shacks, Breck said: "Now that there are two of us, we can guard more of the perimeter. The sector most likely to be attacked is the southern sector, where the horse is. That sector is nearest the highway. Men can reach its Negro shacks by walking less than a mile. Loretta is in that sector. So I'll guard it. The second most likely sector to be attacked is the northern sector. My house, of course, is there, as is the house where you once lived and where Nancy now lives. That's the sector you know best, Al, so you can guard it. To attack it they would have to walk at least two miles through the woods, and much of the sector is bluffs which they wouldn't try to climb at night."

"You're giving me the safest sector," Allen said.

"Who knows?" said Breck. "It may be the most dangerous sector. My house or barn could be their objective."

Breck explained the whistles, where three of them were placed, and how he hoped the whistles alone might cause the Kluxers to retreat. "I have a whistle for you, too, Al," he said. "We'll get some blankets for you out of the house, and coffee, and the shotgun you like to use. You mustn't spend any time in the house because it could be a trap. You find a spot in the woods for your blankets and coffee and extra ammunition. Then you move around, watching, listening. Carry the whistle with you, and if you see anything, set it off. Run away from the whistle the instant you set it off because it may draw fire. When I hear your whistle, I'll come to help you."

"What'll I do if I hear a whistle or gunfire in your sector?" asked Allen.

"Stay where you are. If you ran to help me, I might mistake you for one of them. You can recognize me because I'll be on the horse or in the truck. Even if I'm afoot you can recognize me by the way I move. But I couldn't recognize you. So you must stand fast and be alert."

"Suppose," said Allen, "that I see a man running toward your house or Nancy's house or a Negro shack with a fire bottle? Do I shoot to kill him?"

"No," said Breck firmly. "Shoot over his head. Holler at him. Threaten him. But don't kill him."

"You mean that I've got to watch a Kluxer burn down your house and I'm not to kill him?"

"Yes, I mean that," said Breck. "You're not to kill any man unless he's trying to kill you and you can't run off. If any other sort of killing has to be done, I'll do it. You're what the Marines call a 'point man.' Your job is to watch and listen, to sound an alarm, to fire warning shots and then run. You're an all-state halfback. You can outrun any Ku Klux in the county. So you run!"

At 8:45 P.M. a Ku Klux informer telephoned a message into the Birmingham office of the FBI. It was: *10:30 tonight.* So at 10:25 Clay Wilbanks got out of a Hertz Chevrolet on the highway west of Ellenton. The Chevrolet raced off; and Wilbanks faded into the woods. At 10:30 he saw an approaching car blink its lights twice. He stepped out onto the highway and was picked up by the driver of a 1961 Ford.

"There was a meetin' tonight," said the informer. "In the woods back'a Cane Creek Church. It's just over."

"How many men?" asked Wilbanks.

"About forty. They come in nine'a ten cars. The cars was hid in the woods, and guards was staked out."

"What went on?"

"Vernon was late gittin' there. He said nine o'clock but it was mighty nigh nine-thirty when he showed up. So there was a lot'a jawin' about Breck Stancill and the TV and how Breck had'ta be tended to. The preacher quieten'd 'em down and said Breck ought'a be let alone if he'd run his niggers and his two cunts off. The nigger cunt agitator and the white cunt that Old Willie put the blacksnake to."

"What'd Vernon say?"

"He tried'ta put his foot down against action. He said he'd just had word that Breck'd run his niggers and cunts off this week."

"Did the men believe that?"

"Some did, some didn't. Some said that anyway Breck's niggers ought'a be burnt out so's other niggers'd git the message and haul ass for Chicago. There was a lot'a jawin' and yellin' that 'we want'a Klux,' and Vernon kept puttin' his foot down."

"Are they going to follow Vernon's order?"

"Naw, they ain't. Not all of 'em. Most of 'em's down at Awful Annie's now gittin' ass at the company's expense. Most of 'em'll go on home. But a few of 'em—I figure about six or seven—is gonna go Kluxing. Fer ya'see Vernon never did git around'ta orderin' 'em not'ta go. He told 'em not'ta go. He told 'em hard. But he didn't threaten nobody with a Klan whipping if they went. Then he talked about the big meetin' that's coming up Saturday night. He told everybody'ta be there and'ta bring all his family and friends. Then him and the preacher got in his car and drove off."

"And you think six or seven will go to the mountain tonight?"

"I'd bet my bottom dollar on it. They got hards on'ta singe black asses. Free ass at Annie's ain't gonna satisfy 'em."

Clay Wilbanks paid the informer, got out of the car, and was picked up by his partner. The two agents weighed the information.

"Well," said Wilbanks, "we could go tell Breck that Kluxers may be coming. But he knows that. So there's no way we can help him."

"No way I can see," agreed the partner. "He needs police protection. We're not police. Only investigators."

"Yeah," said Wilbanks. "All we can do is wait till the shooting's over, then go count the bodies."

"If there's shooting, who'll get shot? Breck or the Kluxers?"

"Hard to say," replied Wilbanks. "Breck is handicapped by humanitarianism. He doesn't want to shoot them. They know it. That may get him killed. On the other hand, Breck was trained never to fire a warning shot and never to hesitate in a killing situation. So when he sees them coming after him with guns, he may react like an old Marine. He may shoot first and not quit shooting till they are all dead."

At 2 A.M. Breck began to feel that they were not coming. About 1 A.M. Big Track had come up on the mountain and reported that he could find no sign that they were coming. He had talked with some of them at Annie's; when they left Annie's he followed them; and they went home. At midnight Big Track had telephoned Hardy, and Hardy had said: "Tell Breck to go to bed. He's got nothing to worry about." After reporting to Breck, Big Track went back down the mountain, saying that he'd watch the roads for another hour, then go home.

Astride the palomino, Breck noticed that he seemed to be catching cold. The temperature had dropped to about 45, and he felt the chill through his tan corduroy hunting coat. He took off his hunting cap, pulled down the ear flaps, and replaced the cap snugly over his ears. He decided that once more he'd ride along the western slope of the mountain; then he'd take the truck and horse home, find Allen, and they'd quit watching and go to bed around three. Today was Thursday, and Kluxers, as well as he, would need to be at work at seven. Allen would need to be in school at eight.

As the horse picked his way along a firebreak in the moonlight, Breck thought of his peaceful years since 1946. Until 1964 no one disliked him. A few people talked about his not going to church, about his not having a wife, and about where he found his sexual comfort. But no one thought harshly of him. His associates always seemed glad to see him. He was liked at the American Legion Post, which he visited several times a year. He didn't participate prominently in politics, but he made no secret of his votes. He didn't like the Democratic Party because in Alabama its slogan was WHITE SUPREMACY. Many of its leaders were racist demagogues. In 1948 he voted for Thomas E. Dewey for President. He voted twice for General Eisenhower, and in 1960 he voted for Richard M. Nixon. He didn't vote in 1964. There was no contest in Alabama. The only candidates on the ballot were Wallace and Goldwater; and Wallace was supporting Goldwater.

For state and county candidates Breck voted in the Democratic primary which, in effect, was the election. In 1958 he voted for Wallace for governor. The Ku Klux Klan was being revived to enforce White Supremacy, and in 1958 the Klan supported Wallace's successful opponent. To vote against the Klan, Breck voted for Wallace. By 1962 Wallace was the Klan's candidate for governor; and by 1964 he was the Klan's candidate for President. In 1962 Breck voted against Wallace; in 1964 he publicly called Wallace a piss-ant. It was Breck's contempt for Wallace, along with his inherited contempt for the Klan, which made him the first personal enemies of his life.

Like all men who live on the land, Breck Stancill felt close to his forebears. The century and a half between 1815 and 1965 seemed scarcely more than a lifetime to him. He felt as close to his great-great-grandfather, Fowler Stancill, as if they had planted trees together or ridden together with General Jackson. He felt as close to his great-grandfather, Landers Stancill, as if they had stood together against the visionless men who led the South to ruin. The Stancills, from Fowler to Breck, were landed Americans who loved the Union; who regarded slavery and White Supremacy alike as economic and social evils to be ended, not perpetuated and romanticized; and who wanted the South to heed the wisdom of Jefferson,

Madison and Jackson, not the folly of Calhoun, Yancey and Wallace.

At the head of a draw Breck reined the horse into a clump of young trees and stopped. He pushed the flaps up off his ears and sat there listening, searching the slope. As he listened and watched, he found himself remembering his first killing situation. It was on a now-forgotten island in the Solomons. He was eighteen. He and two other Marines were manning an outpost. They were in a hole, partially covered, and the jungle was around them. Suddenly, not a hundred feet away, appeared two young women, naked, their hands high above their heads. They walked slowly toward Breck, begging in Japanese, saying that they were camp women, hungry, and they wanted to surrender. They were naked, not to be sexually attractive, but to show that they carried no grenades. They twisted their bodies to show that no grenades were plastered to their backs.

Breck hesitated to kill them. He had been ordered not to hesitate: the danger of concealed grenades was too great. But did the order apply to little, hungry, naked women, begging for mercy!

Breck shouted for them to halt, to lie down, to go away, but they didn't understand. They kept coming, and he kept hesitating. When they were within a few feet of him, he squeezed the trigger and the stream of steel reduced them to a writhing mess of blood, hair, guts and flesh on the jungle floor. Then Breck saw the four grenades. Around each middle finger was a ring. Behind each hand hung a grenade. Had he allowed the women to take one more step, with quick moves they could have pulled the pins and hurled the grenades into the hole.

Breck remembered how he vomited from the shock of that killing, and from realizing that his hesitation had almost cost two lives he was responsible for, along with his own. That experience helped him survive the war. He never hesitated again.

Now Breck heard the Klansmen coming. He heard them before he saw them. Then he saw them. Three men . . . coming up the rocky draw through a thin stand of trees. They were the length of a football field from him, walking briskly toward him. Each man had a shotgun in one hand and a carton for carrying bottles in the other. Fire bottles.

Breck looked for other men. He had thought the party

would be larger. Was it a divided attack? Were other men coming up the east slope? Or up the south road?

Breck's hands tightened on the 12-gauge automatic shot-gun. He eased off the safety lock. His left hand reached down the barrel and turned the polychoke to full choke, to reduce the spread of the buckshot and make the charge deadly at longer range.

As with the Japanese women, he would ask the men to turn back. Sixty yards from him they would cross a rock bed and be in unobstructed view. He would shout for them to stop, to turn back. If they hesitated, or broke for cover, firing at him, he would try to kill them. But first, in a last gamble to avoid killing, he would give away his advantage and risk an unequal fight.

In a soothing undertone he said to the horse: "Ho, Dan, steady." The horse was trained to gunfire. He wouldn't move. Breck looked down the gun barrel. At sixty yards the men would be twenty feet below his level, so he would adjust his aim for downhill shots.

Breck inhaled deeply to shout. Then he heard the whistle. The direction told him it was Loretta, and she was a mile away. Other men had come from the east or south and were attacking the shacks.

The three men heard the whistle, stopped, then began running, not back down the mountain as Breck had hoped, but up the mountain, to close the pincers.

Breck fired three shots—*pow! pow! pow!*—then wheeled the horse and started moving as fast as he could along the firebreak, through the woods. He assumed that the three men behind him were dead, or would be dead before help could reach them. He had fired at their belt buckles from fifty yards.

When he was half a mile from the southernmost shacks, Breck saw firelight. From a quarter of a mile he saw that three shacks, including Loretta's, were wrapped in flames. From two hundred yards he saw the silhouette of a man between him and the flames. From a hundred yards he saw the front door of Loretta's shack open and Loretta come through the doorway with her mother in her arms. At the same instant Breck saw the man raise a gun and fire two shots at Loretta. From the back of the running horse Breck fired three shots at the man and saw him go down.

When Breck rode into the yard and jumped off the horse,

Loretta and her mother were lying on the porch, their clothing afire. Breck dragged Loretta off the porch and carried her into the yard, beating out flames on her dress. He hurried back for her mother, but he couldn't reach her through the flames.

Breck was risking being shot by Klansmen he assumed were still in the area. His horse had run off, and he had thrown down his gun when he went for Loretta. Silhouetted against the flames, he was an easy target. But no shots were fired, and Breck's risk had been for nothing. Loretta was dead. The buckshot had struck her in the eyes and forehead, all but decapitating her. Her mother's body was being incinerated.

Retrieving his gun, Breck moved behind trees and circled the other burning shacks, looking for Kluxers. The five old Negroes who had occupied these shacks had lost all they had, but they were unhurt, and they were huddled together, wailing. When Breck found no more Kluxers, he returned to the man he had shot. He was still alive, with a curious expression of surprise on his youthful face.

"What's your name?" Breck asked. "I know your face, but I don't know your name."

As though he hadn't heard the question, Tag Taggart said: "What'd'jah shoot me fer? I wasn't shootin' at you. I was just . . ." Then he died, and Breck had orphaned his four ragged-assed kids and widowed his twenty-six-year-old wife.

Twenty-five minutes after Loretta blew the whistle, Allen Bascomb came galloping down the road on Breck's horse. He had disobeyed orders, left his post, and was running down the road to help Breck when he met the horse running home. "Gosh, Breck," said Allen, "when I saw Dan running loose I sure thought you'd been shot."

"Not tonight," said Breck. "Take the truck and drive back up the road. Tell everybody that the burning and shooting are over. And tell them what happened."

Thirty-five minutes after Loretta blew the whistle, Breck heard the rising-and-falling scream of a siren.

Big Track was coming.

Now begins worse trouble, thought Breck. The killing situation between me and Big Track.

HATTIE

AS BRECK WAITED for Big Track, the moon disappeared and left Stancill's Mountain in darkness. Illumination came only from a searchlight and from the embers of three shacks which had housed Negro-Americans for seventy years. In the embers of one shack the cancerous body of Susan Sykes was roasting, and Breck had moved upwind to avoid the stench. The bodies of Loretta and Tag lay in the yard, twenty feet apart. Tag's face was uncovered; Loretta's was covered by the blanket from Breck's truck. Five old Negroes, stunned, weeping and displaced, huddled together near Breck.

Big Track, his searchlights blazing and rotating, raced up to the scene and stopped, leaving all his lights on. He jumped out and shouted to Breck: "Is my boy all right?"

"He's not hurt," said Breck.

"Where is he?"

"Up the road in my pickup."

"Anybody else hurt?"

"They murdered Loretta and her mother." Breck motioned toward Tag's body. "There's one of them. I don't know his name."

Big Track walked over and threw his flashlight down into Tag's face. "It's Tag Taggart. A damn good boy."

"I suppose he's a Christian and a patriot? That he has a yard full of ragged-assed kids and a hard-working wife?"

"Yeah. Four kids and a good wife." Big Track walked toward the car. "I got'ta start calling."

"Before you call anybody," said Breck, "who told you there was trouble up here?"

"The Forest Service. They called me at home twenty minutes ago. I was just'a goin' to bed. They said they could see firelight up here. I come as fast as I could."

"Did you tell Hattie you were coming?"

"Yeah. She's standin' by."

"Has she called anybody yet?"

"Naw. She's waitin' for me'ta tell her."

"Then, first," said Breck, "I want her to call my lawyer in Tuscaloosa."

"I got'ta let her call Maybelle first. And let Maybelle know that—that you're all right. Then Hattie can make your call."

After Hattie had called Maybelle, Breck gave Hattie the lawyer's name and telephone number and said: "Ask him to come as fast as he can." While Hattie was making the call, Big Track said: "Breck, what'd'ya have'ta shoot Tag for?"

"He asked me that same question," said Breck. "Just before he died. He couldn't understand why I had shot him."

"Lot'ta folks ain't gonna understand. Tag was a good boy. Never been arrested in his life. If a man ain't breakin' in'ta'ya home in Alabama, or threatenin'ya with a knife or gun, the law don't give'ya no right'ta kill him."

When Breck said nothing, Big Track continued: "I don't see no evidence that you shot Tag. When there's shootin' in the woods at night, it's hard'ta tell who shot who. Nobody can say what buckshot come out'a what shotgun. I ain't'cha lawyer, Breck, but I'm'ya friend. You ain't shot nobody. Don't say'ya did."

Over the radio Hattie said: "Track, tell Mister Breck the lawyer's on his way. I got him out'a bed."

"Okay," said Big Track to Hattie. "You got'cha pencil? Make a list. There's been a little burnin'n'shootin' up here. Don't make it no bigger'n it is. Tag Taggart's dead. So's the nigger gal, Loretta. Same one the agitators raped. Three shacks been burned down. A sick nigger woman, Loretta's mother, didn't get out'a one of 'em. I'm proceedin' with the investigation. Call Hardy first. Then Butt Cut. Then the state troopers. Tell the troopers I'm gonna need extra men'ta help with the demonstrations in town and the inquest up here on the mountain. Call the coroner. Tell him'ta get up here and bring his hearse for Tag. Tell him'ta bring a nigger hearse, too. Call the district attorney. Yeah, git Trixie out'a bed and down there with'ya. The papers and the TV boys will be calling. Tell 'em there's been unlawful killin' and the sheriff and the coroner and the district attorney are tryin'ta figure out who shot who and why. I'll be standin' by."

While Big Track was talking, Allen arrived in the truck. When Big Track finished, he said: "Son, what'd'ya see or hear?"

"I was in the woods up close to Breck's house," said Allen.

"The first sound I heard was a whistle. Breck had told me about the whistles, and I thought the one that was blowing was at Loretta's house. Just after the whistle started blowing I heard shots. Then a second whistle started blowing, and a third, which was close to me. Then I saw the fire, and after four or five minutes I heard more shots. Breck had told me not to run toward any shots. But I was afraid he needed help so I ran anyway. I was running down the road when I met Prince Dan going home. I caught him and rode him down here. Breck was here with Loretta and the dead man. Breck told me to take the pickup, turn the lights on, and go back up the road and tell the Negroes and Nancy that it was all over. That's all I know."

"Okay," said Big Track. "You can't help this investigation. You don't know nothing. You just stay here at the car and handle the radio for me. We'll let folks think you come up here with me just now."

"What about the Negroes and Nancy?" asked Allen. "They'll say I was here before you got here."

"They won't say nothing. When there's shootin', no nigger ever sees or hears nothin'. Breck'll tell Nancy what to say. Won't'cha, Breck?"

"Yes," said Breck. "I see no reason why anyone should be told that Allen was up here during the shooting."

"Well, that just leaves you, Breck," said Big Track. "You was at home asleep when you heard whistles and shootin'. You jumped in your pickup and come runnin' down here and found three shacks afire and Tag and Loretta dead. That's all anybody knows. Agitators might'a come in here'ta burn out Loretta for sayin' they raped her. Tag might'a been trailin' the agitators. The agitators set the shacks afire and shot Tag and Loretta. That's how it looks'ta me. Looks like the investigation is about over."

"What about my horse?" asked Breck. "There he stands. If I ran down here in the pickup, how'd he get here?"

"Let's put the horse in his stable," snapped Big Track. "Al, you ride him and I'll follow and bring you back. Quick! Breck, you stay here and stop everybody till I git back."

Allen was running toward the horse when Breck barked: "No! Don't get on him, Al!" Then Breck lowered his voice and turned to Big Track. "We won't do that, Track," he said firmly. "I'm going to ride the horse right now, but not toward the stable."

"Where you goin'? You ain't supposed to leave the scene till the coroner gits here."

"I'm going to another part of the scene," said Breck. "Allen told you he heard shots immediately after the first whistle began blowing. I fired those shots. At three men. About a mile from here, on the west slope. I didn't observe the effect of the shots because I rushed back here and shot Tag while he was in the act of shooting Loretta. Until now I haven't had time to consider the men on the slope. They all may be dead. Or they may be alive and bleeding to death. If we hurry we may save them. I can't get there except on the horse. You can't get there except by walking. Let's go."

Big Track's jaw had dropped. "Good God, Breck! You mean you ambushed three good men?"

"It depends on how you look at it. Maybe I ambushed three good men. Maybe I protected lives and property from three criminals who were committing armed trespass with intent to commit arson and murder. Maybe Tag here was a good Christian patriot. Maybe he was a raping, burning, murdering criminal. No matter how you look at it, the crime committed here tonight can't be covered up. The time has come for uncovering. Then you and the coroner and the district attorney can decide whose acts were lawful and whose unlawful. Let's go."

Big Track didn't know what to do. He had never seen Breck act so hard and unreasonable. He didn't want to have to try to stand against Breck. Instead he wanted to continue to feel that Breck was standing behind him, ready to help him and his family, as Breck had done for eighteen years. "Now hold'ya horses, Breck," he said. "Let's don't do nothin' reckless. We can't leave here right now. We're waitin' for the coroner and the troopers and Butt Cut."

"Allen can receive all visitors."

"Yeah, but hell," said Big Track, "even if you and me found a wounded man in the woods in the dark, we couldn't bring him out. We need a basket and men'ta carry it."

"We can give first aid. You can bring a man out on the horse if you need to. Let's go." Breck walked to his horse and mounted him. Allen handed Breck the shotgun and a light. Then Hattie's voice came on the radio. "Track, the coroner and the troopers and Hardy are all on their way. But I can't locate Butt Cut. His wife says he ain't been home all night. Annie says he ain't down there."

"Oh, Lord!" Big Track groaned. "Did'ja hear that, Breck?"

"I figured Butt Cut was with them," said Breck. "If he came with Tag he got away. If he came up the west slope he may be dead."

"You mean'ya killed my deputy, too?"

"I may have. I fired once at each of three men at fifty yards."

"Then'ya killed 'em," said Big Track. "You ain't never missed nothin' as big as a man with that gun at fifty yards."

Big Track got a shotgun and a light from the Wildcat. He said to Allen: "Now, son, we ought'a be back in thirty minutes. If we need stretchers and stretcher bearers, we'll fire two quick pistol shots, then keep firing ever' few minutes, and throwin' up our lights, to lead help to us. You stay here at the radio and meet ever'body. And get this: *don't repeat nothin' that Breck said'ta nobody!* Just tell 'em all'ta stand by, that me and Breck's gone'ta investigate some more shots he thought he heard."

"I understand, Dad," Allen said.

Breck and Big Track moved off, Breck riding the horse at a walk, and Big Track walking behind.

As Breck and Big Track proceeded along the firebreak, through the woods, Big Track couldn't easily converse with Breck because Breck was on the horse ahead of him. Moreover, Big Track had to hold his light down and watch his step to keep from stumbling. So Big Track kept thinking: Why the hell didn't Breck git in bed like me and Hardy told him to? If he'd a just got in bed at 2 A.M., there wouldn't be no serious trouble now. They'd'a sneaked up here and set fire to a few worthless old shacks, then run on off. Hell, if Breck hadn't'a give fire whistles'ta these niggers, Tag'd'a never shot Loretta. I can see it all just as plain. When Tag set the shack afire, Loretta started that whistle'ta blowin' like a catamount a-screamin'. That scared Tag, and when he seen the gal coming out'a the shack he lost his head and raised up and shot her. So, goddam it, Breck's'ta blame for all the shootin'. He just wouldn't do what his friends begged him'ta do.

"Hold on a minute, Breck," Big Track called. "Stop a second and let me say something." Breck stopped the horse and Big Track caught up with him.

"Now, Breck," said Big Track, "we can still smooth this over. Nobody wants'ta accuse you'a killing nobody! Remember'ya Constitutional rights! When this shootin' was goin' on, you was at home asleep and tryin'ta git out'a bed and put'ya leg and'ya pants on. You didn't shoot Tag. And now me and you's goin' over here'ta see about some shots'ya thought'ya *heard!* If we find anybody dead over here, *you* didn't shoot 'em! They was shot by niggers or agitators or *persons unknown.* It's my Constitutional duty'ta keep remindin'ya of that. Have we got that straight?"

"I won't travel that road any farther with you, Track," Breck said coldly. "I helped you smooth over a Ku Klux rape. I did it because you didn't kill the victim and because I thought the surest way for her to get out of this county alive was to cooperate with you. Now she's lying in dirt with her head shot off, and I'm partially to blame for it. So are you. If you had arrested the rapists instead of covering up for them, there wouldn't have been any killing here tonight."

Big Track was stunned. "Good God, Breck!" he exclaimed slowly. "You're tryin'ya best'ta commit suicide! I'm tryin'ta save'ya life and what'ya got. For God's sake, keep'ya mouth shut till'ya lawyer gits here and tells'ya what'ta say."

"Come on," said Breck impatiently. "Let's find these men." The horse moved off, and Big Track again fell in behind. It was then that Big Track began to see that Breck could not be saved. Hell, they've got to kill him for killing Tag, he thought. They'll ambush him, and take this mountain for Tag's widow and orphans. And if Breck accuses them and me of the rape, they'll double-sure kill him.

Big Track asked himself: Since Breck's sure'ta be killed, why don't I kill him right now? With him dead the trouble'd all be over, and nobody'd never know who shot who. Big Track's right hand tightened on his shotgun. Then he said to himself: I couldn't never do it. I just couldn't shoot Breck off'a that horse. I ain't got it in me.

When Breck found the spot from which he had fired at the men, he and Big Track moved forward with their lights, searching for bodies. What the lights uncovered looked like a concrete floor on which three hogs have had their throats cut. The three men, one of whom was Butt Cut, were dead. They had died hard, their guts torn with buckshot. Because they had fallen on an expansive, flat rock, their blood, their gut fluids, and the gasoline from their fire bottles had not disappeared into the ground, but had collected in shallow pools into which the bodies had thrashed in protracted agonies. The

forms were scarcely recognizable as men, so smeared were
they with blood, gasoline, and gut contents.

Big Track took off his hat. "Lord God Almighty!" he
groaned. "I ain't seen a human mess like that since *Korea*."

Breck did not take off his cap. "I remember a mess like it,"
he said. "When I cut two naked Japanese women in two.
They had long hair, and it got mixed in with the blood and
guts."

"Pore old Butt Cut!" said Big Track. "He hated for you'ta
belittle him, Breck. Now you *really* belittled him! You tore his
guts out and let him die kickin'n'floppin'. He sho' is a mess."

"It's hard to stop men with buckshot and not make a
mess," said Breck. "Who are the other two?"

"Coupl'a boys who work for the company. This'n's a truck
driver. That'n's a trimmer. Damn good boys. Never been arrested in their lives."

"More widows and orphans?"

"Yeah. You done run'ya score up'ta four widows and a doz-
en or more ragged-assed orphans."

After a moment Breck said: "Well, fire some shots. Let's
get the coroner and the others in here so they can look and
clean up."

"Before anybody else looks," said Big Track, "I'm gonna
tell'ya one more time. Nobody who sees this sight is ever gonna excuse the man who done it. So *you* didn't do it! *You*
didn't shoot nobody. You just *heard* shootin' goin' on. And
don't you never tell nobody nothin' different! You understand?"

"I understand what you're saying."

"You goddam better understand! Because if you done this,
by God there ain't no way'ta keep you out'a jail, or keep you
alive, and there ain't no way'ta keep this mountain from bein'
divided between all them widows and orphans and their
lawyers."

Big Track pulled out his automatic pistol and fired two
shots into the air.

At 9 A.M. on Thursday, six and one-half hours after the
shooting, a Gallup poll would have shown that 99 per cent of
Atoka County's 11,642 white citizens knew that "the most
awful crime in the history of the county" had been committed. *What was this crime?* Murder. The murder of Sheriff's
Deputy Butt Cut Cates and three good men who were trying
to help him enforce the law against agitators and outsiders.

The four had been "ambushed" or "bushwhacked" and "murdered" or "butchered" or "massacreed" on Stancill's Mountain.

Who were the criminals? Some white citizens would have answered they didn't know. All others would have answered: "Agitators, outsiders and niggers."

Was anyone else killed? About half the whites would have remembered hearing that two Negro females were also killed by the agitators, and that one of them was "that nigger gal the agitators raped last Sunday night."

Was any other crime committed? Most whites would have answered no. A few would have remembered hearing that "two or three old nigger shacks was burned down by agitators."

Was Breck Stancill involved? Not one citizen would openly have accused Breck. The few who hated him were afraid to accuse him openly, and the many who either liked him or did not dislike him were incapable of believing that he could commit "the most awful crime in the history of the county." He was no outsider or agitator or bushwhacker. "He wouldn't'a had no cause'ta kill."

Was the Ku Klux Klan involved? Not one citizen would have said yes. How could the Klan have been involved? The conflict was between the law and the agitators.

But what about last evening's telecast? It reported a conflict between Breck Stancill and the Klan. Wasn't the awful crime a result of that conflict? No white citizen would have answered yes. To do so would have been to "accuse somebody."

By 9 A.M. about three hundred white citizens of Atoka County were on Stancill's Mountain. Many of them were high school boys because at 6:30 A.M. the county superintendent of education had announced over radio that "due to the tension" all schools would be closed for the day. Several citizens had helped carry bodies in wire baskets. Scores had visited the roped-off "Bloody Rock" and seen where the deputy and two other men were butchered. Others had watched the Negro undertaker recover a charred body from ashes. Newspaper reporters, TV cameramen, state troopers and FBI men were "all over" the mountain.

In Ellenton there were no demonstrators. Josh Franklin and Charles Peck, at their motel in Tuscaloosa, had decided to suspend activities, at least for a day. But in the courthouse and around the square men gathered to talk and wait. Others assembled at the funeral homes where state toxicologists were performing autopsies, and still others congregated at the four-room houses on the edge of town where the widows and or-phans were.

Everybody was waiting for the coroner's inquest, to be held "at the scene" at 10 A.M.

At Breck's home, since 6 A.M., two Negro women had been serving coffee and cake to men who came and went and some-times, stayed to talk in twos and threes, in the living room, in Breck's bedroom, on the porch, in the yard, or in the cars. Among the men were Dr. Parker, Big Track, Hardy Riddle, the coroner, the district attorney, the county judge, two FBI men, TV cameramen, reporters, and a distinguished-looking old man who resembled General Eisenhower and who ap-peared to be known and respected by all. He was Upshur Allgood, Breck's lawyer from Tuscaloosa. All good lawyers had been advising the Stancills since long before the Civil War.

Upshur Allgood defended life, liberty and property. He therefore, disliked courtrooms. He measured his success by how few times in a long career he had been inside a court-room. "Courtrooms," he said, "are dusty, foul-smelling, poor-ly ventilated chambers in which men of property invariably sustain loss. If the goddess of justice inhabits courtrooms, she is a sloven. So the objective, always, must be to avoid court-rooms." His equals and contemporaries called Upshur All-good "Up." All others, including Breck, called him "Mister Up."

Mister Up, in a blue Lincoln Continental driven by his Ne-gro chauffeur-valet, had reached the mountain about 4.30 A.M. Despite his seventy-odd years, he had inspected both scenes of crime, and by six had installed himself in Breck's living room. On his stern advice Breck slept between six and seven-thirty, then bathed, shaved, put on clean khakis and ate breakfast, while Mister Up received everybody and conferred with Big Track, Hardy, the coroner and the district attorney. At nine Mister Up ordered the "darkies" to bring more coffee, cake and whiskey for all visitors, then went into Breck's bedroom. He sat in the only comfortable chair, and Breck sat on the bed.

"Breck," he said, "we are all agreed as to prudent proce-dure. Do you know what a coroner's inquest is?"

"Generally, yes," said Breck. "Specifically, no. I've never attended one."

"It's the elementary inquiry into a homicide . . . a man-slaying . . . the killing of one human being by another. Homicide is either justifiable or felonious, lawful or unlawful. Usually at the scene of the killing, the coroner selects a jury of what Alabama law calls 'six discreet householders.' They have subpoena power. They hear evidence from the police, from a doctor, from any other persons they choose to call, then they rule whether the homicide was lawful or unlawful. They report their ruling to the district attorney. If the ruling is unlawful homicide, and if there is a suspect, the district attorney obtains a warrant. The suspect is arrested and held for a preliminary hearing before a judge, to determine if he is to be allowed freedom on bond until a grand jury meets and either indicts him for murder or manslaughter, or declines to indict him."

"I understand, sir," said Breck.

"In a few minutes," said Mister Up, "we shall attend such an inquest. Your coroner, as you know, is himself a 'discreet householder.' He's an undertaker, and Hardy Riddle's bank holds the mortgage on his new funeral home. So we shall have discreet jurors for this public inquest which will be watched by TV cameramen."

"Will I be questioned?"

Mister Up pursed his lips and answered deliberately. "No. We shall be present, but the jury will question only the sheriff and Dr. Parker. The sheriff will report that you heard shots and saw fire. He'll describe how bodies were found by you and him. He'll state that the criminals are presently unknown to him. The jury will rule that arson and unlawful homicide were committed by persons unknown."

Breck asked: "Will the slayer of Loretta Sykes be named by the sheriff and the jury?"

"No. These jurors will not want to brand the dead men as criminals. Nor will the sheriff. One of the dead men was the sheriff's deputy. The others were well-regarded, and they leave widows and orphans. These jurors will want to rule only that the criminal acts were committed by persons unknown."

"What about Tag Taggart's shotgun, lying beside him with two empty shells in it?"

"Who can tell the jury with certainty what Tag fired at? Or even that he fired at all?"

"I saw him fire at Loretta."

"But you won't be questioned."

"What about the fire bottles dropped from the hands of the men on Bloody Rock?"

"Those bottles could have been placed there by the killers. The deputy could have been searching for suspected criminals. Would you like to try to convince a jury in this county, beyond their reasonable doubt, that the respected law enforcement officer you slew on Bloody Rock was intent on committing arson and murder?"

"Do you mean," said Breck, "that at this inquest no mention is to be made of the Ku Klux Klan?"

Mister Up raised his hands as if to quiet a multitude. "Now, Breck," he said, "let's converse calmly. At my age I didn't rush over here in the grim hours before dawn to cure the ills of mankind. I came to protect the life, liberty and property of Breckenridge Stancill. Your life is valuable. The law holds that the life of a man of forty-one is more valuable than that of a man of fifty-one, much more valuable than that of a man of my seventy-three years. Your liberty is precious. And while you are by no means rich, you do have a net worth in excess of three hundred thousand dollars; and even in to-day's emaciated dollars that's a sum which merits protection. With the legal authorities of this county I have devised a plan to protect you. I am explaining the plan and urging you to follow it."

"But Mister Up," said Breck, "if the men I killed are not to be called criminals, then I'm a criminal. Can't I be sued by survivors who charge that I unlawfully killed their husbands and fathers?"

"Our motions to throw such suits out of court would be granted."

"Then here is another question. If the men who came up here last night with guns and fire bottles, and who murdered two innocent women, if they are not to be called criminals by the legal authorities of this county, why shouldn't other such men come up here tonight?"

"We've thought of that," answered Mister Up. "Hardy Riddle has made a generous proposal. This afternoon I will advise you to sign an agreement with the Atoka Lumber Company, leasing your land and all your equipment to them for one year. Hardy's wife will move your horse into her pasture and cherish him. She'll look after your home. After we have signed the lease, you will ride with me to Tuscaloosa where you will board an airplane for California, to visit your sisters. Maybe you'll want to visit old and new battlefields in the Pacific."

"What about Nancy Poteet?"

"She's packing now. This afternoon Dr. Parker will move her to a motel in Tuscaloosa. She will be resettled safely and helped. The doctor says she has completely recovered from her traumatic experience. She'll now be able to find a new husband. For her to stay up here any longer would only handicap her."

"And the Negroes?"

"The company will protect them and be generous—for thirty days. The darkies must go, Breck. They are now the responsibility of a Great Society. You haven't done them any favor by making it easy for them to stay here. You got two of them killed."

Breck lowered his face into his hands and rubbed his temples. Mister Up moved to consolidate his victory. "Now, Breck," he said, "any course other than what I advise is without hope. If you speak out at this inquest, you will gravely jeopardize your property, your liberty, even your life, and you will accomplish nothing. I need not remind you that this scene between us has been played before. You Stancills have been intractable clients for us Allgoods. My great-grandfather urged your great-grandfather not to speak out against secession. My grandfather urged your grandfather not to commit murder, but he murdered six men for murdering his father. Your father defied my father and me and lived his life as a wastrel, lusting after wars and whores. You volunteered for the Marine Corps after I had arranged for you to go to the university and serve your country in a less violent capacity. And last night you eviscerated four men whom you could have avoided or over whose heads you might have fired. The girl was already dead when you killed Taggart. So now you *must* listen to me! You *must* not destroy yourself for *nothing!*"

Breck removed his hands from his face and said: "Mister Up, you are giving me exactly the same advice that Big Track gave me before you arrived."

"That doesn't surprise me," said Mister Up. "Your sheriff is an admirable man. He has made the most of his opportunities and adjusted well to his environment. You should have listened to him sooner."

"He's a goddam Klansman, sworn to cover up for the s'nuvabitches!"

"Well, that's not original sin. He's not the first Alabama public servant to place a fat paw on a Bible and swear allegiance to the Invisible Empire. Alabama's contribution to the Supreme Court of the United States swore the same oath. Myself I always despised the bedsheeted boogers. But men must posture so that they may endure themselves. You can forgive Big Track."

Breck got up and walked to a window. He could see Hardy Riddle standing in the yard, talking with the coroner, the district attorney and the county judge. "Mister Up," he said, "do you know why Hardy Riddle and the judge and the public prosecutor are so anxious to be generous with me if only I'll keep quiet and go away?"

"They're afraid of you," said Mister Up. "They've tolerated, protected, used, even reverenced the Klan. They're afraid you might spark a white revolt against the Klan and therefore against them. To put a man with your credentials on trial for killing Klansmen would endanger all Klan-serving demagogues and White Supremacists, as well as all Klansmen, in Alabama. Hardy Riddle and the others know it."

"Yet if I speak out they must put me on trial?"

"Certainly they must. The demagogues and White Supremacists, as well as the Klansmen, will demand it. The jurors at this inquest will be afraid not to rule against you. They'll fear physical and economic reprisal. The office holders will fear defeat. The White Supremacists will feel that not to bring you to trial would be admitting before the world that Klansmen are criminals and that *Birth of a Nation* is a lie. Once you speak out, Breck, the fat's in the fire. For all men who serve and use the Ku Klux Klan, it's damned if they do and damned if they don't."

Breck continued to stand at the window, searching the worried faces of the responsible leaders of Atoka County.

"And remember this, Breck," said Mister Up. "Now they are here at your doorstep, offering generosity. The coroner wants to generously not question you. Hardy wants to be the generous caretaker of your property. The district attorney and the judge want to generously discourage civil suits against you. If you spurn their generous offers, they will not be generous with you again. All of which is to repeat that you must accept generosity, stand mute, and be gone, or risk destruction."

Breck looked at his watch. "We must go," he said. "I'm grateful to you, Mister Up. You have done more for me than an intractable Stancill deserves. I value your advice."

"Are you going to follow it?"

"I don't know," said Breck. "At the scene of the crime I'll look, and listen, and remember, and then decide. Advice is your responsibility. Decision is mine."

Normally, April is the happiest month for a tree farmer. It's the month when the branches of a pine tree do all their growing for the year. Young trees seem to burst upward and outward. In March the farmer can walk through a stand of young trees and see over their tops. In April he'll find these trees a foot taller than he is. Growth can be seen and felt. Breck Stancill loved April. It was the time when he began rising long before the sun so that he and his horse and dog could be working in the trees at sunup. The wildlife was mating, birds were nesting, and the deep green of the pines was adorned with the whites and reds and yellows of dogwoods, azaleas, redbuds, and flowering peach trees.

Now Breck rode with Mister Up through bright sunlight toward the scene of the inquest. Old Negroes stood in their yards and on their porches and waved. Near the scene state troopers had removed a section of fence and were directing cars into a pasture to park. Other cars were parked on the edge of the woods and in the yards of two of the burned shacks. The troopers allowed Breck to park his pickup between two TV station wagons so that he needed to walk only a short distance.

The jurors were to sit alongside the still-warm ashes of Loretta's shack. They were to sit in the yard where four days earlier Butt Cut arrested Loretta. Since the coroner was an undertaker, his assistants had used funeral equipment as furniture for the inquest. They had set up two dozen collapsible chairs for jurors, witnesses and dignitaries. They had set up amplifiers so that the questions and answers could be heard by the three or four hundred persons who would stand and perch in trees to watch and listen.

Breck and Mister Up were offered chairs. Mister Up sat down, but Breck remained standing, leaning on his cane, behind Mister Up. He shook hands with several youths introduced to him by Allen Bascomb. He nodded to Vernon Hodo, who stood with Rev. Mark Alverson. He exchanged glances with Clay Wilbanks, who stood with three other FBI agents. Then Breck stood looking over the crowd, guessing which ones were hostile to him and which ones were friendly. The hostile ones, hard-eyed and hard-handed workmen, were gathered around Vernon and Reverend Alverson. Breck guessed that several of them were brothers of Butt Cut and Tag and the other slain men.

If I stay here, thought Breck, I suppose I shall have to be killing them the rest of my life, like my grandfather did. Or they'll kill me. There is no way to kill four Ku Klux without having to kill more.

The coroner, the jurors and Big Track arrived. They had inspected Bloody Rock. Hardy Riddle, the district attorney and the county judge took seats. The crowd pressed closer. Cameramen, atop the station wagons, adjusted their cameras. The coroner called the inquest to order and said: "We are here to inquire into the unnatural deaths of four white men and two Negro women. Unnatural deaths may be accidental, like falling out of a tree or being struck by lightning. Or they may be suicides or homicides. All homicides are either lawful, like self-defense of killing in line of duty, or unlawful, like murder or manslaughter. Our job is not to indict anybody, or find anybody guilty or not guilty. Our job is to rule on whether, in our opinions, these deaths were lawful or unlawful."

The coroner told the jury that he reached the scene at 4:10 A.M. He described the six bodies as they were shown to him. He told of his external examination, and of how he had ordered the bodies moved to funeral homes for more careful examination by Dr. Parker and for complete autopsies by the state toxicologists. As the coroner talked, Breck looked at the blackened, twisted, partially melted objects in the ashes of the shack in which Loretta and Susan Sykes had lived. An iron bedstead, bed springs, a TV set, a water kettle, a fire whistle, a kitchen stove. Near the TV set, partially covered by ashes, was a loose pile of small tin cans still filled with dirt. They were Crisco and Maxwell House cans in which Susan had grown her prized African violets. Everybody on the mountain admired Susan's violets. Each Christmas she gave Breck one.

Dr. Parker began describing wounds. Punctured livers and pancreases and bowels and aortas and transverse colons. A massive charge of buckshot in the forehead of Loretta Sykes.

Buckshot in Tag's kidneys and hemorrhaging in Butt Cut's bowels. As the doctor talked, Breck looked at the remains of the old typewriter he had given Loretta.

Then Big Track began talking and answering questions. When he had gone home for breakfast, he had changed into a cleaned-and-pressed uniform for this appearance before his constituents and the cameras. As Big Track talked, Breck tried to reach a sensible decision. His best judgment told him to follow Mister Up's advice. He didn't want to lose his life, his liberty, or his property; he wanted to keep what he had. But as he stood there he noticed that, perhaps by chance, the men he was facing were Vernon Hodo, Reverend Alverson and other Ku Klux, while the persons standing beside and behind him were Allen Bascomb and other high school boys.

Breck knew that the Ku Klux knew who did the killing. He suspected that at least one of the men now facing him saw him kill Tag. He knew that the Ku Klux wanted no public or legal confrontation with him. They preferred secret and illegal confrontation. Allen Bascomb knew who did the killing. Breck suspected that the other boys knew, too.

Big Track concluded: "I just can't say right now who done this shootin'. But with all the trouble we been'a havin' with outsiders and agitators, I got'ta believe it was some'a them. I didn't know Butt Cut was coming up here last night. I didn't send him. But this morning good, sound citizens have come forward'ta tell me that in their presence and hearin' last night after midnight, Butt Cut got a tip about some agitatin', and that he was up here lookin' for agitators when him and the other boys was shot."

When Big Track sat down beside Dr. Parker, the crowd believed that the inquest was over and began to stir. The coroner rose and said: "Now before we close this inquest, is there anybody here who knows anything, or saw anything, or heard anything that might help us in deciding the lawfulness or unlawfulness of these killings?"

Breck didn't decide to speak out. He could not have so decided, because speaking out was not a sensible decision for him. He merely quit weighing consequences and acted, as he had done at Bloody Rock. He stepped past Mister Up and stood before the jury, leaning on his cane. "I believe I can help," he said.

The action caused disorder. Breck had not spoken into the microphone, so most people in the crowd did not know what he had said. They began to shout and ask what was going on. The coroner appeared confused and afraid. He looked toward Hardy Riddle and the district attorney and the county judge for advice, but they had none ready for him. Big Track didn't move a muscle except to jam a cigar between his teeth. Mister Up's face was as impassive as Buddha's. He had not been surprised. Finally, the coroner said: "I'll have to ask you all to please quieten down. The inquest is not over. Mr. Stancill says he has something to tell us."

When Breck took the microphone from the coroner, the crowd became so quiet that the whirring of cameras could be heard. Breck said: "I saw Loretta Sykes trying to carry her mother out of this burning shack. I saw Tag Taggart shoot Loretta down. Then I shot Tag. A few minutes before I shot Tag, I shot Butt Cut and the others over at the bloody rock. So I killed the four men. The two women were murdered by Tag and his accomplices who got away. I saw one of them, but I was running to try to pull the women out of the fire, so I didn't have time to kill him."

The district attorney jumped up and asked: "Is the witness confessing that he slew these men, including a deputy sheriff who was performing his duty?"

Mister Up rose and replied: "Mister Coroner, the district attorney is out of order. He is not a party to these proceedings. His presence here is highly irregular. Mr. Stancill has nothing to confess. He is a law-abiding citizen voluntarily reporting to this jury how he was compelled to defend his person, his home, his property, and his innocent tenants against arsonists and murderers and brigands intent on committing arson and murder in the darkest hours of the night!"

"Now, Mister Coroner," shouted the district attorney, "you must not allow Mr. Allgood to prejudice these proceedings by casting slurs on the good name of a slain officer of the law. I suggest that you must adjourn this inquest and report your finding to me on the evidence now before you. The place for Mr. Stancill to defend himself is not here but in a court of law!"

"Mister Coroner," replied Mister Up, "the advice given you by the district attorney offends you, sir. It offends each member of this jury, and it offends the law. No officer of the law was slain here last night. Have you ever heard of an officer of the law performing his duty by carrying a carton of fire bottles through the woods at two A.M.? Only Ku Klux were slain here, after they had set fire to three homes and murdered two innocent and helpless women. The eyes of the nation are on you, Mister Coroner. Breck Stancill is not only an esteemed citizen of this county, he is also a national hero who left his flesh and blood in the sands of Iwo Jima. He stands before you, not to defend himself, but to help you do your duty. It is your proud duty, sir, and the proud duty of these fine citizens who are your jurors, to question Breck Stancill, to inform yourselves completely, then to affirm for all the world to hear that in Alabama a man's home is still his castle, and he has the right and duty to defend it against brigands who come like thieves in the night!"

The coroner stammered: "Well, Mr. Allgood, I-uh, I-uh, this is a very involved situation. I'm just a undertaker, trying to do the right thing. I'm a good friend'a Mr. Stancill. But I-uh—"

The district attorney intervened. "Let me suggest, Mister Coroner, that you take a five-minute recess and make your decision."

"That's what I'll do," said the coroner, relieved. "Everybody remain in order while we take a five-minute recess."

Breck turned and faced the Ku Klux and the brothers of the slain men. He saw hate in every eye. Allen Bascomb and the high school boys moved closer to Breck, as did Clay Wilbanks and the FBI agents. Mister Up came to Breck's side and said guardedly: "That was your day in court. They'll never let you speak another word." Clay Wilbanks spoke guardedly to the other agents. "Breck had a short day in court," he said. "They'll never let him speak another word. He'll be in jail before sundown."

The coroner went to the county judge, the district attorney, and Hardy Riddle for instruction. The four stood apart, in conference. The district attorney motioned to Big Track to join them, but Big Track ignored the signal and continued to sit, chewing on his cigar, by Dr. Parker.

"You know anything we can do to help Breck?" the doctor asked Big Track.

"I can't think'a nothin'," said Big Track, close to the doctor's ear. "I begged him'ta keep his mouth shut. So'd his lawyer. I risked my neck for him. Everybody here saw me try'ta shield him. But he's a man who won't listen'ta *nobody*. Now nobody can help him."

The coroner came back and picked up the microphone.

"The inquest is now open again," he said. "And I want every-body here to know that a coroner's inquest is supposed to be a very simple hearing. A coroner's jury is not supposed to rule on anything much more than that men have been killed by other men. The whole question of why killing was done is supposed to be decided by a grand jury and maybe a trial jury. We want to be fair to Mr. Stancill. He has come forward like a man and told us he did the killing. And I want him and everybody in the sound of my voice to know that not me or any member of this jury is going to pass judgment on him in any shape, form or fashion. But this is not a courtroom, so we can't listen to speeches and a lot of explaining. So in just about one minute more we are going to close this inquest, and then the jury will go to town and report its finding later today to the district attorney. But before we close, Mr. Stancill, I want to ask you one direct question, and I want you to answer 'yes' or 'no.' Don't give us a speech or an explanation. Just 'yes' or 'no,' so we can keep it simple. We've all looked at Bloody Rock, and we all know that it's more'n a mile from where you live. So we can all see that nobody was attacking your real home—that is, the house where you live. The depu-ty sheriff was crossing your land, and you must'a felt that he was coming to do you harm. But unless you asked him, how could you know for certain that he was coming to do you harm? How can we know? So here's my question, and just an-swer with a simple 'yes' or 'no.' Did you ambush the deputy and the men who were helping him? Answer 'yes' or 'no.' "

Before Breck could reply, Mister Up intervened and said: "Now, Mister Coroner, you have taken some bad advice. Be-fore these TV cameras and before the world, you now pro-pose to deny his Constitutional rights to a Marine hero who fought to protect that Constitution. You've been prompted to use a trick word that implies a lie. Mr. Stancill didn't ambush anybody. He was on his own property, a cripple man sitting on a horse, being attacked from two sides by Ku Klux maraud-ers. With your unfair question you are trying to imply that he should have disclosed his position to armed marauders who could have jumped behind trees and had him at their mercy. A crippled man on a horse is a helpless target. That Mr. Stancill chose to meet these armed trespassers a mile from his home was wise and proper. Only a fool tries to defend his home from fire bottles by waiting inside it. Mr. Stancill can-not answer your unfair question 'yes' or 'no,' and I beg you

again, Mister Coroner, to perform your duty and not close
this inquest. Who's in such a hurry? You should hear Mr.
Stancill at length, after which, most certainly, you should hear
any other men who may be present and who may have pertinent
information."

"Well, Mr. Allgood," said the coroner, "since Mr. Stancill
refuses to answer my question, I now direct him to stand
aside and we will hear nothing further from him. However, I
agree that we ought not to close the inquest to any other
man who may have been a witness to this killing. Is there
anybody else who knows anything?"

When Breck stood aside, the crowd again assumed that the
inquest was over. And again there was consternation when
Allen Bascomb stepped before the jury. "I can help," he said.

The coroner looked to the judge and the district attorney
for advice, but they hesitated. They didn't know what Allen
knew. When the coroner said nothing, Allen proceeded: "I
didn't see the shooting, but I was up here with Breck, helping
him guard against the Ku Klux. I heard the shooting, and I
saw Breck before and just after the shooting, and I know how
much he hoped we didn't have to kill anybody."

The district attorney interrupted. "Now, Mister Coroner,"
he said, "you must close this inquest here and now! This
young man did not witness any shooting, so his testimony is
irrelevant and improper at a coroner's inquest. The place for
this fine young man to appear is in a court of law."

"Hear me one more time, please, Mister Coroner," said
Mister Up, fearing that he would be cut off before he could
speak. "This fine young man is trying to give this jury exactly
the sort of evidence that you seek. You have properly raised
the question of apprehension. I congratulate you, sir! Was
Breck Stancill reasonably apprehensive as he faced the Ku
Klux marauders at 2:15 A.M.? Did he have reason to fear that
the Ku Klux were coming to do him harm? This fine young
man stands here before you, Mister Coroner, to tell you that
he and his father, the sheriff, were so apprehensive last night
that, five hours before there was any shooting, they came here
to warn Breck Stancill that his life was in danger! This fine
young man was so apprehensive that he armed himself and
stayed here on this mountain, through the loneliest hours of
the night, to help a crippled United States Marine defend his
life against armed Ku Klux Klansmen bent on arson and
murder! Mister Coroner, you must hear Allen Bascomb. You

must question his father, the sheriff, and other fine citizens here present, who came here last night to warn Breck Stancill against what peaceful Southerners have had to fear for a hundred years: a sneaking Ku Klux attack in the night! You and your jurors must hear your fellow citizens so that you can report to your district attorney that when Breck Stancill was compelled to kill here last night, he committed no unlawful act!"

The coroner uttered only four more words: "This inquest is closed!"

Then he switched off the sound amplifier.

At 7 P.M. on Thursday Breck Stancill was in the Atoka County Jail charged with murder. He had been arrested and brought to jail by Big Track on a warrant sworn out by the district attorney. His preliminary hearing, at which he was expected to be freed on bond, was set for 10 A.M. Friday.

During the hours after the inquest Breck acted on the assumption that the coroner's jury would rule against him and he would be arrested in the late afternoon. He lunched privately at his home with Mister Up while the cooks served a picnic lunch in his yard to Allen Bascomb and several high school youths, to Clay Wilbanks and the FBI men, and to several reporters and photographers who were waiting for Big Track to return and make the arrest.

"You're in grave danger, Breck," said Mister Up at lunch. "Your days as a tree farmer in Alabama are over. You could never work safely in the woods again. Too many people hate you and can kill you with impunity. Others who don't hate you can't understand why you'd let this happen to yourself. The young people who support you only increase the danger to you. They further infuriate the ones who hate you."

"At the inquest I was impressed by the number of supporters I seem to have," said Breck.

"I wasn't impressed," said Mister Up. "Those jurors hated me for defaming dead Klansmen in the presence of TV outsiders. This is a Klan-ridden, White Supremacy society where Klansmen can kill with impunity, but where Klansmen can't be killed with impunity. You refused to adjust to this society, then defied it. You think you had a right to kill a white man because he killed a Negro woman. You think you had a right to kill three white men to prevent their ridding the community of 'old nigger relief-hounds.' You think the death of one black

equals the death of one white. Except for your young supporters you are the only white person in this county who thinks
that way. So there is no hope for you here. From this day on,
in both the criminal and civil courts of this state, we lose all
the verdicts and all the appeals; and we lodge our hopes in the
Supreme Court of the United States and in a new generation
in Alabama. I hope I have years enough and you have money
enough to see it through."

After lunch Breck walked down to tell Nancy Poteet and
her children goodbye. The furniture had been loaded onto a
truck, and Nancy and the children were in Dr. Parker's car.
The house looked empty and forlorn. "Come and see me tomorrow night, Breck," Nancy said. "Or any night, wherever I
am. This will all be over before long, and you can make a
new start."

"Sure, Nancy," said Breck. "You look after yourself and
the children."

Breck returned the tape recorder to Clay Wilbanks. "Did
Loretta record her statement?" Wilbanks asked.

"Yes," said Breck. "I have it safely hidden. Come to see me
tomorrow afternoon. Maybe I'll give it to you."

"You'll be glad to know," said Wilbanks, "that this afternoon we are sending in three Federal marshals to guard the
rest of your Negroes until they can move."

"Yes, I'm glad to know that," said Breck. "Why couldn't
the marshals have arrived yesterday afternoon?"

"Well, you know how it is," said Wilbanks.

"Yeah, I know how it is," said Breck.

Several times during the afternoon Breck noticed a group
of old Negroes standing in his yard. Each time a new group
appeared, Breck stopped whatever he was doing and went out
and stood with them for a few minutes. Nobody said anything. Breck shook hands with each one, and they exchanged
looks and nods. Folks who know never waste words, and they
never say everything is going to be all right.

In the late afternoon Breck and Allen went to the barn,
loaded Prince Dan into the horse trailer, and hooked the trailer to the pickup. The horse was to be placed in Hardy Riddle's barn, and Mrs. Riddle was to look after him. Then Big
Track arrived in the Wildcat.

"You ready, Breck?" he said.

"Soon as I get my bag and lock the doors," said Breck.

When Breck came back into the yard, a photographer asked: "You gonna put the cuffs on him, Sheriff?"

"You know I ain't," said Big Track. "Git in the front seat with me, Breck."

The procession moved along and down the mountain, with the Wildcat leading, followed by Mister Up and his Negro chauffeur in the Continental, three carloads of reporters and photographers, then Allen in the Chevrolet pickup, pulling Prince Dan in the horse trailer.

There was a crowd in front of the jail, including more photographers. But inside the jail there was only Hattie, Big Track and Breck. Hattie was embarrassed, so Breck tried to help her. "Well, Hattie," he said, "looks like I'm a guest in your house tonight."

"We never expected nothing like this, Mister Breck," Hattie said. "We'll do the best we can for you."

"We've emptied out one'a the cell blocks," said Big Track. "Hattie has put a cot with a soft mattress in the Day Room for you. You won't have'ta sleep in no cell, and you won't have'ta sleep on no tough foam rubber laying flat on steel."

"That's kind of both of you," said Breck.

Big Track led Breck through the locked door leading from the office, then into the cell block. "There'll be just one door locked on'ya," he said. "That's the one out there at the office. All the prisoners, white and nigger, is locked in cells, and the cell blocks are locked. You'll have the run'a the jail. Hattie'll feed'ya after she's fed the prisoners. I'll see'ya in the morning. I got'ta git over to my office in the courthouse. Trixie and another gal's been answerin' phones for twelve hours. Folks calling from everywhere about you. Tonight I'll let that Western Union man come in here and bring'ya a sack full'a telegrams. Then I got'ta try'ta git some sleep and git up at midnight and set up with some corpses. Including my deputy's."

"Looks like I've caused you trouble," said Breck.

"You sho' have," said Big Track. "You should'a thought about how much trouble corpses can be. They got'ta be set up with, and cried over, and sung over, and preached over, and prayed over, and buried. You done give me plenty'a funerals to go to, and plenty'a pall-bearin' to do."

"Before you go," said Breck, "there's one more favor you could do for me."

"What's that?"

"Lend me a shotgun."

"You don't need no gun. Ain't nothin' like that gonna be tried. This jail's safe."

"It wasn't safe for Loretta Sykes."

Big Track sighed and rubbed his brow. "Now, Breck," he said, "ain't talkin' got you in enough trouble for one day? If you keep talkin' about some'pin that's done and over with, you gonna git in a lot worse trouble." Then Big Track added: "All right, I'll git'cha a gun." He went into the office and brought a short, 12-gauge riot gun. "Put this under that mattress," he said, "so if that district attorney comes over here he won't see it. Now I got'ta go. I hope'ya sleep good."

Shortly after Big Track left, Hattie brought Breck a glass, ice, water, a bottle of whiskey and the Birmingham *News*. He poured himself a drink and sat drinking and glancing through the paper. Much of the front page was about the killing. He looked at the pictures but didn't read the stories. The overhead light wasn't strong enough for him to read comfortably. He noted that today was the deadline for filing income tax returns and that President Truman, in New York to receive an award from Freedom House, had called the Selma March "a silly effort by busybodies and troublemakers who should have stayed at home and minded their own business." That'll please the Ku Klux, Breck thought.

As the whiskey relaxed him, Breck found himself thinking of nights when he was a child and his mother read *Ivanhoe* to him, and *Treasure Island*, and *The Legend of Sleepy Hollow*. He thought of battle eves aboard ship when he joined in singing "Paper Doll" and "Lili Marlene" and "The White Cliffs of Dover." He thought of nights in hospitals when he and other maimed men told one another how they used to hit home runs and score touchdowns. He thought of holidays in New Orleans and Mobile and Birmingham with women he liked. He thought of the night before last when, bitter and depressed, he had gone to Nancy Poteet. She desperately wanted him to fuck her, and she was afraid he couldn't. At each brief step in the foreplay, from living room to bedroom to bed, he felt her fear that he could go no further: that he must be halted by the recollection that he'd be following a blacksnake. Even when he moved to mount her, she was still afraid that his erection, like her husband's, would collapse before he could penetrate. Only when he drove deep and powerfully inside her did she believe it could happen. She reacted like a wallflower suddenly invited to dance. She called for more and more, and said: "God, you don't know how much it means to me to find out that I can still give a decent white man a hard."

When Hattie returned she surprised Breck both with her appearance and her actions. She had taken off her tan shirt and pants and put on a low-necked black dress. And she had brought him not prison food on a tin tray, but a carefully cooked steak dinner with dishes, tablecloth and a napkin. "Good Lord, Hattie," said Breck, "you shouldn't have done this!"

"I wanted to, Mister Breck," she said. "I couldn't offer you what I have'ta feed prisoners. We feed them on sixty cents a day. That means a lot'a sorghum and cornbread. I couldn't offer you nothin' like that." Skillfully she set the table and laid out the food, adding: "And since I so seldom ever git'ta eat with anybody, I thought you might let me come in after you git through and have a cup'a coffee with you."

"You haven't eaten yet, have you?" Breck asked.

"No, but I got a little some'pin fixed for me in my room."

"Well, that won't do," said Breck. "I, too, seldom ever get to eat with anybody. You've cooked plenty here for both of us. So you bring more dishes and another napkin, and we'll eat here together. You can hear the telephone or radio from here."

"I won't be botherin' you?"

"You'll be doing me a great favor. I can listen to you talk and forget my troubles."

While Hattie was gone Breck tried not to feel resentful. He was a captive guest being intruded upon. He had heard that Hattie traded whiskey, food and cigarettes to some white women prisoners for company and comfort. Now she intended to impose her loneliness, if not her body, on him.

When Hattie returned they made small talk about the food which Breck thought was delicious. "You got'ta remember, Mister Breck," she said, "that I been cookin' twenty-five years. I had'ta start cookin' for my paw and my brothers in the woods when I was seven. I ought'ta know how'ta cook meat and potatoes!"

"Many women don't know how," said Breck. "Cooking is an art, and you're good at it. I'm lucky to have a jailer who can cook."

She smiled at that, and Breck watched her while she ate. She was too tall, her front teeth were too wide, her brown hair was too short, her features coarse, her shoulders too broad, her breasts too small, her hips too narrow, her legs too straight, and her hands and feet too big. Her brown eyes showed too much white, like a cow's. Yet somehow Breck didn't find her repulsive. There was nothing visibly soft about her, but he felt that somewhere within her muscular frame there were feelings which could be hurt and a personality that yearned to be included. She was an unlikely-looking wallflower, but she, too, wanted to be invited to dance.

For an hour Breck listened while she talked, mostly about television shows that she watched: Ed Sullivan, and Jackie Gleason, and Lawrence Welk, and Dean Martin, and Andy Griffith, and Red Skelton, and *What's My Line* and *To Tell the Truth*. She told him about the longest trip she had ever taken: to the state fair in Birmingham last year. Breck felt grateful to her for not talking about jails and killings and Ku Klux. He felt grateful to her for the meal, and for all the hot coffee they were drinking with whiskey in it. He decided to ask some questions. He thought he might be able to help Hattie. He thought she might be able to help him.

"Hattie," he said, "I've often wondered why you haven't left Atoka County. You're a capable, nice-looking woman. You're strong, still young, in good health, and not afraid of work. Why haven't you gone off where there is more opportunity for you to enjoy life?"

"Well, Breck," she said, "I've thought about it. I still think about it a lot. You know the main reasons. I ain't got much education. Some'a the prisoners have helped me try'ta learn'ta talk right and read. I've done some studyin' and I've listened to TV, tryin'ta learn'ta talk. And I got no money. Nothing! I never seen a hundred dollars at one time that was mine in my life."

She poured more coffee and more whiskey and continued: "Then I ain't got it too bad here. I got Big Track, and he's good'ta me in his way. He's got his own family, so he can't pay me much money, and he can't pay me too much attention. And I got my church. You know I sing in the choir. But I am mighty lonesome. And there's things that you know and that folks know that I wish they didn't know. That bothers me a lot. I guess it just comes down to that I ain't got nobody'ta help me go nowhere else."

"Take a city like San Francisco," said Breck. "It's a long way from here. You could go there and make a whole new life for yourself. Nobody would know any of these things that

you wish people didn't know. You could go to vocational
school for a year, study nursing. In a year you could be earning a hundred dollars a week. You'd enjoy your work, and
you wouldn't be lonesome. There are many women in San
Francisco like you, who want to be with other women. And
most people don't look down on them."

Hattie was shaken. She moved along the bench, closer to
Breck. "But how could I git there? How could I go to school
for a year? How'd I git the money? Who'd help me and show
me how?"

"I'll help you," said Breck. "I'll get you the money tomorrow. More money than you've ever dreamed of having. Twenty-five thousand dollars! That's more than Big Track has. People will go with you to San Francisco. They'll find you a good
place to live. They'll protect you and show you how to keep
your money. Nobody here will ever know where you are."

"You mean you'd give me the money? You'd guarantee all
these things?"

Breck moved closer to her, and she lowered her head closer
to his. "Hattie," he said, "I'm in trouble. It may cost me everything I have. But it's an ill wind that doesn't blow somebody some good. You have something that's worth twenty-five
thousand dollars to me. Do you want to sell it to me?"

She swallowed hard. She went out and looked around the
jail office. She came back and closed, but didn't lock, the cell-
block door behind her. At the corner of the table she sat as
close as she could get to Breck. "You talk," she said. "But
talk like we're in a graveyard."

"It's simple," said Breck. "Some of the trouble began right
here in this jail four nights ago. Sunday night. I know most of
what happened. You know most of the rest. I won't ask you
to tell me anything here. Just carry on in your normal manner. But tomorrow night or the next night, whenever I tell
you, you pack a few things in a small suitcase, and you step
out of this jail at 4 A.M., never to come back, and never to be
heard of again. FBI agents will take you to Birmingham and
ask you a few questions. You tell them the truth about what
you did in this jail before you went to church, and who you
saw and what you did when you came back. The agents will
go with you on the airplane to San Francisco. They'll deposit
the money for you and look after you in every way. They'll
give you a new name and social security card if you want it.
That's all there is to it."

"What about you?" she asked. "Will you guarantee all this to me? Will you come and see if I'm all right?"

"Yes," said Breck. "I'll guarantee it all. I'll come to see you as soon as I can."

"Wouldn't I be hurtin' Big Track?"

"I doubt it. He wasn't here during the rape. He didn't kill the girl. Everybody knows already that he covered up for them."

"Then it's Vernon you want'ta git? Him and the preacher?"

"That's right. I want you to identify the Klansmen. I want to prove by you that the Klan did it and did it in this jail."

"It was Vernon Hodo and the preacher. Them and Sy Shaneyfelt and Tag and Butt Cut."

"That's all I want, Hattie," said Breck. "You give that to the FBI and sign it, and I'll guarantee you a whole new life. You'll never regret it."

She looked around guiltily. "Let me think about it," she said. "I'll git out'a here now, and I'll git these dishes out. Nobody ought'a know we spent so much time together. I won't pay no more attention to'ya."

"That's right. Don't cook me any special breakfast in the morning, and don't bring me any more whiskey."

When she was gone Breck walked up and down the cell block, stretching himself. He went into one of the cells and used the toilet. The lights went down, leaving only the blue night lights burning. He came back to the cot in the Day Room and took off his clothes. He took off his leg and put on pajamas. He examined the riot gun and laid it on the floor where he could reach it. Then he lay down and tried to go to sleep.

Several hours later, probably around 3 A.M., he heard a step in the corridor. He grabbed the gun, snapped off the safety and waited. Hattie came through the door. She was in pajamas and sandals, and she came and sat on the edge of the cot.

"I can't sleep a wink," she said. "My heart's beatin' like it's gonna jump out'a my body. Tell me how to go to sleep."

"Just try not to be excited," said Breck. "It takes guts to leave an old place and make a new life. I didn't have what it takes. You have. Just go on back and drink a little warm milk and go to sleep. I'll see that everything is all right for you."

"Will you hold my hand a minute?" she asked.

"Sure," he said. "You've got a good hand to hold."

In a few minutes she sighed deeply, got up and went back to her bed.

ALLEN

FROM NOON to 2 P.M. on Friday the bodies of "four valiant young men" who "gave their lives" on Stancill's Mountain lay in state at the Pentecostal Baptist Church, Ellenton, Alabama. Hundreds of sorrowing citizens passed the open caskets as the organ played "Rock of Ages," "What a Friend We Have in Jesus," "The Far Away Home of the Soul," "Onward Christian Soldiers," and "The Old Rugged Cross." The corpse which received the most respectful attention was that of Sheriff's Deputy Elmer Cates, in a new sheriff's uniform, his casket adorned with the flags of Alabama, the Confederacy, and the United States of America. Flowers filled one end of the church. The largest floral offerings were from a peace officers association, the Alabama National Guard, the Ellenton Gun Club, a fraternal order, and the Atoka County Board of Revenue.

Respectful state troopers handled the crowd, which by 2 P.M. was estimated at three thousand persons. The widows, orphans, parents, and all the other kinfolk filed into the church, followed by as many others as could be seated. The overflow stood outside listening to loudspeakers. As the music faded, leaving only sounds of sobbing to be heard, the Reverend Mark Alverson appeared in a white robe and began the service.

Jesus said, I am the resurrection, and the life: he that believeth in me, though he were dead, yet shall he live: and whosoever liveth and believeth in me shall never die. Let us pray.

Almighty God, fount of all life; thou art our refuge and strength; thou art our help in trouble. Enable us, we pray thee, to put our trust in thee, that we may obtain comfort, and find grace to help in this and every time of need; through Jesus Christ our Lord. Amen.

We Christians are met here today in grateful memory
of four young men who died fighting for our Christian
way of life. We Christians do not sorrow as do those who
have no hope. We know that our loved ones move on
into the nearer presence of God and abide under His loving care. Our Master said, Let not your hearts be troubled. Believe in God, believe also in me. In my father's
house are many mansions. I go to prepare a place for
you that where I am there ye may be also.

I have seen burials in all parts of the world. Chinese
throw bodies out in the fields for hogs to destroy. Hindus
take their dead to the burning ghats. Parsees place the
bodies of their dead on the roofs of their temples so vul-
tures can devour them. Africans throw the bodies of
their wives and children into the river to the crocodiles.
All of them dispose of their dead without hope of ever
seeing them again. They sing no hymns of hope; they
chant dirges of despair. We Christians mourn but not as
those who have no hope. Our dead are only asleep and
we shall see them again.

We Christians believe in our own resurrection to eternal life because we believe in the resurrection of Christ.
We cannot believe that the purpose of creation is fulfilled
by our brief existence on this earth. These four brave
men have not been annihilated. They have not been cast
as rubbish to the void. They have not perished, never to
be met again.

When a man believes so deeply in a cause that he is
willing to lose his life for it, he has achieved a nobility of
life, a heroism. So today we honor the memory of four
heroes. That sweet old entertainer, Sir Harry Lauder, lost
a son in the First World War. One evening he was walking down the street with a small boy at his side. They
passed a home where a service flag, bearing a gold star,
hung in the window. The boy asked what that meant. Sir
Harry told him that the parents in that home had lost a
son at the front. They walked on and suddenly saw the
evening star appearing on the horizon. "Look," the boy
said, "God is hanging out his service flag. He, too, must
have lost a son at the front."

To you grieving parents, to you still-fertile widows
with empty arms, to you sweet children, I say to all of
you, hang gold stars in your windows. Your sons, your

husbands, your fathers died fighting the same God-hating enemy as our men in Vietnam.

When brave men meet death, tears must be shed, but trumpets, too, must be sounded. One of our dead was a uniformed officer of the law. The other three died helping him perform his duty. Our enemies despise the law. They hope to overcome by disparaging and disarming law officers. So let all within the sound of my voice take heed. These young law men shall not have died in vain. What they stood for, we stand for. What they died for, we shall live for. What they gave, we are ready to give. We have grasped the fallen torch. We stand at Armageddon, and we shall do battle for the Lord.

A final word of comfort. The death of young men always seems especially hard to bear. But Our Lord died young. And for these dear departed, I pray, in the words of the poet:

> Let them in, Peter, they are very tired;
> Give them the couches where the angels sleep.
> Tell them how they are missed. Say not to fear;
> It's going to be all right with us down here.

Each of the four corpses was buried in a different country cemetery. So there were four more services, at gravesides, where quartets sang "Shall We Gather at the River," and where preachers sounded trumpets and defied graves: O grave, where is thy victory? Big Track was one of the bearers of Butt Cut's casket, and the honorary pallbearers included every elected official of Atoka County.

Meanwhile, Breck Stancill was still in jail. His preliminary hearing had been postponed until Monday. At 7 A.M., at his home in Tuscaloosa, Mister Up had received a call from the judge. "Mister Up," said the judge, "I'm in a bind and I need your help. I've got to spend most of today going to funerals and buryings. So I want to continue Breck's hearing until Monday. I want to tell the press and the TV that you agreed to the continuance. I hope you can see your way clear to help me."

"I don't see how I can agree to that, Judge," said Mister Up. "Breck Stancill has a right to freedom on bond. He should have been granted bond yesterday, immediately after his arrest. You can grant him bond in five minutes. Surely you can find that much time this morning?"

"It can't be done in five minutes," insisted the judge. "A lot of people will be present, along with all these reporters and photographers. The district attorney must make a show of opposition. You know that. It'll take two hours, maybe three. I just can't find that kind'a time today, and tomorrow I've got to make a speech in Birmingham. At the same time I'd hate to see you make a show of going to Montgomery and trying to go over my head. With all the publicity, that'd be bad for Breck, bad for the county, bad for the state, bad for everybody. So I'm asking you to go along with me. A few more hours in jail won't hurt Breck much. It might be to his interest to stay in jail till all his victims are under the sod."

Mister Up understood the situation. In Alabama the county or circuit judge—the judge of felony court—has unusual power because the state has no intermediate appellate court. The only appellate court is the State Supreme Court. If Mister Up opposed continuance, he doubted that he could go to Montgomery and get action by the Supreme Court before Monday. And such an action would further "contrary" the local judge.

"All right," said Mister Up. "You may say that I agreed to the continuance."

Mister Up then drove to the jail and explained to Breck. "It's the sort of official misconduct we can expect," he said. "I hate for you to have to stay in this jail until Monday. I could seek relief from a higher court, but we'd be further contrarying people we must face. Under the circumstances I think you had better grin and bear another three days. Your sister Stella has arrived from California. She'll be in to see you, and we'll see that you have digestible food to eat and books to read."

The postponement depressed Breck. He hadn't minded the one night in jail. It had given him an opportunity to talk with Hattie. But in the morning he was accustomed to activity. Now he began to notice the bars. Moreover, the postponement belittled him to Big Track and Hattie. Big Track, who heard of the postponement before Mister Up arrived, removed the cot from the cell-block Day Room, along with the gun and all other evidence that Breck was receiving preferential treatment. "You gonna be here awhile," Big Track said. "You gonna have visitors. I can't let the word git out that I'm favorin' you. Not on the day when I got'ta help bury my deputy." Hattie seemed more formal than she needed to be. A man loses face and influence the moment he allows himself to be put in jail. Each day he allows himself to remain in jail he loses more face and influence.

The stylishly dressed woman who left the Atoka Inn and drove a Hertz Chevrolet to the jail looked like a shopper at the May Company on Wilshire Boulevard in Los Angeles. Which she frequently was. She didn't look like she belonged in Ellenton, and she didn't. She had only been born there, and gone through high school there, then she had left. Now she had a son at Stanford and a daughter at Pomona. Her husband earned thirty thousand dollars a year as a bank executive. She hadn't been in Ellenton for twenty-four years, and she had never wanted to return. She had flown to Birmingham and driven to Ellenton only because she was Breck Stancill's sister, Stella.

When Hattie ushered Stella into the cell-block Day Room, Breck and his sister hugged one another, and Breck said: "Thanks for coming."

"We want to help you," she said. "You're not alone in the world, you know. You have two sisters and a mother. And while you seldom visit us, we are still a family. We must help one another."

"Well, let's sit down on these prison benches," said Breck. "You've helped me by coming. You look wonderful. Is your family well?"

"Quite well," she said. "But first tell me what I can tell Mother. She's terribly worried. I have just talked with her, and her attorney has talked with Mister Up. She wants to know if she should come here?"

Breck grimaced at the thought of his mother returning to Ellenton after twenty-odd years as a rich wife and widow in Miami Beach. "Oh, Lord, Stella," he said, "see that she doesn't come. She despised this place for eighteen of the twenty years she spent here. How could she help me now?"

"She has money," Stella said. "Her friends have money. They have influence in Washington. They all want to help you. And Mister Up says everything you have may be seized by the widows of these men you killed."

"It may come to that," said Breck. "For the present there is little anyone can do. On Monday I'll be released on bond which I can post. Time will pass. There will be trials, appeals, postponements. I'll continue to grow trees."

"Won't they try to kill you?"

"They may."

Stella opened her bag and found her cigarettes. Breck struck a light for her. "Do you have regrets?" she asked. "Do you think about if only you had done this or done that?"

"I guess everybody who takes human life has regrets. Yes, I think about the if-onlys and the ironies and the misconceptions."

"Like if only you hadn't come back here after the war?"

"I don't regret that."

"Or if only you hadn't opposed the Klan?"

"I didn't oppose the Klan much," said Breck. "One of the ironies is that five hours before the shooting the Klansmen were told that I would do all that they demanded. The shooting came after my surrender. A few of them still wanted to do some burning and killing."

"Did you encourage the civil rights agitators?"

"No. That's another of the ironies." Breck pointed to a shopping bag in a corner of the room. "In that bag are hundreds of telegrams. Because I kill Ku Klux, people assume I'm a crusader. They don't know that for twenty years all expressions of high hope have embarrassed me. I talked briefly with one civil rights worker. He regards me as a cynic or a sentimentalist or perhaps a fascist."

"And there was no way to avoid killing?"

"No way for me. I believe that a man has a duty to kill to halt or prevent atrocity. I'll go to my grave feeling sorry that I ever had to kill. But I have no feeling that I did wrong in killing the four men who are being buried here today."

Breck and Stella looked into each other's eyes, and she shuddered and wiped away a tear. Then Breck said: "Stella, there is one thing you can do for me."

"What?"

"Tomorrow, up on the mountain, at our old Negro cemetery, there will be a funeral. Loretta Sykes and her mother. Because the last of the Negroes now must leave the mountain, these may be the last burials in the cemetery. I intended to be there and say a few words. Since I can't be there, I'd like for you to take my place."

Stella felt confused. "Oh, Breck, I . . ."

"You'll be in no danger. You can go with FBI agents. Dr. Parker will be the only white person there from Atoka County. The other whites will be Federal marshals, reporters and photographers, perhaps some civil rights workers. There'll be hundreds of Negroes. When the preacher asks you to speak, you can look back to the arrival of Old Ab and Fowler Stancill, and talk about the long and troubled road traveled together by their descendants."

"But, Breck, I can't!" she said. "I don't want to go where I'll need an armed escort. I don't want to speak words which will enrage people. You forget that I've been gone from here for twenty-four years, and that my memories of this place are not pleasant. I've tried to forget the bloody legends of the Stancills. I haven't told them to my children. At the Los Angeles airport I promised my husband that I wouldn't let you involve me in conflict."

Breck was puzzled. "I must have used the wrong words," he said. "I didn't mean to suggest something distasteful. I thought you'd like to go up on the mountain. You could help correct an imbalance. Today the guilty dead will be buried, as Christian heroes, before a throng of whites, including the officials of this county. Tomorrow the innocent dead will be buried, and no white preacher or official will dare to be present. There is a custom at Negro funerals in rural Alabama. When white persons the Negroes respect are present, they are asked to speak. Not to orate, just to speak a few comforting words. That's all I asked you to do: just to give evidence again that we Stancills include Negroes in the human race."

Stella fumbled with her cigarettes. "But my presence there would be defiant," she said. "Any words I spoke would sound defiant. If I were put on television, I'd be projecting defiance over a national network. I refuse to be defiant. Such defiance could only hurt you."

Breck waited for her to go on. "I feel awful," she said. "I came so far to try to help you, and I'm refusing your only request. Try to understand. My life has been so different from yours. Take Negroes. You'd be at ease at a Negro funeral. I wouldn't. In all my adult life I've scarcely seen a Negro except on television. The only Negroes I can recall speaking to were deliverymen. And take guns. You were born with a gun in your hand. But guns frighten me. There has never been a gun in my home. I don't want my son to be . . ."

"Like your brother?"

"I don't want him to have to be like you, Breck. I've always loved you and sympathized with you. But you are a frightening mixture of tenderness and belligerence. You can be so tender with flowers and birds and animals and people, yet you can wait alone in the dark, and take aim, and blast the entrails from your fellow men! God, how can you do it!"

While Stella wiped more tears, Breck said: "Now I appreciate even more your coming here. It took effort. Entering this jail and this cell shocked you. Then I shocked you. Confronting a killer can be shocking, even when, or especially when, he's your brother. Here's a more reasonable request. You go to Atoka Inn and telephone the Atoka Hospital. Ask Dr. Parker or his nurse to please send me two meals a day. Call the Walgreen Drug Store and ask them to send me a tablet and a ballpoint pen. Then you check out, get in your car, and drive as fast as you can to the Birmingham airport. You can just make the nonstop jet. Because of the time difference, you'll be home before dark. Tell our mother and my other sister that I'm well, that I love them as I do you, and that when I need money and influence in Washington, either I or Mister Up will telephone all of you."

After Stella was gone, Hattie Bascomb walked into the cell block and said to Breck: "She's the nicest-dressed woman I ever seen. Is that the way women look in California?"

"That's the way," said Breck. "In a year you'll look just like she does. Except that you're about eleven years younger than she is."

"I been thinking," said Hattie, dropping her voice. "I didn't sleep a wink last night. I'm scared to death! I'm about'ta decide not'ta go. It sounds so awful: just going off by y'self and never expectin'ta come back. Never's a long time."

Breck had assumed that Hattie would vacillate. To deliver her to the FBI, ready to make and sign a statement, he knew he would have to bribe, cajole and threaten her, day and night, until she was out of the jail and on her way. So he said: "If you aren't going to deal with me, Hattie, tell me now and I'll deal with Sy Shaneyfelt. He knows more about that rape than you know. And that tail-shaking wife of his would make him take my money."

"She sho' would," Hattie conceded.

"But you deserve the money. And I don't want you to stay here and get in trouble."

"What trouble?"

"You had a hand in the rape. If you don't help the Federal law, you can find yourself in a Federal prison."

Hattie's knees suddenly weakened, so she sat down. She was again wearing her tan pants and shirt. Her big hands looked red from scrubbing. Breck continued: "There's another sort of trouble I don't want to see you have. The Ku Klux preacher thinks I'm evil because of the nature of my sex life. What happens when he starts thinking about why some white women in this jail live well and others don't? A Ku Klux preacher is always seeing dirty pictures in his mind. Can you see in your mind what that preacher will see you doing?"

Hattie felt hurt. "You didn't talk this'a way last night," she said. "You talked real kind . . . like you just wanted'ta help me git somewhere and be somebody. Now you're gettin' dirty with me."

"No, I'm still talking kind," said Breck. "It's you who have changed your tune. Last night you agreed to help me. Now you're talking about backing out. As your friend, I'm showing you why you can't afford to back out." He got up and closed the cell-block door, then went to his bag and brought a wallet to the table. He sat down close to Hattie and said: "You may need to buy a few things today, just to get ready to travel. So I'll give you a little money on account. They'll give you more in Birmingham, and in San Francisco they'll bank the big money for you."

Slowly, in ten- and twenty-dollar bills, Breck counted out five hundred dollars. Hattie looked at the pile of money, then began feeling of it. "Don't buy too much," said Breck, "or you might cause talk. Be sure and don't buy a suitcase. You can wrap your possessions in a sheet until you get to Birmingham."

Deliberately, Hattie began stuffing the money into her pockets. "This afternoon," said Breck, "while Big Track is at the funeral, a man named Clay Wilbanks will come here."

"I know him," said Hattie.

"I'll talk with him first," said Breck. "Then you talk with him. Do what he says, and what happened to my sister can happen to you. She shook the dust of this place off her feet twenty-four years ago, and she has never wanted to come back. Neither will you."

As Hattie walked out of the cell block, her shoulders sagging, Breck felt guilty. But he, too, could see pictures in his mind. He saw Hattie locking the door of a padded cell on Loretta, and he heard Hattie say: "Now'ya can work at tryin'ta save yourself by usin' them three holes that ever' black bitch is so expert at usin' on a stiff white dick." Breck quit feeling guilty and only felt sad. Then an earlier picture slipped into his mind. He saw Hattie at fifteen, hurrying through the woods to give a dollar she needed for food to a Negro girl to come and suck her paw's stiff white dick. That made Breck feel guilty again.

At 2 P.M., as Reverend Alverson began the funeral service for his fellow Klansmen, Clay Wilbanks appeared at the jail. Hattie took him to Breck, then went out and closed and locked the cell block door. Breck went to his bag and got a package. "Here are Loretta's tapes," he said.

"You took a risk bringing them in here," said Wilbanks. "Big Track should have searched your bag and your pockets, too."

"I figured he wouldn't."

"Are you going to give the tapes to me?"

"If we can agree on procedure. I also would like to give you Hattie Bascomb."

"This woman here in the jail? Big Track's sister?"

"Yes. She can corroborate most of what Loretta says. More important, she can identify the masked men who watched the rape. They were Vernon, the preacher, Butt Cut, Taggart and Shaneyfelt. Hattie put Loretta in the padded cell. After the rape, she put Loretta in the car for Big Track."

"That's what we need," said Wilbanks. "What's her price?"

"I promised her twenty-five thousand dollars and gave her five hundred on account. You'll have to take her to San Francisco and help her get some training and a job. As you suggested, I dealt on a personal basis. I told her the money would be mine."

"No problems there. We have money and babysitters. Any danger of her backing out?"

"Not if you take her tonight while I'm here to push her."

Wilbanks rubbed his jaw, then said: "I can think of a reason for waiting until after you get out of here."

"So can I. But if we wait she'll never go."

Wilbanks still hesitated. "Big Track will blame you when he finds her gone."

"That's another risk I'll take."

"Okay. What's this procedure you want to agree on?"

"Can you get me a copy of your tape of Big Track taking the Klan oath?"

"Yeah."

"Can you have it here by tomorrow evening?"

"Yeah."

"Then here's the procedure I want. You take Hattie out of here before daylight tomorrow. Take her to Birmingham and record her statement. Have her taken on out of Alabama. Tomorrow afternoon Loretta and her mother will be buried. Tomorrow evening there will be a public Klan meeting. As sheriff, but not as a Klansman, Big Track will be present. When that meeting ends, you deliver to Big Track three recordings: Loretta's statement, Hattie's statement, and Big Track taking the Klan oath. Tell him that the recordings are mine, not yours: that they will be used as I decide to use them. Deliver them to him officially, as my property which by law he must safeguard for me until I am released. Make him sign a receipt for them."

"You mean you want him to hear those records while you're his prisoner?"

"I want him to hear them tomorrow night," said Breck. "Because before Monday I intend to try to turn him against the Klan, just as I've turned Hattie. I want him to arrest Vernon Hodo and Reverend Alverson as leaders of the Klan, and institute the case of *The State of Alabama* against *The Ku Klux Klan* for the rape of Loretta Sykes, for the murder of Loretta Sykes, and for armed trespass and arson on Stancill's Mountain."

Wilbanks whistled. "You don't want much, do you? Big Track can't do that. He's a Klansman, himself guilty of complicity in all the Klan's crimes. If he arrests Klansmen, he knows they'll go free and kill him. He can't turn around now and move against the Klan."

"I think he might," said Breck. "He's a big man. If he turned dramatically on the Klan, he could embolden juries and wipe the Klan out. I may be able to persuade him to do it."

"What if you fail to persuade him?" asked Wilbanks. "He's already under pressure to let the Klan take you out and kill you."

"There's no safe way for me now."

"But there's a safer way for you," said Wilbanks. "Don't give Big Track the records. Wait until you are free Monday. Then the FBI will arrest Big Track and his fellow Klansmen, and institute the case of *The United States of America* against

The Ku Klux Klan for violating the civil rights of Loretta Sykes."

"That's the hopeless way," said Breck. "Because it includes Big Track with the Klansmen. The Klan is strong here because everybody believes it includes Big Track. He's the state law, *The State of Alabama*. Making him and the Klan co-defendants confirms the Klan claim that it is an adjunct to the police power of *The State of Alabama*."

Breck paused, then went on: "And there's no hope for me in a Federal Court case of the United States against the Klan. If I'm ever to live peacefully on Stancill's Mountain again, the State of Alabama must be separated from the Klan, and turned against the Klan. Then the State of Alabama must destroy the Klan. The United States can't destroy the Klan. The United States can't even charge the Klan with rape, murder and arson, because those aren't Federal crimes. You know the FBI's limitations. You told me yourself that the FBI can fight the Klan only by recruiting a man and helping him fight. The man to recruit and help here is Big Track."

"I don't believe you can recruit Big Track," said Wilbanks.

"Maybe I can't," said Breck. "But I must try."

At the funeral for Loretta and her mother there were two surprises. The first was the attendance of twenty-three white students from Ellenton High School: five girls and eighteen boys. The second surprise was the speech by Allen Bascomb. He spoke for himself, his fellow white students and Breck Stancill.

The other two speakers were a local Negro preacher, who conducted the funeral, and Josh Franklin, who spoke for the twenty-one outside civil rights workers, white and Negro, who were present. The Negro preacher said man's hope is in glory; that in this world, at best, there is only trouble and sorrow; that in his brief passage from birth to death a man must lay up for himself treasures in Heaven. The preacher said:

> On that great getting-up morning the pulse of immortality will start beating in the grave. The sheeted dead in Christ will come forth. God will drag the deep for his beloved. God will ransack the tomb and tear open the mountains looking for his own. Wherever we lie God will find us and bring us up to the glorious victory. And

we will come up with perfect eyes, with perfect hands, with perfect feet, with perfect body—all our weakness left behind.

Josh talked about freedom now in a better world here on earth. He said that Loretta Sykes hoped to go to Heaven, but that Heaven was not her only hope. She also hoped to be allowed to live in a decent home in a decent Chicago suburb, and with a decent husband she hoped to raise decent children who would be accorded the decent respect of mankind. Josh said:

> When innocent human beings are murdered by Ku Klux Klansmen because they are Negroes, tears must be shed. But trumpets, too, must be sounded. Here in this ancient slave cemetery, so remindful of three centuries of shame, we must renew our vows to bring social justice to this nation here and now. We are bone-tired of attending the funerals of Ku Klux victims. We are sick to our stomachs of smelling the ashes of homes and churches fired from Ku Klux torches. We must vow, we must sing, we must shout, we must march, we must blow trumpets until the walls of White Supremacy fall down.

The speakers were inside the unpainted frame church which seated only the Negroes who lived on the mountain. Amplifiers carried the voices to the fifteen hundred others who stood outside under the trees, and who had arrived in decrepit Fords and Chevrolets. The three whites inside the church were Josh, Dr. Parker and Allen. Outside the church the white students from Ellenton High School stood together and apart from the civil rights workers. When the preacher finished his remarks, he called on Josh to speak, then on Allen. Allen wore his Sunday blue suit, with a blue tie, and he looked tall and determined when he stood up and said:

> I am here, with a group of my schoolmates, to declare by our presence that we are ashamed, not only of the men who murdered Loretta and her mother, but also of any man or woman who is not ashamed of these murderers. We are ashamed of every man who came to this mountain with a fire bottle in his hand. We pledge our-

selves to try to identify and punish any of those men who
may be still alive.

We are ashamed of the Ku Klux Klan. We are
ashamed of every man who has ever tried to prove himself superior by scaring somebody. We are ashamed of
every office holder who has ever sought the votes of Ku
Klux, or done favors for Ku Klux, or been afraid of Ku
Klux.

Every American with a television set knows that the
days of unfair racial separation are over. Now whites
and Negroes go to the same school, play on the same
team, work at the same bench, and fight and die in the
same army. So the existence of a Ku Klux Klan is
shameful.

I am also here to try, in a small way, to represent
Breck Stancill. He was Loretta's friend. He was her
mother's friend. He's my friend. He's the friend of everybody who wants to live and let live in peace.

In conclusion, when I was born my parents lived on
this mountain. I never knew Loretta because she was older than I am, and we didn't go to the same school. But I
wish I had known her. She worked hard, and dreamed,
and aspired, and hoped, and that's the kind of people I
admire. May she rest in peace.

Loretta and her mother were buried in the same grave. At
the graveside the choir of the Ellenton Negro school sang
"There Is a Balm in Gilead," and the preacher pronounced
this benediction:

Almighty God, who art our refuge and strength: grant us
thy light to shine through the shadows of this hour.
Comfort our hearts. Have compassion upon our weakness. Give us the vision of eternal realities, and solace us
with the hope of a better life beyond; through Jesus
Christ our Lord. Amen.

A few hours after Loretta's funeral, about 9:30 P.M. on Saturday, Big Track stood at the edge of a yelling crowd which
was watching scenes from the film _Birth of a Nation_. The
robed horsemen of the Ku Klux Klan were riding through the
night to serve God and save Southern womanhood from the
claws of the beast.

Big Track felt exhausted: from too much worry and too little sleep. His hat was pushed back on his head, and he sagged at the knees and beltline as he chomped slowly on a cigar. He was trying to survive the worst day of the worst week of his life. At 6 A.M. he had telephoned the jail and got no answer. Without his breakfast he had rushed to the jail and found a note tacked to the door of Hattie's room. I'M GONE, TRACK. I AIN'T COMING BACK. GOOD LUCK. HATTIE. He had rushed to the cell block where Breck was, and found the cell block door locked and Breck locked in the rear cell.

"Hattie's gone!" said Big Track. "You done it."

"I helped her," said Breck. "When you find time I'll tell you about it."

Maybelle came and fixed coffee, bread and sorghum for sixteen prisoners. An off-duty city policeman manned the jail's telephone and handled visitors. And all day Big Track withstood attack from worked-up citizens demanding that he stop "all this tension and trouble and killing." About 5 P.M. Vernon Hodo confronted him at the courthouse and told him about Allen's speech at the Negro funeral.

"How's that gonna sound on TV tomorrow?" asked Vernon. "Your own boy sayin' he's ashamed'a you and me and George Wallace and ever' other red-blooded, God-fearin' white man in Alabama? And I hear your sister run off. Who's she talking to? What'cha gonna do about Breck? He killed your deputy, and now he's got'cha boy and looks like he's got'cha sister. What's he gonna do to you?"

The Klan meeting, which began at 7:30, was being held at a drive-in theater so that film could be shown between the speeches, and so that spectators could sit in their cars or get out and stand or sit on benches and eat and drink. Visiting orators, along with Vernon and the preacher, had all made the same speech: Mongrelization! These four men didn't die in vain! Throwing God out'a our schools! States rights! Run them niggers north! Beatniks, whores, punks, liberals, perverts, Reds, nigger-lovers, God-haters! Wallace for President! Stand up for Alabama and the white man's cause!

The film, in addition to scenes from Birth of a Nation, included scenes of the Selma March showing black hands on white teats and tails. State troopers were on film revealing the "real truth" about the march. Each trooper told how he saw a black male clutch a white female, then the trooper stammered and said: "Common decency forbids me to go any further. You good white folks'll just have'ta use'ya imagination."

Now the speeches and the films were ended, and Big Track was glad to see robed Klansmen raising a forty-foot-high cross which had been wrapped in cotton batting and soaked in gasoline. Big Track knew the meeting was about over, and he wanted to go to the jail and talk to Breck about Hattie. The Klansmen set fire to the cross, began marching around it singing "The Old Rugged Cross," and Big Track was hurrying toward the Wildcat when Clay Wilbanks stopped him.

"Sheriff, I must give you this package," Wilbanks said. "It's for Breck Stancill."

"What is it?"

"Tape recordings Breck may want to use at his hearing Monday."

"FBI tapes?"

"No, they belong to Breck."

When Big Track took the package, Wilbanks said: "I'll ask you to sign this receipt for them." Warily Big Track scribbled his name. "Thank you, Sheriff," said Wilbanks. "Good night."

Big Track acted like he had been handed a time bomb. He jumped in the Wildcat and started toward the jail. But shouldn't he hear the tapes before he saw Breck? He decided to go to his courthouse office and listen to them alone. Then he thought of going to Hardy Riddle's house and letting Hardy hear the tapes with him. He called the jail on the radio, and Allen answered.

"Everything all right, son?"

"All quiet, Dad. The meeting over?"

"Yeah. I want'ta talk'ta Hardy a few minutes. Phone him and ask him'ta step out'n see me."

Hardy met him on the driveway, and they went into the basement and spent two hours listening to Loretta and Hattie; and to Big Track being inducted into the Ku Klux Klan by an Imperial Wizard and a Grand Dragon, in the presence of Exalted Cyclops Vernon Hodo and Grand Kludd Mark Alverson.

After hearing the tapes, Big Track felt so exhausted that for a while he could only sigh and shake his head. Hardy said: "Those tapes can't hurt anybody until they are presented in open court and made a public record."

"Breck will present them Monday morning," said Big Track.

"He can't present them if he doesn't appear in court."

"If he can't present them, the FBI will. They've got copies."

"The FBI can't present them unless the Justice Department can bring somebody to trial. That can be hard to do."

Big Track kept wondering how Breck had obtained the recording of the Klan induction ceremony. He remembered that only five men, including himself, were present. Would an Imperial Wizard or a Grand Dragon or an Exalted Cyclops or a Grand Kludd conceal a recorder and sell such a tape?

Hardy said: "Vernon will be opposed to letting Breck use those tapes. Are you sleeping in the jail tonight?"

"Naw, my boy Allen is. I'm hopin'ta hire me a new jailer tomorrow or next day. And a new deputy."

"Well, here's what I advise you to do," said Hardy. "Go home and take a hot bath and go to bed. You've had a terrible week. You deserve a night's rest. Tomorrow is Sunday, so you can sleep till noon. Tomorrow afternoon, when we both are fresh and rested, we'll meet here."

"I guess that's the thing to do," said Big Track.

"Before you go," said Hardy, "tell me exactly where Breck is in that jail."

"Well," explained Big Track, "he's in number-three cell block. The block has four cells and a Day Room in it. Breck's in the rear cell, the number-four cell, and there ain't nobody else in the block with him."

"The entire block is locked?"

"Sure. The cell-block door is solid steel."

"And inside the cell block Breck's number-four cell is locked?"

"It ain't locked with a lock, but it's closed tighter'n hell. We move the cell door with a switch while we stand outside the cell block. We order prisoners to move out of cells and into the Day Room, and back, while we stand safe outside the block, looking through bulletproof glass and talking through a bulletproof baffle. Our jail's safe."

"Suppose the prisoner has a gun?" asked Hardy.

"He can't have no weapon," said Big Track. "Every prisoner goes into our jail buck-naked. He puts on a one-piece suit we give him. If, after he's in, we suspect he's got a weapon, we order him to come out of his cell buck-naked. If he came out with a gun he'd be helpless. Because we'd be standing outside the locked cell-block door. When he comes out bucknaked, we make him walk toward us and turn around slow and spread his hands, while we stand outside and look him over careful. We order him into the Day Room; we close that door on him; then we enter the cell block and search his cell. There ain't no chance for no prisoner to ever pull a gun on us, like on TV."

"Suppose he refuses to come out of his cell for inspection when you order him to?"

"We cut his food and water off till he comes out bucknaked."

"I see how you do it," said Hardy. "I just wanted to be sure that you can stay away from Breck. Don't go near him. He's desperate now. He has become a fanatic. He's a killer. He can kill a man with his bare hands. Somebody might slip him a gun. He might kill himself. He might go berserk and try to kill you. He knows he's got no future. So don't even go in the cell block where he is. Stay completely away from him. Understand?"

"I understand, Skipper," said Big Track. "I thought I knew Breck. But I guess I don't."

At home Big Track found Maybelle waiting to sponge his broad back, and to serve him his pie and his milk and his sleeping potion. Before he fell asleep he mumbled to her: "Everything's gonna be all right, honey. But when I wake up tomorrow me and you's got'ta talk."

Sunday, April 18, 1965, was a sunless, rainy, cold, dreary day in Ellenton, Alabama. Even free men with things to do, and places to go, and television shows to watch, and women to stay abed with, felt dispirited. When Allen Bascomb brought Breck Stancill the breakfast sent over from the Atoka Hospital, Breck said: "Al, I'd like to talk to you a minute when you find time. I need a little help."

"Soon as I finish feeding the prisoners," said Allen.

An hour later Allen came back to Breck and brought the Sunday Birmingham *News*. Allen was excited because his picture was on the front page, with an account of his speech at Loretta's funeral. SHERIFF'S SON DEFIES KLAN. Breck read the story and said: "I'm proud of you, Al."

"I wonder if my mother and dad are proud of me?" Allen said.

"They will be," said Breck. "Here's what I wanted to ask you to do. Take the pickup and go out to my house and bring me some clothes. I didn't expect to be here but one night. So I need clean underwear and my best blue suit and a white shirt and a necktie and my best shoes. Bring them here and if we can master this automated plumbing, I'll bathe, shave and dress."

Allen smiled: "You going somewhere?"

"No, but today I must try to look impressive. A man in jail must work to keep from feeling and looking insignificant."

"Anything else I can get for you while I'm gone?"

"No," said Breck, "but tell me: when are the TV news shows presented on Sunday?"

"At noon and five-thirty and ten P.M."

"Make certain that your father and mother see them."

"You think I'll be on?"

"Sheriffs' sons don't defy Ku Klux in Alabama every day. You'll be on. And telephone calls, favorable and unfavorable to you and to your father, will reach the sheriff's office. Calls must already be reaching your home over what's in the newspapers. See that Big Track has Trixie at the courthouse this afternoon and evening to take the calls. And you go to Trixie and tell her I'm asking her to see that Big Track talks to many more favorable than unfavorable callers."

"You mean we have to persuade Dad that I did right?"

"It's more of what we were discussing last night," said Breck. "All sorts of people try to persuade a sheriff. So even his family and his friends must keep persuading him. Particularly on a dreary Sunday when he's tired and upset."

"Will Trixie do what you ask?"

"I don't know. My asking may cause her to do the opposite. But I must ask. You must ask Dr. Parker to call Big Track and congratulate him on your stand. Doc's on our side but he's busy. He may forget that we need him."

"Sounds like I'm running for office."

"In a way you are," said Breck. "And here's my other request. At the funeral you pledged an effort to identify any Klan criminals who may be still alive. On that point I need to see Big Track today."

"You want me to see that he talks to you?"

"Yes, and that won't be easy. He'll be busy and worried."

"I'll get him to come."

"Suggest to him that he take me out of this cell and sit

down with me in the Day Room. I'm not persuasive talking
through bars."

"Leave it to me," said Allen.

"I'll have to," said Breck.

At 11 A.M., during the church hour, Big Track and Maybelle sat in their kitchen drinking coffee and talking trouble.
In bed and out, they had been talking trouble for four hours.
Since 7 A.M. Maybelle had answered the telephone thirty-three
times, and each caller cursed Allen's parents for not teaching
their son to respect the Ku Klux Klan. Big Track glanced
again at Allen's picture in the paper and said: "If there's any
pore s'nuvabitch in this world who's got more trouble than me
today, he must be at the bottom of a well with his back
broke."

"We'll figure some way out," said Maybelle.

During the time when she hadn't been answering the telephone, Maybelle had heard Big Track's story of the three tape
recordings. Now she said: "It was low-down'a Breck to turn
your own sister against you. It was low-down'a Hattie to turn
against her own brother, to bite the hand that was feedin' her,
but it was low-down'a Breck to come in your jail and buy'ya
sister. How much'ya reckon Breck paid her?"

"I got no notion," said Big Track. "Enough for her'ta git
off somewhere and last her awhile, I guess."

The telephone rang again, and Maybelle absorbed more
abuse. When she came back she said: "What I can't figure is
what made Breck turn against *us*. You saved the nigger girl's
life. You took the Klan oath because you had to. Allen stood
up on the mountain with Breck. After Breck done his shootin'
you offered'ta lie for him. What was it made him turn against
us?"

"Hardy figures it's because he's gone psycho."

"That may be it," said Maybelle. "He ain't lived right. He
ain't never had a woman of his own. A man in the woods as
young as him needs a real woman'ta tend to most ever' night
to help him sleep sound and keep him from goin' psycho.
Breck ain't never had that. He's been a whorehopper like his
daddy."

"Hardy thinks Breck's dangerous now. He wants me'ta
keep away from him. Reckon Breck's dangerous?"

"He may be. Trouble can make a man dangerous."

"Well, the question is," said Big Track, "have I got'ta try any more'ta help him?"

Maybelle poured fresh coffee, tasted it, then replied: "Sure you got'ta try. You got'ta do right. But you got'ta remember that there's a world'a difference between you and Breck. You're a family man and a public man. You got'ta figure what's best for'ya family, and what's best for the people'a this county. Breck's a loner. He don't have'ta figure on nobody but hisself. So you don't have'ta travel no road just because he wants'ta travel it. He's got'ta travel by hisself at his own risk."

The telephone rang again, and it was Allen. He wanted his parents to watch the TV news at noon. He also wanted his father to instruct Trixie Cunningham to begin answering the courthouse telephone by 1 P.M. Big Track and Maybelle carried their coffee into the living room and heard the TV reporter say:

> The news from strife-torn Atoka County, Alabama, to-day is made by the seventeen-year-old son of Sheriff Buford "Big Track" Bascomb. Yesterday Allen Bascomb, with a score of local white high school students, attended the funeral for Loretta Sykes, the pretty Negro girl from Chicago who was slain Wednesday night by men said to be members of the Ku Klux Klan. At the funeral, held in a rural, Negro, slave churchyard, young Bascomb spoke out against the Klan. Here is some of what he said. . . .

The film showed the churchyard, the crowd, Allen standing inside the church, then Allen's face as he spoke. "He sure looks fine, don't he?" said Maybelle. "That's the best picture I ever seen of him. I ain't ashamed of him, no matter how many calls we git." Then Allen was gone, and the reporter concluded:

> This courageous speech by the football-star son of a win-ner of the Congressional Medal of Honor indicates to some observers that the young generation in Alabama may be deserting the White Supremacy flag flown by Governor Wallace and the Ku Klux Klan.

Big Track said: "Yeah, I better git Trixie down to the courthouse. So we can hear what long-distance has to say."

Hardy Riddle, too, had watched the TV news. And instead of going to church he had spent an hour at the lumberyard with Vernon Hodo. He was waiting in his basement when Big Track arrived about 2:30 P.M.

"You look a lot better," said Hardy. "Sleep did you good."

"I didn't sleep much," said Big Track. "Folks started calling pretty early, cussing about my boy."

"That'll blow over. I didn't sleep either, trying to figure how to help Breck and restore peace in this county and get us off'a TV. For a week now TV's made us look worse than Selma or Vietnam."

"It's been mighty bad," said Big Track. "What'd'ya figure out?"

"Well," said Hardy, "Breck's my friend same as ever. His horse is in my pasture now. But he's a hard man to help. After he killed those boys, I offered him the moon if he'd leave and let us have peace. He didn't want peace. So now he's as good as dead. He can't leave the county, and he wouldn't leave if he could. He's willing to kill more of them before they kill him. And the county would go on suffering as the TV capital of blood and guts."

"I tried ever' way'ta help him," said Big Track. "Then he stabbed me in the back: turned my own sister against me. He's a loner gone psycho. He don't think'a nobody but hisself."

"Even if they let him live to get his hearing tomorrow," said Hardy, "he couldn't live till they tried him. If he did, they'd convict him, he'd go to the Supreme Court, get a new trial, and repeat the process on TV till he broke the county. Same story in civil court. Whether he lives or dies, they'll get judgments for more than he's worth. If he stayed alive, he'd appeal and wind up broke. So what we must think about now is the county: the continued, orderly development of Atoka County."

"That's right," said Big Track. "We got'ta let Breck travel at his own risk."

Hardy passed the cigars, and they went through the ritual of lighting up. Hardy asked: "Who'll sleep in the jail tonight?"

"Me," said Big Track. "My boy has'ta court his girl tonight and go to school in the morning."

"Well," said Hardy, "what I'm saying now is not my idea. But let's think for a minute like they're thinking. Suppose you have a prisoner who's your friend. At two-twenty A.M. he wakes you up screaming like he's got a heart attack. You run to number-three cell block, open the cell-block door, touch the switch opening the door to number-four cell, and run in to help your sick friend. But your friend's mentally sick, and he throws a .38 in your face, takes your keys, locks you in the cell block, walks out, and folks find you in the cell block next morning. That happens every week on TV: it could happen in the safest jail in Alabama, couldn't it?"

"Naw," said Big Track, "it couldn't happen. But we could make like it did if that's what everybody in the county wants."

Hardy looked at the ceiling and exhaled a geyser of smoke. "Suppose," he said, "some persons unknown happen to be at the door of the jail at two-twenty and find the door open. They rush through the office and find the next door open. They rush to cell-block number three, find the door open, and rush to cell number four. The cell door opens, they jump in, rescue a friend, lock you in the cell block, and rush out, all in three minutes."

Big Track observed the ceiling, exhaled, and said: "The persons unknown would need'ta recollect that the friend in number-four cell can kill a man with his bare hands, and he ain't gonna welcome bein' rescued."

"They know that," said Hardy. "They'll send a robed-and-masked party of seven good men plus a noncombatant preacher. The two stout boys who'll lead the way will be brothers of Butt Cut and Tag."

"How long will I have'ta stay in the cell block?"

"Thirty or forty minutes. Somebody'll tip the city cops, and they'll rescue you."

"Speakin'a gittin' off'a TV," said Big Track, "we gonna git on TV tomorrow more'n we ever been."

"But it'll be over in two days."

"Breck ain't no nigger or civil rights worker."

"That's in our favor," said Hardy. "Breck has no organized support. The civil rights workers don't like him. Who's going to raise any protracted stink about Breck? No man's death causes talk for more than three days. Unless he's the President."

They smoked in silence, not looking at one another. Then Hardy said: "If folks heard us talking this way, a few of them might call us hard-hearted. But we are only allowing the majority to rule. We are standing aside, letting an Action Squad do what the people of this county want done."

"I think Breck'd agree we're doin' him a favor," said Big Track. "To sort'a git even with him for what he done'ta my sister, I been keepin' him in that one cell since yesterday morning. He'll be feeling mighty disgusted by two-twenty A.M."

"I read a lot," said Hardy. "Most every society provides a way out for the man who just gets himself so fucked up that he has to die a little earlier than he would naturally. In Japan it's *hari-kiri*. That seems like the most decent way, if they'd use a pistol instead of that dagger. In Russia, and many other countries, the jail has always been the place for ending hopeless conflicts between a man and his environment. What'll happen here tonight has happened a million times before, and it'll be happening a thousand years after we're dead and gone."

"Yeah," said Big Track. "And Breck knows he lived twenty years longer than he figured to."

"That's right," said Hardy. "My wife and I both were fond of Breck. But we both agreed that he wasn't a normal man."

"Naw, he wasn't normal," said Big Track.

Since Big Track was a man who could be influenced, Breck's hope during Sunday afternoon and evening was that somebody, from far or near, would influence Big Track to violate his Klan oath, defy Klan discipline, and stand against the Klan. Breck lodged some hope in the twenty to thirty million Americans who would see Allen defying the Klan on television. He hoped that as many as five out of every million viewers would be moved to telephone their approval of Allen, and thereby encourage the father to emulate the son.

But, for some reason, this number of approving calls did not come. Perhaps they didn't come because spring had arrived and people were tired of a winter of televised conflict. Whatever the reason, between 1 and 8 P.M., Maybelle Bascomb at her home and Trixie Cunningham at the courthouse, received only fourteen approving calls. They came from Skowhegan, Maine, and Grant's Pass, Oregon, and twelve intermediate points. The disapproving calls were more numerous. The telecast angered Governor Wallace's supporters in Wisconsin, Indiana and Maryland; and forty-seven of these White Supremacists telephoned their anger. So Breck and

Allen, instead of winning the long-distance poll, lost by 47 to 14. They lost locally 62 to 0.

One person-to-person call from a famous man to Big Track could have converted this loss into a victory. A member of Congress from Alabama could have called from Washington and said: "Big Track, we need more boys in Alabama like that boy of yours." Or President Truman could have called and said: "Big Track, when I hung that Medal of Honor around your neck, I knew that someday you and your boy might run the Ku Klux out of Atoka County."

Trixie Cunningham could have told Big Track about the approving calls and not emphasized the others. But when Allen delivered Breck's request for such help, she snapped: "Breck's made his bed; let him lie in it."

Dr. Parker could have helped Breck and Allen. But when Allen called to remind the doctor to call Big Track, he was told that the doctor had gone to Memphis and wouldn't be back till Monday.

By 6 P.M. these frustrations had caused Allen to begin thinking less about Ku Klux and more about the evening he and Billie Jean had planned. The evening was one to anticipate: they were going to spend it not in a car but in a bed, at Breck's house.

At 6:10 Big Track entered the jail and said: "Okay, son, I'll take over. Go see your gal. Just remember that married men don't go to West Point."

"Okay, Dad," Allen said. "The prisoners have been fed and all the trays picked up and returned to the café. But remember you promised to talk to Breck. I'll stay here and answer the phone while you go talk to him now."

"You don't need'ta stay here," said Big Track. "Breck and me's got a lot'ta talk about. You go on and don't keep'ya gal waitin'."

Allen felt the impulse to insist. As his eyes met his father's, he parted his lips to speak. Then he shook off the impulse and hurried out of the jail.

Big Track relaxed. He had been afraid Allen would insist. Then he busied himself with routine. The city police first brought in a drunk driver, then a Negro caught selling whiskey, and later a wife who had shot her husband. When the police weren't there, Big Track interviewed a woman who wanted to replace Hattie and a man who wanted to replace Butt Cut. Trixie called with a final report on the long-distance poll and said she was going home. Maybelle reported that the calls denouncing Allen had stopped so she was taking aspirin and going to bed. A few minutes before ten Big Track went into Hattie's vacated quarters and turned on the TV set. He got a beer, kicked off his shoes, and sprawled across the bed to watch the news. The report from strife-torn Atoka County was about Breck's upcoming hearing. At the end there was a paragraph about Allen but no picture. After the news came a good movie: *Warlock,* with Henry Fonda as a hired gun.

At 11:45 Allen had returned Billie Jean to her home and he was driving toward his home. He felt elated, tired, satisfied and sleepy. He twice rejected the impulse to go to the jail before he turned around, drove to the jail, and noted that a light was burning in the window of Hattie's room. He stopped and rang the bell at the door. He rang three times before Big Track came.

"It's time you was home, son," Big Track said. He only cracked the door; he didn't open it.

"I wanted to see you a minute, Dad," said Allen. He noticed how reluctantly his father opened the door. When he was inside he asked: "Did you talk to Breck?"

"Sure I talked to Breck," said Big Track. "He's asleep. You go on home and go to sleep. Tomorrow's a school day."

Allen sighed, then said: "This is hard for me to say, Dad. You and I have always told one another the truth. Why aren't you telling me the truth now?"

Big Track felt the impulse to strike, but he had never struck his son. He said: "Well, Al, I guess I got'ta tell you that Breck's turned against me. It's his fault that Hattie left. He paid her to tell him some'pin that could hurt me. It was low-down'a Breck'ta turn my own sister a~ainst me. So I just hate'ta talk to him. How can'ya talk to a man who's been'ya friend and then turns against'ya?"

"Breck hasn't turned against you," said Allen. "I was on the mountain with you when you wanted Breck to hide the truth. Breck doesn't want to hide truth, and I don't think you should either. You're too big a man for that, Dad. You're too big not to talk to Breck."

Big Track knew he was cornered. The last man in the world he wanted to see was Breck Stancill. But now he had no choice. "Okay, son," he said. "I'll go right now. You go on home."

"No, Dad," said Allen. "I'll stay here until you talk, then I'll talk to Breck. I promised him I would."

Breck was lying on the bunk, still in his Sunday suit. For eleven hours he had been dressed and waiting for his chance to influence Big Track. The only lights burning in the cell block were the blue night lights.

Big Track switched on the white lights, opened the cell block door, entered, and closed the door behind him.

"Is that you, Track?" Breck called.

"Yeah, it's me," Big Track answered. He moved along the walkway until Breck could see him. "Al says you want'a speak'ta me a minute." Breck got off the bunk and stood at the bars, facing Big Track. Noting Big Track's uneasiness, Breck knew he had to interest him at once or Big Track would walk away. Breck handed him a typewritten document dated March 26, 1964.

"That's my will," said Breck. "If anything happens to me, I want you to see that Stancill's Mountain goes to Allen."

Startled, Big Track looked at the document. "You mean my boy is'ta git all your property!"

"Yes. I made that will a year ago. My lawyer has a copy."

Big Track swallowed hard. "I never figured on this," he said. "But, hell, you ain't got no property! Ever' dime you got's going to widows and orphans and lawyers."

"You can prevent that," said Breck.

"Me?"

"Yes, you. You are sworn to make each citizen of this county secure in his person and possessions. Surely you can make your own son secure."

"I can't secure nothin' you got. Nobody could. Out there on the mountain I tried'ta secure'ya by keepin'ya quiet. Your own lawyer tried'ta secure'ya. You chose'ta commit suicide and lose ever' penny'ya got."

"I chose to bet on you," said Breck. "I chose to bet that at showdown you'd turn against the Klansmen, arrest them, and charge them with arson, rape and murder. That's why I sent you those tape recordings. If you'll arrest Vernon, the preacher, and Sy Shaneyfelt tomorrow morning; if you'll announce that Butt Cut and Tag Taggart assisted in the rape of Loretta Sykes in this jail and then conspired to murder her, the charges against me will be dismissed. My estate will not be in jeopardy, and it will go to Allen if Klansmen kill me. Stancill's Mountain doesn't belong to the widows and orphans of

criminals. It belongs to me and Allen Bascomb. So I'm asking
you now to take off your Klan robe, switch sides, and stand
with me and your son, where a winner of the Congressional
Medal of Honor ought to stand!"

Big Track wanted time to think. He also wanted Allen to
go home. So he said: "Breck, this is some'pin that's got'ta be
talked out between you and me. Al's come by here after bein'
out with his gal. He wants'ta speak'ta'ya before he runs on
home. So will you just . . . speak a word to him?"

For an instant Breck considered trying to keep Allen at the
jail. From Big Track's uneasiness he suspected that Klansmen
might be coming. Why shouldn't he tell Allen what he suspected and try to use him for protection? Then Breck dismissed the idea. Allen couldn't protect him. Allen wasn't the
State of Alabama: he couldn't arrest Klansmen. Breck was
gambling to win Big Track.

"Send him in," said Breck.

When Allen came in he asked: "You all right, Breck?"

"I'm fine, Al," said Breck. "Your father and I are talking.
Everything's going to be all right."

"Anything I can do for you before I go?"

"No, thanks. And thanks for coming by."

Big Track let Allen out of the jail, then came back and
again stood before Breck's cell. He didn't offer to open the
cell and sit with Breck in the Day Room. He preferred to
stand and talk through bars. "You're talkin' foolishness,
Breck," he said. "You should'a been at the funeral for the
men you killed. Biggest crowd in the history'a the county.
That preacher hung gold stars on all four of 'em and preached
'em straight into the arms'a Jesus. Everybody liked it. If I arrested Vernon and that preacher, they'd be out in five minutes. I couldn't indict 'em, much less convict 'em. Then they'd
kill me. And you know goddam well I'm tellin' the truth."

"I could protect you," said Breck. "You could protect me.
Two determined men have always been able to protect each
other from the Klan. I'd go to Vernon and say: 'Now you
hear this! If Big Track is hurt, I'll kill you! So you better see
that nobody hurts him.' You can threaten him for me, and
we'll both be safe. One man can't protect himself from the
Klan. But two men can protect each other."

Big Track shook his head. "I can't afford'ta threaten Vernon. He belongs'ta Hardy. And Hardy wants peace, not more
threats and more killing. And the Klan has a big followin'.

Not just in Alabama but ever'where. You should'a heard folks on the phone today cussin' Al fer cussin' the Klan. Most ever'body in this county is glad the Klan's on the job. Or they ain't sayin' it ought'a leave."

"You can change that," said Breck. "You're a big man. You're the law. You're a hero. You represent the State of Alabama. If you arrest Vernon and the preacher on the charge that they staged and watched the rape of Loretta Sykes in this jail, you can turn decent people against them."

Big Track put his hands in his hip pockets and stretched. "I got'ta go, Breck," he said. "You done gone psycho. You don't think like folks think. You keep tryin'ta make some'pin *terrible* out'a what happened in this jail'ta Loretta Sykes. Well, folks won't think it was terrible. She was a nigger. She was a uppity Chicago nigger. Maybe she was a nigger agitator. So folks don't care what happened to her. They damn sure don't care if all that happened to her was that she got fucked! And you know I'm tellin' the truth. So quit talkin' horseshit and go'ta sleep."

Breck felt infinitely lonely. "Track," he said, "you're a man with pride. You worry about what President Truman thinks about you. If you don't arrest these Ku Klux, then tomorrow the FBI will arrest you and reveal that you're a loyal Kluxer who allowed the rape of an innocent woman in your most modern jail in the world. What will Truman think of you then? What will your son think? How can Allen go to West Point with a father like you?"

"You're hitting me where it hurts now," said Big Track. "I hate fer my boy'ta have'ta hear that I'm a Kluxer. I hate fer Truman'ta hear it. But I couldn't help it. I joined the Klan because I had to. I didn't like it when the nigger gal was raped in here. I just did what folks wanted me to do. The FBI can't hurt me. If the FBI says I did some'pin, most folks won't believe it. The more the FBI lumps me with the Klan, the more votes I'll git. And you know it's the truth. What grinds your guts, Breck, is the truth about folks, and not nothin' I done."

When Breck dropped his eyes and said nothing, Big Track continued: "I'd like'ta ask'ya one question. Who sold you or the FBI the tape of me takin' the Klan oath?"

"The Imperial Wizard of your Realm," said Breck. "Surely that doesn't surprise you? Selling Klan secrets, like selling sheets, is an old racket of Imperial Wizards. A week after

Hugo Black was appointed to the Supreme Court, a former Klan official sold Black's secret membership papers for five hundred dollars. You were sold out for less."

"The s'nuvabitch!" said Big Track.

Breck was about ready to give up. "All right, Track," he said, "I'll make one more suggestion. My estate is worth four hundred thousand dollars. I don't want Kluxers or their heirs to get it. So if you'll turn around and fight them, I'll give it to you. It won't be a bribe. I'll only be making you financially secure so that you can afford to risk unpopular action. And so that you won't disgrace your son. If you'll agree to arrest Vernon and the preacher, at seven A.M. tomorrow, I'll pay you twenty thousand dollars in cash. After you have arrested them and appeared as a witness for me at my hearing, I'll pay you twenty thousand dollars more. Then each month thereafter, as the fight goes on, I'll pay you five thousand dollars. If my own estate becomes tied up, I'll get it from my mother. I'll make you so rich that you can quit worrying about what folks think."

For a long time Breck and Big Track stood looking at one another. Big Track studied his watch: 12:35 A.M. "Your boy can be proud of you," said Breck. "Truman will be proud of you. You can be a national TV hero. You can stand up like a big man . . . like a winner of the Medal of Honor. You can be Governor of Alabama! Hell, with great leadership this state could be great! We have great forests, great rivers, pure water, pure air, and people who are good except when they are blinded by racist demagogues. Come on, Track! Don't be a stupid, half-assed, red-necked Ku Klux! Stand up with me and your boy and be big and rich and great!"

After another silence Big Track lowered his eyes to the floor and said: "I can't do it, Breck. I can't be big, and I can't be rich, and I can't be great. I believe you'd get me the money, all right. But I can't believe nothin' else 'ya say. I don't believe there's nothin' on this earth I could do that'd save yo' life and yo' property. I don't believe I could change folks. I don't believe I got the guts'ta arrest Vernon and that preacher. And if I did arrest 'em, I believe folks'd just turn me out and shoot me. Money can't do a dead man no good. So I just can't travel with'ya no further, Breck."

Big Track paused, then went on: "I'll tell'ya some'pin else. Some'pin I ain't never told nobody and never will. I didn't deserve the Medal of Honor. I didn't kill all them gooks. I didn't kill half of 'em, or even a fourth of 'em. Maybe I killed two or three. The killin' was done by better men than me who got killed theirselves. I was just the one they found alive and gave the medal to. And that's the truth." Then Big Track added: "I always kind'a figured you knowed that about me, Breck."

Breck leaned against the bars, his shoulders drooping. He had bet on a scrub horse, and he had lost.

Big Track turned to leave and said: "You was my friend, Breck. I was yo' friend. It was you who turned against me and traveled down a road I couldn't travel. Now there ain't nothin' I can do'ta help you. Nothin' on earth. Goodbye and God help'ya."

Big Track left the cell block, slammed the solid steel door, and switched off the white lights. Only the blue night lights remained.

About 2 A.M. Maybelle Bascomb got out of bed and walked to her kitchen for a pinch of baking soda. She was worried and her stomach was upset. Her footfall awakened Allen. He saw the light under his door and wondered why his mother was up. He began worrying and got up. Over his mother's objections he dressed and headed for the jail in the car.

Maybelle telephoned the jail to tell Big Track that Allen was coming. The jail telephone began ringing at 2:20 A.M. It was not answered. Big Track was busy: unlocking the front door of the jail, unlocking the door from the office into the area of the cell blocks, unlocking the solid steel door to cell-block number three, and pressing the switch which slid back the door of cell number four.

The fight in the cell was brief and brutal. Breck struck one blow. With the fingers of his right hand extended and rigid, he jabbed them into the mask of a Klansman. He broke his fingers, and he blinded for life the youthful brother of Butt Cut Cates. Then the robed-and-masked Klansmen rode Breck to the floor, trussed his arms behind him, and hustled him toward the waiting cars. The preacher locked Big Track in the cell block and led the blinded Klansman behind the others.

Allen met the Klansmen on the sidewalk outside the jail. He had no weapon, so he yelled "you yellow bastards!" and attacked like a defensive halfback trying to break up a flying wedge. In the melee Breck shook loose and tried to help Allen by butting, kneeing and kicking. Masks and robes were torn, teeth were spat out. The Klansmen had no choice. They shotgunned Breck and Allen, then fled in the cars, leaving two mangled, bloody and dead bodies. Breck lay in the gutter, face up, his tin leg crumpled under him. Allen lay face down in the street.

Locked inside the cell block, Big Track heard the gunfire. First he felt puzzled. Why would the Klansmen be shooting? Who could be shooting at them? Then Big Track felt scared. If the Klansmen killed Breck in front of the jail, and left his trussed-up body lying there, how could Big Track claim that Breck had produced a gun inside the jail and escaped?

After twenty minutes of uncertainty and dismay, Big Track was released by a city policeman and told what had happened. He ran into the street, fell to his knees beside Allen's body. Then, waving others aside, he picked up Allen's body and laid it on the grass between the sidewalk and the jail. He picked up Breck's body and laid it beside Allen. Maybelle arrived, and she and Big Track sat on the grass, weeping, shaking their heads, and holding their dead son's hands. Big Track's khaki shirt and pants were smeared with blood from both bodies.

This scene was viewed, in turn, by the city police, by state troopers, by the curious multitude, and by the coroner, doctors, undertakers, reporters, photographers, Klansmen and FBI men.

About 10 A.M. Monday, after the bodies had been moved and the blood washed off the street and sidewalk, Clay Wilbanks went to Big Track's house. He was let into the living room where he waited for several minutes for Big Track. He looked at the Medal of Honor, at the flags, and at the autographed pictures of President Truman and General MacArthur. Then Big Track came, and they sat down together.

"I'm sorry about your boy, and about Breck," said Wilbanks.

"Thank you," said Big Track. He had put on a pair of blue serge pants, a white shirt, and a blue tie. He appeared stunned, his eyes red.

"I was just looking at your medal," said Wilbanks. "And at your pictures."

"They're coming down," said Big Track. He sighed, then continued: "Yeah, I'm gonna take 'em down. I'm gonna bury the medal with my boy. He deserves it. I don't. A man who won't stand up with his own boy damn sure don't deserve to wear the Medal of Honor and have school kids comin' around lookin' up to him."

They sat there together for a while, then Wilbanks said: "Well, Track, I hate to bother you at a time like this, but I do have a Federal warrant for your arrest. I'm arresting you and Vernon and the preacher and other Ku Klux for conspiring to violate, and violating, the civil rights of Loretta Sykes, Susan Sykes, Breck Stancill and Allen Bascomb."

"You mean I violated my boy, just like we violated Breck and the niggers?"

"Yes," said Wilbanks. "You violated your son's right to live. You helped kill him, didn't you?"

"I guess I did," said Big Track.

A trip that makes *Deliverance* seem like a picnic!

OPEN SEASON

A novel by David Osborn

Three ordinary, pillar-of-society citizens —Ken, Greg, and Art—take a vacation each year in the woods of northern Michigan. And each year, during that vacation, they kidnap a couple and rape the girl and torture the man. And then —for sport—they set the couple free, only to hunt them down in the forest . . .

A journey that you will never forget—in the most startling, shocking, superbly powerful adventure novel of the year!

Now a sensational shocker of a movie starring William Holden and Peter Fonda—from Columbia Pictures.

A DELL BOOK $1.50

BESTSELLERS
FROM DELL

fiction

☐ **THE TAKING OF PELHAM ONE TWO THREE**
  by John Godey **$1.75**
☐ **EVENING IN BYZANTIUM** by Irwin Shaw **$1.75**
☐ **THE MATLOCK PAPER** by Robert Ludlum **$1.75**
☐ **BURNT OFFERINGS** by Robert Marasco **$1.50**
☐ **ELLIE** by Herbert Kastle **$1.50**
☐ **ELEPHANTS CAN REMEMBER** by Agatha Christie.. **$1.25**
☐ **DUST ON THE SEA** by Edward L. Beach **$1.75**
☐ **PEOPLE WILL ALWAYS BE KIND** by Wilfrid Sheed **$1.50**
☐ **SHOOT** by Douglas Fairbairn **$1.50**
☐ **THE MORNING AFTER** by Jack B. Weiner **$1.50**

non-fiction

☐ **LOVE AND WILL** by Rollo May **$1.75**
☐ **AN UNTOLD STORY** by Elliott Roosevelt and
  James Brough **$1.75**
☐ **THE WATER IS WIDE** by Pat Conroy **$1.50**
☐ **THE BOSTON POLICE DIET AND WEIGHT CONTROL
  PROGRAM** by Sam S. Berman, M.D. **$1.25**
☐ **QUEEN VICTORIA** by Cecil Woodham-Smith **$1.75**
☐ **GOING DOWN WITH JANIS** by Peggy Caserta and
  Dan Knapp **$1.50**
☐ **TARGET BLUE** by Robert Daley **$1.75**
☐ **SOLDIER** by Anthony B. Herbert **$1.75**
☐ **MEAT ON THE HOOF** by Gary Shaw **$1.50**
☐ **THE LEGEND OF BRUCE LEE** by Alex Ben Block ... **$1.25**

Buy them at your local bookstore or use this handy coupon for ordering:

Dell | **DELL BOOKS**
P.O. BOX 1000, PINEBROOK, N.J. 07058

Please send me the books I have checked above. I am enclosing $_____
(please add 25¢ per copy to cover postage and handling). Send check or
money order—no cash or C.O.D.'s. Please allow three weeks for delivery.

Mr/Mrs/Miss_____

Address_____

City_____ State/Zip_____

This offer expires 7/75